Praise for The Quantum (

'A protagonist who cor
thing, but one who feels the Thames would be much improved by a
few crocodiles is something else!'

'Some genuinely laugh out loud moments plus a really engaging
cast of characters, and a meta plot that has me hooked! Cannot wait
for the next one!'

'…a fun take, with engaging characters and good writing.'

'This book was so much fun! The plot has been advancing apace
over the three existing books, and just when you think it's all over,
bam, the author throws a massive curveball! This series always defies
what you expect, and always for the better...'

Amazon

'A very entertaining, action-packed read with excellent
characters and several good jokes - and no doubt some more I
missed :) Reminiscent of *Ash* by Mary Gentle and the *Rivers of London*
series.'

'…a delightfully fun read.'

'St. John does a great job of weaving in real history with fiction
and an alternative history. So much fun!'

'It started interesting and just got better. The twists were
unexpected and added to the story, can't wait for the next
instalment.'

'Picked up the pace and ran with it.'

Good Reads

Also By Eva St. John

THE
QUANTUM CURATORS
AND THE
GREAT DECEIVER

EVA ST. JOHN

MUDLARK'S PRESS

This one's for Mark.

There's a bit of Julius in all of us, but there's a whole dollop of Julius in Mark.

November: Alpha: Clio

Clio Masoud was taking the biggest gamble of her life. She had just convinced the Head of Security for all of Alexandria, Asha Giovanetti, to undergo a delicate piece of brain surgery. The surgeon in charge, Koda Bitsoi, thought he was removing a quantum lesion. But, in fact, it was the block that Anansi had inserted into all Alpha citizens' memories.

Its removal lifted the veil of Minju Chen's deception, the true architect behind the Grimaldi Uprising. Now, Bitsoi repeated the procedure on Giovanetti without knowing why, and he was reluctant.

But Clio didn't care about his ethics. If this didn't work, they'd all soon be dead anyway. No one would believe her, and Julius and Neith were depending on her. Everyone was. Clio Masoud, Alpha's last hope. It was enough to make her weep.

Giovanetti stirred and blinked her eyes.

Bitsoi marched in and administered a restorative, glaring at Clio as he did so. 'She needs to recover slowly from a brain operation.'

'Balls to that,' snapped Clio. 'I need her in play.'

Giovanetti nodded groggily. 'Was there a lesion?'

'Yes,' said Bitsoi. He rubbed his chin as he considered the situation. 'Although I don't understand how. Have you been through the stepper in the past year?'

When Clio and Julius had recovered from their operation, they discovered they had had false memories implanted. Them, and the rest of the world. In a second, they had known they were in mortal danger. Minju would not permit knowledge of her true nature to come to light. But now Clio had no choice. Minju was preparing to enact her end game.

'Restorative,' said Giovanetti, her voice still slurred.

Bitsoi picked up the syringe, frowning, and injected his patient.

She blinked a few times, and winced, then held up her hand as he advanced. 'Just a headache. To be expected, I imagine. Now, Masoud, what the hell is this about?'

'No,' said Clio. 'This has to be a private conversation.'

Bitsoi still had his lesion in place. He thought Minju was their great saviour, Clio couldn't risk it.

'There is no scenario where I would leave a patient I have operated on,' snapped Bitsoi. 'Especially in such irregular circumstances.'

Clio scowled. 'Director Giovanetti, this is classified. Please insist that Director Bitsoi leave the room.'

Now it was Giovanetti's turn to refuse. 'Clio, I have known him all my life. I trust him.' She glared at Bitsoi. 'If a single word of this leaks out, you will be imprisoned. Do you still wish to stay?'

Bitsoi nodded.

Giovanetti turned to Clio. 'Right. Get on with it.'

They were running out of time. This had to happen now.

'First off,' began Clio, 'I am going to ask you a question. Then you are going to feel very sick. Emotionally and physically. You may throw up. Your head will hurt. Are you ready?'

'You're going to ask me a question and my head will metaphorically explode?'

'Yes.'

'Okay.' She rolled her eyes at Bitsoi, as she prepared to indulge the younger woman. 'I'm ready.'

'Who led the recent uprising?' asked Clio carefully.

The word Grimaldi formed on Giovanetti's lips and then the security director paled. The heart monitor raced as sweat broke out across her brow. She didn't vomit, but it was a close thing. 'But Minju!'

'I know.' Clio cut her off before she said anything else in front of Bitsoi.

'Is the pharaoh in danger?' asked Bitsoi, appalled. 'Let me call the custodians.'

'NO!' Clio and Giovanetti spoke with one voice.

'Bast's Balls,' whispered Giovanetti in horror as her memories came flooding back. 'The Glass Wastes!'

'We know. The world is about to end and we need your help.'

Repatriation
Four Months Earlier

Chapter One - August: Beta: Julius

Quite frankly, I blamed myself. I was a total bloody idiot. The thing was, I had been in the middle of an excellent dream. When the summons came through for an emergency step, I stumbled into work, bleary-eyed and full of sleep.

Even when I saw I would be stepping with Ludo Bianco, class clown and all-round waste of space, no alarm bells rang. Apparently, Clio was out getting drunk somewhere, and I blindly accepted that. That we were also stepping over with a custodian, and not just any custodian but Luisa Githumbi, Giovanetti's right hand, had also failed to alert me to an issue.

We all stepped through. I was probably even smiling.

Seconds later, I found myself in Charlie's house. Correction, my house, since I had inherited it. The disconnect was startling and yet I still didn't twig. I thought we were here for a Cambridge mission. I was annoyed, though. The least they could have done was warn me. A wave of homesickness engulfed me, and, for a heartbeat, I would have given everything to stay there. Well, they warn you not to wish for things, just in case it comes true.

'This is a bit rum, Luisa?' I said. 'Might have been nice to warn a chap?'

Githumbi cleared her throat. 'Ludo, if you will, please.'

Things felt wrong. On reflection, I can only wince at how long it took me to reach this conclusion.

'Angel Julius Strathclyde—'

I took a step away from her and bumped into one of Charlie's many bookcases.

'Hang on a minute. I mean, I'm not one for titles, but it's Curator, not Angel.'

The part of my brain that had been still happily resting on a pillow back on Alpha and dreaming of snowball fights was rapidly waking up and panicking.

Angels were the weakest of Alpha society. They were Beta individuals who were terminally ill, with no friends or family, selected to act as messengers. The quantum technology was excellent, but communications between the two realities was difficult, so curators would send people across with messages as a mission was ongoing. It was, however, a one-way ticket. In return for their extraction from their Earth, Alpha cured them, then settled them into a retirement plan. So far, no one had complained.

Ludo's voice interrupted my thoughts. 'We are pleased to repatriate you safely to your home.' He was reciting the words by rote and staring straight ahead, refusing to make eye contact.

Githumbi looked directly at me, her face pained. I had seen her fight Medusa but never seen such anguish on her face.

Ludo continued, but I had stopped listening.

My brain was awake and screaming. 'No, look, hang on. I think there's been some sort of mistake,' I said.

'These orders are directly from the pharaoh. We don't make mistakes,' said Ludo.

'You make mistakes all the bloody time! You allowed an uprising to occur under your bloody noses. You had thieves in the heart of your organisation.' My mouth was now running ahead of my brain. 'This is Minju's decision, isn't it? She's fooled all of you. You all think she's the saviour of the day, but she's conning everyone. Anansi made you forget her role in the uprising. She was behind the thefts and the riots.'

My revelations were falling onto stony ground. I tried again.

'Githumbi. This is a mistake. Let me go back. I can fix this.'

I slapped my brace's emergency recall before she could stop me, but nothing happened. I tried again, but Githumbi's face told me everything I feared was true.

Ludo piped up. 'Angel Strathclyde, your brace has been rendered immobile. Please remove it from your wrist and return it to me. All equipment from the quantum facility is on loan only and remains the property of said organisation.'

'Make me.' I took a step towards him, then felt churlish as he stepped back. This wasn't me, and I retreated.

He cleared his throat and continued. 'Fear not. A cover story for your past year has been established. Your bank account has been generously enhanced, and there is a job waiting for you back at your college. We are proud to inform you that your transition has been designed to be happy and pain-free.'

'Githumbi? Luisa, is this a joke?'

I knew it wasn't. This was my fault. I knew other angels had been repatriated, but I had done nothing to investigate, to protect myself from a similar fate. Githumbi was about to speak when Ludo tried again.

'This is no joke, Angel Strathclyde, but a wonderful-'

'Fuck off!'

Now he really did recoil. I couldn't think if I had ever sworn at someone in anger, but it felt appropriate.

'Julius…' Githumbi's voice was so sorrowful that I wanted to wail. 'This isn't a joke. I wish it were, but the orders were very clear. We're to leave you here. In your home.'

Silence fell between us. It was the middle of the night and the hush from beyond the house was complete. I strained to hear anything, anything that might herald a rescue party, a way out, but I was fooling myself. My brace was immobilised. Whoever was at the other end had severed my return. Githumbi was here to prevent me from doing anything stupid. Ludo was here to read me the terms and conditions. I didn't know what to do, so I fell back on my manners.

'Right, then.' I cleared my throat and tried again. 'This can't be easy for you, either. What happens now? You just go home, back to Alpha, and I go to bed and resume my old life?'

'Pretty much,' said Githumbi, nodding slowly.

I tried to think about tomorrow. I could do this. So long as I didn't think about yesterday.

'Very well.'

There was no need to make this harder for her than it already was. I removed my brace and held it out to Ludo without looking at him. I might feel sympathy for Githumbi, but if I had to engage with that buffoon again, I might absolutely sodding lose it.

Tomorrow I would start planning a way to return. I had no idea how yet, but curators came here all the time. All I had to do was find one and... And what? I didn't have a clue, but it would be something to aim for.

Githumbi stepped forward, her hand stretched out, and I nodded.

'Quite right.' I shook her hand and smiled at her. 'It has been an absolute honour to know you. Please say goodbye to—'

And then I blacked out.

Chapter Two - August: Alpha: Neith

I sat on the marble bench and wept. Julius had been repatriated, and I hadn't been able to save him. If I had run faster, would I have made it? I hadn't bothered to change. I was still wearing my night wrap and was barefoot.

Could I have done anything more? Had it really just been thirty minutes since Minju woke me up, full of mock concern? I had slammed out of my apartment, almost bowling her over in my attempt to get to the step facility in time.

The sun was baking my neck, my head in my hands. The smell of scorched earth and jasmine flowers was already overwhelming. By the time the sun rose much higher the blooms would have curled up for the day and shrivelled away. I felt like joining them.

'Did you hear?' Ramin Gamal, my oldest friend was standing over me. He had followed me out of the facility. 'Sabrina's been put on sand leave.'

'Sabrina Mulweather?' I had to check. She was a junior curator who graduated with Julius. Had the makings of a first-rate curator, one of the best in my opinion, although a little rigid, and certainly the last person I expected to be put on sand leave.

'What in Ra's name did she do?'

'It's what she didn't do. Apparently, she was assigned to accompany Julius back, and she refused. Point blank. Direct order from the pharaoh and she said no.'

I'm pretty sure my jaw fell open. That girl was Alpha through and through, obedience and duty all the way. Of course, she also had compassion and honour like any good Alpha citizen, but I didn't expect them to trump duty.

'Where is she?'

Ramin shrugged. Tapping on Tiresias for a location, it told me she had requested privacy.

'Any clues?'

'You could try Jack's,' said Ramin. 'I hear they're together a lot. I'll come with you.'

I was about to say yes, then remembered that Minju was almost certainly behind Julius' repatriation. Until I knew what I was dealing with, I needed to handle this myself.

'No need. We don't want to swamp her.'

'He's my friend too, Neith.'

I had been so wrapped up in my own distress that I hadn't paid attention to how Ramin was feeling, but his anguished expression said everything.

'Tell you what, you go talk to Ludo. See what he says.' I turned and left the facility.

Ramin shouted something to me, but I wasn't interested in any more small talk. Like Sabrina, I set my brace to privacy, muted my messages, and headed out to Jack's. My feet were beginning to throb now. Had I been thinking clearly, I'd have gone home and put some shoes on. When I sprinted out of my apartment this morning, I hadn't been thinking about my attire. All I knew was Minju had managed to remove Julius, and I had done nothing to stop her.

I needed to talk to Sabrina, see what she knew. But, more importantly, I just wanted to hug her so hard. She had done what the best of us might have hesitated to do.

I was limping. I looked behind to find bloody splodge marks trailing me as I made my way out of the city. No doubt I'd rack up penalties for those as well. My crib sheet by the end of the day would be well in the red. I was so lost in my thoughts, I failed to hear the gentle hum of the cruiser until it hovered down and paused alongside me. A yellow custodian eyed me carefully. A tattered and bleeding civilian was not an everyday incident.

'Can I help you?' she said.

I wanted to get rid of her and shook my head.

'You're bleeding.'

Did she think I was unaware? I wished I was in my uniform. She might be slightly less concerned. Curators, after all, had something of a reputation for recklessness. It was well deserved.

'I'm okay. I just forgot my shoes. I'm heading home now.'

'May I give you a lift?'

I wanted to scream at her to go away, but no custodian worth her salt would leave someone in such a state of distress.

'That would be kind.'

I stepped gingerly into the cruiser and gave her Jack's address. I was surprised she hadn't asked for my name yet, but no doubt once we were moving and I couldn't get out, she would ask. We were hovering about three metres above the ground. I could jump, but I didn't have the energy or the inclination.

We travelled in silence though, until we reached the outskirts of the city and arrived at District 25, or what was more colloquially known as the Floating Towers.

'I can walk from here.'

I didn't want the custodian to know exactly where I was going, and it appeared I had got away without saying who I was as well. I inched out of the cab. My feet, having enjoyed the brief respite, were now swelling painfully. Sodding cacti.

The custodian studied me. 'I can carry you?'

I tried not to recoil. 'That's very kind, but I don't have far to go.'

She nodded, then removed her helmet and sunglasses. 'Curator Salah. Please accept my sincere condolences.'

I jerked in surprise, then chided myself. I had become such a well-known face, I just hadn't realised that meant people knew who I was. Even if we had never met, even if I wasn't in uniform.

'Julius has been a very good friend to us. We have all enjoyed getting to know him. My colleague, Custodian Shorbagy, is deeply distressed right now, and we share his pain.'

She bowed her head briefly, put her fist over her heart and spread her fingers wide to indicate a break.

I returned the gesture. Why not? My heart *was* broken. It then struck me that she would probably know I didn't live here.

'Do you think you could not mention this trip?'

'Of course. Would you like me to wait and I can take you home afterwards?'

It was surprising, the speed with which she was prepared to help me. Perhaps I had become so used to Minju's duplicity and Clio and Grimaldi's crimes that I had forgotten the basic decency of my fellow Alphas.

I shook my head, testing my feet on the ground. 'And how would you account for your absence from patrol?'

'I'd say I was helping a tourist with heat stroke who had become confused.'

'Do you get a lot of those?'

She chuckled. 'More than you can imagine. So it would be no problem for me to wait?'

14

'Don't worry. I don't know how long I'll be, but thank you. And please pass on my condolences as well to Custodian Shorbagy. Julius considered him one of his first friends here.'

The custodian's eyes welled up and she put her sunglasses back on. 'I will be sure to tell him.'

I watched until she was out of sight, then turned towards the Floating Towers.

The towers were a collection of buildings ranging from three to eight storeys and, unlike a lot of the local architecture, were perpendicular rectangles with no flourishes or curves. The simplicity of design hid an engineering feat of great complexity. The towers were built on the islands and land surrounding the Mareotis Delta, an area prone to flooding in the wet season.

Each tower sat in its own pit of water and, through buffering and hydraulics, was kept upright whilst not touching the edges of the pit. About three floors of the tower sat below ground level. When it rained, the pits would fill with river water and the towers would gently rise on the column of water. Every level was watertight, and so no one ever flooded.

The technology came from our Bangladeshi engineers, and had been employed around the world. It was unsurprising that Jack would choose to live here amongst the streams, lush vegetation, and brilliant technology.

I limped across the bridges until I got to his building and stepped inside. The structure felt as firm as any other, and apparently you could only detect the slightest of movements during very high winds, sandstorms or floods. Otherwise, it was totally normal. The buildings also helped stabilise the delta and stopped it from spreading out and drying up. The farmers loved the downstream silt deposits, and the wildlife loved the deeper water channels. Julius had called it a bloody marvel, and he was right. There was so much we had achieved, but I was beginning to wonder about the cost.

I took the lift up to Jack's, then knocked on the door. If he wasn't home, I wasn't sure what I would do. Probably sit down and fall asleep. I knew I should be chasing down the pharaoh and demanding answers, but I was too angry and too bereft right now, and I knew I would screw it up.

The door opened and Jack simply stared at me. Then he surprised me by stepping forward and giving me a massive hug. He ushered me into the flat, calling out for Sabrina.

She came slowly into the corridor. Her eyes were red and puffy and when she saw me, she burst into fresh tears. It was all I could do not to join in.

'Come on, sit down. I'll get some food and drinks and some skin-fix,' said Jack. He waved us through to a beautiful sitting room with a balcony that opened onto the treetops. Beyond the tree line, boats were making their way in and out of the harbour. I sat down on the violet leather sofa, then groaned in horror at my bloodied footprints on the pale wooden floor.

'It will clean,' sniffed Sabrina, 'it's not a big deal.'

This from the curator who was always the most meticulously turned out, and had regularly reported Julius and others for slovenly appearance, from an undone button to a loosely tied binding. I perched cautiously on the edge of the sofa, until Jack came in with a soft cotton throw, wrapped it around my shoulders, and rubbed some skin-fix into my feet. He offered me some figs, then left again, saying he would be back with the tea.

'What happened?' I asked.

Sitting upright, Sabrina prepared herself for an interrogation. I was going to wave her to relax, but was too tired and let her handle this however she saw fit. 'At two a.m. I was woken via a room alarm informing me of an encrypted message from the office of the pharaoh.'

Poor kid, I could only imagine her joy at such an honour.

'What did the message say?'

'I had been selected to repatriate an angel. It was a great honour to have been chosen, but the mission was to be undertaken immediately and not discussed with anyone. If I agreed, further details would be sent.'

'So you agreed.'

'A direct request from Pharaoh Cleeve? Of course I agreed.'

I nodded. I would have felt the same. 'Then what?'

'The second message told me who the angel in question was. I was also told that I couldn't tell him. As far as he was concerned, this was a time sensitive mission, and that we had been selected to step across. Only when we arrived on Beta would his sentence be delivered, then me and a custodian would remove his brace and return without him.'

'Julius.'

'Yes.'

Her voice was flat, her face expressionless. The speed with which her pride must have turned sour. I wondered why she had been chosen, then rebuked myself. It was our way to put society before self. Sabrina was a perfect curator. Presumably Minju had thought Sabrina would carry out her duties, like a good little drone. Minju had clearly miscalculated.

'What did you do then?'

'I tried to contact Sam. Sorry, Chancellor Nymens,' she corrected herself. Sam had always been a very relaxed captain, but now as Chancellor the familiarity was a step too far for the respectful Sabrina. She continued: 'There had to be a mistake. There just had to. I needed him to hear what had happened. And that's when I realised my communication lines had been jammed.'

'You were prevented from contacting anyone?'

Basic protocols for a sensitive subject, but still a surprisingly authoritarian move. Under normal circumstances, we would never breach a secrecy order, but then this was unheard of. A covert repatriation of an active curator.

'Then what?'

She shuffled in her chair, frowning as she recalled the next few minutes.

'Then I queried the order. I asked Tiresias what directives had been passed. I asked, were they certain? I also asked exactly who I was communicating with.'

'And?'

'There was a pause, then my holo-screen lit up.' Sabrina's voice broke, her eyes wide. 'Nolyny Cleeve herself appeared. The pharaoh, Neith! Can you imagine? Told me it was a matter of national security that Julius be removed as an immediate threat and, that as a non-human of Alpha Earth, he wasn't liable to the same legal protections, so no laws were being broken.'

'The pharaoh actually said "non-human?"'

'Yes. She has never even looked at me, and here she was in my room giving me a direct order.'

Bast. Sabrina must have been out of her wits in awe.

'What then? How did you end up on sand leave?'

She reached for a fig, her hand shaking. I pushed the tray towards her and waited for her to compose herself.

'I said no.'

I tilted my head. Sabrina Mulweather was not the sort of girl to say no to a direct order from her pharaoh on an issue of national security.

'No?'

'I said I didn't believe Julius was a threat, and I would not be a party to his removal without due process.' Her voice broke. 'Can you imagine his expression when he was told that he had been thrown out and was never going to return?'

She broke into noisy sobs. I jumped up and sat beside her, hugging her as tightly as I could.

Jack came in with the tea tray, took one look at us and headed back to the kitchen. He returned with a box of sugared jellies and some hankies. We both helped ourselves to the sweets, and I returned to my seat as Jack sat beside Sabrina and poured us all a cup of tea.

The smell of hot mint and the sugary sweetness hit the spot perfectly, and I was able to draw a breath without my throat hitching. Sabrina's distress was a public manifestation of my own grief, and I was determined to keep it together.

'Then what?'

'Well, then there were a lot of threatening words after which I was informed I was under house detention. My communications were disabled. And when I tried to leave my apartment, there were two red custodians outside my door.'

The outrage in her voice when she mentioned the colour of the custodians was priceless. Yellow custodians were for minor civil regulations, red custodians were for dangerous situations.

'What sort of threat did they think I was?'

I coughed out a laugh. 'You are a curator. A veteran of the Grimaldi Uprising. Plus, you had just disobeyed a direct order from the pharaoh. Added to which you were actually trying to leave your house having been told you were under detention. I guess they were taking you pretty seriously.' I had hoped to cheer her up, but the level of her transgression upset her further. I offered her another sweet. 'Go on.'

'I closed my door and waited. At nine a.m. my communications were restored and I received a notification that I was on sand leave for a fortnight. When I opened the door, the custodians had gone. I tried to contact Captain Gamal, but his call was diverted, so I checked the status of Julius and found he was gone.' She trailed off.

I had to nudge her again. 'Then what?'

'And then I came here.'

Jack wrapped his arm around Sabrina's shoulders and gave her a small squeeze as we sipped our tea in silence.

'What's going on, Neith?' asked Jack slowly. 'Why was Julius repatriated?'

I shrugged.

'It doesn't make any sense,' he continued. 'I just thought, with your closeness to Special Adviser Chen, you might know more?'

'How would that give me any further insight?' I might have spoken more harshly than I had intended, but I disliked the implication that Minju and I were friends.

The pair of them sat huddled together. They were little more than teenagers, and I felt the weight of their regard, waiting for me to fix everything.

'Well,' said Jack slowly, 'not your closeness so much as her friendship with the pharaoh. You're moving in pretty high circles, since your recovery. Maybe the pharaoh said something to you or Chen?'

I stared at Jack, trying to see things from his point of view. Was that how he saw me? Mates with the power brokers? I had been out of circulation for six months, had achieved some sort of hero status in my coma, and then when I returned to daily life, I was only being seen in Minju's company. I was a fool not to consider how this appeared to outsiders. I had actively avoided other curators, but I had done so to protect them. A side effect was that they thought I no longer was interested in them. I wanted to clasp my fist over my heart and spread out my fingers. The old gestures were often the most universally understood, and my heart was truly breaking all over again.

'I'll speak to Ramin. We'll get the sand leave removed from your record,' I said, hoping to offer Sabrina a small beacon of light. Her courage had been remarkable, and I didn't want her punished for it.

'You will not!' She sniffed and hiccupped.

'I won't?'

'No, you won't. I will serve my time and then I want it on my record permanently. I want everyone to know what I did and why. I'm not ashamed of it.'

My heart swelled. This was what curators were made of. Piss and guts. And, in Sabrina's case, tied up in a pretty pink bow.

I laughed for the first time that day.

'Don't you dare mock me, Neith.'

'I'm not mocking you. I bloody love you, Sabrina Mulweather. You are the very best of us and I am honoured to know you.'

The fight billowed out of her, but she gave a weak smile and poured everyone another drink as tears continued to roll down her cheeks.

'Now what?' she asked. 'Because this isn't right.'

'There's a lot not right at the moment,' muttered Jack.

'What do you mean?' I demanded. Jack, despite his age was highly placed within the engineers and at the heart of the new quantum advancements. It was possible that he too may know more than he was letting on.

He drank his tea, then studied his cup. 'Nothing.'

I wasn't going to press him. He had been tortured by Grimaldi and hadn't said a thing. If he didn't want to talk, he wouldn't, and yet I was worried. Was I so compromised that he couldn't trust me?

I put my cup down slowly. My time here was done. I would learn nothing more and my presence might even be compromising them. Standing up, I returned the shawl to Sabrina.

'I'll let you know if I hear anything else. Trust me, I will be arguing for Julius' return. As you say, I have friends in high places. Let's see if I can put those connections to use.'

I needed to leave. Jack's expression was wary and conflicted. I could tell my simple presence was causing him issues.

Sabrina went off to find me a spare pair of her shoes, and I wondered just how often the girl stayed over.

'There isn't a day that goes by that I don't thank you for my life you know,' said Jack quietly. 'I will never forget how you gave yours for mine.'

Now it was my turn to look uncomfortable. I hadn't consciously sacrificed my life for his. I was just trying to save him from being abducted. The shot to my head had been an unwelcome outcome. I'm certain that if people had foreknowledge, we might have fewer "heroes."

'Forget it.'

'Never.'

'Well.' I paused. Small talk was useless. 'Then just trust me.'

I needed him to know I hadn't changed, even if I couldn't tell him what was really going on.

'I do, Neith.' He grabbed my hand. 'I do trust you.'

Sabrina came back with a pair of pink party shoes with laces up to the knee. She held them out to me with an apologetic look.

I grimaced for effect and pulled the webbed strapping up over my calves. Bell boots were the absolute nadir in fashion, or at least they were in my eyes. Sabrina, it seemed, loved them. Apparently, they were currently her favourite footwear when not at work.

'How do we turn the music off?'

She wrinkled her face. 'It's integral, I'm afraid.'

Which is how I walked home, bells ringing joyfully at my every broken-hearted step.

Chapter Three - August: Alpha: Neith

I was nearly home when I switched my messages on again. Claiming priority was one from Minju, insisting I get myself over to her office right away. But she wasn't my boss yet. Whilst she had offered me a job, I hadn't started anything. I was theoretically in recovery from my coma and language reacquisition. I still dreamt in Welsh, but other than that I had made a full recovery. I'd be damned, though, if I was going to speak to her right now. I knew she was behind Julius' removal, and I couldn't trust myself to keep up the façade. Not today.

I sent a quick text message.

-Not happening. I'm sick.

I'd never voluntarily taken a sick day in my life, but the last thing I could do right now was listen to her tell me how shocked and outraged she was, and that she would try to fix everything. Minju's text came pinging back. I'd blocked visuals.

-It's what Julius would have wanted.

That made me stop and take a very deep breath. I had to count to ten before I replied and also found myself on sand leave. I needed to stay close to Minju, not tell her she was a sodding snake.

-Sorry. Too ill. Will be there tomorrow.

I then tapped through a request to the med unit and declared myself emotionally vulnerable. That would feed into Tiresias and block all further work-related messages. I scanned the rest of my texts, which were a basic mash-up of *Have you heard?* I was about to switch off when I spotted one from Githumbi. A request to join her at Mithras, a bar favoured by red custodians.

I changed direction and hailed a cab. She had sent the text an hour ago and might have left, but I needed to see her. I was hoping she would tell me what had happened and how Julius had coped.

It had been years since I visited Mithras. I think it had been a bar crawl after graduation. Stepping out of the bright daylight into the shade of the bar reminded me of how taciturn custodians could be. I'd forgotten about the training ring in the corner. A pair were sparring in there at the moment, but it appeared light-hearted. Naturally, as I walked in, everyone turned. The looks weren't hostile, so much as surprised. A few nodded at me, then Githumbi stood up from a table in the corner and waved me over.

With every step my bloody bells rang, and by the time I was halfway across the room I considered flipping into a handstand and walking on my palms. When I sat down, the various conversations sprang back up around me.

Githumbi was a mess. Her pint was half empty, her uniform was unbuttoned, and she was sporting a massive black eye and a split lip. This was Luisa Githumbi. Head of the Red Custodians. No wonder the mood in here was sombre. A server brought me over a pint unasked for, and I took a small sip. It was strong stuff. Much too strong for daytime, and I pushed it away.

'How did that happen?' I asked, looking at her face.

'Clio Masoud.' Githumbi winced. 'Man, she is fast.'

'What does *she* look like?'

'I didn't touch her. She stood there waiting for me to retaliate. When I didn't, she spat on the floor and walked off.'

'Why didn't you?'

'Cos I deserved it.'

She picked up her pint and drained it, then looked at mine. I waved my hand and she drew it towards her. Moments later she was necking it back. I wasn't really sure how to proceed, still processing the fact Clio had lamped Githumbi. I wasn't surprised in the least that she had got in a fight, but I was frankly astonished it was over Julius.

I also didn't expect Githumbi to appear so distressed. When I saw her this morning, she had just stepped back through from Beta, all smart and shiny. But with reddened eyes, my inner voice reminded me.

'Do you want to tell me about it?'

She grabbed a handful of pistachios and began cracking the shells. 'You don't want to try to knock me out?'

I snorted. As if I could. 'I assume you were simply following orders, no matter how distasteful.'

I swear she crumpled. Her shoulders sagged, and she sort of imploded. She downed my pint and was about to wave for another when the server brought it over along with a glass of fruit juice for me, and I smiled gratefully.

By the time the server left, Githumbi had taken control of herself again. 'Do you know the first curator assigned to the job refused? Some chit, barely out of training.'

'Sabrina Mulweather. I've just come from her place. These are hers.' I waved at my shoes.

Githumbi groaned and shook her head. 'The owner of a pair of bell boots has more backbone than I have.' She moaned softly to herself, staring into her pint.

'She knows Julius better, if it helps?'

I don't know why I was trying to console the woman. She had taken my friend away.

'Not really,' she muttered. 'I've tried to kid myself that I was there to be a friendly face. That I would make sure his transition was painless as possible. But it all comes down to the fact that I was too busy following orders.'

'That's how it's meant to be, isn't it?' Red custodians had some of the shittiest jobs and couldn't discuss them. They just needed to get in and get things done. 'Our society thrives when we all work together and do what is asked of us.'

'I should have said no.'

I agreed, but sighed. 'And then what? Someone else would have done it. It would have still happened.'

'But it wouldn't have been me.' She took another gulp, and I wondered at her ability to remain upright, let alone talk coherently. She put her pint back down. 'I wouldn't have to remember our final conversation. The look in his eyes.'

It was too much for me, and I grabbed her pint and took a swig. It was a brutal brew and I choked.

Githumbi smirked at me. 'You stick to your guava milk.'

She had a point. I chewed my lip. 'How was he?'

'Confused. Angry. Distressed. Then furious.'

I raised an eyebrow.

'He swore.'

'Julius did?'

'Yep. Quite colourful as well.'

'Did he say anything? Did he know why he was being repatriated?'

She toyed with her pint and was about to say something, but then changed her mind. 'No, he was as confused as the rest of us. He was raving a bit with lots of wild ideas, but in the end, he accepted his fate.'

In the eyes of a custodian, that was a great honour. When the fight is lost, control your ending. Curators, however, scrapped to their dying breath. We are less dignified. What would I have done in Julius' shoes? Run? Snatched a brace? Then what? Stepped back into a world which didn't want me? Would I even make it out of the quantum facility?

'You said he was raving. What did he say?'

For the first time since I had sat down, I sensed Githumbi withdrawing from me.

'You can trust me,' I said.

She pushed her pint away and shook her head. 'Nothing. It was just gibberish.'

I really needed to know what he said and why she wasn't prepared to tell me. I changed the subject, trying to come at it from another angle.

'Okay. Fair enough. But I'm trying to understand how all this happened. Last night we were all laughing at a party. This morning he's gone. So, who gave the order?'

She was ready to talk, so long as I wasn't asking difficult questions. 'I don't have to tell you any of this, but I am. I don't know why. Guilt maybe. Julius has been an interesting individual and one I could rely on. His actions during the Grimaldi Uprising were exemplary. He fought alongside my custodians, and many reported his actions to me in a favourable light. Some even said he provided cover to help save their lives. I admire anyone who can do that. Especially from such an unlikely ally. An angel professor.'

'But he was more than an angel!'

'I know,' said Githumbi, now glaring at me, 'which is why we are talking. Although I don't think I can help much. I received my orders in the middle of the night for an angel extraction.'

'Why night-time?'

'Less distraction, less protest. Best for all parties. Some angels were reluctant to leave.'

'I thought only those who wanted to go left?'

'No, they have all been returned. Julius was the last.'

That was news to me. I wondered if it was common knowledge, something I had missed during my coma.

'Hang on, even the princes?'

The princes had only recently arrived having been removed from an uncertain future in the Tower of London.

'No, my understanding is that returning them will cause even more disruption to the timeline.'

'Are they any safer here?'

Githumbi blinked. 'They're children! Why wouldn't they be safe?'

'Well, why are angels being returned?' I demanded. 'I don't understand.'

She glared at me and took another swig. 'Neither do I. But that's not my job. I'm just here to protect our society.'

'From angels?'

The idea that a bunch of old age Betas would pose a threat to anyone was ludicrous. 'Has Julius' extraction been on the cards for a while?' My face clenched in anger.

Githumbi pulled away from me. 'No, that was the odd thing.' She eyed me carefully, and I tried to relax. 'I had already asked if he was going to be repatriated. If he was, I was going to speak against it. But Asha assured me his fate had already been discussed and resolved. Julius was to be treated as one of us.'

Asha Giovanetti was Director of Security for all of Alexandria. If she had vouched for Julius, then the order had to have come from a higher source.

'So, what changed?'

'No idea, but last night I received a message to assemble a small team for an immediate repatriation. It was Code Ouroboros, so I couldn't discuss it with anyone but my boss.'

It was useless asking why she hadn't alerted me. An Ouroboros Code is serious stuff and rarely ever spoken about.

'And before you ask, of course I queried it. Asha was really cross that I was double checking. Apparently, intel had emerged proving Julius was a Quantum Threat Level Ten.'

'I don't know what that means.'

I had missed so much in my sodding coma, but I wondered if these changes were public or covert. My money was on covert.

'It means there was evidence he was in contact with other Dimensional Subjects.'

I shook my head. 'No. That doesn't work. Firenze classed this Earth as out of bounds. And Julius doesn't have the ability to make contact.'

Firenze was a sort of superhuman from another reality, a third Earth that put our own accomplishments to shame. Firenze herself was some sort of blend of human and quantum intelligence, fashioned by that Earth's Leonardo da Vinci. We barely understood the quantum dwellers, known as gods, but she had insisted they leave Alpha Earth alone. Julius wouldn't have been able to communicate with them even if he had wanted to. Firenze was not someone to be contradicted.

'All I know is what I was told. The order came directly from the pharaoh. There had been a cabinet meeting, and it was determined that time was of the essence.'

'But what about a trial? We could have presented evidence.'

I was getting really agitated. Minju had at least a six-month head start on me. As I lay in a hospital bed, she had been back to her old tricks.

'I asked the same thing. Trust me, Neith, I was as unhappy about this as you are now.'

'So why wasn't there a trial?'

'Stop shouting and sit down. I'm trying to tell you.'

I glared at her, but she was right. Shouting at her would not solve anything. Especially in a pub full of custodians who were now all staring at me. I slid back into my chair. I knew Minju was behind this, but I couldn't for the life of me work out why. She genuinely liked Julius. For her to get rid of him meant he had discovered something, or she thought he had. What was it?

'There was no trial because he had already been reclassified as "Angel" and, as such, he wasn't subject to the same laws or safeguards as the rest of us. I ran through the laws as we headed towards his apartments looking for a loophole, but angels have pretty much the same sort of protection as rhinos. Sentient independents. We have a duty of care to them, but they don't make any demands on us.'

'He's a human being! Not a fucking pachyderm!'

I had jumped up again and was pacing, my bloody bells ringing merrily. The other patrons were now politely ignoring me, but I wasn't fooled. I stood still

35

and rubbed my face in my hands, then sat back down again.

'I'm sorry, Luisa. I know this isn't your fault. And I appreciate you were looking for ways to save him.'

In fact, it was astounding that she had tried to countermand her orders. I just wish she'd have stretched it a tiny bit further to call me. My thoughts must have been clear.

'It was an Ouroboros Code, Neith. I did everything I could. You weren't the one who had to say goodbye to him. You didn't have to look him in the eyes and shake his hand as you administered the brain fog.'

I had been in the act of placing a nut into my mouth but now it fell onto the table.

'You wiped his memory?' I whispered.

'Standard angel protocol. It's irresponsible to let them remember us. Not to mention cruel.'

'You don't think its crueller to remove us from his memory?' My voice was rising, and I sat on my trembling hands.

'You feel the cruelty because you remember. He doesn't. We implanted a false memory for the past few years regarding a foreign assignment. All paperwork and computer records were manipulated. He has a healthy bank balance and a job to return to. When he thinks back over the recent past, he will find himself uninterested, and will focus instead on current events or historical ones.'

I wanted to weep. He was gone and now, even if I could visit him, he wouldn't know me. It was cruel indeed, but as Githumbi said, he wasn't the one who would feel it.

'If you want to know more, you'll have to ask the pharaoh and find out what changed her mind.'

I went to stand up.

Githumbi waved her hand. 'There's no hurry. Besides, the pharaoh is on a scheduled rest day. Even you can't interrupt a rest day with work.'

She was right, but I wanted to do something. I wanted to kick down Minju's door, slam her up against a wall and beat the truth out of her. I tried to relax. I couldn't do that either, but I couldn't sit still. I needed to find out what had made Minju's tail twitch at the party. Julius had said something last night which had disturbed her. Less than six hours later, he was gone. I couldn't ask Minju, which only left two other people. I was going to have to go and talk to Clio, then talk to the pharaoh.

'Whatever just crossed your mind, don't do anything stupid,' said Githumbi. 'I will not hesitate to detain you if you do something beyond code.'

I snorted. 'Don't worry about me. I'm Neith Salah, I never break code.'

She tipped her head, then shrugged. 'Come on, I've had enough to drink. Time I went home.' She stood up and followed me out to the street.

We walked in silence for a bit and headed along the concourse, the bright sun blinding us. I waited for my contacts to adjust, as she slid her sunnies into place.

'Thank you for coming to see me Neith, I just want to say again how incredibly—'

A bang shattered the airwaves, brutally interrupting her commiserations, and our eyes locked in horror.

Githumbi tightened her holster, pulling it into battle mode. 'Are you armed?'

'No.'

Of course I wasn't. I was a curator, not a custodian. I had no licence to carry weapons on Alpha. From the holster, she pulled a second smaller laser and threw it at me as she sprinted towards the noise.

I instinctively caught the laser, but other than that, remained frozen. Paralysed. The second I heard the noise, I flashed back to a moment of searing pain in my head. My world exploding in a sea of blood and agony.

'Salah!' shouted Githumbi over her shoulder. 'Gunshot!'

There were hardly any people in Alexandria who were trained to recognise the sound of a Beta weapon. Even fewer who had actually been shot. Githumbi looked back at me. A curator would have stopped and come back to my aid, would have talked me through my paralysis, helped me with my fear. Githumbi shook her head and ran off.

A second later, I discovered I was following her. Sweet Ra, she was fast. My goal now was not to get caught up in my memories, but simply to catch up with her. She was running into danger and I had to help, my wretched boots ringing out my arrival.

At first, we were the only ones running, although I could see concern on a few faces. It had been six months since the battle, but memories run deep and a single noise can shake you out of your complacency. As we got closer, people were sprinting past us, away from Hope Plaza.

Githumbi was running with her laser drawn and I did the same, looking up and around at the overhead walkways and hover cars. Memories of flying horses and tentacles kept flashing past.

I began reciting the seventeen times table and focused on the here and now. There had only been one gunshot. Our braces were not reporting any other incidents, although they were now chiming an alert for all citizens to stay in place and take shelter. Those running past us weren't paying much attention, and would no doubt be fined later.

We emerged into the plaza, where a small group of people were kneeling around something on the ground. Everyone else had fled. My sense of horror mounted as I realised what they were staring at. The pharaoh lay on the ground, face up, her eyes open, staring vacantly. Around her turban, a pool of blood and brains plumed outwards. The blood was already congealing as it passed a piece of skull with black hair attached and globs of grey brain matter.

I rocked on my feet as my skin prickled with a searing heat. The light was funny, and a huge bucket of water was smashing from side to side inside my skin. Waves of nausea flooded through me and I knew I was going to faint.

'Salah. Focus.'

Githumbi's voice was a remote echo, over the roar of my heartbeat. I watched as she reached into a pocket and held something out to me. I swayed, wondering if I would fall onto the shattered body at my feet. Would I land in the gobbets of brain or the blood? Was this what I had looked like when I had been shot in the head?

Githumbi took a quick step towards me and shoved whatever was in her hand into my mouth. I tried to spit it out, but she clasped her hand over my mouth as the pill fizzed and dissolved on my tongue. A flush of iced electricity shot through my limbs. Focus rushed through me and I snapped to attention.

'Are you okay?'

'Yes.' I felt utterly discombobulated, but alert. It was a strange sensation.

'Good. The pharaoh must have been shot from above. Secure this area whilst I set up a search grid.'

She ran off towards the closest block. As custodians and medics ran into the plaza, I shouted directions, then slumped against a planter as the experts took over. The rejuvenate was wearing off, and I leant over and vomited into the flowers.

The air was warm, the sky was blue, Julius had gone, and the person charged with dispatching him had just been assassinated. What had he said at the party to freak out Minju? What had he said to Githumbi that she called ravings? I needed to speak to Curator Ludo and see if he would tell me what Julius had said when he was repatriated. Then I needed to see Clio.

I didn't care about the shooter. I knew Minju was behind it, and because I knew that, I also knew that the shooter would never be found. Not alive anyway. The killings had begun again.

Chapter Four - August: Alpha: Neith

I slunk home. This felt like the worst day of my life, which is saying something, considering I once got shot in the head. This was shaping up to be a blistering August and, despite all the clever environmental deflectors, nothing was stopping the heat pouring in from the distant Sahara. I wasn't even in my second skins. When Minju had banged on the door this morning, I had raced out in a vest and sarong. Thanks to Sabrina, I walked home in a sarong, vest and high heels. I also had the blood of the pharaoh on my hands.

Githumbi had failed to locate the shooter. This alarmed almost everyone. Githumbi was one of the best. If she couldn't track them down, they had to be good. Only I was unsurprised. I gave my statement to the custodians, then returned home.

Opening the door to my flat, I stepped into the embrace of cool air and closed the door behind me. I removed the bell boots and slipped out of my clothes, throwing them in the bin. They were covered in blood and brains, and I could never wear them again without flinching.

In the bathroom, I covered myself in Dead Sea mud and lay down on the cold glass bench until the mud caked and cracked on me. As I lay prone, I tried to process the day. I had lost Julius, and Minju was still plotting. I didn't know who to trust. Minju had assassinated the pharaoh without blinking and I was terrified that if I spoke to anyone, they could also be got rid of. As could I. I had died once. I didn't fancy a rerun.

The mud pulled on my hair, and I called out for a rinse.

Thin jets of water needled my skin. I sat up, scrubbing all the mud away as it ran out through the glass mesh.

'Bath please.'

'You have reached your allocation for this month.'

I groaned and placed my head in my hands before addressing Tiresias.

'I've been in a coma for six months, borrow from that allocation.'

'Thank you for your frugality. But there are no bathing roll overs. Three a week is your limit. Do you wish to apply for extenuating circumstances?'

How curious to consider my coma as an act of frugality. How impressive of me. I was too tired to be angry.

'Yes.'

A moment later, my taps began to run. I hadn't even had to explain my request. No doubt Tiresias had run through today's events and considered it acceptable.

I added some salts and sank down into the warm water.

'Neith,' said Tiresias, 'would you like me to call a friend?'

I shook my head, then remembered I had disabled visuals.

'No. I'm fine.'

'Can I get you something to drink? Some food?'

Tiresias was in full care mode. This might go on for a while if I didn't nip it in the bud.

'No, thank you. I'm fine, but tired and shocked. I acknowledge my distress but will cope. I have food and drink in the kitchen. I don't require deliveries. I don't need to make an appointment with a listener. I don't need any chemical support. I would also appreciate no further interactions.'

'Will you be wearing your brace for remote monitoring?'

'No.'

I was a seasoned curator. The chances were that Tiresias would now leave me alone. It might sulk, and it might add a mark against my name, but hopefully that would be the end of it.

'Thank you, Neith. Your preferences have been noted. Please take care of yourself.'

With a sigh, I slipped under the water, and when I re-emerged, the room was silent.

I lay in the water until it went cold, then grabbed a dressing gown and headed into the kitchen for some pancakes and a beer. Settling down onto my sofa, I switched on the broadcasts.

Naturally, all channels were issuing health warnings before allowing access, and there was the standard, alternative selection of films and funnies. I clicked on the news and flicked until I found a channel where the journalists weren't openly weeping.

The Golden Mean was our most rigorous platform and was proudly boasting that Minju Chen would join them soon, to share her thoughts and feelings on the shocking death of her close, personal friend.

I flicked the settings from hologram to 2D on the programme console. The idea of Minju in my room right now was more than I could stomach. They had switched from outside broadcast, where they had been asking citizens how they felt, and moved into the studio where the presenters were sitting on a sofa.

Both stood and hugged Minju as she entered the studio. Minju's back was to the camera, and her thick spotted tail hung sadly, the tip resting on the floor. As they broke apart, she took her place on the sofa and curled her tail onto her lap. Really, she never made such a show of her tail, but it was hard to watch her now and not be reminded that she used to be a curator and sacrificed much for her country.

'Greetings Minju, Honour to your hearth and home,' Jude Mwangi spoke sorrowfully, and was echoed by her co-presenter and life partner Jonas Mwangi. The nation's favourite couple. We had followed them from their engagement to the raising of their children, whilst they entertained and informed us. Their investigative programmes on the consumption of curds were astonishing and prompted a national change in diet.

I listened to their fawning tones and cringed.

'Today had been a most dreadful day,' said Jude sorrowfully.

'A dreadful one,' echoed Jonas as he wiped a tear from his eye. 'And terrifying.'

'It is, it is,' said Minju. 'There are so many things to be scared of.' She stroked her tail thoughtfully. 'What were you thinking of in particular?'

Jude leant forward, her necklaces swinging freely as she took a deep breath. 'Well, we haven't found the murderer.'

'Luisa Githumbi is Asha Giovanetti's finest custodian,' said Minju forcefully. 'And she was on the scene. Evidence of great skills to get there so fast.'

'And yet, despite her speed, she failed to find the murderer,' interrupted Jonas, his voice deep and thoughtful. He turned and looked straight down the camera, making eye contact with the entire nation. 'And we are left facing the threat of a random murderer.'

'How dreadful,' murmured Minju.

'It *is* dreadful,' said Jonas. 'And you are right, it is disappointing that Githumbi was right on the scene and yet couldn't locate the shooter.'

'What are you suggesting?' said Minju. 'That Githumbi was the assassin. Preposterous!'

Jonas recoiled. 'No. Absolutely not. I would never suggest Githumbi was responsible for the assassination of our dear, sweet pharaoh.'

I watched in horror. The more they said it, the more it was becoming a thing. Were people up and down the country watching this and now wondering if Luisa Githumbi was to blame? What was Minju thinking? Githumbi had said Julius was raving when she escorted him home. Was it possible he had uncovered Minju's duplicity and now Githumbi was a target for Minju's attention? She had got rid of Julius. Was this why? Had Julius somehow discovered Minju was behind the uprising? And if he had, was that what he had said to Luisa? Was she next? With the pharaoh gone, Minju could lie all day long about her orders.

Minju's tail was flicking in her lap, and she was stroking it in absent minded agitation.

'I am glad to hear it. Luisa Githumbi deserves our gratitude and respect. If the time has come when she can no longer carry out her job, we must help her acclimatise into a new role. But we must never, *never* cast aspersions on her previous exemplary record.'

Wow, I thought, how to destroy someone whilst praising them.

'Who do you think is responsible? If they simply disappeared, could they be—' Jude stopped and looked around the studio fearfully. She wasn't faking it. 'Could it be one of those "others?"'

'The ones from Beta Earth?' said Minju, her face pensive.

Thank God this wasn't a projection, I might have punched her. She knew damn well those quantum beings didn't originate on Beta Earth, and the Beta Earth angels had all been sent home. Although I didn't know if that was public knowledge. Minju carried on dripping poison.

'Who knows? All I know was that my dear friend Nolyny was concerned that the threat was not yet passed.'

She paused and hung her head low. Even I leant forwards, waiting to see what she would say next. Her hands grasped her tail, her small fingers sinking into the fur. She cleared her throat, borrowing Jonas's trick as she stared into the camera.

'It grieves me to see how cruelly she has been proved right. We are once again under attack, when all we have ever tried to do is support Beta Earth.'

Now Jonas looked positively alarmed. 'So, this could be the work of one of the angels?'

Sweet Bast, did that ninny think octogenarians would come at him with their crochet needles?

'No,' said Minju, shaking her head vigorously. 'At least, I don't think so. Nolyny had been, very quietly, re-settling all the angels back on their own Earth.'

'That's news!'

Jonas turned to Jude. 'Did you know this?' then asked the audience the same thing. There were excited mutterings in the crowd, and Minju shook her head quietly.

'The pharaoh didn't want to alarm the general population, but there had been meetings with the United Nations Symposium, and it had been agreed that the safest places for everyone was in their own reality.'

'Wow,' said Jude breathlessly. The show's viewing figures would be through the roof tomorrow.

'I know,' said Minju. 'Every day she was thinking of us. Her waking thoughts were our protection.'

There was a quiet hush as her image was projected into the studio, smiling and waving at some ceremonial function.

'And now every angel has returned. Does that include Julius Strathclyde?'

I grabbed another beer and inhaled half of it, not even tasting it.

'I can't comment on the whereabouts of Strathclyde.'

49

'Oh, you bitch,' I shouted at the screen, grateful that the windows were closed.

'He surely can't have been responsible for this. Isn't he a friend of yours?'

'Indeed he is, and I wish he was here with me right now. Who knows, he might be able to help explain this mindless violence. He always has such charming insights into brutality.'

Minju was the very picture of distress whilst she gently savaged Julius' reputation. Jonas leant across and patted Minju's hand. I idly wondered when Minju would have him bundled into the back of a lorry and shot for his patronising familiarity.

'But Special Adviser Chen, we are no closer to understanding the assassination of this wonderful leader. Or indeed why Custodian Githumbi claimed the killer disappeared.' He turned to the audience and raised his hands, palms up. 'Are you certain we can trust her?'

Minju slowly nodded her head. 'She is the best of us. Besides which, at the time of the shooting she was with the extraordinary Neith Salah. And she, I would trust with my life.'

I hadn't seen that coming. Then I laughed. I hadn't seen the bullet coming either. I looked at my beer and decided I might be a little drunk. I threw the bottle at the screen and had the infantile pleasure of watching the beer dribbling down Minju's image. Cleaning the screen with a cloth, I stared in disgust at Minju as she extolled how brave, how noble, how prepared I was to do what was right. I was even prepared to lay down my life. I snarled at the screen, flung myself back onto the linen sofa, and grabbed another bottle of beer.

'Sacrifice is something you yourself understand, Minju,' said Jude earnestly.

Minju dipped her head. 'My sacrifice was nothing compared to Neith Salah's.'

'We are grateful for all of our curators and custodians. They take care of our society at huge personal sacrifice.'

There was a warm round of applause from the audience, and Minju graciously tipped her head in their direction.

Jonas quietened down the audience. 'But we must move forward. Who do you think will be our next pharaoh?'

Minju rolled her eyes. 'I have no idea. Who would want such a cursed position?'

Jonas and Jude nodded at each other, then smiled at Minju.

'What about you?' said Jude.

Minju laughed, then wiped a tear from her eye.

'You don't want me, a failed curator, a terrified archivist, a grieving friend.'

Jonas patted her hand again, and I found myself wondering where I should send the flowers for his funeral.

'I don't think others see you in that light. You were a brave and courageous curator. During the uprising, you never left your post, and were prepared to defend our acquisitions with your life, and you have always stood by your friends. Look how you defend Githumbi and Strathclyde, when others may doubt them.'

Minju smiled and patted his hand before placing it back on his thigh.

'You are too kind. And yet we must look forward and get someone in place quickly. Who that will be, better minds than I will decide.'

As the show moved on, Minju left the stage and a stream of guests followed, all sharing accolades and anecdotes of the late Nolyny Cleeve, and each and every one of them suggested Minju would be an excellent pharaoh.

I fell asleep surrounded by bottles and regret.

Chapter Five - August: Beta: Julius

I stretched and grabbed around for the alarm clock. First day back at work and I was looking forward to it. America had been invigorating, but God it was good to be home. However, by the time I left the house I was thoroughly unsettled, and I put it down to first day nerves and being back in Cambridge.

I'd been overseas for so long that little things seemed odd to me. I'd put milk on my cornflakes as I always do, and then found the milk tasted better than I could ever imagine. It was as if I hadn't drunk the stuff in years. My clothes felt wrong. My behaviour was bizarre; when I went to pick my shoes up, I shook them. Then, when I asked myself what I was doing, I appeared to be looking for scorpions. My tweed jacket was oddly heavy. And, when I slung it on, I struggled to button it up over my chest, and it pulled across the shoulders. However, when I stepped outside, the cold air hit me like a sledgehammer and I was grateful for the jacket, trying to pull it closer around me.

As I walked to work, I was surprised by how many people were wearing shorts and t-shirts, and I wondered if I was coming down with something. Given that it was August, their dress was entirely appropriate. It was me that was out of sorts. When I crossed the street, I looked upwards and nearly collided with a group of cyclists. Something was missing from the sky, and I couldn't quite place it.

By the end of the day, I was really unsettled. I'd relaxed back into the job with apparent ease. I picked up my lecture schedule and discussed the next paper I planned to publish. It was all as I expected. But equally, it felt wrong. It became markedly worse when we got to the pub, and I went and got the drinks in and saw a brew called King Arthur's.

'What's that about?'

The barman cocked his head. 'Coronation special, in't it? Mind you, it's so bloody popular I reckon it's going to become a regular.'

'Coronation?'

What the hell had I missed? His expression said the same, and I explained I had been away for a while. Although I was still confused. Surely a British coronation would have made the news worldwide? This made no sense.

'Prince William's.'

His words baffled me.

'Bloody hell, mate, were you living under a bush?'

I laughed weakly.

'It was one hell of an event. Almost outshone the Queen's Jubilee. Remember that, do you?'

At least that was something I did remember. It had been several years ago and had been incredible. Charlie and I had gone to a street party and dressed up as corgis. To quote Charlie, it was bloody good fun. We also celebrated when she hit one hundred. I had wondered how much longer she could go on, but apparently her time ran out whilst I was abroad. For the life of me, though, I couldn't bring it to mind.

'If the Queen died, why didn't Charles come to the throne?'

It was a fair question. The line of succession was pretty clear: Elizabeth, Charles, William, George.

'Poor sod, on hearing of her death, he promptly had a stroke.'

'No way!' That was shocking, talk about unlucky. 'Did he die as well?'

'Nope, but he renounced his claim. All a bit sad, really. Poor chap is quite ill with it. Finds it hard to speak. Felt like he didn't have it in him to be king.'

'Christ. Imagine waiting all that time, and then having to let it go the minute you receive it.'

'Noble is what it is,' said the barman as he placed the pints in front of me. Realising I couldn't carry ten drinks, I called Giles over and he ferried the drinks back and forth, whilst the bartender continued to bring me up to speed.

'So, Prince William is king,' I said slowly, and was relieved when the barman nodded. At least I had got that right. 'Then who is King Arthur?'

'Ah yes, well what you might not know,' began the bartender, happy to proclaim himself an expert on royal nomenclature, 'is that the royal family has a habit of changing their names when they get crowned. Well, the men do anyway. Arthur is one of William's middle names, and he picked that.'

I absent-mindedly passed Giles my pint as the barman continued. Something was really wrong. Why couldn't I remember something this momentous?

'It made quite the headline. A new Camelot and so on. Still, with the recent policy shifts on immigration, welfare, EU trade and travel, things have felt pretty good around here.'

I continued to stare. Absolutely none of this made any sense. Well, it did, just not why I couldn't remember it. Nor why the idea of a King Arthur made me feel so jittery.

'You sure you're alright?'

I suggested the jetlag was catching up with me, and returned to the table, where I surreptitiously got everyone to share their favourite coronation stories and absorbed all I could. After just one pint of King Arthur's, which was incidentally delicious, I made my excuses and headed home.

It wasn't just me that felt wrong. There was something off about Cambridge as well, if that was even possible. Everyone seemed happy. Not inanely grinning or some weird Midwich thing, but just relaxed and smiling.

As I walked along in the warm evening, a cyclist hit a pothole and came off his bike. It wasn't a bad tumble, but two taxi drivers stopped and offered him a lift, redirecting traffic until he was happy to ride on. One of them grabbed some spray paint from the cab and drew a big warning circle around it. It was a nice thing to do, but just felt off. I couldn't work out what was wrong with me. Jet lag probably and maybe I'd eaten something a tad iffy.

I put my key in the door of my terrace house and I wondered when it would feel like my home and not Charlie's. Charlie was my best friend and had died following a car crash in Germany a year or two back. My shock at the loss of someone so vibrant as my best friend was compounded by the fact that he had left me his house.

The following morning, I was disappointed the jetlag hadn't passed, and headed in to work nursing a low-level headache. Trying to come to terms with a misaligned world. For example, the pothole had already been repaired and there was none of the usual congestion. Had the bike lanes finally been fixed? My equilibrium was shaken further by an encounter with a strange man in a coffeeshop.

My students made a habit of wandering everywhere with a cup of coffee surgically attached to their hands, and I decided a takeout might be just what I needed. I made the dreadful mistake of asking the person who was pouring the drinks to surprise me. Apparently, they were a barista, and it took years how to learn to be a master barista, which did indeed surprise me. I had mistakenly presumed that making a cup of coffee involved pouring hot water over ground coffee. My second surprise was that having said *surprise me*, they chose to poison me with a concoction of cream, sugar and, I know this sounds incredible, flavourings.

I sipped and winced whilst I waited for my toasted panini, and wondered when I had become so old.

'You should try The Hole in the Wall on Trinity Street, properly decent coffee.'

I turned to look at the speaker. He was a very well-dressed older Black man. Frankly, he was one step away from sporting a bowler hat, his oxfords were polished beautifully, and his crisp white collar and cuffs peeked the perfect distance out from a dark navy suit. At a guess, I would say he was in his late sixties, but if he said he was fifty, I wouldn't have protested.

He smiled and nodded at my cup. 'Please forgive my intrusion, but I couldn't help but notice your distress.'

I laughed and put the cup down, then pushed it away. Lowering my voice, I turned away from the counter. 'On Trinity Street, you say?'

'Tanzanian beans, which you know are the best. Yes, yes?'

We nodded in agreement, two mutual fans of the Tanzanian flavour profile, although I wasn't sure when exactly I had become an aficionado.

'Well, if I ever see you there, I shall have to buy you a drink,' I said.

He shook his head, but his eyes were twinkling. 'There's no need. To be honest, they aren't a patch on Pyg's and their locusts dipped in sesame seeds, but who is, hey?'

I looked at him, puzzled. 'I'm afraid I've been away for a while. Are they new? Worth a try? Although I have to be honest, I don't think I'd be a fan of locusts.'

He laughed, shaking his head, but there was an expression I couldn't quite interpret. 'Well, you never know. Dipped in honey and sesame seeds with a few chilli flakes. They really are delicious.'

I raised my eyebrow. 'With all that gunk on top, I imagine you can't taste the locust at all.'

He roared with laughter, and a few of the patrons turned around. He gave them a charming smile and waved an apology, and they smiled back. Maybe he was a regular, but some people just exuded confidence.

'Very good Julius, tell them that next time you are in Pyg's.'

Again, the reference sailed past me. 'You'll have to tell me where this fabulous place is.'

He shook his head and reached inside his breast pocket, pulling out a silver card case. He opened it up and handed card to me.

'Here, should you ever wish to share a coffee,' he said, inclining his head. 'It has been a pleasure meeting you.' And with that, he left.

I was about to comment, but my panini was called and by the time I returned, there was no sign of him. I left the café and wondered about the oddness of a random stranger suggesting we meet up for a coffee. Why had he even been in the café? He hadn't ordered anything. Briefly I wondered if he was a runner for The Hole in the Wall, poaching customers, but then I dismissed it. That man was no runner. He was a company executive, an owner, a leader. Whatever he did, poaching patrons in a coffee shop turf war was not part of his brief.

I was almost at work, still playing over the strange conversation, when I realised, he had called me Julius. I hadn't introduced myself, and the barista had written Justin on the cup.

As soon as I was settled, I pulled his card from my pocket and googled him. 'Marcus Carruthers. Alexandria Company.' As I had suspected, he was the CEO of a team of Loss Adjusters. It was a very plain website. Clearly, they weren't looking for business. It had the confidence of a page that said, this is our name, this is how you can contact us, now go away. No links out, no social media. No photos even of staff. Just a one-page website. Quite refreshing in this day and age of feverish attention-grabbing sites.

It didn't help me, though. Why on earth would the head of a loss adjusting company be interested in me? And how did he know my name? Tucking his card in my pocket, I headed in to work. I had lots to do before term started and the undergraduates arrived.

Chapter Six - August: Beta: Julius

Three days later, I was dragging myself towards the weekend. We were working half day this Friday, and I was relieved to be heading home. Work had lost its appeal. Ever since returning from America I was dissatisfied with everything. I was running through a lecture for a colleague on ancient views of the underworld and my mind kept drifting, like I had forgotten something. Essays I marked for overseas students struck me as flawed, but I couldn't say why. At lunch, I dropped in on a guest talk in the science labs on particle physics. I had no idea why, but for the first time all week I felt calmer. I cheered myself up by popping into the Fitzwilliam Museum on the way home. I had always loved museums and found wandering through the exhibits to provide a wonderful escape from the here and now.

As I wandered through the artefacts gathered from all around the world, my stomach lurched, a cold sweat broke out across my skin. I all but ran back out onto the pavement and walked home as quickly as possible, trying to avoid the bins that hadn't been collected. The smells from the bloated bags made me heave. Seconds later, I was on all fours, vomiting into the gutter.

I stood up, panting, and wiped my mouth on the back of my sleeve. When I got home, I would make an appointment with the doctor. This was clearly more than jetlag.

A door opened from one of the terraces and a woman came towards me with a bottle of water.

'Are you okay?'

I was momentarily stunned. Vomiting strangers were usually best avoided. 'God, I'm so sorry.'

I ran my fingers through my hair and patted my shirt down. My fingers ran over a wet patch on my sleeve, making me wince in disgust. Bad enough that this should happen in broad daylight, but that I should be witnessed and then forced to endure small talk.

The woman held the bottle out towards me. 'Here, take it.'

I paused.

'Would you like me to call an ambulance?'

I must have looked worse than I realised, and I shook my head violently. 'Sorry. It's a bug I think.' I laughed sheepishly. 'But yes, the water does look appealing.'

She held it out to me again, and I took it, thanking her as she smiled and headed back inside, reminding me to recycle the bottle when I was done.

Helping her fellow man and the planet at the same time. I wondered if she had a tick list on her phone. Chiding myself for an ungrateful thought, I drank the water and headed home. By the time I got to my front door, I felt so wretched that I just wanted to crawl into bed. I put the key in the lock when I heard someone call my name.

'Professor Strathclyde.'

One of my neighbours dashed across the street. She was leading a large black dog, whose tail was wagging violently. I bobbed down to stroke the dog and felt a wave of calm wash over me. I stood up, smiling.

'It's Mrs Wilson, isn't it?'

Mrs Wilson was a formal old bird. I assumed she had a first name, but I didn't know what it was. Besides, we hadn't been neighbours for that long. I'd only moved in for a week or two before I started working abroad.

'I was going to ask a favour of you, but you look tired.'

'Just a touch of jetlag, I think. Nothing to stop me from helping a neighbour.'

Mrs Wilson eyed at me suspiciously.

'That's what comes of flying. I've always said it's no good. And now they're saying it causes global warming. I heard one woman say they spread chemicals through the air, but I don't think that makes sense. They'd poison themselves as well as everyone else.'

Oh dear. I really wasn't capable of maintaining a conversation on the evils of aircraft.

'The favour?'

I cut her off with a smile and hoped she would remember she needed something from me and wouldn't consider me too rude for stopping her mid-stride.

'Oh it's Dippy, here. I promised to walk him for young Mr Jupp. I always do on a Friday afternoon, but my niece has called and needs a babysitter. I've said I'd drive over, but I can hardly bring a dog with me.'

Looking at the dog, I wondered who on earth called a Doberman "Dippy?" But if I was honest, I quite liked it. They had an unfair reputation as lethal guard dogs. Dippy was reassuringly gentle, plus his floppy ears were an improvement on the rigid cropped version that led to a more alarming aspect. He tipped his head and looked at me expectantly.

'Of course I can take him. When is Mr Jupp due back, and which house does he live at?'

If it felt unusual that I would willingly take a strange dog for a walk, or that my neighbour would even ask it, that only went to show how the spirit of the country had changed. We were doing more nice things for each other. Maybe the barman had hit the nail on the head. We were in a new golden age. An Arthurian Age. For some reason, that made me laugh.

I took his lead and couldn't help but be touched by the speed with which he came and sat by my side. I unlocked my front door and threw my bag inside, switched into a pair of trainers, then headed off.

'Come on, Shuck.'

Mrs Wilson called out from across the street, where she was getting into her car. 'His name is Dippy.'

Of course it was. Where did I get Shuck from? This dog was not at all fearsome, and I felt bad at perpetuating the stereotype that Dobermans were difficult breeds. There was a sharp flare of pain in my head, and I swallowed two more pain killers. This past week I had taken to carrying the tablets with me.

We headed down to the park and went in the direction of the river. Dippy was obviously a regular of the circuit, as lots of dogs came up and said hello. I got a few funny looks and had to explain that I was dog sitting, not napping. Each time I gave a little laugh, and they politely laughed back. It took a while to realise that it was probably my eyes that were causing consternation. I'd had a cricketing accident at school which had caused a pigment discolouration. It didn't hurt, but it did look odd. It even caught me out, which is why I guess I'd started to wear contacts, but it was a routine I couldn't get used to, although I'd obviously been doing it for decades. Maybe this week wasn't the week to ditch them.

Eventually, the painkillers lost their battle with the headache, and I headed home to see if I could sleep it off. I knocked on Number 34 and Mr Jupp answered the door.

He was younger than me and had an office job somewhere. It wasn't the ideal set up for a dog like

Dippy, but he was doing his best. Dippy now bounded into the house and started running up and down the hallway, waiting for his supper. My neighbour stared at me in concern. 'You look like death!'

I smiled politely, saying the jetlag was catching up with me, then headed across the road to bed. I slept without dreams.

Chapter Seven - August: Alpha: Neith

A week later, Minju Chen was unanimously elected pharaoh. After her appearance on the Golden Mean, my only surprise was how long it had taken. I straightened my collar. I was wearing the ceremonial uniform for curators. Even though I had been informed I could no longer be one, I hadn't yet decided what I wanted to do. Now I was standing at the front of the administrative buildings waiting to meet the new pharaoh, and a formal invitation from the Pharaoh of Alexandria required that I dress appropriately. My ceremonial uniform was as good as it got.

A couple came up to me, hugging me tightly. That had been happening a lot since I left hospital. It was beginning to really hack me off. I had done nothing special. All I had done was fail to dodge a bullet, wake up, and learn to speak. I gave them a brief hug and explained I was late for the pharaoh. They were visibly impressed, and I dashed into the building as I saw another couple approach.

Inside the complex I was treated to similar smiles and whispered mutterings, but here at least people were actually working and didn't break off from their job to hug me. It was unnerving, though, and I hurried along the corridors until I reached the senior administration wing. The large double doors were closed and two red custodians stood in front of them. I didn't recognise either.

I had never seen these doors closed before.

'Is there a problem?' I said.

'All visitors to this wing are required to prove their identity,' said the taller of the two. From the tattoos on his face, I guessed he was from the Steppe Lands. An individual with closely shaved hair, leaving only the single back plait favoured by the Vans. His companion, another Van, with another plait, held out his scanner to where I should have been wearing a brace.

'Where is your ID?'

That stumped me. I hadn't been asked to show my ID in years. At work, everyone knew who I was and, as a society, we had little need for security checks.

'My name is Neith Salah. I have an appointment with the pharaoh in five minutes.'

'Not without ID you don't.'

I stepped back. 'Are you going to explain to the pharaoh why her meeting was cancelled?'

'Yes. I will explain, that per her instructions, an individual trying to storm the building without proper clearance was not permitted entrance.'

'Storm the building?' I laughed at him. 'Joking, are we? How exactly do you think I'm going to storm the building? Batter down the doors? Fly through the air delivering lightning bolts?'

The second custodian spoke into his brace. 'Assistance required at the Welcoming Gates. We have an unidentified individual threatening to use powers. Code Red.'

My jaw fell open. 'I was joking. Sarcasm. Heard of it?'

'All I heard was a threat to storm the building.' He turned to his companion. 'What did you hear?'

'I heard a stranger threaten to use banned technology to overthrow the government.'

I looked between the two of them, my mouth catching flies, then drew a deep breath. 'Right.'

They both placed their hands on their lasers.

'Tiresias?' I called out. He was always listening in public spaces. 'Please, can you confirm my identity?'

'Certainly, Neith Salah.'

I relaxed. For a moment, I thought Tiresias might have also lost his head.

'And what is the purpose of my visit here?'

'You have an appointment at noon with Pharaoh Chen.'

I had been staring at the custodians the entire time. Whilst we had been talking, ten more custodians had run into the corridor, their boots stomping on the marble floor, sealing my exit. As I turned, I recognised one or two of them and gave them a quick smile and a wave.

'Twelve custodians for a woman who's been in a coma for six months. I am flattered. Now, you heard Tiresias.' Any humour in my voice now bled away. 'Step aside.'

The first guard slowly removed his laser from its holster.

'No one comes through these doors without ID.'

'My ID brace?'

'Yes.'

'My Tiresias ID Brace.'

'Yes.'

'The same Tiresias that just confirmed my identity?'

He sneered. 'No brace. No access.'

I was keeping a very close eye on his shoulder. If he was going to shoot me, I would see his muscles bunch. The situation was getting out of control. I was in a narrow corridor with twelve red custodians. In a fight, my chances were nil, but that wouldn't stop me. I was furious, trying to stay calm.

'Tiresias. Please send my regrets to the pharaoh. I have forgotten my brace and can't attend the meeting.'

There was a moment's silence, and then Minju's voice came across the airwaves.

'Stay there. I'm on my way.'

I raised my eyebrow. As the door swung open, I noticed the second guard had placed his hand back on his laser. Behind me, all ten had also done the same.

'Minju,' I shouted. 'Stay where you are!'

She walked through the doors, and all the guards came to attention, their hands still on their lasers.

'Minju, the custodians are preparing to attack. Get back.'

This was insane. Had I wandered into another coup? One that Minju wasn't controlling and why was I warning her, anyway? Maybe old habits died hard.

She smiled, walked up to me, and gave me a hug.

'New safety protocols. We have been running through pharaohs at an alarming rate, so I thought some new procedures might be a good idea.'

She turned, her thick tail brushing one of the columns, and addressed the men. 'Thank you, custodians. You are a credit. Custodian Suebi, I am particularly impressed by your refusal to admit Neith Salah. That is exactly what was asked of you. I will ensure you receive a commendation. Now though, Neith, come with me. I've got a lot on today, and you've delayed me.'

She turned, and I gingerly passed between the two custodians. He glared at me, but I could see from the pink flush on his skin that he was proud of his commendation. I moved quickly to catch up with Minju, who was already striding towards her offices. There were more red custodians scattered along the way, standing outside various offices. As she passed each one, they placed their hands on their lasers.

'My fellow administrators are no less important than me. I want to spread the sense of safety.'

The sense of fear was more likely.

Before we entered her office, one of the custodians standing outside went in. We stood briefly until she returned and declared the room empty.

'Weren't you just in there?' I asked, surprised.

'I know. They are taking the security details a little forcefully, but I made it a condition of taking the offer. I'm not as brave as you, Neith. I said I wouldn't dream of being pharaoh unless they allowed me direct control of the custodians. Of course, I knew they wouldn't agree so I wouldn't have to be pharaoh, but they said yes. So,' she gave a small laugh. 'What could I do? I backed myself into a corner and had to become pharaoh. I gave them a whole list of things, hoping to put them off, but Bast and Balls, they said yes to all of them.'

'How did Giovanetti take that?'

I was curious. I had been hoping that she might be someone I could turn to in my fight against Minju.

'She was delighted. I must say I do enjoy working with her. She sees things the same way I do. Confided that she was relieved, quite frankly, to only have to report to one person rather than a committee. Plus, we both agreed that rebuilding custodian numbers is a priority in our current climate.'

I murmured noncommittally and scratched her off my list of people I could rely on. Giovanetti was being given more power, more troops, and more budget. Everything a general needs to do their job. As Minju spoke into an intercom, I waited to be offered a chair. Normally I'd have sat down, but this wasn't just Minju. This was the pharaoh, and you respected the office, if not the individual.

Finally, she waved me into a chair. Within seconds, a teenager walked into the room carrying a tea tray. He gave me a shy smile, a clumsy bow to Minju, then left again, having not said a word.

I raised an eyebrow.

'I thought it was about time that we let teenagers see what goes on in politics. We need to be more open, more inclusive.'

'Aren't we already?'

'I'm talking about them really getting a feel for politics and the future.'

I nodded, because I was supposed to. A new youth movement during a time of political instability and cultural upheaval. What could possibly go wrong?

'Now, first things first. I'm sorry to sound stern, but I have to insist that you wear your brace at all times in future.'

That was a step too far.

'Since when? They aren't compulsory.'

Minju frowned, and I remembered how she used to terrify us as cadets when we were learning our skills. Woe betide the cadet that drew the attention of Archivist Chen.

'Of course they aren't compulsory, you just won't be able to access any government building without one from now on.'

I drummed my fingers on the arm rest. The last thing I wanted was to wear a device I knew could be hacked.

'Tiresias runs a full body scan of anyone approaching the building. Just add facial recognition to the subroutines?'

'And who runs Tiresias?' she asked, and I felt the tide changing around me.

'The Engineers.'

'Indeed.'

Now here was something that we could agree on. I didn't trust the engineers either. They'd been hiding a secret from the whole of society. They were even aware of the potential of other Earths, and had failed to share that information. Could this be common ground between Minju and myself that I could exploit? I wasn't smart enough to join the engineers, but maybe Minju could bend the rules? She'd been smashing enough recently. Once I was inside, I could act as a double agent. See if I could recruit any to my cause.

'You don't trust them?'

Minju paused and drank her tea before placing the cup slowly back in its saucer.

'Do you remember in hospital, when I came to see you? You said the threat hadn't passed. You said we weren't safe.'

I nodded. I remembered lying there, terrified that she would somehow discover that I alone knew the truth of her. That it had been her and not Grimaldi behind the coup.

'I knew then I could trust you. I knew you could see the bigger picture. And that is why, Neith Salah, I have a mission for you.'

'Work alongside the engineers?'

The wretched woman actually laughed at me.

'As what? Their cleaner? No, there isn't a position that I could get you into that bloody Hypatia wouldn't be immediately suspicious of. And you certainly don't have the IQ for an actual engineer. No, don't look at me like that. Neither do I.'

I had been momentarily affronted. Anyone working at the mouseion was the brightest and smartest of their generation, but some of us were brighter than others. She was right to chide me. I was being churlish. We all played to our strengths, and it was no good me thinking I was good at everything. Nor that I knew best. As brilliant minds went, Hypatia Smith, First Engineer, was the best and Minju was smart enough to know that.

'Fair enough. What did you have in mind?'

'I want you in charge of the team selecting which artefacts we might consider returning to Beta Earth.'

'You're still going ahead with that?'

She cocked her head, then tapped a finger on the table as her tail gently swayed back and forth. I could see the tip of it come in and out of my range of vision behind the desk.

'It is essential. The engineers have forced us into a position of complacency and superiority. As a society, we need to be aware that there are others out there. And some of them are more powerful than us.'

'But what good does returning their pieces do for us?'

I was surprised to find myself making this argument. Julius had already convinced me of the right of it, but I still wanted to know what Minju's reasoning was.

'We need to forge new alliances. At first, they don't need to know about us. We can return things anonymously and then, when we reveal ourselves, we will have already demonstrated our goodwill. As Julius said, it's the right thing to do. I thought you would approve?'

'I do. I'm just surprised that *you* do.'

'Think what we can learn from each other.'

I was stumped. I loved Julius dearly, but what on earth could his planet teach us besides a good heap of suspicion? I thought it through. Suspicion, and fear, and warfare. Ah.

'You see, don't you?' said Minju, her face blossoming in delight. 'We can learn to develop our own arts. This will be a golden dawn for Alpha. We will create our own beauty. In fact, I have already altered the budget to enable a huge push into the artistic fields. We will build new campuses for artists, grant scholarships, give recitals and concerts. All Alpha made. It will be wonderful.'

It was hogwash.

'Sounds expensive.'

'But worth it.' Her eyes were shining with excitement. I couldn't see the catch. Maybe she genuinely meant it and I had spent too long with Julius, but I had learnt to accept nothing at face value.

'Hang on, though.' I could see a problem with her scheme. 'I thought the archivists were in charge of drawing up the list of potential artefacts to be returned?'

'They are.'

'So how can I be involved?'

Minju smiled at me, like a mother about to award her favourite child an extra treat.

'Because, Neith Salah, you are going to become an archivist.'

Chapter Eight - August: Alpha: Neith

I walked out of the offices in a daze and didn't even pay attention to the custodians who had given me such grief on arrival. I was going to be an archivist. Well, a potential one. That was Ramin's term for workers who changed careers. It was a new phenomenon for us. We weren't big on change, but following the attempted coup, loss of life, and revelations of other Earths, we were learning to adapt quickly. People, of course, did change careers, but not at the scale of the past year. So, despite having not gone through the exams or basic training, I was going to be an archivist with a lot of catching up to do.

'Neith!'

I turned around to see Shen Jiaqi, my old social studies tutor and now Head of Population Well-Being. Shen was a short elderly man who had spent a lifetime eating marzipan dates and drinking sweet juices. No amount of excellent health care could take care of a lifetime of indulgences. I liked him. He made me smile, and he didn't care what anyone else thought of him. When he had first entered the lecture hall, he had declared that he was older than us, wiser than us, and had nothing to prove. He also said he could be bribed with a properly candied lemon peel. It was hard to work out what shocked us the most, but Clio had laughed out loud and I relaxed a little.

Now he was being flanked by two red custodians walking behind him. 'I heard you were in the vicinity,' he said. 'How are you?'

'Very well, thank you.'

I looked over his shoulder to his escorts.

'Oh them,' he said, having caught my glance. 'I have to admit I haven't quite got used to them myself either.'

'Then why bother?'

'To protect the pharaoh.'

'I don't follow.'

'Well, Giovanetti was insistent that Pharaoh Chen should have an increased guard given the dreadful assassination of Pharaoh Nolyny.'

He placed his fist over his heart and splayed his fingers out wide. I mirrored his gesture. My shock and grief had been genuine. Cleeve may have been a ninny, and probably a puppet, but no one deserved to be murdered.

'So Giovanetti insisted you had guards as well?'

'Who can argue against a swarm of locusts?'

I had forgotten his tendency to speak in riddles. The more I thought about it, the harder it was to understand. I shrugged, then apologised for my slowness.

'Minju refused a security detail, saying she was no more important than any of us.'

Ah, I understood.

'And you all volunteered to have guards?'

'Exactly, a butterfly may hide on a corpse—'

'But only if the corpse stays still.'

'Exactly!' He beamed at me and I bowed, pleased to have earnt his approval. I still didn't understand the butterfly thing. It had something to do with the fact that you can't rely on death. I think. Which, of course, made no sense. Death was inevitable. I was reminded that I had always thought him a little deranged. This encounter changed nothing.

'And so, in order to have Minju properly protected, you all have guards as well.'

Canny old girl. Now all the directors were regularly seen with custodians. It gave a sense of superiority, but also emphasised the need for vigilance. Divide and conquer, breed fear.

'Do you not think the population might be alarmed to see so many people being overtly protected?'

'On the contrary, I think it's reassuring them. Well, I won't keep you. I hear you are going to be in charge of the artefacts assessment. I was delighted when Minju proposed you. We all were, actually.'

'Ah, so there was a vote then?'

'Well, not a vote as such,' said Shen. 'Nothing formal, but we all agreed, if that's what you are wondering. Pharaoh Chen told us she thought you would make an excellent candidate, and we all agreed.'

'Even Arcadi?'

We had never got on. She thought I was loud and reckless. It wasn't my fault that I had fallen in her trifle after my back somersault at a sunrise festival had gone awry. I swear Clio had flipped me faster on purpose.

'Arcadi resigned last week. A few have, actually. Retiring to tend to their grapes is how they put it. When we wither, we shall wane.'

'Indeed.' I had no idea what he meant, but it was curious and something to investigate when I got home. Arcadi's resignation. Not the withering and waning.

Saying our goodbyes, I headed back to my apartment. I had to hug three more couples on the way home and, in the end, jogged the rest of the way, despite the dress uniform. I felt sullied just being in Minju's presence and didn't wish to contaminate anyone else. As I jogged along, I was reminded of the horror on Julius' face the first time a stranger had hugged him. Every time I thought of him, it hurt a little less, and I realised that my memories of him could be a comfort rather than a cruel reminder. I knew he would support me in my efforts and would understand my actions.

As I got through the door, Tiresias welcomed me home and read out the various messages I had received. Mostly congratulations on my new appointment, and invitations to parties and events. Sabrina and Jack were having a declaration, and I felt I should go to that, but until I felt I had a strategy to deal with Minju, I wanted to avoid spending time with people I cared about.

I didn't want to create collateral damage. Besides, I was certain that after their declaration, there would be a Union. I'd attend that instead. Hopefully, after all this mess was resolved. I slumped onto the sofa. How was this to be resolved? How could I do this on my own? I needed help, but I did not know who to approach. Everyone was completely enamoured with Minju right now.

Tiresias chimed again, and I smiled as I accepted a hologram from Ramin.

'Hello, Squid Face!'

I stuck my tongue out and laughed. 'Is that how you greet the new Chief Potential Archivist for Assessment of Interplanetary Repatriation of Artefacts?'

Now it was his turn to laugh. 'You are going to need the world's largest name badge for that title.'

'I plan on hiring a donkey to carry it around for me.'

'Yes, I can see you and a donkey would be suitable companions.'

'Oi! That's a squid and a donkey you've compared me to. What next, oh camel breath?'

Just trading insults and jokes was lifting my spirits. I couldn't remember when I had last felt this light-hearted.

'You've got to admire Minju, though,' said Ramin. 'She has a knack for doing the right thing.'

I stared at him.

His face fell. 'Sorry, that was tactless of me. But Neith, you know you can't be a curator.'

I remained silent. Let him think I was cross about not being a curator. I mean, I was, but that had become irrelevant. I had bigger goals, and I had fleetingly thought I could rely on Ramin. Now I saw that there was no way I could involve him. I knew he'd support me. He might even pretend to believe me, but if he failed to genuinely take on board how lethal Minju was, she might get rid of him and me before we had a chance to blink. One simple blunder, no matter how minor, could be our downfall.

'Look, let's go out,' he said. 'Hire a boat and sail down the coast. Take a few days out. What do you say?'

I wanted to say yes with all my heart, but shook my head. 'Sorry Ramin, I start work in a few months. I have a lot of learning to cram in.'

'I can come over and help you prep?'

'No, I'll be fine on my own. Tell the others I'll be keeping my head down for a while as well, will you?'

My rebuff had been stronger than his generosity warranted, but I knew that for now, he was safer away from me.

He was about to try again when I interrupted him, saying I had to crack on and disconnected the call. I had just enough time to see his shocked expression, then the room was empty again.

I was just changing into my swimming gear when the door chimed. He was making this too hard for me. How would I be able to tell him to leave me alone to his face? Flinging the door open, I paused as a courier stood smiling at me, then handed over a box.

As I took it, it beeped, acknowledging the destination delivery, and the courier left again.

Deflated that it hadn't been Ramin, I took the package indoors and sat it down on the table. It was stamped with the Seal of the Engineers, so I guessed it was something to do with work. Maybe archivists needed specialist equipment.

Opening the box revealed a new wrist brace. It was slimmer than my old version and, as I fired it up, I discovered it had far fewer functions as well. Obviously, I wouldn't be stepping over to other Earths. This brace, however, had more features to make itself look aesthetically pleasing. Smaller and sleeker, this was the perfect example of form over function.

'Greetings, Neith. Please specify how you would like me to wake you in the morning?'

I ignored it and placed it on the worktop. Grabbing my towel and nose plugs.

'Greetings, Neith. Please be sure to put me on before you leave the building.'

I rolled my eyes and headed to the front door, which wouldn't open.

'Tiresias. The door is jammed. Please release.'

'Greetings, Neith. Please be sure to put me on before you leave the building.'

I stared at the brace. 'Tiresias?'

There was silence from my flat's speaker, then the brace chirped again.

'Greetings, Neith.'

'What's going on?'

'Greetings, Neith. Please be clearer in your query?'

'Is the wearing of a brace mandatory?'

'Greetings, Neith. No, it is not.'

'Please stop saying, "Greetings, Neith."'

There was silence.

'Have you overridden my house Tiresias controls?'

'Salutations, Neith. This new upgrade integrates all Tiresias functions for a seamless and happy experience.'

'I'm locked in!'

'Salutations, Neith. Please be sure to put me on before you leave the building.'

Okay, it was clear I wasn't getting out of here without the damn brace. Sod the swim, though. I was heading straight to the engineers. This was outrageous. First at work, now at home. This bloody thing would have full access to all my movements and interactions. In the past, this had never bothered me. Since meeting Julius, I had become wary of the technology. In the wrong hands, this was the most powerful of tools. I knew Minju hadn't penetrated the engineers, but I was certainly not about to put any faith in that knowledge. She might be smarter than me, but I wasn't an idiot.

Unless I was. Was this evidence that she didn't trust me? If I railed against it, would that further undermine her faith in me? I needed her to trust me. I was torn. How could I behave in a way that didn't look suspicious, but that also reassured her?

'Salutations, Neith. What colour would you like this brace to be? I can match your current outfit. Or what about something fun? How about a Jackson colour palette? Today is the anniversary of the great delta triumph. What about something to honour that? What about—'

'Black. And don't speak again.'

Shoving the brace in my pocket, I was already walking to the engineers before I even realised it. Because that is exactly what I would do and what Minju would expect.

Rather than walking all the way over to their headquarters, I stopped at one of their service branches. These were dotted all over the city to help residents with technological issues and offer maths drop-in centres and other fun activities.

A young engineer looked up and smiled as I approached.

'Greetings, Neith Salah. How may I be of service?'

I wondered if the engineer recognised me, or if it was simply the face recognition device at the front door. Very few venues openly used this software as it negated the need for preliminary introductions, considered a sign of good manners. Already knowing a stranger's name felt like cheating. Or it did to me, anyway.

'I have a complaint.'

A young family playing on a number block game got up and left the shop. A second engineer came through a door at the side of the shop, smiled at the younger assistant, and told him to tidy up after the family. His name tag pronounced him as 3859-Mike.

'The nature of your complaint?'

Ah, that was better. No smile, just the standard officious engineer response.

'My brace locked me in my apartment. It wouldn't release the door lock until the brace was on my person.'

'Why?'

'Because it's broken, obviously. I don't know, you're the genius.' The last bit was said a tad sharper than it should have been and I mentally acknowledged Minju's comment about me not being smart enough.

'Pass it over.'

I happily removed it from my pocket and handed it across. The engineer placed it on the mat and ran a calibration.

'It behaved correctly. Your Good Habits protocol is enabled. It was simply following that directive. The new upgrade can help citizens achieve their goals. The

Good Habits protocol on this one will ensure you wear your brace at all times. Either you or Tiresias must have noticed your use of the brace is below recommended personal safety levels.'

He paused as he straightened the items on the counter.

'As a curator, I would have thought you understood the gravity of removing your brace.'

'On Beta, of course. On Alpha it isn't necessary.'

'And yet everyone does.'

'Not everyone, Engineer. You are being inaccurate in your statement. Was that exaggeration?'

The engineer flushed, and I smiled back. If we were going to trade professional insults, I was well up for a fight. He stared at me a little longer, then tapped on his keyboard.

'Eighty-nine per cent of the population aged three and above wear their brace for a mean average of eighteen hours a day. You do not. You—'

'Are you about to waste time by informing me of a fact that I am already aware of, and which you do not need to know?'

His lip twitched. 'I do need to know if I am going to switch off your Good Habits protocol.'

'Whoho— back up there, Nelly. You have zero jurisdiction over any of my protocols. Unless you know something I don't? You are an engineer, not a custodian.'

He glared at me again. 'Engineers strive to protect society and help people become the best they can be.'

'Are you a custodian?'

'No.'

'Do you have the right to curtail my behaviours?'

'No.'

'Remove the Good Habits protocol, immediately.'

He tapped on the keyboard again and then returned the brace to me. 'Done.'

'Now, please provide me with evidence that it has been fully removed, not just temporarily neutralised.'

He raised an eyebrow. 'Because you'd understand the working schematics of a Tiresias sub-routine?' He didn't scoff, but Great Ra it was close.

'No sweetie, because if I have to take you to a disciplinary for poor service and non-compliance, I will have evidence to present.'

For a moment, a flash of fury crossed his face then he gathered himself and returned to a blank expression. 'As you wish.'

My brace pinged, and I saw I had received a locked security file, plus a recording the previous five-minute exchange. I had a quick look at the file — couldn't make head nor tail of it — but smiled and thanked him.

'Have a great day, Mike.' I shouldn't have done that, but I knew it would annoy him. Some engineers still loved their numerals more than their names, and I knew 3859-Mike was going to be one of them. It was disrespectful of me, but he started it.

As I left the building, I put the brace on my wrist. I had done what Minju had expected I would, but now I needed to show her I could be trusted. I would have to start wearing the damn thing all the time and try to work around it, and hope to all of Julius' gods that she hadn't worked out a way to infiltrate the Tiresias data banks.

Chapter Nine - August: Alpha: Minju

Minju Chen looked out across the park and rooftops towards the mouseion and the lighthouse beyond. As expected, Neith Salah had immediately requested a brace modification but, as Minju checked the monitor, she did at least appear to be wearing it as she headed home. Minju walked to the rear window. Work had already begun on the new Arts Foundation. This would be her obvious legacy for the citizens of Egypt and, in time, she hoped its influence would spread far and wide.

For too long, Alpha residents had stagnated artistically, happy to tread water whilst the tide took them further from the shores of creativity. They had become soft and lazy. She had always been aware of the need to change the direction of her society, but since the revelation of multiple Earths she had been galvanised into more extreme action than she thought herself capable of.

Of course, the Arts Foundation would be her visible contribution. Her other project would need to remain hidden for a while yet, until society understood, properly understood, the need for it. Happily, with the vast sums required to build the Arts Foundation in the timeframe she had requested, there was plenty of money to be syphoned off into Project Dance; a pretty sounding name that disguised its true function, and could be easily explained as part of the Arts Facility if overheard or investigated.

'Tybalt Jones is here, pharaoh,' said Tiresias.

Minju shook herself out of her plans for the future. Today was where she needed to focus for now. She had just dealt with Neith and was undecided if she would be able to properly bring her onside. She desperately wanted to. Neith Salah would be an excellent figurehead, but was also a very dangerous person to have hanging around. Tybalt Jones, on the other hand, was completely committed to Minju's plans. He possessed a remarkable lack of care for the skins of others. His own, he treated with utmost attention.

He walked in: a small, unprepossessing man, his friendly smile belying the depths of his aptitude for cruelty. His one affectation was a pair of glasses and a scar, both utterly unnecessary. When Minju had queried them, he said the glasses kept his ears warm. It was a ridiculous answer. Another time she overheard him saying it kept the bugs out of his eyes when he ran. Privately, she thought he wore them to make other people uncomfortable, or off balanced, just like the scar. If they were focusing on the glasses, they were ignoring the man. That was typical of an engineer.

She knew she would need brilliant minds on her side and had spent years searching out those engineers who had been quietly dismissed from the department. She needed the ones who bore a grudge. Of the many that she had gathered up and kept tabs on, Tybalt Jones was the best for what she needed.

'Jones, welcome. How was your journey?'

'Long, convoluted and uncomfortable.' He flapped his jacket to make a point. Sand drifted onto the wooden floor, but Minju ignored it. Jones was simply making a point somewhat peevishly. She hadn't selected him for his charm, after all.

'Excellent. If it were easy, everyone would do it.'

He waited for her to pour him a glass of water and, when she didn't, he poured his own. Minju smiled as he failed to pour her one.

'Have you forgotten your manners out there in the wastes?'

Wrong footed, he poured her a glass, scowling as he did so.

'Now then, let's have a progress report.'

'I need more money and more staff.'

'Money I can get you, people are trickier. What do you need them for?'

'Some for the science, most for the labour. This thing won't build itself, you know.'

He gulped at his water, then poured a second glass before helping himself onto a seat. Minju was amused to see that he wiped it down before sitting. Fastidious oaf.

'If you are working to the timetable you promised me, you should soon have all the grunts you need. Finding suitable technicians is a harder project, as you well know.'

'I've already provided you with a database of all those deemed worthy of approaching, with a risk ratio attached.'

Minju rolled her eyes. The problem with Jones was that he might be a brilliant former engineer, but he was an idiot when it came to understanding people. All the algorithms in the world could only suggest who had the right sort of criminal tendencies. Since the great glyph dénouement, people felt reassured that all criminals had been identified, which was of course nonsense.

When the so-called gods arrived on Alpha and set up two teams to find the missing codex, they had created havoc. One of their many intrusions had been to openly identify people's criminal intent. Good guys got a pyramid, baddies got a crown. It had been incredibly juvenile and had destroyed years of carefully built concealments and subterfuge. Minju was instantly revealed as a bad sort. But happily, she had manipulated Anansi into altering everyone's memory.

Now, everyone with a crown had been identified and re-educated. They were a waste of time for Minju's requirements. She needed people who had been hiding amongst the pyramids. In the first twenty-four hours, the number of people self-reporting as "good" without independent verification was enormous. People could just stay at home and send a text self-registering as a non-criminal.

Giovanetti had quickly spotted that the system could be abused, and asked anyone who hadn't yet registered to do so with a secondary witness, or submit to a visual registration. She then requested that everyone who had initially declared themselves do so again, but this time with evidence. Whilst people were getting jammed up in the backlog, the glyphs disappeared again. At least thirty per cent of the population had a non-verified status and no doubt the vast majority of them were squeaky clean. But Minju knew the dodgers lurked among that number, those smart enough to duck the system. Smart and scrappy. Her sort of people.

And, of course, having a genuine triangle didn't mean that you couldn't be turned in the future.

'I'm watching three more people at the moment, and will approach them soon. One wrong step and the project is placed at risk. Each time I have to dispose of someone, it draws suspicion. So we move slowly.'

'In which case you have to ensure I have the money. I can't be impeded on both fronts.'

Minju sat silently for a while, considering Tybalt's demand. Currently, he was indispensable, but if he continued speaking to her like this, he would find his days after mission completion very short indeed. And possibly painful as well.

'Have I ever refused your request for money? How much do you need?'

The figure was eye-watering.

'We need more platinum, uranium and lithium. A lot more and we have to source from all around the globe to allay suspicion. I've had to open new mines in secret in Cornwall. Have you any idea how difficult that is?' he asked.

'What cover story are you using?' Minju didn't really care but she was curious to see how he solved problems.

'We're calling it a tin mine.'

'Smart.'

'Indeed, but you know the Cornish. The poetry is endless and they hate anyone digging holes in their land. The environmental levees are crippling.'

It was a queer facet of Cornish culture that every time a shaft was dug, a poem had to be written and then performed by the local community every Friday for four weeks. They called it penance and Minju wholeheartedly agreed. She was deeply suspicious of oral recitations.

'The money will be in your account by the time you get home.'

He stood up and brushed his clothes down.

'Now, if you'll excuse me, I have to go and have my cells washed.'

He wanted no sympathy, and Minju offered none. Both knew that the speed with which the project was being undertaken was risky to those involved. Jones had contracted cancer in the first few months. Now he came back once a month for treatment. His doctors could only keep the cell degeneration at bay, rather than repair them. They were unaware of their patient's daily exposure to radioactive materials. Tybalt told Minju he didn't care. This would be his life's work, his crowning glory. By his own reports, the project would be stable within the month, and then the cell washing would actually start to take effect. He just needed to hold on that long.

Minju watched him leave. She admired his dedication to the project. And how could she comment on the high death toll taking place in the Glass Wastes, when he himself was prepared to risk his own life? She transferred the money to him, then meditated for half an hour. Two difficult meetings back-to-back, and soon she would approach a curator she felt certain she could bring on board. For that, she was going to need all her wits.

Chapter Ten - September: Alpha: Neith

It had been a month of me palming off Ramin's invitations, but now he threatened to come and sleep on my doorstep. In a moment of weakness, I had said yes. My loneliness was making me selfish for the company of friends.

The sky was blue, but filled with fast-moving clouds. Autumn had arrived and soon the rains would come, but for now we could still dine outside without fear of being drenched. Autumn rains were incredible, but better observed from indoors.

I'd picked Al-Journo's, a popular restaurant amongst the tourists. It wasn't a place I would normally dream of eating at, but I knew Minju was probably tracing my every step. Since the brace debacle, I wore it everywhere; I didn't want to look suspicious. I had made my protest, exactly what was expected of me and then, like a good curator, I understood the wisdom of the system and wore it anyway. Of course, I had checked that I could leave the flat without it, and I could see the Good Habits protocols had indeed been removed.

What I wasn't able to do was fix the 'Greetings, Neith' message. It seemed some sort of bug that, no matter how many times I reset and overrode it, it came back. When technology goes bad, it can be at the most banal level, but it can drive you to distraction.

So now I was in a popular spot meeting Ramin, all above board. Nothing to see here. Of course, choosing such a visible location had its downsides and, within minutes of sitting down, I was swamped by a crocodile line of school children. Some shrank away from me, others were grateful and whispery, but one or two were shouty and excited. I grinned and signed their school shirts, earning instant disapproving glances from their tutor. I offered to sign his as well, and he took an alarmed step back.

As he shooed his school trip back into line, I saw Ramin had arrived and was grinning at me. I jumped up from my chair and gave him a massive bearhug. I tottered to lift him off his feet but as I looked up at him beaming down at me, it was worth it. I couldn't help myself. I had missed him so much.

'How long have you been standing there?'

'A while. I was looking for you, but you were hiding amongst the rug rats. I swear some of them were actually taller than you.'

I laughed loudly and drew attention as I swatted him. The diners would have loads to talk about when they went home. Not one but two curators, and fighting, in public.

'You should go with them. Maybe they'll help you pass your maths tests?'

Ramin had hated bi-nominal trigonometry and had nearly failed a paper. It was the closest thing he had to an academic flaw and, by Bast, I was never one to let up on that.

'Great Ra, I've missed you! I miss Julius calling me Rami. Bast, I even, and don't laugh at me, I miss Clio.'

I nodded noncommittally and called a server over. Why did Ramin always go to the heart of things? I was trying to avoid him, and he was addressing that avoidance head on. Having ordered some snacks, I switched to small talk and, for a while, Ramin was prepared to play along, although I could see his puzzlement rising. I noted he wasn't wearing his brace. I was paying attention to those who didn't. Were they suspicious that someone was eavesdropping, or were they simply not brace wearers? In the past month, I had become hyper vigilant, but a bare forearm was becoming increasingly rare.

'No brace?'

'No, I'm not at work today. You know you have to wear them now if you enter any building, not just government ones? If you'd chosen an indoor seat, I wouldn't have been permitted entry. Call me a rebel.'

I laughed along with him, Rebel Ramin. It was just so preposterous.

'Hang on,' I said. Something he had just said caught my attention. 'What do you mean you miss Clio? Isn't she at work?'

I hadn't been able to track Clio down but I simply assumed she had been avoiding me.

'Nope, after thumping Githumbi, she demanded a sabbatical and disappeared. It's odd, don't you think? Is there something going on that we don't know about?'

I almost choked and cut him off sharply. 'Sounds typical Clio to me. Plus, the brace abuse was the engineers, and we know they aren't doing that anymore. This is just for our own safety now that we know there are other Earths out there.'

'Yeah, that's the official line, but it just doesn't add up, does it? Betas can't travel here, so they aren't an issue and the quantum dwellers, gods or whatever they are, have been banished, and anyone else powerful enough to visit is presumably going to be smart enough to avoid door security.'

'It's about keeping each other safe.'

Even I winced at the trite lines that were pasted on billboards and on advert breaks.

'Minju says the fall in public disturbances has been wonderful. As a society, we are really coming together.'

I was saved from having to spout out any other hogwash as the food arrived. I really needed him to stop stumbling around this. He was too bright not to find a loose thread soon, and pulling on threads was like pulling on tails. Pulling on one unravelled the tapestry, pulling on the other unravelled you.

I popped a stuffed chilli in my mouth and was disappointed by the blandness of the filling. Tourist fodder. My fault for choosing this place. I tried the ghanoush, which at least was well seasoned, and dipped some pitta in to it. Frankly, it all tasted like ash. As Ramin called the server over for some more water, I snatched the chance to stare at him and drink in every detail. Every laugh line, every memory. I wanted to talk to him so badly. Explain who Minju really was and discuss what she might be up to. And thereby putting him in mortal danger. If he didn't truly believe me, he might accidentally reveal my hand. If I could just gather some evidence, maybe I could show it to him and convince him that the nation's most wondrous citizen was nothing more than a maggot infested snake.

'Hungry?' Ramin laughed, and I relaxed. I was just about to discuss the food when he carried on. 'So these new restrictions, I went to ask Githumbi if she knew anything. Like was it a custodian thing? Because it certainly sounds like it, and guess what?'

I groaned. I had tried to visit her last week, but she was out. I was certain Julius had told her about Minju. I did not know how he had found out, but thought that was the ravings that Githumbi had referred to. I knew something had happened that had really unnerved her, beyond the actual repatriation, and I wanted to let her know I knew. The two of us could work quietly together. But like I said, she was out, and I had got lost in my studies for my new assignment. Trying to bring down Minju, whilst also impressing her, was a fine balancing act. Even though the prospect was boring, I had to be a perfect archivist. I wondered what she had said to him.

'I said, what do you think?'

I shook my worries off and focused on Ramin. 'No idea.'

'She's stopped!'

'What?' My stomach lurched, the chillies and ghanoush mingled unhappily.

'I know. I never thought Luisa Githumbi would end herself. She was so impressive and full of energy.'

His words washed over me. The last time I had seen her, she had been berating herself for repatriating Julius. Then Minju was disparaging her on the national broadcasts. But still, Luisa would never choose to stop. How could she be dead? That power, that energy. That fierce determination to always do her duty. In the shadows of my mind, I saw the swish of a leopard's tail.

'When did this happen?'

'Last Thursday.'

I had called on her on Wednesday. And then she took her own life.

'She didn't even leave a note. That's odd, right?'

Not if she didn't know she was going to die. All thoughts of confiding in Ramin flew up to join the parakeets. Minju had clearly been watching either me or Githumbi. When she saw that we had nearly met up, she put an instant halt to it. Or was I being paranoid? I hated this. I needed Julius. I needed his devious mind to see around all these corners.

'Could Chen's lack of confidence in her, drive her to it?'

'You think Luisa Githumbi so weak that someone else's poor opinion of her would cause her to give up on life?' My anger was palpable.

'Protecting your new bestie?' asked Ramin sharply.

'New bestie?'

'Minju, she's always talking about you.'

I recoiled, then paused and drained my beer. There was only one way to deal with this.

'I will not waste my new boss' time with some sort of nutter's conspiracy theory.'

He put his fork down on the table. 'So I'm a nutter, am I?'

'Bast Ramin, don't get so huffy.'

I knew telling him he was being huffy would annoy him. It was a sore spot for him, ever since school. He frowned at me, and I modified it a bit. It was killing me to deliberately force a distance between us.

'I mean, the theory is nuts, not you. Minju's the sodding pharaoh. I can't just waltz in and ask her to investigate why a custodian who failed to capture the previous pharaoh's assassin may wish to end her life? It doesn't take a genius, does it, to figure out she was ashamed. Even those little kids could work that one out.'

'But Clio's disappearance and the brace thing.'

He was persisting, despite my efforts to steer him off the subject. My desire to save our friendship was putting his life in jeopardy. I needed to put that aside now.

'What brace thing?' I scoffed. 'There is no brace thing. That's Minju trying her hardest to keep us all protected, and Clio buggering off is about the most normal thing that Clio could have done.'

Ramin's lips tightened and I could spot from the tell-tale flush around his collar he was confused and distressed. I needed to push him towards angry.

He sighed and tried again. 'It's all wrong. Julius was repatriated and then the pharaoh who apparently gave the orders was assassinated. Clio, his partner, disappears. And Luisa, his guard, decides to stop living.'

'And what? Do you know how ridiculous you sound? In case you hadn't noticed, I'm still here. So are you. So is Minju, so is Jack, so is Sabrina, so is Sam. All his closest friends are still here. We haven't mysteriously disappeared.'

His entire neck flushed red. I pushed my chair back and threw my napkin on the table, but he pushed on.

'Sam isn't here.'

'Sam's on a well-deserved sabbatical and you know it.'

As a reward for how well he had steered the quantum facility through its recent ordeals, he had been offered a family sabbatical. A year's leave at full pay for him and his family to go travelling. Priti, his wife, had said yes before he had even had a second to think. For Sam, the only thing that trumped the job was his family. As his girls jumped up and down, he'd said he couldn't think of anything he'd rather do and said yes as well.

I was pleased for him. He deserved it, but if he were here, might he be able to help? Could I risk him in a way that I wasn't prepared to risk Ramin? Which was worse, potentially sacrificing a colleague, or hurting my best friend? I knew what I had to do.

'You need to grow up, Ramin. And get on with your job. I have my work to do, and I don't want a performance review like your last one. If I were you, I'd focus on my job and stop chasing silly Beta conspiracy theories.'

I turned and walked slowly out of the café. People hurried out of my way. And, as much as I wanted to run, I needed Ramin to watch me leave as though I couldn't care less about what had just happened between us. Two streets away, I burst into tears.

'Salutations, Neith, you appear—'

I tore the brace off my wrist and smashed it repeatedly against the wall until the supposedly

107

shatterproof coating finally splintered, and the component parts fell to the ground, where I stamped on them and kicked them into the gutter.

I then walked to the closest engineer depot, requested a replacement and returned home like a fine, upstanding citizen. Ready to preserve and protect.

Rebirth:
Julius–October
Beta Earth

Chapter Eleven - October: Beta: Julius

'Julius?'

I looked up from my desk in surprise. I hadn't even heard the knock on the door and there's no way that Anthony Jones, Head of Classics, would have entered my office without knocking first.

'Hello, Anthony. Sorry about that. I must have been miles away.'

My head was pounding, but that had been commonplace over these past three months. Since returning from America, my sense of well-being had steadily deteriorated. Today's lecture had been a disaster, and I wondered if that was why Anthony had come calling.

'What can I do for you?'

'I have spent the past hour dealing with calls from your students.'

'Were they complaining? I can't say I blame them. I am so sorry, it's just these blasted headaches.'

I went to put the kettle on, but he waved at me, telling me to stay where I was.

'No one was complaining.' He filled the kettle up from my little kitchenette and switched it on. 'In fact, they were all very concerned. You're a very popular lecturer, and they are worried.'

'I was fine, just a tad dizzy.'

'Good God, man, they said you started talking in Arabic.'

I looked up in surprise. 'Don't you mean Aramaic?'

I prided myself on my knowledge of the ancient languages. But modern-day stuff I was less certain of.

'No, apparently it was Arabic, although Sheheen said you were using dialectal words that she didn't recognise, and your accent was a bit odd, but otherwise perfect.'

Well, great, I thought. Add another issue to my list of things that made no sense.

'The thing is, Julius, your colleagues are also concerned. Don't think we haven't seen how often you are taking pain killers. Something is wrong. You are always wrapped up in jumpers under your blazer, you shiver constantly. I am insisting that you visit the doctor.'

I nodded. 'Not a bad idea. I'll make an appointment for next week. I have a free afternoon on Thursday.'

'Not good enough,' he said briskly. 'I've informed personnel. I'm placing you on sick leave until the end of Michaelmas. That will give you this month and November to properly recover. Get yourself checked over this afternoon.'

I scoffed, then winced. Anthony passed me a cup of tea and I sipped at it gratefully.

111

'I doubt I'll need that long. Maybe a week or two.' The thought of just doing nothing felt perfect. 'But there's no way I'll get a same day doctor's appointment.'

Now it was his turn to look surprised. 'Since when? Use one of the coronation clinics.' He shrugged. 'There are two here in Cambridge. Or use your own surgery. Since the proper funding, there are no more queues. Good God, man. Is that why you've been delaying? The NHS has been working like a dream. Get yourself checked over. Then come back to work when you feel ready. I've already arranged full cover.'

I finished my tea and placed the cup back in its saucer, trying not to make it rattle as my hand shook.

'Fair enough. To be frank, I would be grateful for a few hours just lying down. I'll go now if I may?'

Having convinced him I didn't need a taxi, I headed out across the quadrant. The wind had picked up, scooting leaves along the alleys. Rain was imminent. I changed my mind and hailed a cab. Some tourists had just hopped out and I decided to take advantage.

'You alright, mate?' The cab driver turned around in his seat.

I must have been a right state, then realised it was probably the eyes. I pointed to them and raised my eyebrows.

'The old David Bowie look? Schoolboy accident. When they said keep your eye on the ball, I took them literally.'

He shook his head. 'No mate. Not that, although ow. I mean, your eye is fully bloodshot. The whole thing's red.'

He pointed to the eye in question, but all I could do was shrug. I mean, it's rather hard to look at one's own eye. I made some fatuous comment about plucking out my eyeball which just seemed to make it worse. After that, he drove me home in silence.

I walked into my house and upstairs to the bathroom mirror, where I could see nearly three quarters of one eyeball had blown red. Little threads of blood traced through the remaining white section. That did indeed look nasty. I wasn't going to call an ambulance. That felt like an overreaction, but I have to confess I was worried. I would call the doctor and ask for an emergency appointment. See what they had to say.

I got as far as the kitchen when I saw a bottle of wine on the countertop. From the fancy label, this was beyond my normal price bracket. Hanging from the neck was a parcel tag on a bit of twine. There was writing on the tag and I read it in surprise.

'Drink Me.'

I didn't remember buying any wine. And why would I have to tell myself to drink it? I checked the back door, but it was locked. No one had come in this way, unless they had a spare key. Maybe one of my neighbours did? Maybe I should change the locks? But if all my intruder was doing was leaving me bottles of wine, that wasn't such a hardship.

I was tempted to open the bottle, but then I remembered alcohol thins the blood, or something like that, so maybe I should wait until after the doctors. I turned the label over.

'Drink me now. You will feel better.'

Medicinal wine. Well, why not? If I was being honest with myself, I was terrified. Splitting headaches, random vomiting and bloodshot eyes were not a great combination. And now I was clearly suffering from amnesia. I had no recollection of how that bottle had come to be in my kitchen. I would have a glass to steady my nerves, then call for an ambulance. If this was a bleed on the brain, a doctor would send me to hospital, anyway. As I pulled the bottle opener from the drawer, it got entangled with the other bits and bobs inside. Various forks and tin openers fell on to the floor in a clatter and I winced at the noise. I was sweating and could feel my hand shaking. I picked up the phone. This couldn't wait. If I was having a stroke, I needed to be in hospital as quickly as possible.

The smell of wine filled the air. I didn't remember opening the bottle, but now the cork lay beside the label saying *Drink Me* and I could smell summer. It felt an odd description, but how else to explain that warm baked earth fragrance? The scents of lavender and roses, honey and almonds being roasted filled the room. I could hear bees and a river nearby and the air seemed full of swallows. I couldn't wait for a glass. Picking the bottle up, I drank straight from the neck.

Immediately, I felt my body pause. There was a sense of stillness and peace from within. This was a very fine vintage. I poured myself a glass and walked through to the front room and settled down on the sofa. The aching thump in my head was receding, and I felt at ease for the first time in months. By the end of the glass, I decided to go to bed. I hadn't been well, but now I was okay. What I needed to do was sleep and everything would be alright in the morning.

As I climbed the stairs, I groaned at my stupid joke about removing my eyeball to look at the other one, which had alarmed the taxi driver. Neith would have laughed along. Clio would have called me a shit-fly.

Smiling, I clambered into bed. I didn't know who these women were or why I had suddenly conjured them up, but just thinking of them made me profoundly happy. Within seconds, I fell asleep and dreamt.

Chapter Twelve - October: Beta: Julius

I woke up and remembered everything. It wasn't a sense of things slowly flooding back. It was simply how we wake up every day and know what happened the day before. There was no flood of memories, or parting of clouds. I just opened my eyes, and I knew what had happened. Including the tears in Githumbi's eyes as she hugged me and said goodbye. Ludo telling her to be professional and I remembered the flash of uncontrolled fury that crossed her face. If I ever got to see her again, I would return that hug tenfold.

For now, though, it was Saturday morning, and I had the weekend ahead of me. First things first. I felt fabulous, but I wanted to check out my eyes. I padded across to the bathroom and smiled in the mirror. Two white eyes. One blue, one brown.

'Thank you, Firenze.'

I spoke out loud, but didn't expect a response. Who else could have been responsible for that bottle of wine? For whatever reason, the wipe Githumbi had administered went wrong. My guess was that after my mind had already been tinkered with by Anansi, and endured brain grafts and splices with Neith, that it wasn't a stable subframe. Jack would probably say my brain was outside of optimal operating parameters for a successful wipe. I don't think they intended to hurt me, but it appeared that I had been heading for a full-on embolism.

I don't know why Firenze had stepped in. Maybe she was curious? Maybe keeping an eye on things that interested her was no effort for a being that could view multiple time streams at a glance? She had promised not to interfere with Alpha, and made everyone else make the same promise. I was very glad to have been on Beta.

I leant my forehead against the cold glass and took a deep, shuddering sigh. Was I truly glad to be here? My hands gripped the basin whilst I tried to think things through. I had been thrown out, ditched under the cover of night. Githumbi's reassurances that no one knew this was coming were slightly consoling. If it was so quick, what had I done? Minju was obviously behind it, and the speed with which it happened suggested that she had this option in place for a while, but hadn't implemented it.

I was about to call Rami for advice when the enormity of it hit me. I would never see him again. Or Neith. Jesus, I was even missing Clio, which I think showed just how rattled I was. Was there a way back? If only to say goodbye properly. To thank them, to tell them how much they meant to me. Was there something I could do? I shivered and grabbed my dressing gown. At least now I know why I had been so cold. Two years living in Egypt would do that to a body.

'Firenze. Can you help?'

The silence continued. Well and good, she interfered to save my life, that had to be enough. I decided to make a coffee and try to work out what my next steps should be. I knew curators visited on a regular basis. The problem was, I obviously couldn't access their steps into the past, and I had no idea where they would be stepping when they made an active retrieval. This was going to require a lot of thought. I'd kill for a cup of Pyg's Cardamom booster. I was two steps out of the bathroom when something about Pyg's rang a bell. I had a memory of it that had nothing to do with Alexandria or the mouseion. Was it from the Fresher's Ball? No, that was Jonty saying the pig roast was a poor choice. Maybe I was clutching at straws. And then I remembered a bunch of straws on a counter and there was the memory. A stranger in a coffee shop talking about how good the food at Pyg's was. There could only be one explanation for that. He was an Alpha resident.

Running downstairs, I patted through my coat, looking for his card. There was nothing. Had I thrown it away? I was desperately trying to remember what it said, his name, anything. I tried all the pockets again, then remembered it was August when I had met him. I had been wearing a summer jacket. Although, I had frozen to death, returning from America.

I stopped short and almost physically felt my brain jolt as it re-categorised those memories of America as nothing more than an illusion. In fact, as I thought of my time in America, I felt no emotional attachment to those thoughts. They were blurred, like the recollections of a second-rate film. This was going to take a while to process. But in the meantime, I ran to the under-stairs cupboard and rummaged in the back until I found my summer jackets hidden under a sea of scarves, hats and winter coats. I really had become quite soft.

My fingers felt the edges of a small card and I snatched at it in relief.

Marcus Carruthers - Alexandria Company

Grabbing my phone, I dialled the landline, praying that someone answered the phones on a weekend. On the third ring, a woman's voice, rather than a computer, answered my call.

'Good morning. This is the Alexandria Company. How may we be of service?'

The old school phrasing caught me off guard for a moment, but I recovered myself and ploughed on.

'Hello. Yes,' I stammered, excited and anxious. 'The thing is, I met one of your colleagues, a Mr Carruthers. He said to call whenever.'

I didn't know what to say. Was she from Alpha? Did she know?

'Mr Carruthers. Certainly, sir. I'm afraid he doesn't work on the weekends, but if I can take some details from you, he will get in touch on Monday. If that's convenient?'

I groaned. The wait would kill me, but what else could I do?

'That would be most kind. Thank you. My name is Julius Strathclyde and I—'

I was about to say I would be available at his earliest opportunity, but she cut me off. 'Putting you through now, sir.'

The line went silent and then I heard Marcus Carruthers' voice, and I could swear he was smiling. 'Hello, Julius. Were you looking to meet up for a coffee?'

My heart was racing. 'Are you a curator?'

There was a slight pause and then he gave a quick, short laugh, surprised by my bluntness. 'I shall send a car for you. It will be with you in half an hour. Oh, and pack an overnight bag. We'll talk soon. Yes, yes?'

As he hung up, I stared at the screen for a few seconds, then flew around the house, grabbing stuff together and shoving it in my bag. I then spent the next twenty-five minutes wearing out a hole in the carpet as I paced back and forth.

Chapter Thirteen - October: Beta: Julius

Two hours later, I was being driven into London. My driver had been courteous, but unhelpful. He was an agency driver and just went where directed. The car was top of the range. I wasn't much of a petrol head, but I knew most taxis didn't normally have this amount of leather, let alone walnut trim and a chiller cabinet. As the door closed with a solid clunk, I wondered if it might also be bulletproof. This was a concierge service for top level clients. Mr Carruthers didn't mess around. We drove past the Bank of England, then turned down a quiet side street and came to a halt. The street's name was Alexandria Lane. Hiding in plain sight.

As I stepped out of the car, the driver handed me my bag and pointed to a large wooden door, with brass fittings. I rummaged in my pocket for a tip, but he smiled as he shook his head. He then got back in the car and drove off.

Looking up and down the street, I felt there was something slightly off with the setup, but couldn't quite place my finger on it. Across the road, a sign for the Guild of Loss Adjustors hung, but the door in front of me was unadorned, except for a small brass plaque: *The Alexandria Company*. I stepped forward, and the door swung open. Marcus Carruthers was standing in the doorway, a ridiculously happy smile on his face for a stranger, his arms outstretched.

'Here, give me your bag. Come in, come in.'

I stepped into a large atrium. There were a few doors leading left and right, a large staircase swept up to the upper floors. Above my head was a large domed roof light filling the hall with light. Hanging below it was a crystal chandelier for evening illumination. In front of me, a corridor heading off towards the back of the house. The building was bigger than I first suspected, and I had an inkling I knew what was off about the street outside. I had a thousand questions, but only one that mattered.

'Can you get me back?'

Watching his smile fade, his expression fell into sorrow. I felt my own misery mix with his as he shook his head sadly.

'No. We are all orphans here. But I hope we can offer you a new family?'

It came unbidden, but I raised my fist to my heart. 'Greetings to your hearth and home.'

He didn't reply, but stepped forward and gave me an enormous hug, releasing me the second my discomfort became intolerable.

About a second, since you're wondering.

I had been on Alpha for almost two years and still found hugging men a tricky procedure. The Alphas really did hug for too long. They also squeezed rather than slap each other on the back. Christ, I remember the first time I had slapped Rami on the back. He thought I was trying to attack him. I'd never hugged Clio, but I imagine she would appreciate the brief and physical approach. Hugging Neith was like hugging my sister. And now I would never hug any of them again.

'Come on. Dawson will take your bag, and you and I can have a chat. I imagine you have some questions? I have thousands, so let's get started. Yes, yes?'

He turned and headed towards the door on our right and into a large office with several desks. A door led from that into a small corridor, lined in linen fold oak, with further doors leading off that until it ended at another oak panelled door. Carruthers swung the door open onto a beautiful and warm gentleman's study. It was a large room with a heavy leather-topped desk and bookshelves to one side. The windows overlooked a courtyard garden and on the other side of the room, two leather armchairs flanked a roaring fireplace.

'You *are* a curator, aren't you, Mr Carruthers?'

He waved me to a chair and sat down in the opposite armchair. I sank into the leather embrace and was surprised how soft and comfortable it was. Everything in this room felt like an antique, but used daily and kept in excellent condition.

'Yes, Julius. I am a curator and please call me Marcus. Coffee is on its way, and then I will tell you all about the venerable history of the Alexandria Company. Unless you would prefer a mint tea?'

I laughed. Of course, that explained my newly acquired hankering for mint tea. Lots of things over the past three months were beginning to make sense.

'I suspect the dental care here isn't as good as Alexandria. I'll stick with the coffee.'

An older lady brought in a tray with two cups and a cafetière. She was a tall woman, with Slavic features, high cheekbones, and bright blue eyes. She had a braid of white hair that fell to her waist. One strand was a darker grey and wove in and out of her plait. Despite her white hair and fine wrinkles, I knew she wasn't someone to mess with.

Marcus choked off a laugh. 'Coffee duties, is it, Marie-Louise?'

'I don't know what you mean. I'm just trying to be helpful.' She huffed at him, then left, having thoroughly scrutinised me.

'Ignore her. You'll meet her again soon, in fact you'll meet everyone. A new curator causes quite the stir. Although I should ask? *What* are you?' He tilted his head and steepled his fingers. 'I assume you aren't actually a curator. Not that it matters. Anyone from Alpha is family here.'

I was about to confirm that I *was* indeed a curator, but he rushed on.

'No, don't answer me. You'll only have to repeat yourself when you meet the others. Let me bring you up to speed and then you can tell all of us about yourself, Alexandria, and the mouseion.'

From the way he spoke, I knew which was the most important thing on that list and it wasn't me or the city.

'So, let's start at the beginning. The Alexandria Company.' Marcus cleared his throat and paused, trying to gather his words. 'You'll have to forgive me. It's easy to reminisce and get carried away. If I start to ramble, just raise your hand.'

I smiled and waved at him to carry on.

'Now, when to start? As you know, we have been stepping for only the past few decades on Alpha Earth, but of course we have been travelling to Beta covering a time period of nearly two thousand years. And as you may be aware, not all curators make it home.'

'We have no records of what happened to anyone pre-seventeenth century. Although there are a few incidents, where we can guess from the historical records, that a curator may have been involved. But, by and large it has been the mantra that if we find ourselves stranded, we just try to blend in and live a good life or end ourselves.'

Marcus paused and took a drink whilst I wondered about those poor curators stepping from sunny, superior Alexandria into the middle ages and getting stuck there. He caught my eye and shrugged, then put his china cup back down.

'Things changed when Finn Thomassen became stranded in Constantinople in 1655. Poor bugger, completely on his own. How he didn't go mad, I do not know. Still, he had something that those around him didn't have.'

'Hygiene levels?'

'Very good! Although I was thinking of foresight. He knew which people to monitor, which markets were going to develop, how history was going to turn.'

'Ah,' I said. Put like that, it was obvious. 'So he made his way to London.'

'Bingo! The start of the stock exchange, the East India company, the birth of an empire that was going to dominate this planet for the next four centuries. Using that knowledge, he built a base and kept an eye out for other stranded curators.'

It was a stroke of genius, really. They could build a tiny empire hidden within the greater wealth and expansion of the British one.

'The first thing he did was try to find any evidence of earlier strandings. Finn knew we'd lost curators in the past, but we haven't been able to find any trace of them surviving. Maybe they were rescued?'

'I'm not aware of any missions to retrieve lost curators.'

126

'No, of course not.' Marcus shook his head dismissively. 'Impossible anyway. What are the chances of the stepper opening a window to the exact same point and location in time?'

Well, at least I had news for him on that score. With Jack's technological breakthroughs in quantum physics, the step could now be pointed at a set time and place. Whether Minju would ever allow a mass return of unindoctrinated curators was another matter.

'Anyway, Finn Thomassen established a home here in this house and started visiting art houses offering his skills as a restorer. He sent out notices on ships with coded messages that only a citizen of Alpha Earth would understand. Pyg's and locusts, that sort of stuff. And slowly, the occasional curator would arrive at this doorstep. In turn, they continued the tradition. Over the centuries, The Alexandria Company has grown into loss adjustors as well as restoration experts. Who better than us to judge the value and authenticity of an item? We are the founding members of the Guild of Venerable Adjustors.'

'So are all loss adjustors actually curators? How many are you?'

'No, not at all. Just us. But we hide in plain sight. We are actually loss adjustors, but also Alphas. There are nine of us at the moment. Obviously, the Alexandria Company employs other staff and our business offices are over on Canary Wharf, but the partners work from this building.'

'This building.' I had to check. 'It's like Downing Street, isn't it? The entire street is one interconnected house. And the same on the other side of the street?'

'You have good eyes. How did you know?'

'Well, unless this is a TARDIS, you are much bigger on the inside. You've clearly knocked through walls. On the outside, some of the front doors just look, well, unused. I could go back and see what exactly tipped me off. But looking at the steps and doorways made me think they were a façade.'

Marcus nodded, smiling. 'Yes, the entire street is ours. We built most of them, and as the other buildings on the street became available, we bought them, and then merged them internally. We also own the street behind this one, so the garden is utterly private as well. No one overlooks us.'

'That must have cost a pretty penny?'

'Don't forget, when you know which way the stock market is going to turn and which area is going to face a property boom, it's child's play to make money. Our family wants for nothing.'

'Except home?'

He sighed deeply. 'Except home.' Pausing, he picked up the cafetière and refilled our cups. I listened to the log crackling and spitting, and thought how bereft they must have felt.

'Anyway, that is how we have thrived. We run our business as loss adjustors and we scoop up stranded curators. I arrived in the 1960s and have now become pharaoh. The title given to the senior partner. Not necessarily the oldest or longest serving.'

I had clearly misjudged his age.

'Ninety-three, as you are too polite to ask. But Sasha Kalo is older than me. She's one hundred and twenty-four. Stepped over from Alpha in 2018, but got stranded in 1944 and has been taking the slow road back. If she returned home now, only seven years would have passed on Alpha, but she has aged many decades.'

It was a double-edged tragedy. A long life, but on the wrong Earth. It was hard looking at Marcus, though, and accept he was as old as he claimed.

He smiled as I continued to stare. 'Better genes, better health care, better medicine. We live about twenty per cent longer than you, on average. Compare your own life expectancy to that of a Georgian?'

I had never really discussed ages back on Alpha. I had just assumed everyone was roughly my age or a bit younger or older. Now I realised Neith could easily be in her fifties. Did she view me as a teenager?

'I know our geneticists back home were looking into whether it's feasible to elongate our life spans further, but I don't know if there is any progress on that.'

'I met a man who was over four hundred years old.'

Now it was his turn to stare at me in astonishment. 'How is that even possible?'

I was about to try to explain meeting Leonardo da Vinci and Firenze on a third Earth, but realised that it might complicate matters. As it was, Marcus held his hand up and shook his head.

'No spoilers, as River would say. You can tell us all about the quattro-centenarian later. For now, we would love for you to spend the weekend with us. I'm afraid you will be rather the centre of attention, and might get a bit hoarse by the end of it. But we all rather miss the homeland and always love to greet a new member and catch up on the news. And I suspect your tale will be particularly fascinating. Yes, yes?'

I wondered where I was going to start. Not only was my tale extraordinary, but Alpha had been through a momentous upheaval, and then there were the gods. Where would I start?

'That's a point. How did you know how to find me? Do you have a way of knowing when steps are about to occur?'

If they did, I could try and hitch a ride back. No sooner had I thought it, than my hopes were dashed. This would have already occurred to them. That they hadn't done it meant it wasn't feasible.

'No, we haven't had anyone from the future, so to speak, arrive back here yet. Which suggests a change in

Alpha is afoot or there are just no more strandings. But more on that later. No, you were an oddity, and we like oddities.'

He rubbed his hands together, a big smile on his face. 'Well, it was Tam who spotted you first. Tam Dawson, he took your bags just now. He was the first to alert us to something happening in Cambridge and rumours of a Fabergé Egg. This was as close to actually being on the scene as a live step was in progress. Gods, we were so close. However, we just missed the team, but we noticed an unusual trail of events running up to what we presumed was the exit point. There were shootings. The local police were involved. And finally you disappeared.'

He paused, shaking his head and drumming his fingers together.

'Honestly, it was one of the worst extractions I have ever heard of, but we think we know what might have caused it.' He looked at me keenly. 'I suspect you might be able to confirm some of our theories.'

I was about to answer him when something occurred to me. 'When you say I disappeared, I was told a cover story had been put in place to explain my disappearance?'

Marcus waved his hand dismissively. 'Solid work, but not good enough to fool a curator on the hunt for clues. You weren't dead. Or at least we could find no evidence of a hidden body. And someone was working

131

very hard to provide a false cover for your whereabouts. The only conclusion was that you had ended up on Alpha and, as you weren't previously ill or dying, we presumed you weren't an angel. Unless you were dying? Did you get caught in the crossfire?'

'Nearly. Neith threw me out of the path of a bullet and yanked me back through the stepper.'

He leant forward and peered at me closely. 'Your eyes?'

I pointed to my left eye. 'Neith's. This one,' I pointed to my right,' is all mine. Or the other way round. I always forget. It's not like I can feel them. Anyway, the blue one is mine.'

'And would this be Neith Salah?'

It was my turn to look at him closely. 'How do you know Neith?'

'Sasha Kalo again. Not only is she our oldest curator, but she is also the most recent to leave Alpha.'

I tried to get my head around it and vowed that, as soon as I had a moment, I would get a pen and paper and try to write this all down.

'Don't worry, it is confusing, but you get used to it.' Marcus gave me a sympathetic smile as he topped up my cup, then continued. 'As each curator gets stranded, they write everything they can remember of the current curator roll call, recent missions, and so on. As Sasha stepped in 2018, she would have known Neith Salah and added her name to the records. Our knowledge comes in strange fits and starts, depending on when the curator is stranded. Some of the older strandings refer to foul play, but we haven't been able to corroborate that. Unless you have news?'

My heart sank. These guys had been living as exiles for decades, polishing their perfect picture of home. No doubt looking around the Earth they were stuck on, feeling derision for its violence, its meanness, its avarice. Now I was going to have to point out that was part and parcel of humanity.

My face must have belied me.

'It's okay. After life here, you won't be able to shock us.'

I didn't share his confidence, but it was the least I could do, bring news from back home.

There was a light knock on the door, and Marie-Louise walked in again. 'Everyone's here, so stop hogging the new boy.'

Marcus raised an eyebrow. 'Ready?' He slapped his thighs and stood up. 'You can meet everyone before lunch, then afterwards you can bring us up to speed.'

We got up and followed Marie-Louise back through the corridors. As we walked, I could hear an excited hubbub of people speaking. Marcus turned to me. 'We only usually meet once a quarter *en masse* so there's a fair bit of catching up amongst ourselves.'

Ahead, I could see an open door leading into a large club room. One entire side wall was glass, lending a bright airy feel to the room. Scattered around the room were recliners and seats resting on a marble floor. Light, bright, and almost like Alexandria.

Marcus clapped his hands and everyone turned to look at us. The attention was mortifying, and I wanted nothing more than to turn my back and run.

I counted nine people, representing a wide cross section of continents. I was easily the youngest person in the room, and I wondered how long people had been stranded here. There were as many women as men. What they did all have in common was obvious wealth and power. Some dressed in suits, others in kaftans, a few in street wear, but every one of them appeared capable of picking up the bill in the Ritz for the entire service without blinking. They also looked like they could knife anyone that added an extra lobster to that bill. I wondered what curators do when they have time on their hands. Loss adjusting can't have kept them occupied.

'Ladies and gentlemen,' said Marcus. 'It is my pleasure to announce the newest member of our family. Usual drill. He will not answer questions until after lunch, but now, please say hello to Julius Strathclyde.'

Chapter Fourteen - October: Beta: Julius

There was a second of silence as the people waited to see if Marcus had finished speaking, and then they exploded into hooting and whistling. The clamour and enthusiasm shocked me. I had been viewing them as some sort of elite powerhouse family. Now they were behaving like winners at the end of the Six Nations, and I burst out laughing. These were curators, these were my friends. In a fit of utter euphoria, instead of saying hello I grinned broadly and proclaimed somewhat tentatively: 'We Preserve.'

It's fair to say the crowd went wild. The roar of our motto was flung up to the rafters as everyone joined in. There was much laughter and hugging, shaking of hands and slapping of backs in the Beta tradition. I was introduced to everyone and promptly forgot all their names, but the stories they told, my God, the stories.

Caught in a landslide, swept away by a tidal wave. Brace failure. Attacked by a leopard. Knocked out by persons unknown, partner missing. Each story was as fantastical as the last as they explained what their mission had been and how it had gone wrong. I was spotting a trend in some of the later failures. Fewer natural events, and more to do with a potentially dodgy partner. Marcus had alluded to that earlier, so they had clearly spotted the same pattern. Soon, I would explain it to them.

After a fabulous lunch held out in the courtyard under heated lamps, we retired back into the clubroom. I sat at one end, and everyone made themselves comfortable. Servers brought in drinks and the doors were closed, leaving just the Alphas inside.

Marcus sat in another armchair beside me. He clapped his hands again. 'I shall lead the questions. Then we'll let Julius catch us up. If that is acceptable? Yes, yes?'

I smiled and gave a tiny shrug. I really wasn't looking forward to this. 'Of course.'

He smiled and returned his gaze over the rest of the room. 'Well, as you all know, we have been tracking the networks for mentions of Julius Strathclyde, and a few months ago, he reappeared in Cambridge. I went to meet him, but it was clear he had been wiped.'

Various heads nodded. This was not news to them.

'Then this morning, he called me up and asked if I was a curator. Bold as brass, and clearly with a restored memory.'

This caused some mutterings, obviously a wiped memory should remain wiped.

'Now, the angels we have been monitoring have all remained unaware of their recent history—'

I cut him off. 'You've been tracking the returned angels?' I had been worried about them when I first

136

heard they had been sent home. 'Are they safe? Are they okay?'

'Yes, of course, although I did want to ask you what caused the change in policy. We have never returned angels before, and suddenly a whole bunch all returned together. In perfect health and living in a retirement home in New Zealand. Can you shed some light on that?'

I put my glass down. 'It's a bit complicated.'

The curators laughed politely but leant in.

'Very well,' said Marcus. 'In your own time. But first, let me establish a few things. You are in fact a curator? We would have welcomed you whatever you were, as an exile from Alpha, but you are, in fact, a curator? And an Englishman?'

This last part was said in astonishment.

'Which is more surprising, that I'm a curator or that I'm English?'

'Both, I suppose. Obviously, we've never had a Beta curator, but we've never had a British curator either. Or at least we hadn't until Sasha's time. That's right, isn't it?'

He addressed a very old woman who was sitting by the fire. She wore a long tribal gown and had her hair wrapped up in a turban. As she had told me earlier, she was also the one whose partner had removed her brace at gunpoint and stranded her in 1944.

Now she smiled at me. 'Yes. Until three years ago, we remained Brit free. Not that they aren't welcome.' She wheezed as she laughed. 'They just have never shown any inclination to do anything so adventurous. I have to say, living in this version of Britain is quite a head explosion. Much more fun.'

There was a lot of very vigorous nodding of heads at this point.

'I quite like them,' said one voice, and was quickly answered by another man commenting on the British habit of colonisation and superiority. He was a large white man with a French accent and an overbearing attitude. The sort of person who liked the sound of his own voice.

He was cut off by Tam Dawson, who had taken my bags when I first arrived, and was now beaming. 'True enough, Pierre, they aren't perfect, but some of them are good fun. I can see why Julius was accepted as a curator.'

I smiled gratefully at him. When I first saw him, I had assumed he was Chinese. Now, from his accent, I placed him as Scottish and realised that for the umpteenth time that my desire to work out where people came from was inevitable, and also utterly futile. They weren't even from this Earth. All other categories were a waste of time.

Marcus grabbed a hold of the conversation again. 'So, Julius. Why did you become a curator?'

I shrugged. 'It looked like fun?'

This was met this with a resounding round of applause. A few glasses were raised in a toast and I smiled back at them.

'Who's the pharaoh?' called out one of the women and was immediately drowned out by another voice. 'How many successful retrievals have there been since Sasha's step?'

Marcus clapped his hands. 'Is this waiting to hear Julius' story? Yes, yes?' He turned to me apologetically. 'I'm afraid we are just a bit overeager.'

'Perfectly understandable. And I'm afraid my story will elicit a hundred questions more, so I am ready for them, but for now I can answer those two.' I turned to the group of curators. 'Successful retrievals. I can't answer that accurately for reasons that will become obvious, if unpleasant. I can tell you, however, that your current pharaoh is Nolyny Cleeve, and her right hand is Minju Chen.'

I knew that would cheer them up, if briefly. Minju was the first curator to rise so high.

'Great Ra! That is most excellent. You have delivered us the best news we could imagine. What an incredible achievement. And one in the eye for everyone who says curators aren't leaders.' He beamed widely and took a sip of water.

'Saved my life, yes, yes.'

There was a wave of warm laughter from the room for a familiar tale.

'Best partner a curator could ever ask for.'

I felt sick. I was about to be the bearer of some dreadful news. And then the penny dropped.

'Dear God, you're Marcus Caractacus?'

A curator still talked about in hushed tones as one of the finest ever to have worked for the mouseion, and not a common name. I should have recalled him faster. In my defence, my mind was still recalibrating.

'The one and only. I've tried to blend in over the years. Changed my surname from Caractacus to Carruthers. Little things like that.'

This room was full of vibrant, healthy, powerful individuals. I wondered if there was ever an occasion where they blended in. They were all in their late middle ages or older, but none seemed diminished by age. Their vitality radiated off them.

'Tell him about Minju's sacrifice,' called out Marie-Louise. I was beginning to recognise her voice. I didn't want to hear the story. I didn't want to hear another reason why people thought Minju was excellent. I had utterly admired her for so long, I felt every fresh betrayal as a personal insult.

'Do you want to hear the story, Julius?'

I nodded weakly and tried an enthusiastic smile as Marcus ploughed on. Eager to heap glory on his partner.

'Juju and I had been tracking a rare sword. The year was 1965, and we had just retrieved it from the hands of a thief who would later be mauled to death by a snow leopard. Now, we should have paid more attention to that detail, dreadful oversight on both of our parts. Just as we were about to head home, Juju had my brace and was recalibrating it to synchronise with her own.'

'What? That isn't protocol.'

'It was our misadventure, according to later curators—' he waved at the room, '—that changed standard practice. Braces back then were cumbersome, and it was easier to remove them to sync them. Anyway, the leopard leapt out of the undergrowth. Its massive paw clubbed me around the head and sent me flying. Juju was holding the sword and both braces and threw herself at the beast. She's just a tiny thing, but I swear I saw the fear in that animal's eyes as she attacked. He drew his claws out of my back and turned and sprung at her. He roared, displaying the whites of his teeth as he prepared to bite down on my diminutive partner. And just like that, as it embraced her, she stepped back to Alpha, saving my life, but abandoning me on Beta Earth.'

There was a collective sigh in the room.

'Of course, I assumed she had died. The leopard had been about to tear her throat out, but a few years later I made my way here to London and found out from Sasha that Minju had survived. She knew I was still alive and sent out messages to me and a few others she knew had been stranded. For a while, she was able to mop a few of us up and she helped stabilise the next generation.' He waved his hand, dismissing what was about to become a very convoluted timeline.

'Anyway, as you can imagine, I was delighted to hear she had survived, although saddened to hear her splice had removed her from service. And now you tell us she's made it all the way to the top! Incredible, but if anyone was going to do it, it was always going to be Juju.'

I nodded weakly. 'Actually, before I begin my story, do you think I could have a glass of red?'

Dutch courage would be required. As my story unfolded, their expressions moved from rapt attention to mounting horror and disbelief.

I explained how the mouseion had been infiltrated by a ring of thieves who were stealing artefacts and selling them on the black market. How the engineers had deliberately been keeping society in the dark about other Earths, and the fact that the stepper had been deliberately nobbled.

When I told them about the two princes, Marie-Louise tutted and handed over a twenty-pound note from her handbag and gave it to Dawson.

'Tam said their disappearance reeked of curator involvement, Marie-Louise insisted we would never be that reckless,' said Marcus with a quick grin.

It was the only highlight in my recitation. With each revelation, there were shouts and questions, but each time Marcus told them to be quiet and to let me get to the end of my story. Which is how I came to explain the Grimaldi Uprising, the attack from quantum dwellers, and that at the heart of all the thefts, the violence, the murders, the attempted coup sat Minju Chen, as she attempted to bring about a new world order. The last act I could comment on was my own repatriation.

'And that's how Firenze saved me and then I rang you up and here I am.'

My voice trailed away into silence. There had been gasps and muttering and moments of excitement, especially when I mentioned the quantum incursion, but overall, they appeared horrified.

'Julius, what you have said is dreadful. I can't imagine ever hearing anything worse.' Marcus had gone pale, and I could see the betrayal of his partner cut him deeply. He had even stopped saying yes, yes. 'I know this is incredibly rude, but do you have any objection to us verifying your statement? All conversations are recorded for the archives to help maintain continuity. Our software will analyse your voice and see if it detected any variations in your speech pattern that might suggest an anomaly.'

'A lie detector?' I asked.

Marcus examined his fingernails. 'That's a rather crude way of putting it, and normally we wouldn't dream of asking.'

I held up a hand. 'Of course I don't mind. What I have said runs contrary to everything you know and believe. Added to which, I am an outsider. What I have said is the truth as I witnessed it, but I am happy to have it verified.'

I knew I sounded painfully formal. I didn't expect them to fully trust me, although I could see in some faces an acceptance. Sasha Kalo, in particular, was nodding along sorrowfully.

'Panoptes, please verify Julius Strathclyde's words.'

'Five minutes buh,' came a disembodied voice.

Marcus smiled at me. 'Our version of Tiresias. I always thought Tiresias should have been named Panoptes. As we waited for this Earth to come online, we were ready to jump onboard. We had quite the party when Tim Berners-Lee was born. Ever since then, we have been sitting behind the firewalls and developing our own code. Certainly not to Alpha standards, but years ahead of Google and the AI systems currently leading the field here.'

'Wait, was that a Norfolk accent?'

'Norwich actually, but close enough.'

'Was there a reason?'

Marcus laughed.

'We based it on a friend. Honestly, it took ages to stop Panoptes from adding *Boy* at the end of every sentence.'

'He still says *Buh.*'

'I tried to eliminate that but Yonni wouldn't have a bar of it. Felt that Panoptes needed a personality.'

Marcus' small talk fell into reflection and I took another sip from my glass.

'Marcus,' a voice sang out across the brittle silence of the room. 'Julius Strathclyde's statement is accurate, right enough, and makes sense of Sasha Kalo's initial debrief in 1944.'

Marcus looked at me with such sorrow that I wanted to tell him I was lying. That it had all been a joke. The thefts, the murders, the civil war, the gods, all of it a massive, poorly conceived gag. I wished it too, but I had been living with the reality of it for too long. He cleared his throat.

'Panoptes, could you ask the servers to come in and take some drinks orders? We're also going to be eating in here this evening, so if canapés could be arranged?'

His words fell into a silent room as he continued.

'Well, as dreadful as it is, I would like to thank Julius for his report and start by apologising to him for all that our world has made him endure. There are not enough words to express our profound regret, but I hope that you accept them?'

They were apologising to me. I could weep. When they didn't go rogue, curators were the best.

'P-please don't. My news is horrible. I don't want to believe it either. Over the past two years, I have valued my friendship with Minju as something to be treasured. I feel foolish at having been manipulated so adroitly.'

I waited in silence as the waiting staff came in, orders were taken and bottles were left. The room emptied and we were left alone again.

'Right, then. Julius, I imagine you are about to face a lot of questions. Then we can work out what to do next.'

'What can we do? We're stuck here!' scoffed Pierre.

'Actually, I don't know about that,' I said, and you could have heard a pin drop as all curators froze and stared at me. 'That is to say, Jack and the other engineers have been making significant advances in understanding the engineering of the quantum technology. We can now control when and where the step opens. Before I left, there were talks about returning some of the saved art.'

'Returning?!' Pierre jumped up, shouting at the rest of the room. 'Are they mad? They can't return artefacts. These barbarians will just destroy it, or lose it, or sell it.'

'With respect,' I said, ice coating my words. 'It belongs to the *barbarians*, and it's up to them what they do with it.' Each word had become more and more

146

clipped until Pierre was glaring at me as I snapped at him. 'It's all very well calling us barbarians, but I think you'll have observed that many museums now have top notch security and controlled environments.'

Pierre scoffed at me. Why was it always the French?

I continued before he could reply. 'Regardless, it is the symposium's decision to only return non-contentious works of art to stable countries with inclusive democracies. My point is—' I raised my voice as Pierre offered his opinion on the total absence of stable countries, '—that we can expect an increasing number of live events as artefacts are returned. We can use that knowledge and try and intercept curators.'

'And how do you know all this?'

'Because I was going to be on the first team.'

That shut him up. His next question shut *me* up.

'So, where is the first drop?'

I shrugged. 'I got repatriated before it was decided.'

'Do you think those two events are related?' asked Marie-Louise as she sipped on a glass of red wine. I noticed we were sharing the same bottle of a very fine Bordeaux.

'No. I've been thinking about that and I think I got kicked out because I got stupid and mentioned that I couldn't find *1984* on the media feeds.'

'And you think that was relevant because?'

'A film that highlights how a government keeps its population in thrall by subverting their news and entertainment channels, exactly as Minju is doing. And mentioning it to Minju herself?'

I recalled how I had been at the party and had let my guard down. Honestly, it was a catastrophic blunder, but I hadn't been aware that Minju was listening to our conversation. I was in the middle of recommending it to the others as a way of subtly trying to make them think about what might be happening to their society when Minju joined us. I'd quickly changed the conversation, but clearly, I had gone too far.

'Bit of an own goal there,' said Marie-Louise as she scrunched up her face.

'Somewhat. I honestly don't know if she knew I was onto her. She had no reason to believe my memory block had been removed. Clio and I are the only people who know the truth of Minju. I suspect that Clio is safe, and she simply got rid of me because she felt a Beta individual was just too high a risk. After all, she had got rid of all the other angels. According to Red Custodian Githumbi, I had been granted leave to stay. But, in the dead of night, following that party, the decision was changed.'

'And a red custodian just told you this?' said Tam, shocked at the lack of professionalism.

'She had just wiped my memory. I imagine she felt I needed to know the truth, even if I would never remember it.'

'Sounds like a good woman.'

'One of the best. I am proud to know her.'

We talked into the evening until my voice grew hoarse and Marcus took pity on me.

'That's enough for today. Can I suggest that we reconvene in the morning? I think we need to plan a welcome committee. Even better, we need to find a way back to Alexandria and put things right. But, for now, let's sleep and catch up over breakfast.'

It was a subdued group that left the room, muttering softly and smiling kindly at me as I followed Tam upstairs. We stopped on the second floor, and he swung the door open onto a marvellous bedroom. The adjoining bathroom, Tam assured me, had a very large bath and unlimited hot water.

'I'm so sorry that your time in our care has been so full of violence and betrayal.'

I tried to protest, but he hugged me and I felt the disappointment of all his decades resting on my body. He turned and left in silence, and I walked into my room and closed the door.

'Good evening, Julius.' I recognised the voice from earlier. 'I am Panoptes. Simply call out if you need anything, otherwise I shall leave you in peace. Breakfast is at seven. Will you require an alert?'

I mumbled that I was fine and set my phone to six am, then slipped into the finest Egyptian cotton sheets and fell asleep almost immediately.

Chapter Fifteen - October: Beta: Julius

Sunday was a day of talk and catching up, and I may have gone on about Neith a bit too much, as Pierre yawned loudly from a sofa in the corner of the drawing room, where we had all retired after lunch.

'Is there a problem?'

I simply hadn't been able to take to Pierre. He was an embittered old man who sneered about everything.

'No problem. I just think your infatuation with Neith Salah is a little obvious.'

That stung. I didn't fancy Neith. I'd never felt an inkling of desire around her, but my God, I admired her. In fairness, I probably did hero-worship her, but I wasn't going to take that from this bitter whinger.

'Neith is worth ten of you.'

Pierre clicked his teeth and sniggered. Even from this distance, I got a whiff of sour breath.

'If I recall, you said the great Neith Salah was going to start working with Minju. Maybe she's not all that, after all? Or maybe she's been turned? Maybe she always was. After all, she was at the heart of the Fabergé Affair.'

I put my glass down. 'Take that back.'

'Or what?'

'Or I'm going to make you.' I wasn't sure about the ethics of punching an old man, but I was prepared to find out.

'Enough,' said Marie-Louise, slapping her newspaper down on the table. The crossword puzzle unfinished.

'All I'm saying,' said Pierre, 'is that she always appears to be nearby when things go wrong.'

'Things would go a whole lot worse if she wasn't there,' I snapped. 'She risked her life saving mine, she saved the life of an engineer by sacrificing her own, she has fought gods and won, she has travelled to other Earths and forged new friendships, she helped expose and bring down a massive criminal enterprise. So when I say we can trust Neith Salah, I mean we can put our lives in her hands and know she will never let us down!'

My heart was racing, my cheeks flushed. Pierre simply smirked at me.

'Well said, Julius,' said Marie-Louise again. 'I hope someday to meet her, but she was before my time. Pierre is simply vexed because, apparently, he tried to date her back in their student days. As you can see, it didn't end well.'

Pierre fumed, and I smiled to myself. Neith didn't need me to stand up for her, but that would never stop me. At least Pierre's hostility was a little easier to understand. I considered telling him we had never been involved, but then I thought there was little point.

'Back to the issue at hand, yes, yes,' Marcus spoke sharply as he walked into the room. We had been resting after lunch, but now we were cracking on with the issue. Marie-Louise tucked her crossword to the side and looked over attentively.

'This ability to choose to step live or select any date is really mind blowing,' said Tam thoughtfully. 'Do you think at some point they might send out rescue missions to bring us back?'

'Unlikely,' said Marie-Louise. 'Timeline disruption again. I think in future anyone who is lost will be immediately rescued. But for previous curators who have lived a life on Beta and affected other lives and events, erasing them from the timeline is again too dangerous.'

'That's not to say you can't step back on a live exchange. The future isn't written yet,' said Tam. 'Only the past is tricky.'

The smile on Tam's face was worth the glare from Marcus.

'Can we try to stay on topic, yes yes?'

There were a few mumbled apologies, and the curators started to discuss how they could make use of this knowledge. An idea came to me and the more I thought about it, the more ludicrous it sounded. Surely it had already occurred to this lot, but no one cared to mention it. I cleared my throat, and the room hushed.

'I know this will have been considered, but does Panoptes track Tiresias?'

Marie-Louise frowned. 'I don't follow?'

'Nubi's balls!' shouted Yonni and slapped her hand on her forehead. 'We're idiots.'

Now everyone was staring at her. Normally the quietest in the group, Marcus said Yonni was usually spending her time thinking up the next step forward. She and Tam were responsible for a lot of the recent innovations that the Alexandria Company relied on. Now she addressed the air.

'Panoptes? Are you capable of tracking all networks, and registering when the Tiresias algorithms are being employed?'

There was silence for a moment. 'Yes. That should be feasible if you tell me what markers to look for.'

'And would you be able to do this in live time?'

' Again, depending on the markers, this should be workable.'

'What's going on?' asked Pierre, and I could see why Neith wasn't attracted to him. Talk about slow.

'When a curator steps over, they invariably use Tiresias to interrogate the local networks. If we can spot the digital incursion, we can intercept the curator and say hello!'

Tam and Yonni were already heading to the door. Tam shouted over his shoulder, as Yonni was already running down the corridor.

'We'll start interrogating the programming language. Keep the food and drink coming, remind us to sleep now and then.'

As they left, the air of excitement in the room was buzzing.

'Thank you, Julius. Sometimes it takes an outside point of view to shake things up. I can see why Minju was worried about you.'

I couldn't add any insight into computer languages or programming, so I scanned the networks for mentions of Clio instead. It was mad, but I was worrying about her. She was the only person on Alpha who knew Minju's true nature. What if Minju had found out and got rid of her? My disappearance should have put Clio on high alert, but would that have goaded her into action or retreat? The best thing I could do was go back to Cambridge and wait for any breakthroughs with Panoptes.

Chapter Sixteen - October: Beta: Julius

The following morning, I got in the car and we pulled out into the London traffic. The Monday rush hour was in full gridlock as we crept out of the city. My head was reeling. I had learnt, or rather, remembered, so much in the past few days. Ever since Firenze had restored my memories, I was trying to re-balance all I knew to be true. Meeting the stranded curators was a new piece of information. If I could only find a way to be useful to them and get involved, I may find my way back. I was so lost in my thoughts of how to find excuses to return to London that I looked up in surprise as the car was pulling up and we were once again in Alexandria Lane. Marcus stood on the steps in front of the main door.

I stepped out of the car as the driver retrieved my suitcase from the boot.

'Have you had a good rest?' asked Marcus. It had been all of twenty minutes since I'd left. 'Something's come up,' he continued, taking my bag from the driver. His expression more serious than I was used to. 'Let's step inside.'

This time, the main hall was filled with bags and suitcases. People were heading in and out of doorways, various pieces of sturdy cases gathering on the marble

155

floor. Kevlar cases were unlikely choices for shirts and ties. As the staff placed them on the ground, bracing themselves against the weight, I guessed their contents were something altogether more deadly.

I turned to wait for Marcus. The minute we had stepped back inside, a few people had come up to him, tapping on iPads, asking questions, receiving instructions. Most were around my age. A mix of men and women and nationalities. Given their age, and the fact I didn't recognise anyone, I would guess these were not curators, but staff employed by the Alexandria Company.

Finally, Marcus turned to me. 'Right, sorry about doing this to you on your first day of work. Follow me and I'll brief you. Then you can join the team. Yes, yes.'

His words made no sense, but I played along as we both walked down the corridor to his office. As soon as the door closed, he grimaced and shook his head.

'Looks like things are moving faster than we thought.' He gestured to a seat, and we both made ourselves comfortable by the fire. 'We have just received reports of the discovery of a golden crown, and have been asked to authenticate it.'

'Why us?'

He blinked, then chuckled. 'Because we are the Alexandria Company. We are the world's number one authenticators. For a side hustle, I'd like to think we carved out a very good niche for ourselves. UNESCO, the British Museum, the Met, the Louvre. If there is an object of art or antiquity that needs verifying, we get the call.'

I was impressed, but not surprised. What else to expect from a collection of Alphas stranded here over the past three centuries? If they weren't so damned ethical, they'd probably be running the whole planet by now.

'Do you think this is a returned artefact?'

'Yes, yes.' He nodded quickly, pleased at not having to explain himself. Why else had I been called back? I knew nothing about Beta authentications process. 'The issue is the item and locations. You see, we have been asked by UNESCO to verify the artefact. They say it resembles a crown of Silla.'

I whistled. These crowns were works of exquisite beauty from the ancient Korean kingdom.

'You see the problem, yes, yes?'

Indeed I did, because the last Silla crown I had seen was on the shelf in Minju's office.

'So, Alpha have started the repatriation sooner than expected.' I shrugged. 'But this is good, isn't it?'

I couldn't understand his countenance. He hadn't smiled once since he met me at the door.

'The problem is where it has been found. Apparently, it was discovered in a series of caves near the ancient site of Bactria.'

That didn't sound great, although Bactria was ringing alarm bells. The discussions back on Alpha had been most emphatic that, if and when anything was returned, it would be to a stable and free state. Not some cave in the middle of nowhere.

'And Bactria is where exactly?'

'It's located in the Jowzjan region, on the northern borders of Afghanistan. Julius, I'm afraid this is going to be tricky.'

Chapter Seventeen - October:
Beta: Julius

I had been uncertain of my inclusion in the party, but Marcus said there was no time like the present to get me involved. I was a partner, after all. And, as a recent arrival, my combat skills were excellent. It didn't need pointing out that the rest of the partners were all in their seventies and above.

We arrived at a private airport and were now on a Lear heading south. The whole experience had been surreal. Passport control had been little more than a cursory glance, security was a breeze and then we were out on the tarmac heading towards a sleek white plane.

I was staring around the plane like a fanboy. Never in my wildest dreams had I imagined I would travel anywhere on a private jet. History professors travelled second class and, if it was available, third. Now I was sitting in a leather swivel armchair on a cream carpet. No wonder millionaires liked private planes. This was amazing. I examined my passport again, and Marie-Louise chuckled.

'I hope you didn't mind us cloning it?' She sipped a glass of wine. 'We didn't have time to retrieve your real passport.'

I scratched my head.

'You have concerns?'

'What if someone notices it's a forgery?'

Marie-Louise scoffed, as Marcus rejoined us from the back of the plane.

His moustache twitched. 'Do you doubt our abilities, Julius? It was plain sailing through the airport, although I think you should probably try not to adopt a stammer. It draws attention.'

The stammer had not been affected. I didn't know what was wrong with me. Although I suspect the lack of brace, skins and the safety net of Alpha power behind me may have had something to do with it. On each mission I had thought I was nervous, edgy, capable. But it was all a lie. I had been lulled into a false sense of security. Now, without the ability to step back, it all felt a bit too real.

'And compared to London, Kabul will be a walk in the park, yes, yes?'

'They probably won't even check,' said Marie-Louise darkly. There had been a great debate over her inclusion. Marie-Louise's argument had boiled down to: screw them. I was sympathetic to her viewpoint, but if we were to inspect this item and work out how the hell they had actually received it—no one believed the cave story for a second—then we were going to have to employ a lot of soft soaping. No matter how distasteful.

It was inconceivable that Afghanistan could have deteriorated further since western troops had

160

withdrawn, but it had. Naturally, there was international hand-wringing, but not much else. I had visited Kabul with Charlie on a cycling holiday after uni. We'd travelled across the Stans, and it had been incredible. The beauty of the landscape and the kindness of villagers to two daft English boys cycling past was wonderful. We ate well, sometimes like kings, as villagers would throw a feast for us. Other times it was one step above rancid and, on one occasion that resulted in two days of constant sprints to the bushes, actually rancid. Bowel movements aside, we had the time of our lives. My recollections of Afghanistan had been of a proud people teetering on the edge. McDonalds and goat carts rubbing along, side by side.

After the fall of the Taliban, it had splintered into several fighting factions but the dominant force presently termed themselves the Ilkhanate. Given the Ilkhanate was once a historic empire that covered vast areas of land beyond just Afghanistan, the UN was watching carefully.

The plane began to descend. Looking down on the tarmac, a fleet of open top Jeeps swarmed towards us. Standing in the back of each were men holding machine guns, goggles on their helmets, wearing full riot gear. One hand gripped the roll bars, steadying them as they rested their other hand on their guns in readiness.

'Marcus, I think we're in trouble.'

Marcus peered out the window and shook his head. 'They're ours. Or rather, the current ruling party has sent them to safeguard our arrival.'

'Are we in danger?' I wished I could deploy skins, but I would have to make do with the Beta equivalent. I was wearing Kevlar under my handmade suit. An outfit hastily arranged for me back in London, but it wasn't the same.

Marie-Louise laughed bitterly. 'Well, Julius, we're in the world's most lawless country. The UN no longer recognises it. The borders are closed to all but a handful of visitors, and public executions are a daily event. But no, this should be a walk in the park.'

Her sarcasm was not subtle.

I smiled across at her and tried to boost her spirits. 'We preserve.'

'Well gosh, thank you for that, Julius. I feel so much better.' Getting up from her chair, she walked to the back of the plane readying the equipment.

'Ignore her. She hates this place, we all do.' Marcus stood up as well. 'Now, let's get going and see exactly what they have found. I sincerely hope it's a fake. Yes, yes?'

'Does that happen much?'

'All the time. Sometimes it feels like, "Oh it's Tuesday, time to declare this Lowry is a fake." And we've now flatly refused to authenticate the Mona Lisa anymore.' He raised an eyebrow.

162

'Ah yes, well, that was a bit of an accident.'

Honestly, we hadn't meant to set the Mona Lisa on fire. Putting my foot through the frame in an attempt to put the flames out was an unhappy by-product. Thankfully, it turned out to be a fake.

'That was quite a lot of an accident, dear boy. When we were called out to assess the damage, we were astonished they had been so clumsy.'

Retelling that episode to the exiles had been somewhat embarrassing. They were less concerned about the damage to a fake than the fact that the mission had got out of hand. But then, they had never had to deal with Loki or Anansi.

'So, what happens now?'

'Now we head to wherever the crown is being stored and run our tests. Some tests will take hours, but with a fair wind behind us, we should be out of here within twenty-four hours.'

The wheels touched down, and the plane slowed to a halt. Grabbing my bag, I joined the others walking down the steps. Heading into the bright sunshine, the smell of baked earth, wood smoke, and aromatic oils from the cedar trees engulfed us. I was transported back to Alexandria as the scent of scorched air rose up to greet us.

I turned towards the two curators, and was unsurprised to see a momentary relaxation in their expressions as they welcomed the familiar climate. Then their expressions snapped back to alert.

It was colder than normal, the late autumn rapidly cooling down. All around us the mountains loomed, encircling the city and its airport, a claustrophobic ring of white menace, as winter was preparing to encroach.

From the base of the steps, we walked a few yards across the tarmac, past the Jeeps and into waiting black Humvees. Marie-Louise sat silently, gloved hands in her lap, head bowed. Her long yellow woollen coat was buttoned up, but she had refused a hat or scarf. Her long white hair shone in defiance. I stared out of the bulletproof glass and waited for Marcus to re-join us.

As the door opened, I noticed that, like myself, Marie-Louise's hand had moved to the location of her gun. Her skirt was a wraparound, and her gun was strapped to her thigh. She had told me earlier where it was placed in case I needed to access it in a hurry. The idea of rummaging around the thighs of a lady the age of my grandmother had filled me with horror. I could imagine Granny cuffing me around my head for the lack of respect. As it was, Marie-Louise cuffed me around the head for being an idiot.

'Do you want to die for the sake of my modesty?'

She had a point, and I knew the location of all her weapons. I just hoped to God it didn't come to that.

As the door swung open, Marcus stepped inside. 'Everything's settled.' He handed us two walkie talkies and then spoke into his. 'Let's go.'

I had got used to him saying yes, yes at the end of instructions and questions. The lack of verbal tic was just another indicator of the level of tension running through our small team.

'Huh.' I shrugged as we drove away.

Marcus cocked his head.

'We didn't even go through the airport. No customs, no passports. Is it always like this when you travel?'

'Sometimes, depending on the level of secrecy surrounding our mission. But this?' He gestured towards the window. 'This is just Afghanistan.'

Kabul was a mess. There was a Ferris wheel operating, its brightly coloured seats swinging in the breeze as each pod was occupied with men and boys laughing in delight, their rifles strapped to their backs. Further on, a goatherd scurried in front of a shattered marble and glass storefront, its luxury contents long gone. As he ran to herd his flock away from our convoy, the goats ambled into the store in search of mischief. Gesticulating wildly, he spat on the broken sidewalk and rounded up his flock again.

Further on, we drove through a market. The stalls were set on the side of a dual carriageway, the shops behind them burnt out. Trade was brisk as men filled shopping trolleys and carts. A Jeep carrying five men in the back drove alongside us. Marcus cracked open the window a fraction, and the Jeep veered away. They were happy enough to harry a convoy of armoured cars, but they weren't idiots. They didn't know who or what we were, but they rightly assumed we outgunned them. From a distance, they waved their guns at us and fired a few shots into the sky. None of the pedestrians flinched.

Everywhere I looked, I could see the ravages of a war-torn city that never rebuilt itself. Instead, it had reverted to a way of living more suited to the mountain villages. And of course, not a single person was female. After the mandatory burka, the only option to further hide the female form was to ban them entirely from public life. Between eight and nine in the morning they were apparently allowed out, under escort, and under those choking gowns, and that was it. They also needed to explain their reason for being out. Shopping and socialising, or just for the sheer hell of it, were not permitted. I sighed and felt the full weight of my futility settle on my shoulders.

'This is truly a dark time. But, as we have seen through the centuries, it will pass.' Marie-Louise spoke sadly. As a curator, they were used to travelling through some of Beta's most horrific acts or barbarism, but then they got to go home. The next time, they would be strolling through the Enlightenment. Now they had to live with the daily misery of human suffering. I wanted to say sorry, but didn't want to piss her off any further.

She leant over and patted my knee, repeating herself. 'It will pass. In the meantime, we do what we can to help. And I personally like to make those that deserve it, suffer.'

She smiled sweetly at me and I flinched.

'But not today, Marie-Louise?' said Marcus gently. 'If this crown isn't a fake, we have other concerns, and won't require your level of special circumstances. Today we just need your skills in metallurgy.'

Marie-Louise gave a dainty shrug and folded her hands on her lap.

'Okay, we're nearly here. We can relax when we're through the gates,' said Marcus.

Marie-Louise scoffed.

'We can relax a bit,' he amended.

The scenery was beginning to change. Whilst we were still in the city, there were fewer buildings. This was once the province of embassies, now long gone as we approached a fortress. The walls were a good ten metres high. I could see soldiers walking along the top, to and from the gun turrets positioned at each corners.

'Are those rocket launchers?' said Marcus to Marie-Louise.

'Surface to air missiles.'

I felt my stomach twitch, then my training kicked in. I slowed my breath and ran through a series of micro stretches. This was just another mission. I'd been to worse places. Sure, I had no escape route and was woefully under-equipped, but I was still a curator and I trusted my body and my instincts. Until we were back on the plane, I would be on full alert.

'I thought this country was poor?'

'Have you visited North Korea? There's always an outside superpower happy to prop up a rogue state.'

As we approached the gates, I could see the wall was made of huge, whitewashed, stone blocks. It gleamed, but was incredibly intimidating. The car came to a stop.

'Why have we stopped?'

'Checking for bombs strapped to the car,' said Marcus.

He picked at his fingernails whilst Marie-Louise yawned. As we waited to see if we were sitting on top of a bomb, I decided to ask questions. Those gun turrets were alarming.

'Who is bankrolling Afghanistan?'

Marcus sighed deeply.

'We thought it was Russia,' mumbled Marie-Louise, as if our very proximity to the compound might allow us to be overheard. 'But with those stingers, I'm not so sure. Things might be on the change.'

The idea of Afghanistan being about to embark on a regime change did not fill me with confidence. Especially since I was driving into the main government seat of power.

'What do you think, Marie-Louise? Should we decline their invitation?' Marcus sounded serious.

Marie-Louise tilted her head, considering his suggestion. 'Well, we're here now. I wouldn't wish to appear discourteous?'

'Quite right. Very well, party of three for the Ilkhanate. Yes, yes?'

His eyes twinkled, and I felt the tension of the car relax slightly. Although I noticed that Marcus and Marie-Louise were running through the same pre-fight-or-flight exercises that I was doing.

'Now, Julius. You are here to learn the trade. See how we act as authenticators. You are also the muscle.'

Now it was my turn to snort. I was in the presence of two of the mouseion's finest curators. What use was I?

'I'm not joking, Julius. I am in my eighties, and Marie-Louise is a lady. Are you really going to stand by and watch as she has to fight off her attackers?'

Marie-Louise stared at me haughtily. I was convinced that despite her age and size, she still had the ability to make grown men weep, but then I pictured someone punching her in the face and flinched. They may have been exceptional, and mentally they were

169

clearly in their prime, but physically? In terms of strength or speed, I was better than either of them. The idea of being responsible for their safety made me feel sick and I took in a deep breath.

'I will protect you with every ounce of my ability.'

I knew I sounded stuffy, but I wanted to impart how seriously I understood my instructions. Christ, I wished Clio was here.

'That's the spirit,' said Marcus.

'Trust me,' said Marie-Louise. 'We are here to assess the crown, then we go home. In. Out. Done.'

Having determined that the car was free of explosive devices, we drove forwards and the heavy gates closed behind us.

I returned Marie-Louise's smile.

What could go wrong?

Chapter Eighteen - October: Beta: Julius

Once inside the walls, we were in a large compound. There were buildings on all sides, and the central plaza was large enough for two helicopters and three tanks to sit on one side of the square. On the other side was a row of Lamborghinis and Bugattis. Just the basic kit for a third world dictator.

'I thought the Ilkhanate acted as a council,' I said, examining the compound. 'This has the feel of an individual fiefdom.'

'It does, doesn't it?' said Marcus. 'Eyes and ears peeled. We'll be passing on details to various governments when we get home.'

The car door was opened from the outside and a man dressed in western clothing smiled in at us. 'Greetings, welcome to Kabul.'

His accent was crystal clear, and he spoke the Queen's English like one raised on Eton's rugby pitches. I wondered where he went to school. He stepped back to give us room to leave the car. Marcus, then Marie-Louise, and then me. I kept my eyes on his face as he took in Marie-Louise's yellow coat and unbound hair. If he found her appearance abhorrent, nothing in his demeanour gave him away.

We stood to one side as a team of men ran forwards and unloaded our luggage and lab equipment onto trolleys. One man dropped a case, and Marie-Louise turned and shouted at them.

'If that is broken, I'll know who to blame.'

A man stepped towards her, spat on the floor, then called back to his companions. The men spoke quickly in Arabic, their coarse laughter an indication of their words.

'And I'll thank you not to talk about me in such a manner.'

Our host shouted at the men, who quickly returned to the building, our luggage and equipment with them.

He then turned to Marie-Louise, pressing his hands together and issuing a short bow. 'Did you understand what they said, or did you guess?'

'I understood.'

She had slipped into Arabic and was employing a local dialect. It was good to know that my language acquisitions were still intact as I followed her perfectly.

'In which case, my apologies are even greater. This was not how I would have had you welcomed. Women are the greatest gift on this Earth.'

'We are not a gift.'

Our host smiled and was about to reply when Marcus stepped in.

'Thank you for meeting us. I'm Marcus Carruthers.'
I noticed he had replied in English, which struck me as

a good idea. If we spoke in English, some of them might forget that we could understand them.

'Ah yes, I am delighted to meet you, Mr Carruthers. I have read about your skills. We are honoured that you have come to verify our treasure. May I ask, is your Arabic as good as Madame Black's?'

So he knew who we all were.

'Madame Black is the linguist amongst us. My command of Arabic is decent. Whereas Professor Strathclyde's is mostly archaic.'

He turned and smiled at me, ignoring Marie-Louise.

'Yes, Professor Julius Strathclyde. I have enjoyed reading your papers. Your insights into the clash between folklore and nascent religions in the Middle East are most interesting. Cambridge must be devastated that you have chosen to work in the private sector. At Oxford, we nurture our talents, not let them slip away.'

Good grief, was he really trying to play university one-upmanship in the middle of an Afghanistan compound?

'And yet, you appear to have left as well,' I said with a smile. 'Although you have the advantage over me?'

'I know. I went to Oxford.' He laughed as though we weren't surrounded by tanks and ground-to-air missiles.

'No, I meant I don't know your name.'

'My manners. You are right. And so very Cambridge to insist on good form before academic endeavours.'

He made me sound like a dilettante.

'I am Prince Suliman. Welcome. Come inside and we will eat and drink. Then I will show you to your accommodation. And then, when you are happy—' he looked at me, '—you can start working?'

'An excellent plan,' said Marcus. 'Lead on.'

Walking towards the buildings, Suliman addressed Marie-Louise.

'It's irregular, but we have accommodated you next to Mr Carruthers and Professor Strathclyde. I suspected you would refuse to sleep in the women's quarters?'

'You are a man of remarkable insight,' Marie-Louise said crisply, then returned to silence. She placed her hand on my arm, leaning heavily against me, as we walked towards the shelter and out of the cold wind.

So the roles were set. Marcus was the bluff old school bon-viveur, Marie-Louise, clever but frail old lady, and me, an affable academic with no real-world experience. And the prince was the genial host.

Fair enough. I hoped for the next twenty-four hours there would be no need for any of us to reveal our true natures.

Chapter Nineteen - October: Beta: Julius

'That is none of your bloody business!'

Prince Suliman snarled at Marie-Louise, all pretence of civility gone. We had been in this room all of five minutes and the gloves were off. The previous evening had been spent wading through the minutiae of hospitality, making nice with the prince and breaking bread with him, reminiscing about college and British buses. From there, we had been shown our rooms. We met no one as we walked along the airy corridors and I wondered if that was deliberate, so no one would be forced to endure seeing Marie-Louise in men's quarters.

This morning we were escorted to breakfast and then on to our task. Our equipment had been brought into a room that had two long bench tables in it, good lighting, and an array of plug sockets running down the centre of the tables. On either side of the room were two large sinks. I would guess this acted as a science lab for students, although I couldn't see any evidence of gas supplies.

As kids, we used to slip a school bag onto the nozzle of gas and then fill the bag up. It was always an empty threat, but one time a boy did actually set fire to the bag. He not only lost his eyebrows, his friend's schoolwork, but also his place at school. He wasn't expelled, but his parents were informed that maybe this school wasn't the best fit for him. And that was that. Money talked a lot, but you needed a lot of money to cover up incipient fire starters.

Last I heard, he was working for Formula 1, working on proprietary fire-retardant clothing. Which goes to prove there's a place for everyone. My place now seemed to be calming down an incandescent French woman before she exploded.

'The problem is, old boy,' I said, stepping in, 'we need to know more about its long-term environment.'

Suliman turned to me, perhaps eager to engage with a man.

'Connard,' muttered Marie-Louise under her breath. I winced and hoped the prince didn't speak French. Given his expression, he clearly did. Mind you, from her tone of voice, you probably didn't need to know the language to know you had just been deeply insulted.

I hurried on. 'You see, depending on where it's been, will have had an impact on the physical item. We are about to run tests on it, and our very first duty is to do no harm. Therefore, it is essential that we know some basic details. Were the caves granite or limestone? Could they have ever been waterlogged? The calciferous deposits alone could render our calculations out by a magnitude of scale so as to make the findings nonsensical.'

I came to a halt. I had no idea what I was talking about and I decided to quit whilst I was ahead. I hoped I was ahead.

'Professor Strathclyde is completely correct,' said Marcus. 'We will need some basic information. We don't require the actual location where this crown was found, but we will need to know the surrounding strata.'

Suliman stared at both of us and then nodded. 'This makes sense. However, I do not have the authority to release that information. Please wait here and I will return presently.' He picked up the crown.

Marcus winced. 'Not like that. It's too fragile for you to carry it in your hand. What if you bumped into someone and dropped it? Plus, the acids in your hand could be eroding the surface. You should have cotton gloves on.'

'I suppose you would rather I just left it on the bench in front of you?'

The three of us nodded quickly, but he laughed and walked off, the crown held down by his side. Marcus followed him to the door and peered out into the corridor before closing the door.

'Two armed guards on either side of the door. Now we wait. And Marie-Louise, I know this is abysmal, but please?'

'If you knew how it felt—'

'I arrived as a Black man in Britain in 1965. I know exactly how you feel.'

Marie-Louise took in a deep breath and then let out a noisy sigh. 'You are right, I am wrong. I was just overwhelmed by the occasion.'

'I know. This is a tragedy. I feel your pain.'

I watched the two of them console each other. When the crown had been brought into the room, Marie-Louise had gone pale. It had been in the glass box that now sat unoccupied on a side table. The crown itself was a thing of beauty, and far smaller than I expected. It was more a diadem. Six inches wide and, from its solid band of gold base up to the tendrils of leaves at the top, it must have been eight inches tall. For this to have stayed on a head, the person either didn't move a muscle or it was sewn into the hair. It was easy to think, given its size and delicacy, that it was for a woman or child, but that was a very twenty-first century way of looking at things.

Similar crowns had been found in the Silla region, in Korea, as well as the Tillya Tepe caves and Persian treasuries. These had been worn by male rulers, according to recovered wall paintings and manuscripts. The Chinese had a treasury of such documents that they occasionally shared with the outside world and, with my enhanced Alpha knowledge, I knew that these crowns were generally for men.

As the crown was removed from the glass box and placed in front of us, we had stared in wonder. Tiny articulated leaves and acorns swung back and forth, the burnished gold glinting in the light. Acorns were fashioned from lapis lazuli and pearls, and the berries from tiny rubies. As I said, it was breath taking.

Now it was gone again, and I wondered at the curators' dismay.

'Is it a fake then?'

Marie-Louise shook her head sadly. 'No, that is the genuine article.'

'But how—'

'Call it a sixth sense, Julius. When you've been doing this as long as we have, you just know. Of course, we'll run all the tests, but this item hasn't aged correctly and has a whiff of Alpha about it. Besides which—'

Marie-Louise sniffed and wiped a tear away.

Marcus walked over to her and gave her a hug. 'Chin up, old girl.'

'Less of the old,' she laughed weakly.

I wondered if Neith and I had a future like this. I had no idea what these two had been through these past few decades, but I'm glad they had each other. I felt awkward in the face of her tears and wasn't sure what the problem was. She glanced across at me and gave one of her little gallic shrugs.

'The last time I saw that crown, it was on this Earth and had just rolled under the throne.'

I stared at her in horror. This was exactly the scenario that curators back home had been discussing; what if the pieces that they had rescued were returned? Marie-Louise had been the curator dispatched to save the crown from imminent destruction. She had brought it back to Alpha and yet, here it was, back on Beta.

'Its wearer had just been spared the weight of his existence. His head rolled one way, his crown the other. Obviously, I was standing too close and got covered in arterial blood, which was as repulsive as it sounds, but nothing compared to the amount of crap I had to wade through to escape the inferno of the throne room. I literally had to crawl out through the sewers and then, and only then, could I hit the return button on my brace.'

'So, this is one of yours?'

'Yes. I risked my life to rescue it and now my Earth, my mouseion, has chosen to return it to the—' She bit off her words. Her promise to Marcus to hold her temper was catching at her. 'To our gracious hosts, the Ilkhanate. Murderers, torturers and rapists. Blessed be.'

A silence fell over us and I felt no need to break it. I had no idea why an artefact had ended up here. Before I left, the talks had been extremely clear about which countries would have items returned. It was a tiny list, and Afghanistan wasn't on it. Neither were any of its neighbours.

The door swung open and an older gentleman walked in. He was wearing long green robes with embroidered bindings similar to those of a Mongol khan. His hair was covered by a small headdress with a feather sticking out from behind a stone in the centre of the turban. This went beyond traditional Afghanistan dress. Power dynamics were changing.

'Welcome to my home. I am Omar.'

No title, no surname. It wasn't even a certainty that this was his real name, but whoever he was, he was in charge. He turned to Marie-Louise, speaking in perfect French.

'Madame Black, I apologise most humbly for the way you were spoken to. You would do me the greatest of honours if you could accept that we still have a lot to change, and you don't dismiss us as ignorant dung sweepers.'

Marie-Louise inclined her head slightly, but didn't smile. Having apparently decided that was as good as he was going to get, he turned to Marcus.

'Mr Carruthers, thank you for travelling all this way to authenticate our crown.' He clicked his fingers, and a man walked in carrying the crown on a silver tray. The man turned to Omar waiting for directions, who glared at him. 'Put it on the table.'

The tray was placed reverentially, and then, with another quick look at Omar, the man slid out of the room again.

Prince Suliman sidled in behind and stood close by Omar. He was sweating and kept trying to catch my eye.

I ignored him. If he was in trouble, he was on his own.

'It is my pleasure,' said Marcus. 'Tell me. Are you from further afield than the crown? Your dress isn't local.'

'Ah, but in fact, it is. I was born in the Ilkhanate region as my father was and his before him. Once our family ruled in Il-Khan. That is in the past, of course, but we are proud of our heritage.' He laughed politely and carried on. 'The crown was discovered after a slight earthquake, revealing a small treasury of artefacts, close to the Bactrian discovery.'

'There are others?'

I understood Marcus' concern. If there were more, we needed to know what the hell was going on.

'All in good time. Let's authenticate the crown first, and then we will know if we are dealing with a clever forgery or something else.'

'If we could see the other items, it would help establish if the items were sympathetic to each other?'

Omar shook his head, but smiled as he did so. 'Just this one for now.'

He was bluffing. I was certain. This was all he had, but it sounded like he was expecting more. What the hell was Alpha up to?

As Marcus asked a few more questions regarding location, Marie-Louise started setting up the equipment and showing me what order we would be working in.

'I didn't see Mr Strathclyde on the staff page of your website?' said Omar.

'We don't have a staff page on our website,' countered Marcus in the same smooth tones.

'But he is employed by you? I would hate to think your government was sneaking in a peeping Tom?'

I stood there feeling like an idiot as the two men discussed me. I was about to explain that I was simply a Cambridge professor when Marcus cut me off.

'Professor Strathclyde is one of our partners.'

'Ah.' Omar studied me then turned back to Marcus. 'That's twenty partners, isn't it?'

'I lose count myself. Now, shall we begin?' Marcus turned towards the crown, cutting off any chance for Omar to continue fishing about the Alexandria Company. 'I am keen to establish the veracity of this item and, if it is genuine, get it into an environmentally controlled atmosphere.'

'I shall leave you to it. There will be two guards.' He shook his head and laughed. 'My apologies. Two *assistants* outside the door. Should you need anything, they are at your service.'

And with that, he and Suliman left. The prince hadn't said a word the entire time, and I wondered if it was all an act to lure us into a sense that Omar was our benign host and that Suliman was a fool, or whether Suliman was really going to get chewed out later.

Marie-Louise continued to plug in devices and then gestured at me to open another case.

'We can talk freely. I've switched on the jamming device. They'll be videotaping us as well. There are cameras above the door and the window. So long as you keep your head down or away from the lens, they won't be able to lip read.'

'Well done, Marie-Louise,' said Marcus. 'Julius, pass me that pack of swabs. The pack with the blue stripe. Not the red. Don't want to melt the gold, do we?'

I laughed weakly and handed over the correct one. As he gave me instructions, we all settled down on our stools and got to work. I didn't get to touch the crown itself. My job was to place swabs in phials and then record the results.

'So, what now?' asked Marie-Louise.

'I can't think why, but Omar is clearly expecting more treasures or indeed already has them. His dress is also alarming.'

'In what way?' It was unusual for this area, but I couldn't see the issue.

'Honestly, you Betas know nothing of your own history,' said Marie-Louise.

'He was dressed as a leader from the great Mongol empire. The talk of his forefathers, the crown itself. If I had to place bets, I would lay money on the fact that he is preparing to expand the Afghanistan region into its traditional homelands and then beyond. Far beyond.'

I tried a quick recap on Afghanistan's history and had to concede the point that my history is woeful.

'And those are?'

'Well, Ilkhanate, the land he just claimed as his ancestral home, once stretched from Constantinople to Islamabad.'

'But isn't that currently Pakistan?'

'Indeed it is. I think Omar wants to take back Pakistan.'

'But doesn't Pakistan have nuclear weapons? What have the Ilkhanate got?'

She took a deep breath and then sighed.

'It would appear that the Ilkhanate have Alpha Earth.'

Chapter Twenty - October: Beta: Julius

After that rather dire pronouncement, we worked in silence. Gradually, the tests confirmed what they already knew. This was the genuine article.

'What are you going to do about the Carbon-14 test?' I asked. As the crown contained pearls and ivory, it could therefore be dated.

'What's your concern?' asked Marcus.

'What about the bomb curve?'

The nuclear explosions of the mid-twentieth century had doubled the amount of C14 in the atmosphere.

'Only applies to organisms alive at the time. These pearls and ivory aren't affected.' He paused as he stopped writing his notes. 'Besides which, if it was ever an issue we'd just fake it.'

'You can't just fake a Carbon-14 test,' I protested.

Marie-Louise looked up from her telescope. 'Why not? Is your denial based on ethical outrage or scientific disbelief?'

I was about to reply and realised that they almost certainly had the technical know-how to be able to alter or obscure their findings. Which left me with the ethical outrage. I was about to get into a debate that even I wasn't sure I agreed with, when the floor shuddered and I heard a distant whump.

Marcus and Marie-Louise stared at each other.

'If those mother—'

There was a second whump.

'Julius,' said Marcus. 'Protect the crown.'

Marie-Louise pulled out her phone as Marcus dashed around the equipment, ejecting microchips from the sides of the instruments and throwing test tubes into the sink. Liquids spilled across the broken glass.

Whoever Marie-Louise had dialled had answered on the first ring. 'We need evacuation now. The compound is under attack. — No idea. — Two bombs. Given the vibration, I would say air attack—'

She paused as we heard rapid fire and an explosion.

'They've just deployed their stingers and I think it's blown up. — No, I can't see anything. I'm going on vibrations. — Okay.'

Whilst she was talking, I had unbuttoned the cuff on my left shirtsleeve. Gingerly picking up the crown, I slid my hand through it and moved it up my arm until the band squeezed past my bicep. It was surprisingly heavy. Those bands of gold were clearly solid and must have been onerous for whoever wore it. The pretty, fluttering leaves made it appear light and ephemeral, but this was a serious statement of power.

Marie-Louise nodded. It was irregular, but if we were about to run, this felt the least worst option. At least both my hands would be free. I'd have given anything for my skins right now, but my Asher and Burberry shirt sleeve would have to do. I slid the sleeve carefully back over it.

'Okay, time to get out of here,' said Marcus. He had pulled out one of the equipment cases and was now ripping out its base, revealing a hidden layer beneath. I was hoping for a serious collection of guns. Instead, he pulled out a dress. Marie-Louise scowled, and I turned back to Marcus.

'What's going on?'

'No idea, but this place is under attack. I suspect a regime change is on the way. We are travelling as three British subjects. I don't wish us to become regretful casualties or hostages.'

I shook my head. Neither option was one I had any intention of entertaining. 'No, I don't think so.'

'Agreed,' said Marcus, handing a garment to Marie-Louise. She sneered, but slipped into it without comment. He then threw a desert robe over himself.

Marie-Louise's robe covered her entirely, as it was designed to. Whilst I stood there in a handmade suit straight out of Jermyn Street.

'No disguise for me?' I hadn't been expecting a pair of comedy glasses and a fake moustache, but I felt somewhat exposed as I heard distant gunfire rattling across the compound.

'It's not perfect, but hopefully you'll get taken for someone important.'

'On whose side?' I asked.

'Whilst they're trying to work that out, hit them,' replied Marie-Louise.

Sometimes being a curator was less about diplomacy and more about getting the hell out of a place.

'Marie-Louise, what's the exit strategy?' said Marcus as he tucked a knife into the sleeve of his gown.

'We have air support and ground support, depending on how they can get to us. All of our trackers are activated, so if we get separated, they can follow us individually. However, with dodgy stingers on the battlements, they aren't going to fly in for us. Which means we have to get out of here.'

I rubbed the back of my ear where my tracker had been placed and then covered by a layer of fake skin on the plane.

'Leave it alone, Julius, it won't fall off,' said Marie-Louise with a smile. Or at least I think she was smiling. Who could tell under that long black face panel? 'Now, I hear gunfire. That's our cue to leave.'

I was cursing myself as a fool. I had paid no attention to the situation I was travelling to. Admittedly, I'd had little notice, but I should have asked more questions on the plane. I had been so focused on the history of the crown that I had failed to pay attention to exit strategies. I mean, everyone knew how stable Afghanistan was, right?

'How are we getting out?' I hated asking. I felt like an amateur.

'The tunnels.'

'There are tunnels?'

'In a place like this? Almost certainly.'

'But you don't know where they are?'

'No, but I suggest we don't climb up any stairs trying to find them.' Marcus grinned at me. 'Ready?'

I grinned back. 'Ready.' The adrenaline was pumping through my body, pre-fight jitters making me buzz.

Leading the way, Marcus opened the door and peered out. Our guards had fled and the corridor was empty.

I pulled out my gun. Unlike my normal Alpha weapon, this one would kill. There was no temporary incapacitation option. Just stop dead.

'They'll kill you without thinking about it,' said Marie-Louise, sensing my concern. 'I mean, they might shoot me first, for the fun of it, which will give you time to stop dithering and return fire. But I'd be grateful if that didn't happen.'

I winced at her tone, but felt she had a point. A volley of gunfire and shouting came from the left, so we turned right and ran down the corridor, all of us carrying guns, although again, Marie-Louise's was concealed. I'd love to see the look on anyone's face who tried to corner her.

At the next junction, I smelled cordite and burning oil. Turning down a short corridor, we came out into the open-air compound we had crossed yesterday. It was a scene of devastation. The helicopter was now a lump of torn metal, black oily flames blooming out of the fuel tank, and a blade hung broken over a shattered cockpit. To the left, a tank lay on its side, one of the caterpillar tracks torn from its roller.

'There! 'Marcus pointed to a corridor on the other side of the plaza where people were all running in the same direction. They were clearly heading towards an exit. We came to a gap in the corridor and sprinted across the plaza. As I ran, I saw with dismay that he and Marie-Louise were far slower than me, and having to run between the burning pieces of debris to try to get cover. Despite appearances, they were two octogenarians, and running across an open square was causing them issues.

Little pinging sounds spat up marble to my right, and I span round. From the top of the wall, a shooter was aiming at us. I paused and took aim, covering Marcus and Marie-Louise. My aim was spot-on, and the gunman fell backwards over the parapet. One less bad guy. Another shooter was taking aim at us from above.

Marcus didn't even stop, just ran whilst he sprayed the gunman with bullets.

'My aim isn't what it was.' He shouted over at me. 'Wish I still had your skills.'

'I can only pray I will be as fast as you at your age.'

Really, they were impressive for a pair in their eighties.

'If you two could stop the chit-chat.' Marie-Louise had now overtaken Marcus and was making a beeline for the passageway where we had seen the crowd running.

Ahead of us we could hear women's voices raised in protest and the occasional gunfire. We ran forward, passing into the corridor where a small crowd of women in black robes and two men with guns were standing at the top of a staircase. There was a crumpled form in front of them, blood seeping out of her robes. Two women were crouched down beside her, wailing loudly.

I pushed through to the front and Marcus launched into rapid street Arabic.

'Move aside, we all need to get out of here. They are about to breach the gates.'

'You two can go down. She waits here.' He pointed his gun at Marie-Louise.

'Absolutely not!'

'Not a chance,' I said.

Marie-Louise was silent, but I suspected if it was quieter, I would hear her teeth grinding.

'The women stay here. It will slow the attackers down.'

I stared at him in dawning horror. 'You plan to leave the women as fodder?'

The second gunman shrugged and spat on the floor.

'It is their duty—'

He gurgled to a halt as both men fell to the floor. The noise of the gunfire ringing in my ear. I span around to the women who had all moved quickly away from one smaller burka clad form. Gun smoke gently trailing out of two holes in her outfit.

'What?' shrugged Marie-Louise. She then turned to the women and told them to get a wriggle on. As the distant gunfire came closer, they didn't need urging twice.

The walls shook and a deafening roar blew along the passageway, forcing a cloud of dust ahead of us.

'The front gates have gone,' coughed Marcus. 'Time to leave.'

Shouting at the women to run faster, Marcus and Marie-Louise urged them on down the stairs. I picked up the machine guns and slung them over my chest, then covered the rear of our party as we ran along a lower corridor. At the end of the corridor, the party clustered around a hole in the floor. The women moved as quickly as they could, feeding themselves down into the chute and then down a rung of steps. I paced backwards and forwards, my gun trained on the far end of the passageway. So far, our luck was holding. Whatever this fight was about, the incoming force was unconcerned about escapees.

Finally, it was my turn and as I hung from the rungs, I pulled the trapdoor closed over my head and we plunged into darkness.

The women remained silent, but I saw mobile phones, their small screens of light illuminating the way. We were a little group of black clouds moving quickly and quietly through the tunnels, illuminated by pinpricks of light.

After five minutes of running, the group came to a halt. The women had reached a branch in the tunnels and whispered about which way to go.

'What's the problem?' I asked. I was keeping an eye behind me, but so far there was no sign of pursuit.

'The women think the left-hand branch heads of out the city out onto the plains,' wheezed Marcus. 'The right-hand branch comes up in the city somewhere.'

'And?' I couldn't see what the issue was.

'If they head out of the city, they will be in the tunnels longer and they will also stand out like a sore thumb. A group of women beyond the city confines,' said Marie-Louise, nearly as out of breath as Marcus. 'It's not permitted. They could be shot on sight.'

'The right-hand path it is, then,' I said.

'It's not that simple. They are concerned more guards will be watching the other end and will shoot them as they emerge.'

This bloody country.

'Okay,' I said. 'We go right, but Marcus and I will lead the way. If there are guards, we'll overpower them and signal when it's safe for you to come up.'

'Not going to happen, Julius.' Marcus held my forearm, gently wrapping his fingers around the hidden crown. 'You forget why we're here. We preserve.'

'My dear Marcus,' hissed Marie-Louise. 'There is no way I am leaving these women.'

'Sod the crown,' I said. 'I'm not leaving Marie-Louise to cope with these bloody butchers on her own.'

'I won't be on my own. I have twenty very angry women with me.'

'And you'll have me,' said Marcus.

I breathed a sigh of relief. 'Right, that's settled. We protect the women and get them back to their homes and a place of safety.' I thought about it. 'Relative safety.'

'We will,' said Marcus, 'but not you. You need to get out of the city with the crown intact.'

Far behind us, the metal trapdoor clanged open.

'Discussion over,' ordered Marcus. 'Run. You are fitter, faster and stronger than us. Get out into the desert and hide until the evac crew finds you. We'll get

195

the women into the city and then rendezvous with you if we can.'

The women were already moving, quicker this time, but still in silence. Marie-Louise stepped forward and kissed me on the cheeks, the fabric brushing against my skin, and then joined them. Marcus shook my hand, then hissed at me to run.

Chapter Twenty-One - October:
Beta: Julius

I ran silently, my torch picking up the uneven floor, a small pool of light in the darkness. Behind me, I heard the patter of gunfire but no screams. I prayed that whoever had stormed the compound would decide the tunnels were empty. I also prayed that Marcus and Marie-Louise met no resistance at their exit. And finally, I prayed I would soon reach mine. As was the nature of prayers, I had no idea if anyone was listening. I had been running for half an hour. I was in leather soled Oxfords, dressed in an Armani suit, had a priceless gold crown on my forearm and two Kalashnikovs strapped to my chest. I wondered who was taking my divinity lectures back in Cambridge.

A few times, the tunnels split. Each time I checked the floor and took the path with the fewest footprints. I was having to weigh the risks of running along a dead end and having to backtrack and bump into any potential pursuers, or pop up from a tunnel to a welcoming party. I felt either option challenged my life expectancy. As curators, we were trained in combat, but that always suggested a failed mission. The primary rule being not to engage in the first place. And honestly, I was fine with that. I had no wish to fight the Ilkhanate or indeed, the people that they were running from.

Trust me, the enemy of my enemy is not my friend. He's just as likely to kill me on sight. If this was the start of a foreign invasion, would Marcus have been informed? As it was, we were running blind.

The tunnel ended abruptly at a metal ladder. I paused to regather my breath. I wasn't totally knackered, but I figured I had been running for miles and, if I was about to be ambushed, I'd like a fighting chance. I climbed the iron rungs. The top of the shaft was sealed off by a trapdoor with a round wheel. As I wrenched the wheel with one hand, it creaked and groaned. In the movies, these things were always well oiled.

Having announced my imminent arrival to whatever waiting committee might be above, I pushed the lid up and it fell open with a resounding clang, just in case no one had heard the squeaking.

Night had fallen quickly, and the cold desert air filled my lungs. I held onto the ladder and listened for any sounds, my head safely out of view. After a minute of silence, I held one of my rifles up above me and poked it up into the air. I was holding it by its middle, clearly unable to fire it. I hoped that anyone watching would realise I wasn't trying to shoot them.

'Show me your other hand!'

The voice was male and speaking in a local dialect. No doubt they had covered all exits as they fled the compound. This could get tricky.

'I can't,' I shouted. 'I'm holding onto the ladder.'

There was a pause whilst he thought about this.

'Who are you?'

I tried to play all the scenarios out. The problem was I had no idea who he was, so didn't know which way to go. Eventually, I fell back on the ancient failsafe.

'I'm a guest.'

There was silence for a second and then some muttered cursing. So far, I had only heard his voice, and I was praying that he was a lone sentry.

'Throw your gun towards me, then exit the tunnel slowly.'

This felt like progress. I threw the gun out, twisted the second gun so it was on my back rather than across my chest, and slid the safety off my handgun before I returned it to its holster. I was beginning to shiver as I cooled down from my run and the sweat chilled my skin.

I crawled out of the shaft and scrambled up onto my feet and peered into the dark. It was a clear night and a full moon. Over by a boulder was the comforting flicker of a campfire. It looked like he was alone.

He was barely older than my students. If he was out of his teens, I'd be amazed. He was also skinny, and I felt confident that I could overpower him if need be. However, at the moment, he was pointing his own Kalashnikov at me and I didn't feel like testing out his reflexes.

'What's your name?'

'Julius.' I kept my hands in the air. He might be a kid, but even a baby can kill with a gun in their hand. 'How about you?'

'Shut up. What happened to the women?'

Time to tread carefully.

'The ones the guards were stopping from entering the tunnels?'

He screamed up at the night sky, then rushed towards me before I could say anything else. He swung the butt of his gun at me and I raised my left arm to block. There was a sickening thud as his gun connected with my arm and the hilt bounced off. He stared at me in astonishment as I pivoted and kicked him in the knee. As he collapsed, I snatched the rifle from him and jumped back.

'Stay down,' I shouted. He was crying now and seemed to have given up any sense of fight. My arm was on fire and I was trying to determine if it was broken.

'Did you kill them?' he sobbed.

I was still pointing a gun at him and wondering why I was bothering. He was a teenage boy crying in the dark.

'Kill who?'

'The women. Did you kill them?'

'No.'

He wiped his face. His arms were wrapped around his knees as he rocked back and forth in misery.

'Did you leave them there?'

'No. We took them with us.'

He wiped his face again and his breath caught.

'What about the guards left to prevent their escape?'

'Them, we killed.' I shrugged. I was holding all the weapons. I hoped that was enough.

'You saved my mother, my sister?'

I barely had time to nod when he jumped up and hugged me, sending shafts of pain up my arm. The next second he was dancing and laughing, his feet kicking up dust and flecks of snow.

Laughing, he pulled me towards his fire and squatted down, offering me a cup of coffee from a tin cup.

'What happened? Where are they? Who are you?'

His questions tripped over themselves and I wondered how he had coped, knowing that his family had been used as a human shield. I soon explained what had happened, and he wept some more. My arm was throbbing and I was desperate to tend to it.

'You need to go. I will wait. If your pursuers leave the tunnel, I will shoot them.'

'What if they are here to overthrow the Ilkhanate and free the women?'

'I am Ilkhanate. They will kill me if I don't kill them.'

The logic was simplistic, if brutal.

'Head towards the moon. When you reach a tarmac road, turn left and walk along it.'

'Will that take me to the border?'

'No, the border is too dangerous. This road takes you inland. You say your friends can track you. Inland is safer. Take care through the mountain pass. Many patrols. And bears, and wolves, and sometimes leopards. After that, you should be safe.'

I stared at him and then, realising there was nothing to say, I returned his rifle to him and set off towards Mordor.

By the time the sun rose, I had only covered thirty miles. It felt like one of my more brutal training sessions back in Alexandria, although the threat of bears wasn't part of the usual obstacles.

My arm had swollen up as I jogged along, and I was freezing. I was tempted to ditch one of the rifles but, despite the weight, I felt the more gun power the better. Lots of traffic had passed in the night. Trucks driving towards the city full of loud, jubilant men, firing at the sky as they got their first glimpse of the Kabul skyline. Turning around, I could see a red glow rising. The city was on fire.

Traffic leaving the city was silent and travelling with their lights off, using the moonlight to show them the road.

Each time I heard an engine, I ran off the road and hid behind the rocks. I had no idea what was happening there, but the politics of this region were not my issue. I just needed to get away and pray to God that Marie-Louise and Marcus had also escaped.

As the sun rose higher, I knew I'd stand out like a sore thumb and decided to find shelter for the day and sleep. I was also desperate to see what damage had been done to the crown and my arm. I trudged through the scrub. There was more snow on the ground, but nothing recent and most of it had blown away. I found a collection of rocks and clambered behind them, trying desperately not to disturb any scorpions or snakes. Did they even emerge in the cold? Or were these brief moments of sunlight a time when they would emerge in their thousands, desperate to grab what little warmth was available to them? Thoughts of tiny venomous creepy-crawlies helped keep my mind off the wolves, bears, and leopards.

The sun slowly crept around the rocks and my skin began to warm slightly. It wasn't much. In fact, it was barely anything. If I didn't get rescued soon, I was in trouble.

I looked at the arm of my suit. The dark red stain had now dried. I was torn. I knew removing my clothing would start the bleeding again, but I was concerned by the constant pain. I had a horrible feeling that part of the crown was embedded in my skin. I felt confident my arm wasn't broken, but I was less convinced about the crown itself. I was certain it had snapped and was sticking into my flesh.

I gingerly peeled off my jacket and swore. My shirt sleeve was red and as I had pulled the jacket sleeve away, the bleeding had started again. Rolling up my shirt sleeve, I carefully removed parts of the crown. A section fell to the ground. I left it there as I examined the piece that had been jammed into my arm by the young fighter's gun. Wincing, I pulled it out. I could do with a few stitches, but that was the extent of the injury. That said, it hurt like stink, and I would give anything to be wearing my lovely Alpha skins, oozing with nanobots. Instead, I removed my tie and wrapped it around the cut, and then rolled my sleeve back down. Having decided I wasn't broken beyond all recognition, I turned my attention to the crown.

All those delicate leaves and acorns were now thick with blood. The gold was covered in gravel and dust where a section had fallen on the ground. I looked at the three pieces. So much for me taking care of the precious artefact. I had a small bottle of water and considered cleaning the crown, but my own parched throat reminded me I had no other food or water with me. The crown would survive. I might not.

I cradled the three broken sections of the crown into themselves, placed them on my other arm and then settled down into the shade of the rock and fell asleep.

Chapter Twenty-Two - October:
Beta: Julius

The helicopter harness dug into my groin, ensuring the last part of my body free from pain, joined in the agony.

I had woken from my fitful sleep as the temperature and light fell away and headed down onto the unlit tarmac road. As I had been limping along the silent road, I could hear the rotation of a distant helicopter and I saw a set of lights in the sky rushing towards me. A harness was being winched down from an open door and Marcus was hanging out, his face illuminated from the interior of the helicopter. Why they couldn't bloody land was beyond me, but I didn't care. A rescue was a rescue, and I thought I'd enjoy hanging in the air, the weight off my feet. Now all the weight was pinching my fundamentals, and I wondered when I could just wave the white flag.

Once onboard, Marcus whipped out a first aid kit whilst Marie-Louise took the crown from me and placed it in a Kevlar case.

'You couldn't have blocked his attack with your other arm?'

'My other arm was reaching for my gun.'

'And?'

'He's Beta raised, Marie-Louise. He isn't ambidextrous.'

She shook her head and muttered about Beta limitations as she carefully sealed the case and pressed a button on the side.

'Aren't you going to clean the blood?'

'No, I've just pressurised the case and filled it with argon. That will stabilise any decay until we get home. Then we can start to repair your ministrations.'

'Come on, Marie-Louise,' chided Marcus gently. 'It was the lad's first solo retrieval. He did fine.'

I felt like a boy scout who had been given a badge for effort rather than attainment. Effort didn't cut it. It was results that mattered.

The gel that Marcus had rubbed into my arm had deadened the pain without making me feel sleepy. I had a thousand questions, but I'd wait until Marie-Louise stopped tapping her foot.

'Sir?' A man approached with a phone and handed it to Marcus. He spoke into the receiver.

'Good morning, Brian.'

Marie-Louise's body stiffened and her tapping stopped. She tilted her head slightly in order to hear the other side of the conversation.

Marcus was now quietly nodding as the speaker on the other end appeared to have a lot to say.

'It is our intention to go home and change first, secure the crown and—' He paused, listening to the speaker, and then continued. 'Very well. We shall see you later.' He closed the call and pinched the bridge of his nose. 'We're joining Brian for supper.'

'I guess that was inevitable,' grumbled Marie-Louise. 'The man has no elegance. Imagine not even letting us shower first.'

I felt sorry for her. She'd killed God knew how many men in the past day, her mission was in tatters, and now she was going to have to go and play nice with some mysterious figure that could demand the attention of the Alexandria Company.

'No use you looking at me like that, child,' she said. 'You'll be coming as well.'

'Surely not?' I asked in alarm.

'Almost certainly. Brian will have a car waiting for us on the runway in London. No one will escape his attention. And you are a new face. That will be most tantalising for him.'

'Who is he? MI5, MI6?' I paused. That was as far as I knew about government organisations, and I presumed this was the British government.

'Neither of those. Nothing so grand. He works for the Foreign Office. Hospitality Division.'

That sounded relatively harmless. Someone in charge of gift bags and handshakes. I wasn't fooled though. I was reminded of Orwell's Ministry of Peace. Hospitality suddenly felt rather ominous. Was he interested in us because he knew who we were, or because of our recent jolly in Kabul?

'Does he know about Alpha?'

Marcus shook his head. 'No. At least, probably not. We've heard nothing to alert us.'

'You bug him?'

'Julius, don't be so melodramatic,' said Marie-Louise as she patted her hair. 'We don't bug *him*. We bug everyone. GCHQ isn't the only one listening in to your calls, your texts, your posts.'

I paused. I really needed to spend more time at the Alexandria Company and work out how far their influence spread.

'Don't worry, yes, yes.' Marcus smiled. 'We don't interfere or direct. Much as I wish we did. We merely hide and stick to our original mission. Preserve treasures and rescue abandoned curators.'

After a short while, the helicopter landed on an unlit runway and we moved briskly across to a waiting aeroplane, and were soon up in the air again. The reach of the Alexandria Company was even more impressive than I had imagined. I was torn between sleep and food, but as a table was laid out with linen and crystal, I was reminded that I hadn't eaten in forever, and sometimes a man just has to eat. Five minutes later, I was fast asleep.

Chapter Twenty-Three - October: Beta: Julius

We landed at London City Airport and were driven into town. There had been a bit of a scene when Marie-Louise wouldn't relinquish the case with the crown in it. Nor, when requested, would she open it, or say what was in it. Marcus remained tight-lipped, and so I sat there and smiled as the staff of HM Customs railed at me. Eventually, after a terse phone call, the official came back and waved us through to the car. The past forty-eight hours involved gunfire, blood loss, and uncomfortable sleeps. I just wanted to go home, but the mission wasn't over yet.

'A little honey now and then, Marie-Louise,' said Marcus. 'It goes down wonders.'

'As does the courtesy of a shower and a change of clothes.'

'You showered on the plane, and you are in fresh clothes.'

She tutted. 'It doesn't count. I wanted to bathe.'

We drove into London in silence. The curators had briefed me to say as little as possible, and only confirm what was widely known. Brian, apparently, would have to work for the rest.

The car drove past Whitehall and pulled up in a nondescript road full of tall nameless buildings with identical facades. I was surrounded by my government and felt deeply uneasy. I loved my country and had no wish to lie or obfuscate. I also didn't wish to be treated as an enemy combatant or, even worse, a deranged fool.

We were met at the door by a beige civil servant, a short man with a put-upon expression, and I dismissed him. How could this be the man that had made Marcus and Marie-Louise come to attention? However, as he shook my hand and introduced himself, I rapidly recalibrated. From his little smile as he said hello, it was obvious that he also knew I had discounted him. I could only plead tiredness for my poor initial observational skills.

We walked along a carpeted corridor and Marcus and Marie-Louise were waved into a comfortable reception room.

As I stepped forward, Brian held up his hand. 'Ah, would you give me a minute with Professor Strathclyde? You two have security clearance, but it's Julius' first time here. Just need to run through some paperwork.'

Marcus was frowning, but Marie-Louise shrugged and sat down and read one of the magazines. Deciding there was little I could really do, I smiled at Brian and followed him back out of the room. We walked down a lengthy corridor and up a flight of steps. The next corridor was less grand. Parquet wood floors and doors with frosted glass inserts.

We walked into a room and an alert immediately pinged. A woman had been sitting at a desk just inside the room. Standing up, she approached us with a security wand and waved it over us. Sure enough, the wand beeped as she swiped it over my sleeve. Holding my arm out, the guard inspected my cuff, then removed a small white "button" from the inside section of the fabric. I winced as he held my arm. Marie-Louise's painkillers were wearing off.

'Not today, you don't,' said Brian into the receiver and then handed it back to the guard, who placed it in a small vial and left the room. I hadn't even been aware I was wearing a bug, but no doubt Marcus or Marie-Louise had placed it on me as we arrived in Whitehall.

'Right then, Professor Strathclyde. Who the bloody hell are you?'

Brian Hastlethwaite dragged out a chair and waved me to sit down on the chair opposite. We faced each other across the plain table. I really did want to go home and sleep, and I was hankering after a bath almost as much as Marie-Louise.

'What do you want to know?'

'How long have you been working for the Alexandria Company? Why were you selected to go out to Afghanistan? Where is the Fabergé Egg? Where have you been for the past two years?'

I stared at him and steadied my mind. As a curator I had some training in interrogation techniques, but generally we stepped back to Alpha before they were required. Now I needed to be calm and as honest as was possible.

'Three weeks, subject knowledge, no idea, America.'

'Bollocks.' He glared at me. 'You're certainly arrogant enough to be one of them. They all have that same air. Of knowing something I don't. So, what do you know that I don't?'

'Really?' I scoffed. Now he was being silly. I had decided that this aggressive blustering northern act was just that. Oh, he may well be a loudmouth, belligerent Geordie, but he wasn't a fool.

'Do you expect me to say something about me not knowing what you don't know? Are you hoping to lull me into some misguided sense of superiority?'

He bit off a laugh and shrugged his shoulders. 'Always worth trying to kid the other side that they are smarter than you are.'

'No worries there,' I said. 'I'm smart enough to know when I'm not the smartest person in the room.'

'Flattery, is it? 'Fraid that won't work on me either, sunshine.'

'It's not flattery when it's the truth.'

213

He opened a file in front of him and began reading through it. 'You have an embarrassment of degrees, speak multiple languages, many defunct, and you are a professor at Cambridge. And you still think I'm smarter than you are?'

He didn't know half of my talents thanks to my time on Alpha, but this man put me in mind of Minju. Unassuming, sitting in the heart of the British political establishment. I bet he didn't even have a decent title. He'd be an assistant or an undersecretary, maximum.

'In most aspects, yes, I think you are.'

I meant it. I knew a lot of stuff. But with regards to British politics, he was miles ahead. I decided to turn the tables and try to get him to share some information.

'But tell me, because I am also really curious about my new employers. What do you make of them? I signed up because the work sounded interesting. Help establish provenance of lost artefacts, but are they goodies or baddies? Have I hitched my wagon to the wrong sort?'

I tried to sound open and sincere. Just us fellows together.

'A bit of quid pro quo, is it?' said Brian with a smirk. 'You scratch my back, I'll scratch yours.' He tilted his head. 'Very well, I'll play along. The fact is, I haven't decided yet.'

I noticed he said I, not we. Whoever he was, he was in charge. What of, I didn't know.

'The Alexandria Company has always been on our radar.'

'Our?' I wanted to see if he would say more about exactly who it was he worked for.

'Me, my predecessors.' He smiled, and I knew he wasn't going to tell me anything beyond what he had already decided to share. I was a trained curator, not an interrogator. I'd just have to do my best.

'And you report to?'

'The British government, obviously.'

Helpfully vague. I raised an eyebrow, and he shrugged, then decided to be a bit more forthcoming.

'We keep an eye on things. From time to time, we notice organisations trying to set up shop on our soil and we decide if they should stay or go. Sometimes Mossad or the CIA, for example, will run a mission on our territory. We either aid or obstruct them, depending on whether their goals are in line with our preferred outcomes or not.'

'And if they aren't?'

'We tell them to bugger off.'

'What if they break the law?'

'We don't care about the bloody laws. Our job is hospitality. We either make sure they have an invitation and see that they get all that they need. Or,' he paused, 'we don't. We judge it on a case-by-case need.'

'What if they're wearing trainers?'

He laughed. 'Yep. View me as a bouncer. That works. If your face doesn't fit, you can't get in.'

'And the Alexandria Company, does their face fit?' I was curious about how the government viewed the curators.

'Ah, their face fits, all right. But you know when someone is almost certainly wearing a wig? They're like that. Something about them seems slightly off-key.'

'You've just admitted to not caring about the law.'

'That's different. Besides, I know what laws are being broken. With this lot, I know they are wrong, but I don't know why.'

I thought about it. Brian didn't feel like a threat, but he was certainly someone to be very wary of.

'Well,' I said thoughtfully. 'They've been in business a long time and remain a private company. That can lead to an air of secrecy, I suppose.'

'No, it's not that. This is London. We are awash with powerful secret societies. And not one of them makes me itch.'

'What makes you itch, exactly?'

'They do nothing. They just restore and evaluate artwork.'

I leant back in my chair. 'Isn't that their job?'

'Yes. But their reach!' Now his mask slipped. 'They travel anywhere, they are always first with knowledge, their technology is unmatched. Hell, they could take over a country if they so wished. Maybe even this one!

But no, they just pontificate about whether a painting is by Botticelli or Joe Bloggs.'

'And that's an issue?'

'Yes,' he snapped, slapping his hand on the table. 'They are too powerful, too rich, and too clever to be doing nothing.'

I could see his point of view. To a Beta, their behaviour was deeply suspicious. I tried to make them sound a bit better.

'I understand they support various charities and outreach programmes.'

'Huge red flag!'

'It is? Why?'

'Because with their influence, they could eradicate the issue, not ease it. But they don't. Why not? Why refuse to change the status quo?'

'So they make you itch because…' I sought for the right word. 'They're too lazy?'

'Lazy? Do they strike you as lazy? You've been with them these past three years.'

I interrupted him. 'Three weeks.'

'Don't play games with me. You've been involved since the Fabergé Affair.'

'I assure you—'

'Whatever.' His eyes bore into mine, and for a moment I felt the full force of those sworn to protect His Majesty's realm. Brian Hastlethwaite was not playing about. 'In the time you have known them, do they strike you as lazy?' he repeated. More insistently this time.

Now it was my time to lean back. 'No, not lazy.'

'Exactly, and that's why I itch. They don't appear to be on anyone's side.'

'And that's a problem?'

'If I don't know what side they are on, how can I take a position on them?'

I shrugged. I could see his problem, but thankfully it was his, not mine.

'And now there's you. The first new partner in years, and you don't fit the bill. Every other member on the board has a faked alias and backstory, but you. You are exactly who you say you are. And that makes me itch as well.'

The idea that I was personally making this man itch was alarming. I had just faced down a new Afghanistan militia and hadn't felt this level of concern.

'So, do you want to explain how you came to be working for the Alexandria Company?'

What could I say other than the truth?

'Marcus Carruthers approached me in a coffee shop in Cambridge. Suggested I might like to work for them. I thought it over. Went up to London for an interview and decided that I would give them a go. I have to confess the last forty-eight hours have been more challenging than I was expecting.'

Brian stared at me, then drummed his fingers on the table.

'Your academic speciality is ancient religions and language dispersal. Is that correct?'

'Yes.' I couldn't help but feel this part of the conversation was about to go off the rails. I didn't like his smile.

'Two days ago, you entered the Ilkhanate Government Compound in Kabul. Shot various trained soldiers, evacuated a group of female civilians, smuggled out a priceless artefact and successfully fled into the desert, evading patrols and capture.'

'That was mostly Marcus and Marie-Louise.'

'Two pensioners?'

I exhaled. 'We just got lucky. You make it sound more than it was. I have to tell you I was petrified.'

'You were bloody James Bond, is what you were. Do they teach that in Religious Studies?'

Silence was going to be my best option.

'We have aerial footage of you running across a compound and accurately shooting two snipers. Did you learn to do that whilst learning how to conjugate Latin verbs?'

'You have footage?'

'Of course we have bloody footage.'

I wondered whose satellite they were using to watch Kabul, or maybe it was a British one. I was beginning to discover that I knew less than nothing about the true level of global surveillance.

'So, I ask you again, Julius Strathclyde. Who are you and where have you been?'

I remained silent and shrugged. I had already said all I was going to say, and knew that the more I said, the more I was likely to slip up. After staring at me in disgust, he pushed his chair back.

'Right. Let's join the others and run through a proper debrief of whatever the hell this little uprising was, that the three of you happened to stumble upon.'

We walked in silence back to the reception, where Marcus came to his feet.

'I say, Brian, that was a bit rude. Yes, yes? Professor Strathclyde has only been working a few days with us. Somewhat unnecessary to take him off for a grilling.'

'Worried that Strathclyde may have given the game away? Frustrated that you couldn't hear anything?'

He placed the broken listening bug on his desk and raised an eyebrow at Marie-Louise. She tipped her head and blushed prettily. I don't think anyone was buying the doe-eyed act, but Marie-Louise was a lady who brought out your manners whether you wanted them or not.

'Well, you can't blame me for trying,' she smiled. 'You broke the rules of hospitality first. No rest, no refreshment. Then stealing away one of our team for an interrogation. It really is very naughty of you.'

'I have to agree with my colleague,' said Marcus. 'It is most unbecoming.'

'I don't give two rats' hairy bollocks if I'm unbecoming or not. I don't trust you lot and that's all there is to it.'

Marie-Louise yawned, whilst I studied my fingernails.

Marcus shrugged. 'So, now what?'

'Now show me that bloody crown.'

Without hesitation, Marie-Louise placed the case on the desk, removed her handcuff, and opened it up. A small hiss of gas escaped and the crown could be seen resting on the grey padding. The white gas dissipated, revealing the crown in several pieces, covered in blood and grit.

'Whose blood is that?' demanded Brian.

'That's not relevant. We will take this back to our labs, clean and repair it. By that time, I am sure conversations will have taken place as to what to do with this,' said Marcus. 'I presume Afghanistan, Pakistan and India all claim it should be returned to them?'

'And South Korea and Macedonia. We are expecting China to get involved any minute now.'

'Ah, yes. Tricky.'

'They claim that it was originally the property of one of their emperors and was stolen. They also claim that they offer a stable home for it.'

'China. Home to the great uprising where millions of artefacts were broken, melted down and generally destroyed?' asked Marie-Louise.

'They cite that as a regrettable blip in a long and steady civilisation, respectful of their long-standing cultural heritage.'

'Stability through repression is not to be boasted about.'

'Oh, I agree, but it does make life easier,' said Brian, a shade too wistfully for my liking. He gave himself a quick shake. 'Still, that's not how we do things here. And despite the appeal, we're British and we do things better.'

I wanted to point out our own colonial past wasn't anything to boast about, but I felt that might fall on deaf ears. He reminded me of a mother standing in front of her child charged with war crimes, pointing out that he was a lovely child and always sent Christmas cards to his grandma.

Brian was well aware of Britain's history and didn't care. His job was to protect and support the country, and that was what he would do.

Marcus cleared his throat. 'I imagine the British Museum is also going to put in a claim.'

'All the major museums will, once they know it's up for grabs.'

Marie-Louise closed the case and re-pressurised it. 'Well, we'll leave the politics to you. We'll be in touch when it's repaired.'

She stepped back and rejoined me and Marcus.

'I take it we can leave now?' asked Marcus. 'Your colleagues have debriefed us whilst you were talking to Julius, and now you know as much as we do.' Brian snorted, but Marcus ignored him and continued. 'We are private citizens who were on a routine authentication job, that went catastrophically wrong. We have spoken to our government and explained what happened and have helped Military Intelligence understand the situation based on our amateur observations. If there's nothing else, I think we are done? Or shall I phone Harry?'

Brian smiled. 'No need to disturb the Prime Minister. These briefings are beneath her attention.' He walked over to the door. 'Oh, and she doesn't like being called Harry. Just so you know.'

Clearly, he was delighted to be able to put one over on Marcus. Marcus stood up and brushed up some non-existent crumbs from his sleeve.

'Well, not by outsiders, obviously. Friends and family are fine. I used to babysit her back in the day, you know.'

With a small tip of the head, Marcus sailed out of the room, followed by a smirking Marie-Louise.

I paused. I wanted to tell Brian that he could trust them, but didn't have the words. He watched them head down the corridor and then turned to me.

'I hope we never meet again.' With that, he entered his office and shut the door in my face.

We were driven home in a ministry car and remained in silence until we got back to Alexandria Street and into the safety of our own building and headed straight for Marcus' office.

'Well, that was disappointing,' said Marie-Louise. 'Yonni will be most annoyed.'

'Agreed,' said Marcus, 'but it will help her raise her game.'

'What's that?' I asked.

'The fact that Brian knows our identities are assumed. Yonni works really hard on them. Creates several every year. Starts them in childhood and then literally grows them. Develops CVs, passports, driving licences. She even hires actors occasionally to be the identity for a week or two so people can say they've actually met them. I wonder if Brian has worked it out, or is guessing?'

'Informed guess would be my deduction,' said Marcus. 'Julius' identity is rock solid because the genuine article always is. A fake, no matter how good, is never perfect.'

'I thought Brian crushed the bug?' I asked, surprised. It looked pretty obliterated to me.

'That thing,' laughed Marie-Louise. 'It was positively medieval. I'd have been appalled if they hadn't found it.' She shook her head. 'No, it does them good to think they have outsmarted us. As it happened, you were wearing three other bugs, including the subdermal tracker behind your ear.'

I thought about it. Of course, their technology was going to be better. Even isolated from Alpha, they had superior knowledge as to what was achievable, they had deep pockets, and their own labs at the far end of the street.

'So, how does Yonni know what identity to create? You don't know what curator is going to be stranded?'

'Not quite true. Sometimes we do know. For example, I was stranded in 1965. I knew a colleague from a step the Alpha year before would fail to return from the 1970 disaster.'

'But you only had a few years to create the identity. You couldn't grow it from birth.'

'Indeed, which is why Yonni makes so many each year. Various genders, skin tones, countries. I'd say she has hundreds of aliases on file, including the ones that were passed down to her. We've been doing this for a while, remember? Then when a curator becomes stranded, we scoop them up and offer them an identity closest to them. And, being curators, they slip into the new identity with ease.'

It made sense. When we were working on Beta, we always had to pretend to be someone else. There probably wasn't a group better suited to assuming a new identity. We could give George Smiley a run for his money. I thought of Brian again, a mouthy, disgruntled northerner at the heart of the government's diplomatic missions.

'Right, let's get clean,' said Marcus. 'Julius, there are fresh clothes in your room and we'll get the arm properly tended to. The others are on their way, so we can brief them and work out what the hell to do. Let Brian deal with tribal uprisings. We have bigger problems.'

I headed upstairs. For all Marcus' dismissal, I felt certain that the days of keeping Alpha's presence a secret from the British government were drawing to a close.

Revenge:
Neith–October/November
Alpha Earth

Chapter Twenty-Four - October: Alpha: Neith

I pushed back from my desk and sighed. I had always suspected office life wouldn't suit me, and so far, I was right. This was the end of my first week, and already I was dying of boredom.

My desk was at the far end of a large office. There were three other people in the room, all archivists, all working quietly. Yesterday, one of them hiccoughed, the second one giggled, the third one tutted, and silence was restored. They did talk, but at times of mutual agreement. When Minju had introduced me to them as their new boss and as a Potential Archivist, they had all formally shaken my hand, smiled pleasantly, then ignored me and went back to work.

At first, I thought they were offended at having a Potential placed above them. After the second day, I decided they didn't care. I would either prove myself, which would be good, or I would fail and move on, which would also be good.

Now I just had to learn how to be an archivist. I'd spent the past two months taking micro courses, reading and testing, then reading some more. No need for anything as alarming as physical training. Combat training for archivists no doubt dealt with photocopiers and tricky box cabinets. They were surprisingly old school.

Every day my new team steadily built a pile of paper reports on the central table. Each time one of them placed a report on the pile, the others stopped what they were doing and clapped softly.

The excitement was killing me.

Sui-hu stood up and came over to me. She was a young woman in her mid-twenties, with long black hair that shone like a mirror. At the moment, it was held back in two clips and a toggle.

'Potential Archivist Salah—'

I held up my hand. 'Please, just Neith.'

Being a potential was still a new idea, but it was catching on. However, I couldn't get used to not being Curator Salah, so I had asked them all to call me Neith. I didn't think they approved. Sloppy classification and all that. Instead, she just nodded and carried on.

'We're going for drinks later. Would you like to join us?'

I slapped my hands on the table. 'Now you're talking!'

Sui-hu stepped back and Fuad and Hinks looked up in distress.

I apologised, although I wasn't sure what for, and whispered that I would be delighted to join them. Friday Night was Shots Night, and it was time I let my hair down with my new workmates.

I had been deliberately distancing myself from my former friends. It had been a month since I had provoked Ramin. He had contacted me twice since then, but each time I rejected his call. The news that Luisa had been killed terrified me. I didn't believe for one second that she had voluntarily stopped. I didn't know if she had been killed because I had approached her, or because she accompanied Julius back to his Earth. Either way, I needed to move carefully. I had to protect my friends, but couldn't do this on my own. I had considered approaching Ludo, but saw with a sense of deep unease that he had been promoted to Ramin's partner. In every way Ramin outshone him, so his appointment was deeply suspicious. It had been announced on the newsfeeds, a surprising event in its own right. Internal work decisions rarely made the news.

I had now taken to watching the news daily and discovered it was increasingly driven by personality, rather than policy. Ludo was a rising star. It was about who people were, more than what they were doing. It was odd, but I couldn't see the harm. If anything, it was nice to see more of my fellow Egyptians.

I returned to my study notes, smiling. It was time to get back on the camel and start mixing with people. I was becoming paranoid trying to second guess Minju and work out what she was up to. So far, I had drawn a blank and made myself a social outcast in the process.

My screen buzzed, alerting me to a message from Minju. Another person I was avoiding.

-How has the first week gone?

-In line with expectations. Am going out for drinks with the team later.

-Excellent. I'll book a table at Khamouns. See you at eight.

I reread her message, then typed back.

-Our messages must have crossed. I'm going out for drinks tonight. Another time?

I needed to stay friendly.

-Tonight's fine. See you later.

The icon indicated she had now left the conversation and was not to be disturbed.

Great, the night would just be heating up and I'd have to slope off to have dinner with the boss in the city's swankiest restaurant. I'd be lucky if my new colleagues didn't pelt me with beer bottles as I left the bar.

At the end of the day, they all approached me, smiling and chatting. Work was over and it was time to relax.

'So, where are we going?' I asked. I knew it wouldn't be Blue's or Pyg's, and I was keen to discover somewhere new.

'Home,' said Fuad, looking at me, puzzled. 'To change clothes?'

I rolled my eyes. I forgot lots of people like to dress up on a night out. Laughing an apology, I explained that curators just turned up in whatever they had been wearing during the day. They gave me the address, and we arranged to meet out the front in a half hour.

I ran home. Half an hour was barely enough time for a party outfit, but I knew how to improvise. I didn't have much fancy wear, but slipped into a killer red dress with slits on either side, heeled boots in day-glow yellow to contrast with the dress, and slid on a pair of diamanté gloves. It was nothing I would normally wear as a curator, but I wasn't one anymore, so I may as well get used to it.

For a final touch, I applied a hologram filter to my hair, consisting of swallows and butterflies darting around my face and in the column of air above my head then consulted the mirror. Not too subtle, not too bold. Perfect.

When I arrived outside the club, the three were already waiting for me and we all stared at each other for a bit. Shua-Hi had removed her hair clips. Fuad had changed the colour of his belt and Hinks appeared to have possibly added lipstick. Possibly.

'I thought you were going to change?' I asked.

'We did,' said Hinks. 'We can't wear our work clothes out.'

'But they're identical!' I protested.

The three of them laughed.

'No, look,' said Fuad. 'Hink's outfit has two pockets, and Shua-Hi has pink stitching on her hems.'

232

I blinked, certain I was being pranked, but decided to take it on the chin. New girl hazing and all that.

We walked into the bar and I saw something I had never seen in a bar before. A carpet. And I don't mean the sticky sort that you have to pull your shoe from, I mean the soft fluffy sort that you get in penthouses. There were some cats on velvet sofas being patted by patrons, and on the stage four singers were humming in a close part harmony. Everyone was staring at me. I turned off my holograms.

'Wow, the place is jumping,' whispered Hinks excitedly. 'I love Pentra. Their harmonies really shake the working week out of you!'

I followed Hinks in silent astonishment, my fluorescent heels sinking into the deep pile. People had stopped staring at us now, but I could still catch the odd person sneaking a peak. I couldn't tell if it was my colours, my expanse of skin, or my jewels that were causing the issue. Looking across a sea of beige cotton robes, I suspected it was everything. We headed towards a table, but there were already cats on the chairs, so we moved over to one in the corner.

Shua-Hi grimaced. 'Sorry about the noise.'

I think she was referring to the humming. I was still trying to get my head around the place. It was insane. I had never been anywhere so restrained, and I had been to Lutheran funerals.

As we sat down, a server came over and exchanged a few words with the team. They were clearly regulars and the mood was friendly and convivial.

'Welcome, what will it be tonight?' She tapped on her pad, ready to place our order.

'Well, we have a new colleague,' said Fuad, smiling at me, 'so we thought we'd celebrate. How about some Rooibos?'

Hinks and Shua-Hi laughed and then nodded.

'In fact,' said Hinks, 'I'll have some fresh grated ginger in mine.'

Shua-Hi gasped, but then agreed, and Fuad quickly asked for the same.

I was beginning to think this wasn't a prank.

'Isn't Rooibos a tea?' They came out on a Friday night to let their hair down and drank tea?

'Yes.'

'Is it alcoholic?'

'No,' said Hinks, puzzled. 'But we are having it with ginger.' They all smiled at me again. Shua-Hi kept twisting a strand of hair through her fingers.

'Ginger, hey? Wild!'

No one noticed my sarcasm.

'What beers do you have?'

The table next to me fell silent. As did the one next to them. I was sitting in the centre of a spreading circle of censure.

'I apologise. Is this a sobriety bar? I am so sorry.'

Now the server looked flustered.

'Please don't apologise. We serve anything. Our aim is to make our patrons happy. I will bring a beer.'

She left quickly and I apologised to my workmates again.

By the time she returned, we had moved on to an appraisal of the band and everyone's favourite songs. Apparently, if we were in luck, the band would invite people up onto the stage to hum along. The excitement was palpable, if inexplicable.

I picked up my beer. It was a bottle of Stubbies. I hadn't had a Stubby since high school. It was everyone's first drink, about as low alcohol as you can get. One girl drank an entire keg of the stuff and swore blind she was actually drunk. But then that was typical of Clio.

I raised my bottle to their teacups, and we spent a genteel evening discussing the merits of cat groomers and vocal harmonies. I mostly listened. The room began to empty until we were nearly the last ones left. Hinks was yawning and trying to pretend she wasn't.

'Time for bed, I think. I have to be up early tomorrow.'

'Plans?' I enquired, and was pleased to see her look proud, if somewhat sheepish.

'I'm taking part in a knitathon.'

The other two clapped their hands and scolded her for not telling them about it. She blushed some more and said she didn't want to brag. It was then agreed that the night was over. The others would attend as observers and cheer her along. I wondered if the late-night bar was still open. Maybe I could grab a drink and drown my sorrows. I checked my brace and swore.

'It's seven thirty!'

'Seven forty-five, actually,' said Fuad apologetically.

I blinked.

'I know! That's what ginger does for you. Party!'

The three of them linked arms and, laughing, gently headed out of the bar. I followed in a daze. Saying good night to each other, we headed off to our own accommodations, and I was still laughing to myself when I remembered I had a date with Minju. Hell, there might even be booze.

Chapter Twenty-Five - October: Alpha: Neith

Khamouns is one of those places you go to, to be seen. If anything, I was now underdressed. I flicked my holograms back on, and a host of swallows dived around me. I liked swallows; they made me feel safe. Hirundine shielding. I received a few claps from passers-by and, as I approached the queue for the restaurant, one of the hosts waved me forward.

'No need to queue. We've been told to keep an eye out for you.'

As I was waved through, the crowd parted for me and the flash of holo inscribers lit the air. My image would no doubt be on all the entertainment channels within minutes.

Inside, there were fewer observers. The place was heaving with diners. On the stage, the band had just burst into a ragtime rendition of an old Hebrew spiritual, and everyone was chanting and whooping in time. I followed my server towards a small dais. There were a few dotted around the room. Anyone sitting at these tables could be clearly observed and noted. Theoretically, it was first come first served for these spots, but it was funny how it was always the most famous of our society that sat there.

Minju was seated alone on her dais and, seeing me, she jumped up and waved wildly. Anyone who hadn't already clocked my entrance certainly did now as I climbed the two steps up to our table.

'See,' she shouted over the band, 'I knew you'd be free by eight o'clock.'

'Why didn't you warn me?' I smiled as the server placed a Serengeti Surprise in front of me. I knocked it back in one go.

'Your first night out with the archivists. How could I spoil that?'

The server brought me a second Serengeti, which this time I sipped. They served them at double strength in here.

'I wouldn't have thought this was your sort of place, though?'

'You forget, I used to be a curator myself.' She raised her glass. 'We preserve!'

I raised my own, but didn't drink. I hadn't forgotten. I hadn't forgotten a single damn thing about Minju Chen.

'Even so, this isn't the normal sort of curator hang out.' Sure we liked noise, but we really weren't fussed about the attention.

'Agreed,' shouted Minju. 'But barely anyone has seen you in months. You are the hero of the Battle of the Gods. People want to see you and say they were there when you first came back to public life.'

Indeed, lots of people had been taking pictures and holos. Several people had approached our table, but Minju had been waving everyone away. It was curious that she referred to it as the Battle of the Gods, rather than the more popular Grimaldi Uprising. She was obviously trying to change perceptions, but to what end?

'Come on, let's order.' She waved for the server and, having suggested that the chef surprise us, she also asked if the band could turn it down just a notch.

Within seconds, they did just that. Minju might just be a little old archivist, forced to become the pharaoh, but everyone was doing what she suggested. This woman was born to rule. How had I never seen this? It was only now, when she was acting without a filter, that I could see how effortlessly she handled it.

'There, that's better,' she said as the volume dropped. 'I think I was an archivist too long.'

I thought about it and wondered how she had made the transition herself. I knew I was struggling, and I asked her how she managed. The more I got to know her, the more ammunition I had.

'It wasn't easy.'

She paused and her face fell flat. For the first time, I had the sense that I was seeing the real Minju. I suspected she was being honest.

'When I was spliced and removed from my post, I was devastated. I wanted to tear down walls. My

239

partner was lost. I had abandoned him. I wanted to destroy everything.'

I found myself nodding in agreement. 'You saved his life, though.'

'Did I? You know I searched the archives and there was no trace of him on Beta. The leopard had attacked him before I wrenched it off him. He clearly didn't survive his wounds.'

There was no point in trying to disagree with her. It would take a very special curator to survive a leopard attack, then settle into making a new life on Beta. I shuddered. We had all been warned about how to adapt and survive, but even for a curator, it was an adventure too far, living full time on Beta. And Minju had to live with that knowledge, as well as the fact she could never be a curator again. Early attempts to step with someone featuring a splice of non-human DNA were disasters. Each time, the quantum stepper tried to lock onto, and separate, the two DNAs, resulting in painful death every time. Minju could never go back.

'Someone laughingly suggested I could be an archivist, and I realised it was perfect for me. I could hide from sight and avoid talking to anyone. I knew the tail was no great shame, and yet I found it very hard to embrace. There were more of us back then, Kiki with her wings, Tabouline with his carapace, curators with whiskers, ears, one arm, three hands. Gradually, though, there were fewer and fewer of us. You know what I'm talking about.'

She patted my hand, and I was horrified to discover how alike we were.

'My splice has only been an eye and some language issues. And, of course, it was human DNA. I could still step.'

She waved her hand at me and narrowed her eyes. 'Do not make light of it. No one knows what it is like to suddenly play host to DNA that is not yours. To have alien thoughts and feelings occupying your attention. So many of us went mad. Those of us who survived were stronger for it.'

She stopped and sipped her cocktail whilst I pondered her words. My splice had been with Julius, a human, and whilst I found myself folding socks in times of stress and occasionally swearing in Welsh, I hadn't suffered too much. Although, I had begun to view Alpha society in a new light, and I didn't know if those were my thoughts and feelings or Julius'. How much worse would it have been to absorb animalistic instincts and responses?

'And so the archives were perfect for me,' she continued. 'I hid in the basement and gradually learnt to accept my lot. I even enjoyed it. As you might. Like me, you carry the burden of a splice and you are without your partner.'

I choked as the chocolate-dipped seed went down the wrong way. Thankfully, my spluttering gave me time to regroup. This was not a friendly chat with a mentor, this was my enemy. I knew she liked Julius. In fact, I would say he viewed her as a close friend. But that hadn't stopped her from removing him. I decided to be obtuse.

'Clio left of her own accord. Nothing I did had any impact on her choices. I regret them, but they were not my fault and I won't feel guilty about them.'

I felt guilty about them every day.

Minju tutted and shook her head.

'I wasn't referring to Clio, but to Julius. Although yes, you have been unlucky. Do you ever think you are to blame?'

It was a rhetorical question as she quickly moved on, but for a second I was reeling from the truth of her observation. Of course I was to blame. I had not done enough to save either of them.

She tapped her finger on the table. 'Stop that. You know what happens when your world turns inside out and rips you apart?' She leant forward, her expression fierce. I wanted to get up and leave but she was mesmeric.

'You get back on the camel?'

She leant back and snorted. 'You look at the universe and decide that from here on, the world will turn according to your desires. You will take control and stop being everyone else's puppet.' She sipped her cocktail and studied me over the rim of her glass. 'You know what I mean.'

I didn't know if I agreed with her. Maybe my losses were all too recent, but I was getting some insight into Minju's philosophy. It wasn't comfortable. I could see she was about to continue, but something changed her mind and she shook her head.

'Whatever. Now, tell me how the plans for the artefact's selection are progressing.'

The server arrived at that moment and presented a sharing dish of the finest seafood. I smiled in pleasure. I loved seafood, and could smell the butter and garlic as it oozed down the side of lobster. She cracked open a prawn, the juices running down her fingers as we chatted about the job.

'How many items have you proposed so far?'

I put the crab claw down. 'Honestly, I'm hands off at the moment. The team is building a whole stack of reports. I thought when they had finished, I could review their choices and we could discuss them then?'

She pursed her lips. 'You understand I picked you because of your specialist insight. You may have even been the curator who rescued some of these choices. I know there is going to be a lot of pushback from all factors. This idea of repatriation is important for our society, but we have to move this really slowly.' She waved a crab claw at me. 'You and I both know that there are plenty of places on Beta that are just not suitable recipients.'

I dabbed butter off my chin. 'Don't! I have to say most curators have huge reservations about this.'

'It's okay, you can say openly hostile.'

'Well.' I took a deep breath. 'It's just, you know. We risk life and limb to save these artefacts, and now we are simply returning them?' I shrugged. I knew the opposing argument. Julius had been very eloquent on that point. It was just a bit of a hurdle.

'But there have been world debates about this. The world's chancellors, leaders, pharaohs, queens, emperors, everyone agreed. It is time to move our culture forwards and as we run the quantum facility on behalf of the world, it's down to us to put forward the first list for proposal.'

I had missed all the talks. Apparently, there had been months of live footage. Still, it was a done deal now. In our benevolence, we would start returning the odd item if we felt the country was now in a position to properly protect it. I knew this was being done at Minju's instigation. I just couldn't fathom why.

We wouldn't tell Beta about us. We'd just leave the artefacts in safe places. Call us Father Christmas. I'd made that joke to Julius, but he mumbled something about St Raffles rather than St Nicholas, but I tended to switch off when Julius started talking about saints.

'Penny for them?'

'It's nothing. I was just thinking about Julius. Whenever he felt conflicted, I often ended up siding with him. But, of course, that was usually when things went wrong.'

Looking back, I shouldn't have had that third Serengeti Surprise.

'Julius did have that effect, didn't he?' said Minju thoughtfully. 'I miss that about him.'

I quickly agreed and wished I hadn't spoken out loud. Things might have gone wrong, but they always seemed to work out better when we saw things from his point of view. Except for his stance on chips. Thick, greasy, salty, vinegary potatoes were not something that anyone should eat.

Julius had the unique ability to see our world through a different lens. He was the first to spot the problems in our society and was also the first to notice that our systems were being abused. No wonder Minju needed him gone, no matter what she said. Her plans had been derailed once. She wasn't about to let that happen a second time.

'I plan to announce the list at the opening of the Arts Foundation this November. I want people to have renewed faith in themselves. I want them to see that we are no one's inferiors, that our art will be superior to Betas.'

'I agree. It's been a rough time for all of us. The Grimaldi Uprising…'

As I hoped, she took the bait.

"That was nothing. What could he have achieved without those quantum god things? That is where the threat comes from, not from within. We need to remind ourselves how superior we are and get ready to defend ourselves.'

I screwed my face up as I thought about it and broke off some garlic bread.

'And how will doing better at art do that?'

'Small steps, Neith. Let's give our population back their sense of pride, then go from there.'

Minju as Chief Morale Officer made sense, but I didn't know what she was hiding. I could almost take her words at face value if it wasn't for the fact that I knew what she had done so far. Only I knew of the killings, the thefts, the truth behind the attempted coup. Even now people were being monitored, key players being assassinated. This was not all in order to launch a new Arts Programme.

I changed the conversation and we talked of banal things. Nothing to cause me further discomfort. Each time I felt grateful for her concern, I had to remember she had probably manipulated the conversation that way in the first place. As the meal came to an end, I noticed Minju catch someone's eye behind me.

'Neith. Would you mind if the Pharaoh of Sudan came and said hello? He's been hovering all evening.'

I looked across at her in shock. 'Of course. Please don't avoid your friends on my account.'

Minju grinned impishly at me. 'As if he's here to see me. He wants to say hello to you. Probably wants to thank you.'

This was stupid. I had just been doing my job. And not particularly well, given that I had been shot in the head. I leant across the table so that I could whisper. I didn't want to offend anyone.

'Is it really necessary?'

Minju put her glass down. 'Of course not. I shall tell him you are too tired. I'm sure the people of Sudan will understand.'

I groaned. There was absolutely no way I could be so discourteous.

'No, of course I'm not too tired. I'd be delighted.'

Minju gave a mock sigh of relief. 'That's my girl. Duty first.'

For the next half hour, I shook hands with half the customers in the room. Out of the corner of my eye, Minju gave imperceptible nods and shakes, as to who could approach, tell me I was wonderful and smile for the cameras. She was orchestrating everything until I was about to call an end to it.

'That's enough now, I think.' She called over a server and asked him to fetch her shawl. 'I'm so sorry, Neith. You got a bit mobbed there, didn't you? It didn't occur to me so many people would want to meet you.

Next time we'll go somewhere quieter.' She looked at me in sudden alarm. 'I apologise. That is, if you want to meet up again? I had a lovely evening with you and it was such fun to relive my youth with someone I can relate to.'

She wrapped her shawl around her shoulders and managed to make herself look small and fragile. 'Of course, you probably had a very dull evening, listening to an old lady witter on about the past, and then got mobbed by the press. You must have been terribly bored.'

I laughed. Honestly, what else could I do? She was clever, charming, and entertaining. An evening with her was certainly not boring. As we reached the exit, an official car had pulled up for her and she offered me a lift home.

'The walk will do me good. Clear out those cocktails.'

'Very well, but do me a favour?'

I tilted my head. Was this what the evening had been all about?

'Have a look at the reports your colleagues are compiling. I've never known archivists to work ahead of schedule. There are already so many reports. It seems…' She paused, looking for the right word. 'Unexpected. Humour an old lady. We need at least fifty suggestions by next week so the board can start whittling them down.' As she sat back into the seat, she rested her elbow on the side and smiled at me. 'Incidentally, I expect you to be on the podium with me when we announce the shortlist to the world.'

'Why me?'

'My dear, who better?'

Tapping the driver's shoulder, the car pulled up into the sky and headed off into the night whilst I stood there gaping like a fish.

Chapter Twenty-Six - October:
Alpha: Neith

Last night at Khamouns with Minju had been a nightmare. I had failed to understand what Minju was up to and ended up feeling some sympathy for her. Then I remembered all the people that had died so far, and I knew Minju wasn't finished.

It had been three months since she had got rid of Julius. I hoped he had settled back into his old life. My money was on the fact that he'd spent last night out with friends doing nice professor stuff, although I had no idea what that was. But I bet he had slept soundly and hadn't had a cup of tea where someone poured the milk in first.

I didn't resent him for his fresh start. I just missed him. I was fed up with having to manage Minju alone, but it was better than losing anyone else.

I'd had a tonic before bed, to bolster my liver, and felt refreshed and ready for action. Picking up the first report that the archivists had been diligently compiling, I settled down to read. The pile in the centre of the tables was gratifyingly large, and I was happy that we could present the suggestions ahead of expectations, no matter what Minju thought. Sometimes a new boss just shook people up a bit. They wanted to impress or please or show off, but I had heard that productivity could often improve when the team dynamics were slightly altered.

I grabbed a coffee and opened the first report. I had to confess, I was anxious. Would it be a treasure that I had rescued? Maybe something too exquisite or fragile to part with? Or might cause problems to Beta Earth if returned? I supposed that was my job. To filter the choices made by the archivists. I would have a quick peek and then go back to my training.

I flicked through the pages of the first report in confusion. Clearly, I had picked the wrong report. I pulled another one towards me, and as I flicked through it, my sense of bafflement increased. By the time the team arrived, all together, all precisely when the clocks chimed, the table was strewn with open reports. Not a single one contained an item for repatriation.

'What is this?' I held up a report at random.

The three of them stared at me. Shua-Hi slowly unwound her scarf, hanging it carefully up on the hook before approaching me.

'May I?'

I passed the report over to her and waved at the other two to sit down. She flicked through the report, nodding as she read the paper, then placed it on the table.

'This is Fuad's assessment of the Binomial Cataloguing System. As you can see, he has been very thorough in his research and rates it highly as one of the proposed methods of cataloguing.'

I looked at her blankly, then across at Fuad, who was now flicking through his report nervously.

'Have I missed something?' he asked, and sagged in relief when Shu-hi told him everything was in order.

'So what's this, then?' I picked up a report from the table and read out the heading. 'Assessment of the P'tok Classification System.'

I wished I hadn't asked as the three of them explained, at length, that they had been collating and assessing bloody classification systems, rather than actual artefacts. This was a nightmare. In their words, they needed a proper foundational approach before moving on to the initial assessments. Anything else would be reckless. For the past few months I'd been learning how to be an archivist and hadn't once thought to check on their work. My first assignment and I was tanking. Thank Ra, no one would be paying attention.

No wait, that's right, the entire world was paying attention.

I let out a very audible groan.

'Right, kettle on, we are going back to basics.'

'P'tok basics or Binomial Basics—'

'Saladin basics?' asked Fuad hopefully.

'Neith Salah basics. We start with coffee.'

An hour later, we had filed and catalogued the reports and now all three were looking at me, waiting for my leadership. Or to fall flat on my face.

'Okay. Here is what we are going to do. We have treasures from five continents. We will pick ten items per continent. Those ten items will be selected from the various countries within that continent.'

I felt embarrassed that I had failed to announce this when I had first arrived. They were just working so judiciously, I assumed they were already briefed. I clearly wasn't used to office work.

'We've got more European than American artefacts,' said Fuad in alarm.

'I know, but we don't have time to be nuanced or proportional. We have a week to draw up an acceptable list.'

'It's not enough time,' he protested.

I wanted to point out that they had had two months, but that wasn't going to be constructive. I needed my team to feel motivated, not chastised. Besides which it was not their fault that they had not been properly managed.

'What about their Middle East artefacts? Surely, we can't risk them?'

I sighed. This went to the heart of my concerns, and that of every single curator.

'That's not down to us. I'm certain that the steering board will not repatriate items into a region that has shown recent evidence of destroying, hoarding or losing artefacts.'

I knew this was the right thing to do, but had so many reservations. At least I would get to be on the steering panel. That was a bonus. I couldn't make my mind up about Minju. There had to be an angle, but I couldn't see what it was. I wished I could ask Julius. He'd have an interesting take on it, but as far as he was concerned, she was lovely little old Minju. Proud, brave, honourable. Pah!

I must have said that last bit out loud, as they all jumped.

'Sorry. It's just this is a big task, so let's crack on. First things first, let's eliminate all the items of monumental importance or fragility. Or anything that will destabilise political systems.'

'So, we're not returning the Samarkand Scrolls.'

'We are never returning them!'

'Or the Mary Papyrus?'

I nearly spat my coffee out. 'Anything remotely religious or political stays off the list.'

I felt the room relax. We all cared greatly about our responsibility to Beta. It was a fine balance. We could neither improve nor harm their development. And so the day unfolded as I set the team off to study each continent and pick out books, jewels, paintings, pieces of music, even clothing. As I walked home, I was even whistling. A day spent amongst the greatest of Beta treasures can raise anyone's spirits, and it actually felt good to think that we would soon be sending these treasures back with their rightful creators.

Julius would be proud of me. Now if I could only work out what Minju was planning for Alpha, I'd feel a lot happier. I hoped whatever he was doing, he was having a good time.

Chapter Twenty-Seven -
November: Alpha: Ramin

Ramin was quietly stewing in his own dissatisfaction. It was November now, and he still had failed to make up with Neith. She was behaving like a camel's arse and he missed her. Last night, Xandro had accused him of talking about Neith even more, now that they weren't seeing each other. It had resulted in quite a row. Ramin had told him he had nothing to be jealous of. Xandro said he wasn't jealous, but it would be nice to have a partner who at least pretended to be more interested in him, than someone who wasn't even talking to him. They'd slept in separate rooms and headed in to work without their usual morning kiss and goodbye.

This was all Neith's fault. He didn't understand why she was shutting him out, and wondered if he should speak to her doctors. This could be a symptom of her brain damage. It felt unlikely, but he had no other explanation.

Ramin let out a deep sigh. Who was he kidding? The row between him and Xandro was completely his fault. He was obsessing over Neith. Maybe it was time to let her go?

'Rough night, Rami?'

He spluttered. Ludo Bianco was lounging against the door frame, one leg crossed over the other, a wet smile on his face, and a bunch of papers under his arm. They weren't even in a proper clasp. Never had Ramin seen a smile he wanted to punch more.

'It's Ramin. Not Rami. Captain Ramin Gamal.'

Ludo's smile widened. 'Co-Captain Ramin Gamal, remember. We're partners in crime now.' He laughed and walked into Ramin's office, heading for the stuffed dates that Ramin had for guests. He placed the paperwork on the side then, pouring himself a small espresso, came and sat opposite Ramin.

'So, Ramin,' he stressed the second syllable. 'What's on the agenda for this week?'

Shortly after Sam's sabbatical, his temporary replacement, a woman called Sabui, who was something of a bean counter from Human Resources, had taken over the job. Shortly after Julius' repatriation, she had appointed Ludo Bianco as co-captain of the curators. Ramin had protested that with a depleted workforce he had less to do and didn't need or want a partner. Financially, it made no sense either, and yet Sabui insisted.

It was then made clear that with fewer curators, they were an even more valuable resource. Every step would now have to be scrutinised and double checked. Only if both captains agreed on the risk factor could the step proceed.

Ramin had pointed out that Ludo had limited experience and wasn't even top of his class. In fact, a proper analysis would suggest he was closer to the bottom. If not the actual bottom itself.

The bean counter had told him that Ludo had other talents. Ramin wrote a letter of protest to Pharaoh Chen. He didn't want Minju to be unaware of developments at the mouseion. She had replied with a curt note saying Ludo was her appointment as she was aiming to make the curators more egalitarian. Ramin had read the note, decided that egalitarian must now mean the lowest common denominator, and tried to live with it. And now the fool was about to put his feet on Ramin's desk.

'Ludo, how many times do I have to tell you? Please keep your feet on the floor.'

Ludo had a habit of wearing a short tunic without under-garments. He thought it was hilarious if a breeze exposed him, and of course, putting his feet on the table also left himself exposed to the elements. Ramin wasn't a prude, but it was just so unprofessional.

'Cool beans, Ramin,' said Ludo as he sat straighter in his chair and rearranged himself. 'Now, what is this week's rota looking like?'

Theoretically, they were supposed to plan this together, but it was all Ramin's work. Ramin ran through the list and waited until Ludo had nodded, agreeing that everything was in order.

'And rescuing the Koh-I-Noor during the Blitz. You're good with that?'

Ludo ruffled his hair. 'What? Oh, are you testing me?' He laughed loudly. 'No trips to the Blitz for us at the moment. Way too risky. What did you actually have in mind?'

Ramin explained he had recommended rescuing some paintings from an act of vandalism at the Met, whilst wondering if Ludo had even clocked that the Koh-I-Noor was not actually on the list of lost items. And this man was considered his equal?

'Right, well, that all seems in order. I give my permission to have that signed off.'

Ramin stared at him, then nodded slowly. Ludo was a fool, but he was harmless. An idiot promoted above his station. What damage could he do? Then he remembered Chancellor Alvarez and shuddered. That idiot had almost destroyed the mouseion itself.

As Ludo left, he swung the door closed, despite Ramin's open door policy. Ramin got up, muttering to himself about oafs and idiots. Walking across the room, he noticed that Ludo had left his paperwork by the coffee pot. The man was a fool. Only important documents got printed out. It was a peccadillo of the pharaoh that the more important an item, the more likely it was to be handwritten and burnt upon receipt. Her distrust of the engineers and their observation of the Tiresias network was all-consuming. Ramin

259

sympathised, but felt paper documents were just as prone to misuse. Ludo's folders were a case in point. He loved walking around with them. It showed how important he was. At least, that's how he viewed it. Leaving them by coffee pots just showed how completely incompetent he was.

Picking them up, Ramin left his door closed and turned to his desk. What was so important in the set of notes? As he read through, it appeared to be about the new Arts Facility, although, as this was quite a detailed breakdown of costs, he imagined there was a need for privacy. He was about to close the document when he noticed a figure that accounted for thirty percent of the entire spend.

'Tiresias, what is Project Dance?'

'Project Dance is part of the new Arts Facility.'

'Why would Glass Wastes be in a bracket beside it?'

'The Glass Wastes is an area of land deep within the Sahara...'

'Yes. I know that. Is there some new work going on there?'

'No. The Glass Wastes is a restricted zone under the Mali Convention.'

Tiresias droned off and Ramin closed the query. Maybe it was an art installation? He tapped his brace and called his boss.

'Sabui, are you certain Ludo is the right person for this job? He nearly signed off on a step into the Blitz, missed the fact that the Koh-I-Noor is not on the list, and just now left some confidential written material by my coffee pot.'

Ramin listened as Chancellor Sabui explained that Ludo was probably just playing about and that he had left the papers for Ramin to read. Maybe Ramin had forgotten he had asked for them?

'I'm not senile, Sabui. If I had asked for a breakdown of figures for the Arts Foundation, I would have remembered. They have nothing to do with me. Or Ludo, I would have thought?'

There followed another lecture about confidential documents and the need not to discuss them.

'I thought there was also a need to not leave them lying around?'

This was followed by a few words on solidarity and ethics.

Ramin yawned. What did a bean counter know about solidarity?

'If there's anything else?' said Sabui sharply, hearing Ramin yawn.

'No, nothing. Oh yes, there is one thing,' said Ramin. His curiosity had been piqued by Project Dance. 'Any idea if something is going on in the Glass Wastes?'

'No idea at all. Why?'

'It was in the costings.'

'The costings I have just told you at length not to discuss?' she said sharply. 'Ramin Gamal, maybe you are not the right man for this job?'

Ramin rolled his eyes, reassured Sabui that the curators were in the safest pair of hands whilst he remained at the tiller, and signed off.

A second later, the door flung open and Ludo ran into the room, staring wildly about until he saw the folder on Ramin's desk.

'Thank all the small dangly things! Thought I'd sodding lost that. Sabui asked me to deliver that to the pharaoh. They'd both slice my 'nads off if they thought I'd lost it. Do me a favour. Let's keep this between us boys, hey?'

And as quickly as he had stormed in, he headed back out again. This time leaving the door wide open. In the corridor, Ramin could hear Ludo calling out. 'Make way. Man on a mission! Coming through. Mind your backs.'

Ramin sighed and wondered how he could make amends to Xandro. Living with an idiot was hard work. As his mind wandered, he called on Tiresias again.

'Can you download everything you have on the work plans for the Arts Foundation? No hurry, send it home. Can I have the 3D modelling option?'

Xandro was an architect, he might be able to explain what could account for having so much money being spent on it.

The more he thought about it, the more uneasy he became and decided to send Neith a hologram. He really needed to talk to her. Maybe a warning would grab her attention?

Chapter Twenty-Eight - November: Alpha: Minju

Minju watched as Sabui left her office. That she had come in person had alerted Minju to a problem. The scale of the problem momentarily stunned her. That Sabui had entrusted the finance plans to Ludo Bianco, who had then allowed Ramin Gamal to read them, was beyond the pale. Minju could scream. Ludo was perfect, but he could hardly be trusted with secure information. She was tempted to fire Sabui for such a tactical error, but the fact was Minju had so few people she could truly rely on.

She pinched her nose and then decided there was no real harm done. They were always going to get to this stage and, in fact, this might have made her life easier. Gamal had just placed his neck in his own noose. Now she had to find out where Neith's loyalties really lay. She had huge hope for her. She knew that the younger curator loved her Earth as much as Minju did, and knew she would sacrifice anything to keep it safe. Now it was time to see if her protégé could see that this was necessary to save her home.

She tapped on her brace, then swung around in her chair, taking in the view from the window.

-Jones. We need to move things up. Don't let Jack off-site.

Her tail flicked as she listened to his excuses.

-Bast! I don't care, threaten to end his little fiancé. That will make him play along. I know. How unlikely to have an engineer in love. So easily manipulated.

She tapped her fingers on the desk.

-I'm glad to hear it. What's the current fatality rate?

As Tybalt Jones reeled off the figures, Minju interrogated her data pads. At this rate, she would have to speed up new personnel to replace those lost.

-Excellent. More money is on its way, and soon you'll have all the personnel you can handle.

It had taken all her resources to rebuild the network that Asha Giovanetti had destroyed. Every name on the ledgers had been tracked down by the Director of Security and prosecuted, but Minju knew a few had been using aliases and proxy bidders that had never been traced. Asha had been brilliant, but Minju had been fast and managed to re-establish the beginnings of her network. She had been approaching them anonymously. Of course, none of them trusted an unknown source, but she knew they were hooked, and with what she was offering they would instantly come on board.

But first, she needed to strengthen her position. Pharaoh was not enough. She needed something more permanent. The Roman Empire had a system to introduce a dictator now and then. Now it was Egypt's turn.

She hung up on Jones, then told Tiresias to summon Neith to her office. Whilst she waited for Neith, she called Sabui and informed her that Ludo was about to get a promotion. Incompetence should never be rewarded, and she was annoyed. It was so Beta. She was looking forward to a new world order where she could appoint the best people for the jobs. But for now, she had to appoint the ones that would help her achieve her goal.

The project out in the Glass Wastes was coming along on schedule. Loss of life had been within tolerable margins, and still no one knew about it. It was infuriating that Ramin Gamal had stumbled across it. He would not stop digging until he had the puzzle solved, at which point he'd blow it out of the water.

Time to put Neith to the test.

Chapter Twenty-Nine - November: Alpha: Neith

I was sitting at my office desk, wondering if classification systems would ever excite me, when my brace vibrated. Someone was trying to send me a hologram. As it wasn't an actual call, I hit accept. In the past two months, I had blocked all face-to-face calls. In fact, I had blocked all calls that weren't work related. Considering Githumbi's murder, I no longer viewed Sam's yearlong sabbatical as an act of good fortune. Ramin was right. People were being moved and replaced. That he had to share his job with the idiot Ludo was evidence things were changing. Of course, Ramin didn't know who was behind it, but I did.

As I checked the brace, I saw it was Ramin. I had been studiously screening his texts and, happily, he appeared to have stopped talking about things being wrong. So long as he didn't draw Minju's attention, I felt I could keep him safe.

I tapped the brace and my room was full of jellyfish. Clouds of small white jellies floating up into the corners, large blue and red ones, their tendrils drifting below as they bobbed past me. Everywhere I looked, I saw jellyfish, and I shuddered.

At school we had various codes, as I'm sure all kids do, or at least all kids that grow up to be curators. We had lots of complicated dead language codes and maths ciphers, but we also had symbolic codes for speed. These couldn't be cracked. You simply had to agree on certain words and meanings and then only you knew them. Jellyfish meant to proceed with extreme caution. Unseen danger ahead. T-Rex meant danger present. But that was less used as we were often too busy running or swearing or basically trying to extricate ourselves from whatever mess we had just got ourselves into.

From the floor of the department, Shu-hi was staring at my office. Her eyes were wide as she coughed, and Fuad and Hinks followed her glance. God knows what they made of it. Maybe they simply filed it under mad things curators do now and then. Other crazy things I had done in the past few months had been to drink my coffee from the wrong mug, drink my coffee at the wrong time of day, wear orange and pink together, doodle, make paper aeroplanes, fail to organise my notepads, sign my name with a flourish and sneeze on a Tuesday.

One of those was made up, but you'd never know which one.

They lived their lives differently to me. A room full of holographic jellyfish was just another thing.

What had Ramin discovered? What danger lay ahead? I had been spending all my free time at work, or in Minju's company, and I hadn't discovered a thing. I was certain it had something to do with the Art Foundation, as that occupied most of her time, but every time I visited everything seemed above board. In fact, it was incredible. There was such a wonderful buzz about the place. It was giving people something to talk about and visit as it was being constructed. School trips were a daily feature as it rose up, and the builders and architects were glowing with pride. And who could blame them? As each building connected to the next, and the glass walls and walkways spread out, it was clear this would be a new step forward in modern design.

Perhaps this was Minju's goal? Maybe she was done with skulduggery, and would actually focus on something positive? Or maybe she had simply been conning me over these past months? Ramin's jellyfish suggested I had been hoodwinked.

Jellyfish meant I was in imminent danger. Had he sent a shoal of krill, it would have meant he was the one at risk. We'd tried to think of something that was always in danger and went with the bottom of the food chain. So, if this was a warning rather than a call for help, it could wait. I knew I was in a dangerous situation. Now I needed to work out how to meet him without Minju listening in. I didn't even want our locations to overlap. I switched the hologram off. Tomorrow, there was a gala down by the lake. I knew Ramin was likely to be there, as were thousands of others. It was also a good place to disengage the brace.

269

Amongst huge crowds, the fine tuning could become blurred. It was the perfect location to talk to him. Relieved that I had a solution, I pulled the next stack of suggested artefacts towards me. Today we were focusing on American treasures. I'd been delaying Asia. That list was overwhelming and several of my favourites were on it.

My brace pinged again. I sincerely hoped it wasn't more jellyfish. Instead, it was a summons to call on the pharaoh at my earliest convenience. Any time within the next five minutes.

Whatever Ramin had discovered, Minju knew. It couldn't be a coincidence. I pushed my chair back and took a deep breath. Was this the end? Was it jellyfish or krill?

As I walked into the main office, Fuad cleared his throat. 'Archivist Salah, about the jellyfish?'

I shook my head. 'I was just trying out a new meditation technique, but I'm not sure. What do you think?'

The others joined him as he shook his head vigorously. 'Oh no, much too distracting.'

I smiled. I quite liked these three. I'd even let Hinks teach me how to knit, although it had been touch and go at the beginning when I remarked knitting needles made excellent weapons.

'I'm just popping over to see the pharaoh. I shouldn't be long. Whilst I'm gone, can I ask why the Sangorski book isn't in the American art file?'

They stared at each other and then quickly returned to their desks to investigate why it hadn't made the cut.

As I arrived, Ludo Bianco was leaving the building whistling. He ran up to a crowd of sightseers and offered to take their photos, then managed to include himself in a bunch of them. After that, he hailed down a hover and set off towards Cairo. As it pulled away, the hover glittered and the crowd below cheered. Little wonder, golden glitter was a very expensive celebration. The people below had just had their personal accounts credited with nights out galore. My heart sank further as I proceeded towards Minju's offices.

This time there were even more guards present, but they waved me through. Minju was dressed in full ceremonial robes. Braids hung from the black epaulettes, and her white tail stood out against the blue silk gown.

'Archivist Salah, I have some disturbing news. Please.'

She pointed to a chair as she returned to her own and sat. Her face was severe and her tail was swinging. As she caught me looking, her tail stilled, but I knew it was an act. I made a show of turning away and took my seat.

271

'First, I have to know the nature of your communication with Ramin Gamal just now.'

I paused and wiped my palms on my legs. For Minju to reveal her hand like this, something was changing. I was done with subtlety.

'What do you mean by monitoring my calls? This is strictly forbidden.' I jumped up from the chair and paced back and forth. 'You have no right to listen in on my calls. You—'

'We aren't listening in on your calls. We're keeping tabs on persons of suspicion. And this morning, just after a security breach, one of them called you. Now…' She had remained seated the whole time I had stormed back and forth. 'What was the meaning of a jellyfish hologram?'

I stared at her blankly, then came to a halt. 'You're monitoring Ramin?'

She nodded her head slowly, watching me carefully. 'Now, please sit down and explain the jellyfish?'

I returned to my seat. She might be lying. I was certain she was monitoring me, but for now her focus was Ramin. I had to play along and see what I could do to protect him.

'It's a joke. We used to throw them at each other during basic training for a laugh. We haven't been talking much these past few months. I think this was his way of trying to say hi.'

'And why haven't you been in touch? You and Ramin have been close, as you say, since childhood. What has been the nature of your rift?'

'There is no rift. I just wanted some time to myself,' I mumbled, sounding pathetic even to my own ears. 'Wait. Did you call him a person of suspicion?'

'Since the Battle of the Gods, the authorities have been monitoring the population for further signs of disturbance. Hundreds of lives were lost that day, Neith.'

'But Ramin had the triangle glyph.'

'And? Who says people can't change their nature? Who knows how those events played out in an individual's mind? Maybe they thought the government handled things badly? Perhaps they think they can do a better job? Even now, your friend could be planning to overthrow the elected democracy and run things their way.'

'That's nonsense. Ramin would never do that.'

'Really? So why has he been communicating with traitors? Why has he been trying to access state funds through back channels? This morning he was found with classified documents, and the first thing he did was try to access further classified files.'

This was my fault. I should have found a way to warn Ramin without telling him what was happening.

'He's captain of the curators. Maybe he saw something concerning and wanted to check it out? That's what I would do.'

'Would you, though? Or would you hand the report to your superior and highlight your concerns to them? Because that's how it's supposed to work, Neith.'

'Come on Minju, you know curators are a bit different.'

Things were getting desperate if I was trying to appeal to the old buddies together network.

'I do know, and I know that many of them were at the heart of the artefacts black market trade. In fact, Ramin's partner Paul Flint was up to his eyeballs in the corruption.'

That was outrageous. Minju had been the player behind the player, and she knew the true story. Even now, I was having to play along with her game.

'He was being blackmailed! We've been through this. We were all exonerated. And Clio has been rehabilitated. Bast, Ramin had the triangle.'

I was repeating myself now, but I was desperate.

'And what does a triangle indicate, anyway?' asked Minju. 'We're to take the word of some quantum dweller? A personification called Loki, that by Julius' account is one of the greatest tricksters in the pantheon. We should believe this entity over our own legal system?'

She had a point. It would be like Loki to screw it up just for fun, but the glyphs had felt accurate.

'Do you have any idea how many people went into exile or ending, protesting their innocence?'

'Well, they would, wouldn't they?' I said.

'But what if they were right?' Minju leant forward, her face angry. 'I was hugely troubled by this action of ours. Our citizens had their rights removed in the blink of an eye, and we went along with it like colony ants.'

I had never thought about it this way. Of course, she was arguing for the criminals, but she was correct. We had ceded our authority without even blinking.

'What does Giovanetti say?'

Minju snorted. 'She deals with security, not justice. As far as she's concerned, lots of criminals were taken out of the system and that's a good thing. If some innocent people got caught up, then that's someone else's screwup. And if there are others out there that dodged a bullet, well, now she's onto them.'

Which sounded like an eerily astute assessment of Giovanetti.

'But Ramin isn't one of them. I just know.'

What the hell had he discovered?

'I'm sorry, Neith, but his behaviour has been too suspicious. He was at the heart of the Fabergé incident. Someone gave the orders to strand you and Julius in the fourteenth century, when you were recovering the *Inventio Fortunata*. Someone tipped off Grimaldi that it was time to stage a coup. On each occasion Ramin was loitering on the edges.'

'But so was I! So were you!'

Minju paused and sat back in her chair, studying me closely. I knew I was floundering, and suggesting outright that she could have been behind things was a dangerous claim for me to make, but I was panicking. Ramin was in Minju's sights, and I needed to deflect her.

'Neith, you're being irrational. Your own life was compromised several times and, as much as I would love to save Ramin, I was an archivist at the time. I had no access to any of the systems that Ramin had at hand.'

'But he's innocent,' I wailed. My tone of voice had become desperate, and I couldn't see a way to save him. Minju was holding all the cards.

'And we will give him time and space to prove it. Unlike other citizens, we will ensure he gets a full and public trial.'

'Then I will stand by his side and argue in his defence.'

'And damage yourself in the process?' She looked at me sadly. 'I had hoped for more. The country sees you as the way forward. Changes are coming, and I wanted you to help reassure the population that everything will be fine. If you stand by a convicted traitor, how can I have you by my side?'

And how could I stop her plans from a distance? I tried to think of a compromise. That she was preparing to remove Ramin from the board suggested her plans were gearing up. I had to remain on side. Was this the moment when I could finally get her to trust me and confide in what she was doing?

'Okay. Let me make a deal. Put him under a quiet house arrest. Call it sick leave or a sabbatical. Keep his name free of suspicion. Monitor him constantly, but don't prepare a trial.'

'But isn't a court case better?' asked Minju, surprised.

'No, we've seen how evidence is fabricated. I won't have his name dragged through the mud again.'

This was ridiculous. I wanted to scream at her that she was the one fabricating the bloody evidence, but then she'd just get rid of me as well.

'He won't be happy. He'll want his day in court.'

'Well, he'll just have to cope,' I said. She pursed her lips together, thinking through options.

'Maybe he'll cope better with it if he hears it coming from you.'

'What?'

That wasn't going to happen. Was she mad? There was no way I was going to tell my oldest friend he was fired and under suspicion of being an enemy of Egypt.

'Yes. That would work,' she mused, and I swore to myself. I had danced into a corner.

277

'You shall be the one to tell him he is placed under concealed arrest and charge him with crimes against the state.'

'I can't do that. I'm an archivist. I don't have the authority.'

'Good point.' She tapped the intercom. 'Please draw up the necessary press release. I am appointing Neith Salah as my Special Adviser, with full custodian powers.'

My blood froze.

'You need to go now, Neith. I know this feels brutal, but I trust you to do the right thing. Not for me, not for your friend, but for your fellow citizens and your country. Go now. If he is still in post in one hour, I will send a troop of red custodians.'

I controlled my face, trying to mask my fury. With a curt nod, I stood up and left her offices. As I walked towards the quantum facility, two red custodians followed me.

'What are you doing?'

'Orders. We are here to protect you, Special Adviser Salah.'

I glared but continued across the plaza. I would deal with them later. First, I had to save Ramin.

Chapter Thirty - November: Alpha: Neith

My escorts were drawing attention as I approached Ramin's office. No doubt that was all part of the plan. Spread concern wherever I went. Idly, I wondered who Minju would replace Ramin with, and then realised I'd already seen him celebrating on his way to Cairo. Ludo Bianco was the perfect puppet for Minju to have in place running the step. With Sam on sabbatical, she had unfettered access to whatever she wanted. But what exactly was that?

Heading into the facility, I was greeted with smiles that quickly slid off faces as the two custodians came into view. Ignoring any greetings, I strode through the building. I knocked on his door and my heart sank as I heard Ramin's cheerful tones call out. I was coming to destroy him and he was smiling. Walking into his office, I felt my stomach heave as he jumped up and rushed around the desk to give me a huge hug. It was only when he saw the custodians that his smile wavered.

'You two wait outside,' I said.

'Our orders—'

'Balls to your orders. I am Neith Salah and in a fight I could destroy you. And if you tried to rise up, Ramin Gamal would finish you off. Wait outside.'

They looked at each other and then decided on the smarter course, pulling the door closed behind them. I knew Minju was monitoring everything, so now I had to put on a performance of a lifetime.

'Ramin Gamal, you are under arrest for espionage and crimes against the state.'

Ramin took a step backwards, blinking rapidly. 'Neith, are you drunk?'

I ignored him and carried on in a monotone. Determined that no distress should affect my vocals. 'You will go to trial in due course. But for now, your reputation is to be upheld, so long as you remain silent and do and say no more to jeopardise your future and the security of this country.'

'Neith, the jellyfish were for you, not—'

I cut him off. This was exactly what I was worried about. That he may unwittingly reveal what he had discovered. It was clear that he didn't realise his office was bugged.

'I know. But I'm not a child anymore, Ramin, I don't need silly holos sent to cheer me up. What next? A cobra?'

Cobra had been our ultimate keyword. It meant death is imminent. We used it on the rarest of occasions. In pretend situations or potential expulsions. It never meant this is high risk, or anything vague. It meant your next step could be your last. Choose wisely. We treated it as our most solemn code word. Now I prayed he remembered. Nothing gave him away that he noted my words, but then he was Ramin, a brilliant curator. I knew Minju would look for anything out of the ordinary.

'But you can't arrest me. I've done nothing wrong. Neith, you have to—'

'Enough!' I rubbed my brace and hoped to Bast that he saw what I was doing. 'I don't want to be involved in whatever moonshine you have cooked up. You're facing treason for espionage. Do not drag anyone else into this. If you speak to anyone, they will receive the same treatment.'

'And you're okay with this?'

'With you destroying all that we've been trying to achieve these past few months. Pharaoh Chen has been working day and night to try to fix things. To build a better society, today. Leading us into the future, securing us from the past.'

Even listening to her slogans was making me retch, but I had to shut Ramin up.

'But Neith—'

'One more word and I will call the custodians in to gag you. Is that clear enough for you?' I was gripping my brace so hard I thought it would crack.

Ramin's face flushed red and his eyes shone. I had never seen him so distressed or so angry. His brace pinged and an override message began to broadcast.

'Ramin Gamal, you are placed under quiet arrest, whilst you await trial. An advocate shall be assigned when the date is decided. Until then, you are to speak to no one of your recent activities or enquiries. If you do so, you will be ended without trial.'

I gasped. The carpet had been well and truly pulled from under my feet.

'Tiresias. There is no law that permits this.'

Ramin and I stared at each other in horror. I was trying to save Ramin, but even I didn't know how high the stakes had become.

'Pharaoh Chen has just signed an executive order that was ratified by the assembly. It was broadcast fifteen minutes ago.'

That's why she was all dressed up. She was making an address to the nation, and I had played into her hands and delivered up Ramin.

'Ramin. I know you are innocent. I will advocate for you.'

In that moment, all my intentions fell apart. I didn't care about Minju, I didn't care about society. Staring at Ramin, I realised that sometimes no matter how big the picture, it was the tiny detail that counted. I wasn't a hero. I didn't save societies, but I never ever abandoned my friends. All I cared about was saving Ramin.

'Incorrect, Special Adviser Salah. Advocates may not be known to the accused,' said Tiresias.

'Since when?'

'Today. It is part of Pharaoh Chen's New Dawn act.'

I had watched Ramin's expression choke as he heard my new title, and some of the fight left his face and was replaced with betrayal.

I took a deep breath. 'Say nothing. Do nothing. It's the only way to stay safe. I will get to the bottom of this. Let me walk you back to your apartment.'

'I'd rather you didn't.' He all but spat the words at me.

'If I walk with you, everyone will presume the custodians are there for me. Not actually escorting you.'

He blinked once and then stood up and grabbed his bag. He placed a framed image of himself and Xandro climbing a mountain into it. Next to it sat a picture of all of us in a bar. Jack and Sabrina were chasing shots, Julius was laughing into the camera and I was leaning on Ramin, his arm slung around me. He watched me as he picked up the picture and slowly tore it in half, throwing my image in the bin. Without taking his eyes from mine, he placed the picture and one or two other pieces into his bag. Then, sealing it, he strode out of the office, leaving me and the custodians to catch up with him.

Chapter Thirty-One
November: Alpha: Neith

The following day, I woke in despair. Ramin had come closer to finding out Minju's schemes than I had, and it had cost him his career. I dared not ask him what he had uncovered, in case it cost his life as well, but I could feel things slipping away from me. I truly believed Minju now trusted me, but at what cost? All I had achieved was a list of artefacts that could potentially be returned to Beta and alienated all my friends.

I was failing. It was a bitter pill, but I couldn't do this by myself and yet I had no other option. I was a woman of action. As team leader, I co-ordinated everyone's efforts. I relied on others in the team for their insights and intel. Ramin, with his ability to see the long game, Julius' ability to out-think the opponent. Clio for her instincts. My skill was leading, but with no one to lead, I was adrift. All I had was action. Until I knew what Minju was about, I had nothing.

I had just finished my morning exercises when Minju requested I come in to see her early. I had been planning for an extended meditation session, but instead placed my brace on my wrist and headed in to work. Whatever Minju's plan was, she hadn't revealed it yet, although I was pretty convinced that banishing

Julius had been the first step. Cleeve's assassination was the second. Then the purges began. Sam was gone, Githumbi was gone, Clio was gone, although I doubted Minju had anything to do with that. I imagined my onetime best friend was making trouble somewhere.

Now Ramin was under house arrest, and still I didn't know what Minju's plans were. I was certain Minju was holding him in place for something. I wondered if her constant discussions about the pharaoh's assassination meant she was lining him up to be the fall guy. Or using him as leverage over me. Because she had to know, if push came to shove, and shove came to blows, that I would stand side by side with Ramin, taking down the whole bloody structure. I still hadn't worked out what her end goal was, though. Most of her attention was focused on the new Arts Foundation. The speed of the build was astonishing, but given the amount of money being thrown at it, that was hardly surprising.

Every other broadcast either rejoiced in how great and creative we were, or urged viewers not to be scared of the terrifying reality: multiple universes all poised to attack. 'Pharaoh Minju and her dashing team will protect you from the monsters.'

I couldn't see how the Arts Foundation fitted into all this. What were we going to do, paint them to death?

I noticed my stride had become sharper and, judging by the way people were avoiding me, I was frowning. I desperately missed Julius and Ramin. I wanted them by my side, all of us working as a team, but had to cope alone. Letting people see I was unhappy was foolish. I slowed down and tried to whistle. Deciding I sounded like an idiot, I made the rest of the journey in silence, smiling at the occasional passer-by and stopping for a few photographs. Over the past month, the questions I was asked had moved away from my exploits to those of Minju. Did I really know her? Had she really been prepared to fight to the death for her exhibits? Was she just like Captain Janeway? I asked them if they had seen *Alien* yet? There was some emphatic nodding as they pictured Minju as Ripley. Imagery that slayed me. Neat, fastidious, elegant Minju as Ripley. Besides which, I was thinking of The Bitch.

I activated the photos into holos and waved to the tourists. I was an hour early, but as soon as I entered the building, my brace beeped and, instead of her office, I headed towards the central meeting room as requested. The double doors slid open as I approached. The room was dim, but as I walked in light shone down as the doors slid closed behind me.

'Sweet Bast!'

The horror in my voice was clear, and my second skin instantly slid across my entire frame. In front of me on a raised dais stood Minju and, standing in a line behind her, stood six Roman soldiers in full armour.

The man standing beside her was another Roman. Behind all of them hung a line of floor to ceiling pennants akin to a Beta dictatorship.

At my utterance, the Roman's hand had gone to the pommel of his sword. I moved my feet into a combat pose and noticed that the six men also minutely adjusted their stance as well. I noticed they also had lasers on their belt clips but still favoured the sword. That would be their undoing.

Seven Roman soldiers against one curator. One curator whose oldest friend no longer spoke to her, whose lifetime partner was a murdering traitor, and whose ersatz brother had been permanently banished. I was in the mood for a fight and I didn't rate their chances.

'Neith, it's okay.'

I watched Minju's face change from pride to alarm as she tapped the soldier on the arm, muttered to him, and rushed down the steps towards me. The soldier followed her, but she turned round.

'Gaius Cinna Sulla. Are you deaf? Do you question me? Neith Salah can be trusted with my life.'

That was another bet I wouldn't make, but I relaxed my position a little. I noticed they did the same. It would be fair to say that the tension in the room was far from laid back.

'Neith.' Minju was standing in front of me. 'It's okay, they are here to protect me. This is my new personal bodyguard.'

'Minju.' I paused. This was momentous. 'They look like Romans. Real Romans. Not Alphas dressed up.'

I felt panicky. I was almost certainly in the presence of real Beta warriors. It wasn't who they were that worried me, but what the hell they were doing here? These were not angels. And if they weren't, then what in Great Ra's name were they?

'It's too much, isn't it?' She patted me on the arm. 'Let's return to my office and discuss it.'

I let her lead me towards the door when three of the soldiers overtook us and led the way down the corridor, the other four bringing up the rear. As we walked along the building, a few early workers gasped and we had to stop several times to reassure people that everything was okay.

Some joker by the coffee pots called out '*Salvete!*' and people began to relax. There were even a few nervous laughs, as the ancient Roman greeting was called out. And there was me, right in the middle of it, presumably adding my endorsement to this display.

We entered her room and she dismissed the soldiers to her outer office. Even their captain, who eyed me narrowly as he left the room. I reckon I could still take him out in a fight, but I knew when I was standing in front of a hardened warrior and one who wouldn't seek to delay or stun. He would simply kill and move on.

'Pharaoh Chen. What on Earth are they?'

By now Minju was pouring hot water into a tea pot and adding leaves. The scent of bergamot filled the air. Julius' s favourite. I was momentarily distracted, which I imagined was Minju's intention.

'Minju, the Romans. They are Romans, aren't they? Real ones. Not any of our lot in fancy dress.'

She brought the tea tray over to the low table and beckoned me to join her. I sat down and resolved to say nothing more until she explained herself.

'Was my display over the top?' she said, pouring the tea. 'I do apologise. I thought you might appreciate the drama, but I can see now that I took the wrong approach.'

'Minju. They're Romans. How?'

She took a sip from her cup and waved at me to do the same. I drank and smiled sadly.

'I miss him as well, you know,' murmured Minju with genuine remorse. 'I'm just so grateful we could save him. Return him home before people associated him with the War of the Gods.'

It had nothing to do with me, but I had noticed that the narrative had been changed and was beginning to twist. Very gently, Julius was being forced back into the role of dangerous Beta, rather than a valued member of our society. However, Minju knew Julius was my weak spot. She was stalling.

'The Romans, Minju?'

She sighed and placed her cup on the table. A tendril of steam rose into the air and wavered as she sighed deeply.

'They are the price I have to pay to be pharaoh.' She shook her head sadly and I decided to play along.

'But you didn't want to be pharaoh?'

'I know. I said it was too great a responsibility. I said I didn't have the skills. I said I feared being killed.' She took a sip of tea and continued, observing me. 'Do you remember when I told you I would only become pharaoh if the committee could guarantee my safety?'

I nodded.

'Well, they assured me I could have as many red custodians as I wanted to protect me. I said I wouldn't do it even if I had a single Roman soldier. Then they said, what, just one? And I said, well maybe a few more, as a joke.' Her eyes were wide. 'You have to understand I was joking, but they said that was acceptable and suddenly there I was agreeing to be pharaoh. I mean, I could hardly say no to them after that, could I?'

I shook my head emphatically, agreeing with her. Clever little Minju. They didn't stand a chance.

'But I still don't understand where you found a bunch of Romans.'

Minju took another drink as she continued to study the city below. The silence stretched out until she put her cup down. 'I can trust you, can't I, Neith?'

I looked her in the eye. 'With your life.'

She paused again. I still didn't know if she did actually trust me. I mean, I suspected that Minju Chen trusted no one, but did she still doubt my memory?

'Good. Well, it's about time you knew, anyway.' She settled back into her chair. 'Switch your brace off, would you? I never really trust them.'

I placed the brace reluctantly on the table. I was wearing my skins, and had done ever since the assassination. It was rare for a curator to be wearing skins on Alpha outside of training, but I didn't know what Minju was planning. Now, with a bunch of squaddies in the next room, I felt even more exposed, but I nodded in agreement and placed the brace on the table. I had a blade strapped to my thigh and darts on my upper arms, plus two wow-bangs concealed in my hairband. They should buy me a few seconds.

I leant back and nodded at her to proceed. My face, the model apprentice. Waiting to learn at the feet of the master.

'We've been bringing Betas back through the step.'

I spluttered on my tea and leant forward. I must have shouted because Gaius ran into the room. I jumped up, but Minju waved us both back into our positions. Gaius and I stared at each other. I was

291

impressed with the speed that such a big man had got to her side. He had also not attacked me, meaning he had properly assessed I was not a threat. At that moment. From his stance though he hadn't fully discounted me. Mind you, the way he was looking around suggested he viewed the entire universe as a threat.

As he retired to the outer room, Minju cleared her throat.

'Well, I do seem to be startling you today, my dear. I apologise. Ever since the War of the Gods, it was Pharaoh Cleeve's great concern that we were incredibly vulnerable to attack. Not just from our own people, but from other Earths as well. You yourself discovered that there aren't just two Earths, but a multitude, and many of them more powerful than we are.'

'But they've never bothered us before. And how does bringing Betas over here help us?'

'I said exactly the same thing to Nolyny, but she determined we were at risk. And we needed warriors trained in combat.'

'So, you just went back to ancient Rome and grabbed a bunch of soldiers?'

'Not a bit of it.' She leant forward and puffed out her chest. 'These are the Ninth Legion. Or what's left of them.'

I shook my head. We didn't study the Romans at school very much and, until recently, they hadn't figured in our popular culture. As a curator, I had never stepped back to ancient Rome.

'The Ninth! Neith, this is Britain's missing legion. An entire Roman legion travelled up to defend Hadrian's Wall and was never heard from again. In fact, it was Julius that gave me the idea. When he and Clio returned with the two princes, I realised I could maybe retrieve the ninth without upsetting the timeline. This was meant to be.'

I was speechless. Minju had a platoon of Romans as a personal bodyguard that she had transported to her side, and presumably the general council was fine with all this. Julius had said we were sleepwalking into our own nightmare and I finally understood what he meant.

'Captain,' Minju called out, and the Roman walked into the room.

'Please introduce yourself.'

The soldier turned towards me. 'I am Gaius Sulla.'

'Ask him anything,' said Minju. 'We have no secrets in this room. Special Adviser Neith is my valued colleague. You may trust her with anything.'

I imagined the minute I left the room she would tell him not to trust me an inch. A dog could only have one master and his was a leopard.

'Tell me, centurion. Are you happy?' I was having trouble calling him captain, everything about him screamed his Roman lineage. His lip curled as I continued to speak.

'I am trying to assess if your human rights have been violated,' I said. 'We treat the removal of angels with great care, and you are not our typical angel.'

'I am a soldier, not an angel. When the Empress arrived, she fought by our side, attacking the tribes. We were down to our last contubernium, and she made me an offer. Now, my men are saved. We are away from that stinking British latrine. We have a new mission. The sun is warm and our bellies are full. Yes. We are happy.'

He had a point. I turned my attention back to Minju. 'How did you get them back? Weren't you worried about splicing?'

'I took a box full of braces. Plus, Jack has been working on the splice effects. I think you and I will be amongst the last generation to suffer from splices. Clio was a recent benefactor of this. As were the two princes.'

That was a good thing, but I wondered if Chen was planning on bringing over more people? I would have to ask Jack, whose idea it had been to work on the splice effects.

'Centurion, you are a Roman. How are you, knowing Rome is no longer the great empire it was and you are now sworn to protect a female with a tail?'

Minju's tail twitched and I raised a hand. 'I am sorry, Minju, but I don't trust him with your safety. He's a Roman!'

'There is no Rome anymore. Now there is Empress Chen.'

'Pharaoh Chen,' I corrected.

He shrugged his shoulders. What did a title matter? Power was power. Minju had been running the show for years and barely anyone knew her name beyond the quantum facility.

She sipped her tea again and dismissed Gaius.

'Really, Neith. His simplicity is what I trust. I am his leader. He is a soldier. He will follow my orders. Woman or not, tail or not.' She said the last bit with a slight challenge in her voice. 'I know you view me as a frail archivist…'

I snorted, but she carried on, politely ignoring me. 'But I used to be a curator, just like you were. Until my splice removed me from active service, I excelled in quantum missions. If my country now asks me to step forward in its hour of need, how can I say no?' She looked at me fiercely. 'What would you do?'

A shiver ran down my spine. I finally understood the depth of her motivation. She wasn't doing this for money or power. She wasn't doing this for recognition or glory.

Minju Chen was doing this because she believed in it. The passionate conviction of a patriot.

I shuddered.

Chapter Thirty-Two - November: Alpha: Neith

Two nights later, I sat and stared at the wall. It was getting to be my routine. Minju was building a new world order and everyone was blind to it. Julius had once explained to me that if you put a frog in hot water, it would jump straight out, but if you put it in a pan of cold water and slowly heated it up, it would stay in the water and die. At the time, I had been astonished. What sort of culture dreamt up ways to torture frogs? I was so transfixed on the society that thinks like that, that I had utterly failed to grasp the message behind the story. Minju was boiling us alive.

There was a knock at the door and I got up carefully, grabbing my laser from the bench. It was unusual for Tiresias not to announce a visitor, and I wondered if a centurion had been dispatched to assassinate me. An assassin that knocked. Right. I was losing my marbles.

I cracked the door open and saw Sabrina Mulweather with her finger on her lips staring at me. I stared back, and for a few seconds we looked at each other in silence until she lost her patience and waved at me to get out of her way. I was going to speak, but she shook her head fiercely and banged her finger on her lips, three times quickly in succession. Opening the door wider, she slipped inside, stood in a corner, and gestured at me to obscure my windows.

I did as she bid and turned to see that she had now moved to the middle of the room and was tapping away on her brace. She then opened her bag and handed a new brace to me. It appeared identical to my existing one. She pantomimed that I should place it on my wrist and then remove my current one. Once my old brace was sitting on the counter, she brought out a small pen-like device and, placing it against the old brace, clicked a button. The light on my old brace switched off at the same moment that my new brace lit up, and Sabrina let out a deep sigh.

'You have to save Jack.'

'Again?'

She burst into tears and I felt dreadful.

'I'm sorry, you caught me by surprise.'

I had no idea what she was doing, but I couldn't risk her talking to me and saying something that might get back to Minju. 'If you have concerns about his whereabouts, you should report them to the proper authorities.'

She did a double take and then shook her head. 'It's okay. Your new brace isn't recording. It's synthesised your average noise routines for the past five nights and is now running an augmented soundscape of what you'd be up to if I wasn't here. It's also blocking any remote listening devices. As is mine.'

'Did Jack—'

'Yes. He's been busy. These braces appear identical, but send dummy information back to Tiresias. You can also switch the locator device off, as I have, but don't do it too often, just now and then. It will register you as being at a location within a few metres or a few miles, depending on your setting.'

The sudden sense of freedom made me giddy, but for her sake I still needed to be cautious. I headed to the fridge and grabbed some beers.

'Do you have any wine?'

I rolled my eyes, but returned with an Italian white that Julius liked. In fact, the only wines I had were for guests. There was even a bottle of Merovingian that I had bought as a treat for Julius. I hoped he would understand, I doubt he'd approve.

'Why does Jack need saving? And why is he making covert braces?'

She wiped her eyes, and I wondered if she was always crying, then tried not to be churlish. It was easy to forget with her love of silly shoes and fancy frocks and her desire to be the teacher's pet that she was also a very brave, intelligent and resourceful curator. Who was dating our society's finest engineer. I checked her rings and was relieved to not see a pledge band. I had isolated myself from everyone. I wouldn't have been surprised if I hadn't been invited to their nuptials. As it was, I was caught off guard by how relieved I was.

She took a sip of wine and then looked for a coaster to place her glass on. I shook my head and she sighed, pulling a napkin from her bag and placing it on the counter. I wasn't sure what one more stain would have done, but that was Sabrina for you. Always living by her standards, not yours.

'He's been working away a lot. At the beginning, he was really excited. He said what he was doing was revolutionary. Naturally, he wouldn't tell me any details.'

'Did you get any hints?'

'I didn't ask!'

I clenched my teeth. This was the closest I had got to discovering what was going on, but Sabrina was having a fit of the privates. If Jack was working on something in secret, I bet Minju knew about it. This could be the break I had been looking for. When I had spoken to him in his house just after Julius had been repatriated, he had been concealing something. Why the hell hadn't I pursued that avenue of investigation? Before I could berate myself any further, I reminded myself that he was an engineer and engineers shared nothing.

'Carry on.'

'But recently he was becoming quiet, irritable. He started doing odd things. And then he gave me this.' She waved her brace at me.

'So he thought someone was spying on him? Did he say who?'

She shook her head.

I hissed. 'Bast, Sabrina. Why didn't you ask?'

She glared at me, then her face crumpled. 'I did! But he said he didn't know, plus he didn't want me to know as he was trying to protect me.'

Nubi's balls. What was he thinking? Sabrina was brilliant. She could have helped him.

'Then a few weeks ago, he got really anxious. He was having nightmares. He kept shouting, *Not Grimaldi*. I suggested he go back to therapy, but he just laughed. He was losing weight and stopped sleeping. Two days ago, he didn't come home.'

Two days ago, Ramin had been arrested for something he discovered, and Minju had introduced a swathe of new laws and punishments for the protection of Egypt's citizens.

'Have you reported it?'

'Of course I've bloody reported it.' She knocked back her glass and held it out for a refill. 'I was told he was working on a project and would be home in a few weeks.'

I didn't like the sound of this and I could see why Sabrina was freaking out, but I hoped she was exaggerating the issue.

'So, why are you so worried?'

'Because he told me if he ever failed to come home and not send a message, then I was to understand he was being held against his will. An engineer! With no court or governance.'

I thought of Ramin, imprisoned without process, and wondered how many more there were.

'Okay, but why come to me?'

'Because Jack said I could trust you and Ramin, and that was it. And I can't get hold of Ramin.'

I groaned. I needed to find out what had happened to Jack. But how could I do it without alerting Minju, and keep Sabrina out of things?

'I've been studying the employment records and you've been working nonstop for weeks,' said Sabrina. 'You can request a day off and go investigating.'

'You did what?'

I was horrified at her stupidity. If I requested a day off, it would look suspicious to a woman like Minju. She might start investigating who else was interested in me.

'Are you insane? Jack warns you he is being watched and that something is wrong with the system and you go and pull up my work files!'

'No, Neith Salah. I am not insane. Pharaoh Chen released a press report yesterday praising you and your team for your unstinting efforts to get a list of artefacts to be announced on the Arts Foundation launch day.

It's public knowledge and no traceable search was undertaken.'

She glared at me and I shrugged, annoyed with myself for under-estimating her.

'Right, you clearly think I'm over-reacting, but I'm not. Jack said something was wrong and I believe him. I want him back and I don't know where to begin. He said with you, but clearly that was a mistake.'

She knocked back her glass again and stood. 'I'd be grateful if you didn't mention my visit to anyone.'

She picked up her miniature valise that matched her shoes. The holograms jumped from boots to bag and back again. She had set them to autumn leaves to match the weather. I remembered when Clio used to add holographic fish to our fingernails. Life had seemed so innocent back then.

'No, look.' I paused. I didn't know how much to say. 'Jack's my friend. If you're worried about him, I'll start digging around. But in the meantime, don't do anything else, okay?'

Something in my tone clearly tipped her off as she sat back down again.

'You think something's wrong as well, don't you? Shit. Sorry, I didn't mean to be vulgar. But you do, don't you? I came in here full of worries and forgot to assess the room. You know something.'

This is what happens when you underestimate curators. They take your legs out. There was no point prevaricating. She was trained to spot lies. I wondered how much longer Minju thought she could hold out before people started to question what she was doing. Her concealed past was becoming less of an issue when her present-day actions were causing concern.

Was this Minju's plan? Try to become what? A dictator before anyone objected. And to what end? She was already a beloved ruler. What more did she want? She said she wanted to protect us, but wasn't she already doing that? Her new Arts Foundation was making people feel good. But I knew there was more to it than that. I decided to go with half-truths and see if I could shield Sabrina from Minju's true nature.

'Okay yes, I've felt something was off for a while and frankly, I'm relieved that Jack thought so as well. So I am going to find him and then talk to him about it.'

'And what shall I do?'

'Nothing. Talk to no one. Don't discuss this with anyone.'

'And if you disappear?'

Bast, I did not like that question.

'Shall I go and warn the pharaoh?'

'No!'

'Oh sweet Ra, do you think she's at risk? We can't handle another security breach. Is that why you've been working so closely with her? To protect her?'

I took a really deep glug of beer and nodded.

'Yes. I'm trying to protect her. So do not approach her under any circumstance. We don't want to tip off whoever is behind Jack's concerns.'

Sabrina's face went still and her eyes lost focus. I watched as she ran something through her mind. She eyed her brace carefully as her breath caught. The blood drained from her face and she steadied herself against the counter.

'It's Chen, isn't it? You think Pharoah Chen is behind Jack's disappearance. Only she would have the clearance to monitor all movements. Jack wasn't worried about another outsider, was he? He was worried about her! That's it, isn't it? Are you mad? Have you both lost your minds?'

Like I said, never underestimate a curator.

'Sabrina, I'm sure you're right, I've lost my mind. But just play along and say nothing to anyone. And don't approach Ramin. He's under silent house arrest.'

Her jaw fell as she tried to gather her shock. Ramin was a powerful figure in our society, not to mention well-loved. She had also fought alongside him during Grimaldi's uprising and hero-worshipped him a little. In her worldview, Ramin was gold.

'What? On whose authority.'

'Pharaoh Chen's.'

She took a deep breath.

'I've got to go. My locator disruptor shows me taking a walk. I need to make that true.'

Her face was sombre as she tried to digest what she had just deduced. I had confirmed nothing, but at least I felt she would now act without blundering.

'Regarding Jack, have you any idea where I should start looking?'

She pulled her coat around her, fastening it against the November winds, although sometimes I thought that a fool's errand. This was the start of the sandstorms, and nothing could stop the wind. Even a pretty little red and blue number with holographic leaves falling from the sleeve. Sabrina adjusted her hood.

'I have a guess. I sweep the apartment every day. A few months ago, I noticed something odd in the dust, so I began to save it.'

She kept her dirt. That was a new one on me. I suspected she was a neat freak, but this took cleanliness to the next level.

'Over the weeks, it has become more and more apparent.' She paused and looked me in the eye. 'The sand is blue.'

'Are you kidding?'

I wanted her to be wrong with all my heart. The situation was already as bad as it could be, blue sand felt like the straw that would break my back.

Sabrina's voice shook. 'No, I'm not kidding. I think Jack has been working in the Glass Wastes.'

Chapter Thirty-Three - November: Alpha: Neith

So far, my journey had been uneventful. I had hired a rental hover and said I was travelling to Kenya. I told Minju I was taking two personal days before the presentation. She seemed annoyed, but distracted. She was also out of Alexandria at the pan-African Summit. An annual event that shaped the global direction for the year ahead. I knew she was planning on inviting all the heads of state up to Alexandria for the unveiling of the Arts Foundation and wanted to ensure everything ran smoothly.

As I sped out of the city, I passed the beautiful building. The glass-spinners were finishing the domes and finials, the colours shone in the morning sun. Flocks of birds delighted in new resting spots before flying down to the city below or onwards in their migrations either north or south. My own journey was taking me south, and then as soon as I was in the mountains I would turn right and into the Sahara.

The trip to the Glass Wastes would only take two hours travelling at full pelt. Normally, for a journey of this distance, I'd have activated the auto drive function, but as the Glass Wastes was a restricted zone, there were no pre-programmed routes. As you would expect for the site of a nuclear catastrophe. Our early forays into nuclear energy had been messy. Two hundred years later, the Glass Wastes were still uninhabited. No longer poisonous to humanity, they were shunned spaces that were largely feared or ignored. I'd have to do this the old-fashioned way. I flicked over to manual.

My brace was happily passing on telemetry without telling anyone else where I was going. I had set it to display forty-eight hours in my apartment, and once again blessed Jack for his skills and cunning. I just hoped I got to him in time. I didn't think Minju would harm him. The boy was too precious, but what could she make him do?

After an hour, I received my first proximity alert, which broke up the journey. Looking down on dune after dune gets tedious after a while. I tried to entertain myself by spotting animals, but this far into the desert, the only wildlife out in the daytime was too small, and the camel trains avoided this section. I briefly wondered if I would have made a good nomad, living on my wits, focused on one task, honouring the ancient traditions. For a moment, the simplicity appealed, and then I knew I would be bored silly.

Plus, I didn't really care for camels. Never had, never would.

Quarter of an hour later, the warnings had ceased being intermittent and were now a constant drone. I had brought a radiation monitor with me, but so far levels were normal. It was to be expected. The area had been deemed safe decades ago, but still you couldn't fail to twitch. In the distance, I could see a series of double storey buildings emerging out of the mirage. We were right in the centre of the previous nuclear trials and the foundations had remained, providing a structure for these new buildings, but why were they here?

The land below was also changing. Patches of blues and greens swept through red bands, mottling the golden tones. The wind and years had shaped them into ribbons and rivers of colour. As I got closer to the point of the historic explosion, the dunes flattened out and became waves of glass. The extreme heat of the explosions had turned the sand to glass, with the initial blasts from the disaster radiating out into the desert, killing all at the site and surrounding settlements. Thousands had died instantly. Those who survived suffered lingering, painful deaths. Some of the glass waves contained the shadows of the evaporated bodies. It was a cruel and painful place of sorrow, and a reminder to the world that progress was not always positive. Two hundred years later, all had been sanitised. There had been talk of demolishing the waves, but there had been a better argument for it to remain as a monument to haste and folly. Besides which, it was in the middle of nowhere.

As I got closer, I brought the hover down towards the road that had been built to service this new facility.

My approach had been noticed, and I parked the hover and walked towards the complex, stopping as two guards in red custodians' outfits waved me to a halt.

They wore their uniforms poorly and, even from a distance, they smelled bad. Both men were heavily muscled. One was missing an ear, the other had a red puckered scar across his chin. Such disfigurements were rare, but not unheard of, although it was strange to see two side by side.

The man with the scar glared at me.

'Greetings to your—'

He made an unpleasant noise in his throat and then spat at the sand in front of him. I stepped back in disgust.' What d'you want?' he said.

'Si,' grunted his companion. 'Sod off.'

For a moment I had a strange sense of dislocation as I tried to place their accents, then remembered the last time I had heard it I was on Beta. These were late period Romans. It wasn't a time frame we visited much, but that didn't mean we didn't go. It also meant I knew how to deal with them.

I slapped my fist against my breastbone and then saluted. Like true Romans, they immediately reciprocated the gesture, then looked confused. I wondered how long they had been here.

'Step aside. I am here on orders from Pharaoh Minju Chen. I am checking up on Jack Ticona. Where is he?'

309

'We have orders—'

'Did you just contradict me?' I shouted loud enough that anyone standing on the other side of the gate would hear me.

Sure enough, the door opened, and another custodian joined us. Another Roman, so I slammed my fist against my breastplate again. And again, it worked. Ignoring the two chumps, I turned to their commander.

'I am Special Adviser Neith Salah. Do you know who I am?'

The soldier (it was hard to think of him as a custodian) curled his lip. 'I do.'

'I am here to speak to Jack Ticona. Immediately. Please escort me to him now.'

'Ticona is not to leave the compound.'

'Did I say anything about him leaving? I instructed you to take me to him. Or do I need to appoint someone else to take over your position?'

He blanched, and I imagined that life here was confusing enough already. I decided to lean into it and spoke into my brace.

'I, Neith Salah, do hereby formally announce that the new gatekeeper of the Glass Wastes shall be…' I paused and waved the man with the missing ear towards me. 'What's your name?'

His commander widened his eyes in alarm. Clearly, the idea of the one-eared oaf being appointed above him was not going to happen and he quickly relented.

'Follow me.'

He turned sharply on his heel and headed back to the gate. I followed and strode past the gates into a large compound. The buildings had all been hastily erected, and I wondered what they were all in aid of. What I hadn't been expecting was the number of people. The yard was full of people training. Some were running back and forth, others were working in drill patterns, some groups were sparring. All of them were well versed in combat, but all were men. It was an odd sight. The closest I could equate it to was a custodian's training academy, but some weird, single sex version. Where had all these men come from? I had a thousand questions, but any of them would reveal my ignorance. I just had to wait until I spoke to Jack. I was just grateful that he was still alive and capable of receiving visitors.

The buildings were set out in rectangular blocks on either side of the principal glass thoroughfare. At the far end of the compound stood one huge building. I could see it had been built into a glass wave, negating the need for a perimeter wall at this end of the compound. This was clearly our destination. As we approached, two huge blond men eyed us suspiciously. They had thick matted hair and their skin was peeling from recent sunburn. If I had to put money on it these men were Vikings. Even if they weren't, they weren't to be messed with. They were out of place and out of time.

I turned to my escort. 'What is your name?'

'Custodian Paolo, General.'

General was as a high a rank as it got before Emperor, so I decided I was happy with that.

'Why have these men not been treated for their burns?'

'We don't want your foreign magic,' laughed one of the men. 'You can flay the skin off my bones and I still won't ask for help. This is nothing.'

'You can chew on my bones and I won't say a word,' said his friend.

Custodian Paolo shrugged. 'They've only been here a week. They are still adapting. But no one could best them in a fight, so it was decided that they would guard this door.'

I was wearing my skins and was certain that I could probably beat them. Vikings were easy. They were all strength and fury. Speed and agility would put a berserker on his back within a minute. But why were they here? Minju seemed to be gathering her own private army.

The guy with the peeling nose looked at me and laughed. 'Are you looking for a fight, little ant?'

'If I were, I would look for a more worthy opponent.' I spoke without malice and was pleased when he laughed.

'Okay, little ant. I will give you the first strike.'

It was tempting. I could do with blowing off some steam, but I needed to see Jack and find out what the hell was going on. I was about to reply when my flesh tingled. A wave of sensations ran through me. No one else had reacted, but why would they? They hadn't been attuned to this occurrence. I was standing in the vicinity of a quantum step machine powering up. I stared at the three men in horror, and the penny finally dropped. These men hadn't been smuggled in through the step machine at Alexandria. They had arrived here, in the desert where, incredibly, against all laws, we had a second step machine.

Chapter Thirty-Four - November: Alpha: Neith

I sprinted towards the door, my heart pounding in my chest. Paolo lunged at me, but was thrown backwards with a cry of pain as my skins delivered an electric charge. I knew I only had a few seconds before my armour would recharge, so I dropped to my knees and prepared to defend myself.

The taller of the two blond men laughed at me and advanced, but I was ready for him. With a quick movement, I slammed my fist into his groin, causing him to double over in pain. As he fell, I seized the wrist of his companion, who was reaching down to grab me. Using his momentum against him, I pulled him to the ground. Jumping up, I span around and delivered a powerful punch to the back of his head.

I knew I had to be careful not to kill these men, but also needed to get past them. As they lay groaning at my feet, I caught my breath and looked around for any other threats. Seeing none, I ran to the door.

Inside was a large, well-lit empty hangar. Red lights were flashing, and in the distance, I could see a big white wall shimmering. This was a far bigger step than the one I was used to, and there was also no barrier. Was that because this one was safer, or because no one cared here? What in the hell was Minju doing?

'Special Adviser Salah?'

A middle-aged man walked towards me blinking rapidly, as he pushed his glasses back up his nose. An engineer if ever I saw one. No doubt the scar was fake, another eccentric affectation. Which made me think of the custodians who had stopped me on arrival. Those scars hadn't seemed affected, they had felt earnt.

'My name is Tybalt Jones. I am in charge of this facility. We weren't expecting you.'

'The pharaoh has a message she wants relayed to Jack.'

'Oh.' He looked me up and down dismissively. 'Well, he's engaged at the moment, but if you would like to give me the message, I will see he gets it.'

The silence between us stretched out. He was Alpha through and through and going along with whatever Minju was up to. This man was my enemy. But sadly, not one I could punch, as tempting as that felt. Crap, I would have given anything to have Clio by my side at this moment.

'Are you stupid?' I asked slowly. 'Do you think I travelled all this sodding way just to pass on a message to some jumped up shit sweeper?'

I was still reeling from the evidence of a second quantum stepper and was having to work fast to avoid revealing my ignorance.

'Do you know who I am?'

'Yes,' I lied. 'I've read your file and quite frankly, talking to you is a waste of my time. You won't be in your post much longer based on your current performance. You aren't even capable of carrying out a simple task. Now where is Jack?'

Verbal punches were often just as satisfying. Clio didn't agree, but a perfectly landed sentence could deliver awesome results and a feeling of joy. As his face flushed, I smiled. Snapping his fingers, he turned sharply on his heel and I followed him to the operations zone.

As we got closer, I could see he was skirting the outer ring of the step, so at least there was a certain level of common sense in place. Over at the wall, five people stepped into the surface and vanished. The sirens stopped and my skin returned to normal. I noticed the operations unit was behind sealed glass. Some people were more valuable than others, then.

Even from this distance, Jack looked haggard. He glanced up and saw me, but didn't react, returning to his screen and checking on the various readouts. When he appeared satisfied, I saw him mention something to the other operatives in the room and they all turned to observe us.

The door opened as we approached it, and I walked into the room ahead of the paper pusher. The tension was palpable. I cleared my throat. What sort of pressure were these people under?

'Another successful step. Congratulations.' I didn't smile, but I could see the relief pouring off them. 'Continue, please. Jack?'

Jack muttered to a colleague and then walked over to me.

'I have a message from the pharaoh,' I said. 'Where can we speak in private? Also, I want some water.'

Jack turned to Tybalt. 'No water for our esteemed guest? Would you like me to make a note of that as well on my daily report?'

Clearly, Jack also liked verbal punches.

Tybalt blanched and suggested Jack take me to the oasis, where he would have drinks waiting for us. He stepped aside and began furiously muttering into his brace.

'If you would like to follow me, Special Adviser Salah,' said Jack.

He was being incredibly formal. I wondered if he even recognised me. He was so distant. He'd lost weight and gained a weary air. We walked slowly towards a bank of hovers and climbed into one. Seeing he walked like an old man, I wondered about his physical health.

'It's not far, but it's too hot for a walk.'

We lifted off the ground and crept away from the compound and out across the glass dunes. As we ambled along in silence, I wondered about the speed.

Jack was making no effort to talk, and I decided to follow his lead.

At the site, a small team of people were rushing about, placing food and drinks on low tables, before scrambling back into their hovers and zooming back past us, desperate that we should have our privacy. If I had to place money on it, I'd bet Jack went slowly to allow the team to set up our refreshments before we arrived. I didn't rate Tybalt, and imagined that after we had both belittled him, he would gladly pass on his temper to those people who made us wait for our refreshments.

The oasis was a wonder. Terraces had been carved into rock-like glass, providing seating and lounging around a huge pool. In the centre, a column of water gushed up. Any slight breeze allowed the fountain to sprinkle grateful recliners.

'Nice, isn't it?' said Jack in a tired voice. 'The water is piped in from over a hundred miles away. We had it built at the same time the facility was established. I thought everyone could enjoy it. Now it's only used as a reward. After the Mongols drowned a team of Zulus, it was deemed unsuitable for unsupervised use.'

I didn't know what to say.

'Please, I see we have some melons to go with our water.'

A feast had been laid out. It would take a month of Sundays to eat and drink all that had been provided, but I certainly wouldn't be able to fault the hospitality now.

We sat down and he poured me a glass of water. Ice cubes tumbled over slices of mango and guava. I picked out the mint leaves, never having understood the appeal.

I examined Jack. His eyes were closed as he drank his water. I could see a vein on his temple throb, and I wondered how to begin.

He opened his eyes and smiled at me sadly.

'What does the pharaoh require?' His eyes slid to my brace and his face lit up. 'You're wearing one of my braces?'

I nodded.

'You can talk?'

I nodded again, uncertain if he could. Were we being bugged here?

'Thank Ra! Oh, thank every piece of fame and fortune.'

An unusual exclamation for an engineer, but they were an odd bunch at the best of times. He picked up a pomegranate and began to knock the seeds out. I presumed it was safe to talk.

'Sabrina sent me.'

'That's my girl!'

'Jack. What the fuck is going on?'

'You don't know?' He dropped the pomegranate, spilling the jewelled red seeds on the floor. 'But you've been approving all of the artefacts we've been sending back. Pharaoh Chen said you knew all about this.'

Chapter Thirty-Five - November:
Alpha: Neith

I choked on a slice of watermelon and had to wait for my coughing to clear before I could splutter out my shock.

'I haven't approved anything. I'm still finalising the list.'

'Last month's Silla Crown to Afghanistan. That wasn't approved by you?'

'Are you joking?'

Not only was that crown not on the list, but there was also more chance of me reciting Pi to the final digit than there was of me adding Afghanistan to the list of approved countries. Was Minju setting me up, or just using me? My face must have been a picture as Jack stared at me.

'Do you mean you know nothing about the returns?'

'Jack, I know nothing about a second sodding stepper being built. Let alone the repatriations of precious treasures to war-torn regions.'

I was sitting on glass formed by a nuclear explosion under a sterile blue sky, but that was nowhere near as chilling as what Jack had just said.

'What is this?' I whispered.

'What, this?' He waved his arm airily in the facility's direction. 'Just a second stepper that I built. In secret, under the orders of the previous pharaoh, under the label of heightened security, and now Chen has us importing slave labour and weapons on a daily basis. I think she's insane, and I appear to be helping her because otherwise she will kill Sabrina, my parents, my family, my friends, my junior teacher, my polo coach, the person who poured my wine once when I went on holiday. I don't know; that kid I said hi to ten years ago. You get the picture.'

He laughed. It wasn't a good sound.

'But surely those are just bluffs. Threats to make you comply?'

He wiped his hand over his face. 'In the early stages of building this, our accident and death rate was appalling. Several a week. I complained to Chen that we were moving too fast. She walked into the room and randomly shot four people. One of them was a fucking excellent engineer, another was a mother with triplets, the other two were just trying to go about their duty.'

I was speechless as Jack continued.

'She told me she wanted results faster, and she didn't care who died. As she walked out of the room, she shot a man hiding behind a desk. He was the fifth.' He poured another glass of water. 'After that, I received a message from her, reminding me that my work was secret and that she was monitoring everything. Should anyone even hint at a project out in the wastes, she would assume I had been talking. Would start killing people I knew.'

The heat was unbearable, but a cold sweat prickled my skin. Minju was more dangerous than I had possibly imagined.

'What about First Engineer? Is she in on this?'

Hypatia Smith was a terrifying woman, but I had thought she was honourable.

'She knows. Or at least she knows up to a point. She approved the idea of building a second stepper. It meant we could work on the new modifications. But a month ago when Chen started to trade treasures for weapons and men, she began to falsify my report back to First. And of course, I daren't disagree.'

'So, what did you do?'

'I made stuff. You're wearing one of them. It's been relatively easy to work on secret projects here because everything is secret. No one asks what I'm doing. I could be building a doomsday bomb for all anyone would know.'

'You're not, are you?'

'I thought about it, but I decided to do something else first.'

The fact that Jack could invent a doomsday device didn't surprise me. The fact that he was considering it though, terrified me.

'Bast!'

A hover was heading towards us and stopped where the sand turned to glass. Tybalt stepped out of the car and tapped a small hologram box. Minju Chen, in all her official garb, stood by his side looking across at me.

'She can't come any closer,' Jack muttered softly. 'I rigged the glass to create a technology blackout. It wasn't hard. The glass does do strange things out here.'

I stood up, waved at Minju and walked towards her. 'Good morning, Pharaoh.'

'Neith. What are you doing there? I thought you were in Kenya.' She continued to stare as I remained silent. 'Very well, and what are you doing there?'

Her tail was twitching, but I was certain that this time it wasn't for effect. Minju was furious. My number of breaths was now on a countdown.

'Something has been bothering me for a while. Ever since I woke from my coma. Maybe it's because my job was taken away from me, but I found I had more time to think about things.'

'You were supposed to be thinking about which artefacts to return to Beta.'

'Please. I've never had such an easy mission. And whilst I was playing at the challenges of *Do we return this artefact back to a war-torn dictatorship? Er, let me think about that,* I started to look around, and found an equation I couldn't balance. It all slotted into place when I saw some blue sand in your office.'

She flinched then, but at least I had removed suspicion from anyone else.

'Once I started thinking about the Glass Wastes, I noticed other odd things, so I decided to come out and have a look for myself.'

'And?'

'And—' I paused. 'And it's incredible.' I let the awe seep into my voice. 'What you have achieved is unbelievable. For the first time since those quantum beings arrived, I feel we might actually have a chance at defending ourselves. What are your plans?'

I fought to appear enthralled. Sweat was building up along my hairline. I could feel it trickling along my spine, but knew holograms didn't have perfect replication. She was unlikely to spot any nonverbal tells. I waited in silence.

'Very well. We will discuss this tomorrow when I return from the summit.' She turned to Tybalt. 'Please see that Adviser Salah's hover is properly replenished and send her back with two guards for her protection. Actual red custodians please. The others are still undisciplined idiots.'

Tybalt saluted, which was clearly not a new thing, as Minju simply inclined her head before turning to Jack.

'I understand we had another successful step. Please alert me when this lot are returning. They are scheduled for tomorrow. Is that correct? What a busy day that's going to be.' She looked at me meaningfully. 'When they arrive, it's time to move things forward. Neith, I will see you in the morning.'

The hologram ended, and I was left with Tybalt. He fiddled with his glasses, clearly delighted to have caught me out on an unsanctioned visit, but concerned as to how I would react. Minju didn't appear cross with me, so he was uncertain how to treat me. From my body language, he had settled on "carefully."

'I wish to say goodbye to Jack,' I said. 'Go away.'

Tybalt took one whole step back and smirked as two custodians approached us.

'Engineer Ticona has to get back to work.'

Jack ignored him and gave me a huge hug. He was still growing and now towered over me. I'd forgotten that he wasn't much more than a teenager.

He leant down and for a moment I thought he was going to kiss me on the cheek, instead he whispered in my ear. 'Help.'

Reunification

Chapter Thirty-Six - November: Beta: Julius

It had been almost a month since Afghanistan. Each time I saw the family, they burnt with nervous energy. Yonni and Tam were getting closer to identifying the Tiresias signature. They were using every known visit and then searching the databases and algorithms of local networks to see if they could spot Tiresias moving between the code. Occasionally they got hints that something extra was present, but so far, they hadn't isolated it.

Marie-Louise had successfully repaired the crown, and it was now in the hands of UNESCO whilst they deliberated on the best way to deal with it. It had no provenance and no historical evidence as to who made it or for whom. The stones and metals came from various geological locations and the artistry was similar to several cultures. It was a missing link piece of jewellery and all the more important because of it.

In the meantime, I carried on at work very much in a limbo state. High tension, low boredom. I felt out of sorts and only truly relaxed when I took Dippy out for walks across the fields. Only under the vast Cambridge sky could I unwind as the Doberman streaked across the flats, his tail wagging joyfully as he played and bounced.

I was desperate to know what Minju was up to. If Neith and Rami were safe. Christ, I was even worried about Clio. And what about the two princes? How were they adapting? I was their only link to their home, and now I was gone. Every time I thought of Alexandria, I just started into a downward spiral. There was nothing I could do but fret.

So I walked the dog instead. As we headed back to the house, Dippy would pounce on the leaves, and I would shiver in the November wind.

Today, though, I was heading to my other happy place, rummaging around in the archives. Down there, I could pretend I was in the vaults of the mouseion, laughing along with Minju, working alongside her as we catalogued artefacts and gossiped about life back home. She had probably been drilling me for information, but the memory was still a good one. As I headed along the cobbled lanes, avoiding selfie sticks and cyclists, my phone rang and I recognised the family's ringtone. It was cheesy, but Yonni had set it up and said she was quite partial to Sister Sledge.

'Julius. We've just had a live intercept!'

This was an incredible breakthrough. I was about to offer my congratulations when she ploughed on.

'The ping came from Cambridge. Given the threat you posed to Minju, we think it is a very high probability that she has decided to remove you permanently.'

I came to an abrupt halt and had to apologise to the people walking behind me. I stepped left and tucked myself beside a postbox.

'That's ridiculous. Don't forget, as far as she knows, I have no memory of Alpha.'

There was a silence on the other end of the phone and Marcus came on the line.

'Yes, yes. You're probably right, but the Minju I knew was a fastidious planner and meticulous to boot. You are a loose thread.'

I felt Marcus might be over-reacting and I was about to reassure him as he continued.

' We're nearly with you. Find somewhere public and crowded. It will be hard for an assassin to operate covertly.'

With that, he hung up, and I studied my surroundings. I was five minutes from the college and standing in front of King's. There wasn't a busier and more photographed spot in Cambridge. This was as good a place as any to wait, but I felt horribly exposed. I was getting flashbacks to when Neith and I were chased by unknown gunmen. I wanted to head towards the corners and alleyways and hide. Now that I knew so much more about combat measures and counter tactics, I knew staying visible was the best course of action, but my heartbeat was racing. Marcus and I were both banking on the fact that an Alpha assassin would try to be covert in their execution.

'Hello, Professor.'

I turned and saw one of the more attentive undergraduates smiling up at me. I didn't want to ignore her, but if something was about to go down, I really didn't want preppy students caught in the crossfire.

'Hello, Miss Charters.'

Formality seemed to help maintain a distance. Some undergrads were very enthusiastic in their pursuit of learning. My fringe fell over my eyes, so I pushed it back. I really needed to get it cut. It was getting tiresome every time I had to talk to someone shorter than myself. It would help if they didn't stand so close. I wanted her to go away, but couldn't quite bring myself to be rude.

I honestly think British manners will get us all killed.

'Are you waiting to meet someone?' She loosened her collar. 'Only there's a lady waiting for you at the library. She's proper angry.' She giggled, and I wondered who I could have annoyed.

'Did she say who she was?'

'Tall Black woman, looks like she could break you. To be fair, she looks like she could break the entire rugby first team. Boy, is she mad. Professor, where are—'

I didn't hear the rest of her sentence as I was off and running across the lawn. I could hear the porters

331

shouting at me for trampling their precious grass, but I had other things on my mind.

As I sprinted up the steps, Clio's dulcet tones were already threatening to rip the ears off our poor receptionist, and I couldn't help but laugh.

'Psycho!'

Clio span round, scowling, when I barrelled straight into her, throwing my arms around her and spinning her up in the air.

'If you don't put me down this instant—'

Dropping her, I stepped back, a stupid grin plastered across my face.

'Hello, shit-fly. You remember me then? I was told your memory was wiped.'

I tensed, ready to fend off a punch, but she gave me a brief grin instead and then resumed scowling.

'Right. Good, saves me some time.' She turned away, walking back out towards the road, calling over her shoulder. 'Let's go. Work to do.'

Chapter Thirty-Seven - November:

Beta: Julius

She strode off, and I apologised to the receptionist, who was still quivering. When I had finally reassured her that Clio was just a bit brusque, I turned and ran off to catch up with her. She was heading down to the riverbank, and it all felt rather full circle.

'You were going to kill me here?'

She rolled her eyes dramatically. 'I was not going to kill you. Just wound you.'

'I know.' I slapped her on the arm, then stepped away sharply. 'Just teasing you. I think you deserve it.'

She stared at me, and I honestly thought this time she *might* kill me. Then she just shrugged. 'You really are very tiresome. Come on, we need to get home.'

She put her hand into her bag and pulled out a very large bangle.

'And that is?'

'A new way to travel. Will make you sick as a camel, but you won't be traced, and we can go any when/where.' She paused and rolled her shoulders. 'Theoretically. This will be my second step. Jack said it would be rough, and that it wasn't one hundred percent guaranteed, but I needed to get you.'

'You, the great Clio Masoud, need me?' I made a pantomime of being shocked. 'The Beta shit-fly?' I really was enjoying myself.

'Have you finished?'

I grinned at her. Honestly, my reaction had surprised me. Sure, she was a violent, self-centred killer, but I just couldn't help remembering the fear on her face when she saw those spiders. The moment when she sacrificed herself to save me when we rescued the princes. When she had killed Grimaldi for shooting Neith. I could no longer tell if she was a good guy or a bad guy. But, rightly or wrongly, she was my guy.

'I have finished, but we can't go yet.'

'Minju is making a play for the heart and soul of Egypt. I think she is trying to set up a new world order, with her at its head. She's importing Beta soldiers and weapons, and Neith is standing right alongside her. We have to act now before Minju finally wins.'

'What about the others. What are they doing? I was brought across by Ludo and Githumbi. Who are they working for?'

'Ludo is Minju's creature. Luisa Githumbi was murdered. It was made to look like suicide.'

I stopped walking.

'That was my fault. I told them Minju was corrupt.'

Clio turned back to me.

'If Ludo hadn't been present then yes, she may have lived. As far as I know she didn't say anything to anyone.'

I felt cold. Githumbi wasn't a close friend but she was a good woman and she had always treated me fairly. In my panic to return to Alexandria, I had spilled the beans and sealed her death warrant.

'Stop it.' Clio watched me carefully. 'I understand your anger but focus it correctly. Ludo and Minju are to blame and we need to stop them.'

That certainly sounded compelling. I also didn't understand why Neith was working with Minju, but I wanted them as far apart as possible. Even more so now. I took a deep breath.

'Okay, as much as I want to travel on some jerry-rigged prototype quantum traveller stepper, and then pitch straight into battle with a bunch of soldiers, you need to meet some people first.'

On cue, my phone rang, and I answered it quickly. 'I'm safe. No threat.'

'Who's standing by you?'

'Oh, can you see me?'

At that, Clio bristled, then casually dropped down to pick something up off the floor. As she stood up, she stepped towards me.

'There are four people watching us. I'd say they are professionals. Tell them if they value their lives, they stay where they are.'

I sighed and spoke into the phone. 'Did you hear that?'

'I did,' said Marcus, 'but I don't think your companion is a threat to four curators.'

I rolled my eyes and apologised to Clio. This wasn't going as well as I had hoped.

'I'm standing with Clio Masoud.'

She hissed at me as I said her name.

'And she is more than you could possibly handle,' I continued. 'But I haven't had a chance to tell her who you are. Wait there. I'll wave when you can approach.' I hung up and studied Clio. 'Now look, I know you don't like surprises, and this one is huge. The four people you observed are curators.'

She tensed, and a moment later she was holding a slim baton in her hand. No doubt that had been tucked in her coat lining.

'Did they get here before me? Has Minju sent them?'

'Yes and no. These curators are the abandoned ones. The ones that got left behind on aborted steps, the curators who never made it home. Missing, presumed dead.'

Clio's face went blank. 'All of them?'

'No, only the ones that arrived on Beta in the last sixty years or so, but since the mid-1700s they have built an organisation to search out and provide shelter for curators that are stranded. They've been waiting all this time to go home.'

Clio flinched, and as she gulped, her eyes welled up. That, I hadn't expected. She took a deep breath and all signs of emotion passed. Had I not been staring into her face in that exact moment, I wouldn't have seen her pain.

'Can we trust them?' she said.

'Yes. I've been working with them these past months. Can I wave them forward?'

She gave a brief nod, and I watched as four people slowly walked towards us. Yonni and Tam had been reading a map over by the bridge. Marie-Louise peeled away from a tour group party, and Pierre left the queue for the ice creams. Then I smiled as Marcus stood up from the park bench not ten metres from us, making Clio flinch and step back into her fight mode. As she did so, the others all stopped. Only Marcus walked forward, smiling.

'Curator Masoud? I am Curator Marcus Caractacus. Welcome.'

At the name of one of the mouseion's most glorious curators, Clio did a double take, peering closely.

'You got old.'

'Not too old to throw you on your back.'

'I'd like to see you try.'

'Well, I wouldn't.' He chuckled. 'Because I suspect a second later, you'd spring back up, then kick my arse all the way down Trinity Street, then dunk me in the Cam for good measure, yes, yes?' He held out his hand and smiled at her. 'We preserve?'

There was a pause, and I realised that if there was going to be a fight, I would be fighting alongside Clio. Since when had that happened? Clio must have heard me sigh.

'What?'

'Nothing, but these are my friends. They've really helped me. I don't want to fight them.'

'You'd be fighting on my side?' Her voice rose in astonishment.

I shook my head. 'God only knows why, but yes. So please, can you just shake the man's hand, and then we can go and talk?'

Clio glared back at Marcus.

He had now taken a step back. 'Julius. Can I suggest we invite Clio down to London and she can get a better idea of what's going on? I can see there may be some trust issues. And given what has been happening to Alpha these past few years, that is fully understandable.'

'We don't have time to go to London,' snapped Clio.

'We do and we will,' I said. 'If there are problems back home, I have a bunch of curators who will want to lend their support to the battle. Hell, Marcus here is

338

Minju's old partner. So let's play along and follow the nice man.'

'Don't patronise me.'

I wanted to tell her to stop acting like a child, but even I'm not that stupid. We followed Marcus in silence back to a parked car and climbed in. The others all piled into the other car. No doubt to give us some space, and also because no one in their right mind gets into an enclosed space with a furious predator. We drove in uncomfortable silence. At the beginning of the drive, Clio sent me a text.

-What did you tell them about me?

-Not much.

-So they don't know what I did.

-No.

-Why?

-Felt rude.

-WHAT?!

She glared at me. Marcus was politely ignoring our silent conversation by pretending to read the paper. I continued to type.

-I don't believe you should bad-mouth a person if they aren't there to defend themselves.

God knows, Clio's betrayals and crimes were many, and two years ago I would have happily seen her punished for them, but since then, I had started to understand some of her situation. Between Minju's manipulations and Anansi's power, Clio didn't stand a chance. All her weaknesses and vulnerabilities were played upon until she was well and truly stuck on the wrong side. She took a deep breath and was about to text a reply when she swore instead. Shoving her hands in her pockets, she turned her back on me. We drove the rest of the way in silence.

Chapter Thirty-Eight - November: Beta: Julius

We pulled into Alexandria Street. Clio got out and took in her surroundings before walking into the house. Once inside, she spent a few more moments examining the atrium in silence, then turned to Marcus.

'How many exits?' she asked.

'Ten,' said Marcus.

'And how many of them are subterranean?'

I was about to say one as I knew the answer when Tam replied three.

I coughed.

Clio laughed at me. 'Come on, Julius. They've been stuck here for centuries, in London. With all its rain and cold. If they want to visit the buildings on the other side of the street, you don't think they go outdoors, do you? And once you've built one tunnel, why stop there? Rooftop exits are less useful, but I imagine there's one or two of them around.'

'We have a flat roof at the far end of the terrace,' said Tam, smiling. 'Never used, but capable of withstanding the weight of a helicopter if required.'

I laughed weakly.

Clio grinned. 'They're curators, Julius. What did you expect?'

Marcus smiled broadly. 'Right, Curator Masoud, since we are all gathered, I suggest you come through to the salon and meet everyone and say hello.'

We walked into the salon. The sun shone off every reflective surface from the gold inlay, glass tables, and mirrors. The warmth was all embracing, and I swear Clio relaxed for half a second.

'Filters on the window?' she said.

'Yes,' said Sasha Kalo, who had been sitting near the door and watching Clio carefully. 'Just to make the sunlight tone that little bit warmer, less northern blue.'

Clio nodded in approval, and I began to appreciate how much I had missed. These curators had done all that they could to modify this space into something as Egyptian as possible. Alphas continued to impress me. Now, if I could only help save them from themselves.

Marcus walked to the bar and clapped his hands.

'Friends. We have a non-stranded curator! Clio Masoud can get home.'

There was a hell of a lot of cheering and fists banging on the tables.

'Clio. We generally get newcomers to introduce themselves as they join the family, but with your arrival, everything is about to change. Would you like to come and explain why and how you got here? Yes, yes?'

Clio walked slowly to the front. She looked angry, but wiped her palms on her thighs. Why was she nervous? This made no sense.

'Right. Full disclosure. I understand Julius hasn't told you much about me. But I don't believe in duplicity or lies. Not anymore. I'm a warts and all sort of figure, so here are my warts.'

And she proceeded to tell them about her role in the theft of artefacts, that she hung around with Anansi for a year, that she fought with Grimaldi, that she supported Minju.

Her words fell into silence. As she finished, jutted her chin out, ready to pick a fight with the first person who challenged her.

Yonni cleared her throat. 'How were you taken back as a curator after all that?'

'I went through the bokbok process and various other realignment processes.'

Approving mutters rose around the room and a sense of relief flowed across their bodies.

'But it was all camel shit. I lied and faked my way through those tests. I regret a whole lot of what I did. But I missed home, and I missed being a curator. I would do or say anything to get back.'

Now the curators muttered amongst themselves and Clio looked over at me. I shrugged my shoulders. I was still surprised by how brutally honest she was being. In fact, it was the most I had ever heard her speak. Clio not usually being one for the deep and meaningfuls.

'Well, okay Clio,' said Marie-Louise. 'The question is, can we trust you?'

Clio puffed out her cheeks and shook her head. 'Based on my track record, no. But I'm all you've got and, honestly, I need you and I am trying to stop Minju and the rise of a new empire.'

Marie-Louise pursed her lips, the red lipstick falling into small vertical lines. She was clearly unimpressed with the answer, but what else could she do? 'Very well. Now, how do we get home?'

Clio closed her eyes. I watched as the curators, all decades older than us, regarded her silently. She had declared herself a traitor and untrustworthy, but she was also their solution to getting home.

Taking a deep breath, she opened her eyes. 'Don't you have something to say about my record? About cheating on the bokbok tests. About any of it?'

Marcus inclined his head towards the others as they smiled and shook their heads.

'We don't care.' He spoke with a kind smile on his face. 'Clio, we have been living on Beta long enough to know people can behave in really strange ways when under pressure. By Alpha standards, you are an out and out bad apple. By Beta standards, you're practically the reluctant hero. And we don't care. Now, shall we shake hands? Yes, yes.'

Clio let her head fall forwards, her face obscured by her braids. I was holding my breath. Everything hung on her reaction. If she rejected these curators, she and I would have to go it alone. It was the wrong move, but I couldn't abandon her. The tension in the room was absolute, everyone was watching her and then she lifted her face, and stepped forward, her hand outstretched. Soon everyone was crowding around her, smiling and laughing…

… Until Pierre stood in front of her and sneered. 'So, the great Clio Masoud turned out to be a traitor? Colour me unsurprised.'

Clio laughed. 'Pierre Le Brock? Man, I liked you better when you were dead.'

Faster than anyone had time to react, she punched him square in the face, propelling him backwards over a chair. As he fell, he grabbed at the tablecloth, pulling glasses and plates down on top of himself. From the floor, he shouted obscenities at Clio as blood from his nose gushed out through his fingers.

She stood there like she hadn't moved a muscle. 'Sorry about that. Hand slipped. Must be the after-effects of the new brace. I'll be sure to mention it to the engineers.'

'I thought you didn't believe in lies?' asked Yonni with a small smile.

'Oh, white lies are fine. Now, can I bring you all up to speed and then we can plan an attack? That is, if you want to?'

Marcus looked at Clio and back to Pierre as he tipped his head back in an attempt to staunch the blood. A linen napkin was steadily turning red. It felt shocking for such a strong woman to lay out an old man like that, and I felt deeply conflicted.

'Clio! What was that in aid of?'

Clio pursed her lips then turned to Pierre. 'Would you like to tell them?'

He lowered his head and glared at her balefully. 'I said sorry at the time.'

'No, you didn't. And, if I remember, you also passed the blame.'

'That's a lie!'

'No, it's not. Happily, we're surrounded by our peers. Shall we ask them to adjudicate?'

She crossed her arms. Slowly, he pulled himself upright and looked around at the others, who were all agog. Whatever this was, none of them were party to it either.

Pierre dabbed at his nose carefully and shrugged his shoulders as he addressed the room. 'Just a misunderstanding. No doubt Clio and I will laugh about this in years to come. Shall we head through to the conference room? Marcus?'

And with that, he stalked out of the salon.

Chapter Thirty-Nine - November:
Beta: Julius

Marcus suggested we take five minutes to calm down and then head back to the meeting rooms. We were sitting around a conference table. I was wearing new skins and a new brace, and was feeling confident. Yonni had peered hopefully as Clio pulled them out of her backpack and handed them to me.

Clio shrugged. 'I only brought one set for Julius. I wasn't expecting a party.'

She had, however, brought a hologram of the mouseion with the hope of it jogging my memory. She even had some sand in her bag, which she poured onto the table. As the hologram sprang to life, the curators stared like children spying Father Christmas. Some even appeared to have got some of the sand in their eyes.

For a moment, there was silence.

Then Marie-Louise threw her head back and wailed, a high keening sound that was immediately joined by all the other voices in the room as the sound of grief and longing filled the room. They hugged each other as tears poured down their faces, sobs wracking their bodies. Marie-Louise wiped away Clio's tears as she bent down to embrace the smaller woman. Her small bony fingers sweeping across Clio's smooth skin.

I had never seen such a clear example of hiraeth before. The emotions were too raw and too private for me, and I quietly stepped out of the room, away from the pain.

I was sitting in the atrium when my brace pinged.

-Get back in here you, idiot.

I presumed the message was from Clio. When I returned, there were lots of blotchy faces, but they were smiling and laughing as well.

'Oh, Julius.' Marcus came over to me. 'That was so good to get off our chests. I could only imagine how dreadful all that open emotion was for you. But you know the old saying, better out than in. Yes, yes?' He slapped the table in front of my chair and then went back to sit at his place. 'Hurry up and sit down. We have work to do.'

I sat down and he carried on.

'Clio here is very anxious to get you back to Alexandria to stop Minju, but I am asking her to recalibrate her plans.'

Clio was sitting tight-lipped. I knew that expression. She had changed her mind, but wasn't happy about it.

'I can't just bring you all back,' she said. 'It's more complicated than that. Listen.'

And we sat in astonishment as she explained that Minju had built a secret step facility out in the Glass Wastes, and was bringing over hardened soldiers and workers to toil in the compound.

'Soldiers and slaves to build a new Egyptian Empire,' said Tam in horror.

'What is she thinking?' asked Pierre.

'I don't care what she's thinking, we have to stop her.'

There was general agreement around the table, but Marcus quietened everyone down. 'I agree she has to be stopped, but if we understood her motivation, we may find the chinks in her defences. Julius, you said you spent a lot of time in her company. Have you any ideas?'

Over the past months, I had thought of little else. The thievery had always seemed beneath her, but now I saw it for the role it played in a much bigger picture. The thefts weren't for money. They were for control. Not of money and artefacts, but of people and power. The Beta soldiers were part of that process.

I spoke slowly as the idea formed in my mind. 'I know this sounds strange, but I think she is acting in Alpha's best interests.' There was some pretty vocal pushback, and I waved them down. 'No, hear me out. Minju has always wanted to protect Alpha. After her splice, her desire to protect became more assertive, less collegiate. She retreated to the shadows and started to pull strings to ensure that things ran the way she felt they should and manoeuvred herself into a position whereby if needed, she could take control.'

'But that's not the Alpha way,' said Sasha. 'We are better than that.'

'Of course we aren't,' snapped Clio, sparing me having to point out the obvious. 'Minju couldn't have manipulated the system on her own. She found others who were quite happy to disrupt the Alpha way. We have steadily become smug, complacent and moribund. We are stagnating in self-satisfaction.'

'And you think Beta is better?' scoffed Pierre.

'Not remotely, but in some areas they beat us hands down. And on other Earths, they are doing far better than either of us. And also far worse. I have travelled through the multiverse, and I have seen Earths *you* couldn't imagine, but I think Minju has. Is that what you are getting at, Julius?'

All eyes turned back to me. It had been uncomfortable listening to their discussion of my Earth. It was clear that having lived here for decades, some of them had become set in their preconceptions of Alpha Good, Beta Bad. I hoped I could make them see the bigger picture.

'Yes. I think when we had the incursions from the gods, Minju envisaged a greater threat than anything posed by Beta or Alpha's own complacency and she geared up. And Minju Chen is not messing around. A second stepper, my God.'

We all paused and considered how much planning had been involved in that, and how much political power.

'To what end, though?' asked Yonni.

'She's already pharaoh,' said Tam. 'What more does she want?'

'I know this sounds ridiculous, but my bet would be world domination. In her mind, she can only protect Alpha from enemy attack if she is in charge of all of it.'

'Sorry Julius, that doesn't feel—' Tam began.

I cut him off. 'I know, but what else explains this? And, frankly, once Minju has full control of Alpha, I would expect her first move would be to create a vassal Earth. Namely us.'

'But how does she plan to control Alpha? She can only rule Egypt. If she tries to enforce her will on other countries, they will reject her,' said Pierre. He was still scowling and keen to disagree with anything I or Clio had to say. 'Exactly how many soldiers does she plan to import?'

It was a good question and not one anyone had any answer to.

'If only we had a way to intercept one of her illicit steps and have a look at what was going on,' said Yonni, furiously scribbling on a paper pad. 'We need more intel.'

'What about November eleventh?' said Clio, sipping her water.

'You know when a step is taking place?' roared Yonni. 'You might have led with that. We can go home that way. Well, those of us that want to. Some of us may wish to stay on?'

I could see curators considering their options. They had lived here for decades, had built new lives. Some even had families.

'It's not that easy though, Yonni,' said Clio. 'This bangle and the one Julius has will take us anywhere. It is a fully functional stepper. We are not tethered to the stepper in Alexandria, or to the one in the wastes. We can go anywhere. But the brace that transports you back means you'll have to come through a step wall. There will be no air of surprise, just a slew of custodian ready to detain you.'

'And Jack has only made two of your particular bangles?'

'Yes, so far. I mean, he may be making more, but he's been hard pressed to do everything. He has been doing Minju's work behind the backs of the population, and then his *own work* behind *Minju's* back. He is running on empty.'

'Okay, tell me about the step on the eleventh.'

'I don't know much, but according to Jack, Minju has made it clear that lots of items are coming back through the step. The entire hangar will be vacant and there will only be a skeleton staff for processing.'

'Items? Not personnel.'

'I don't know. I didn't ask Jack to break it down. My idea was to grab Julius and take it from there. He's quite good at planning and seeing opportunities that I haven't.'

I tried not to feel too self-important.

'Although his discipline is woeful and his fighting skills are bizarre,' she continued. 'He's more likely to incapacitate you by random tripping than deliver a considered blow. Some proper curators would be a bonus.'

My sense of self-importance was properly restored, but as I caught her eye, she was grinning at me.

'Right,' said Marcus, trying to get the conversation back under control. 'Where is the step on the eleventh?'

'The Kremlin.'

My heart sank. Kabul had been bad enough.

'So, Minju is sending treasures back and forth between Beta and Alpha, and she's working with some seriously unpleasant governments.' I looked across at my partner. 'Clio, is Neith really signing off on this?'

'No idea. I've been lying low. But when I left yesterday, they were gearing up to announce the Grand Unveiling of Artefacts to be potentially returned. No one knows that stuff is already being returned.'

'But Neith must know, surely?'

'How? This new stepper is out in the Glass Wastes, almost no one knows about it. All eyes are on the new Arts Foundation Building.'

Clio had mentioned this already, but I wasn't familiar with it.

'Which is?'

'Chen's shiny bauble. She's using it to usher in a new golden age. Instilling pride and self-fulfilment. I suspect it's also acting as a front for all the money she's been syphoning off to build her secret stepper.'

'I don't like how close Neith is to Minju,' I said.

'Neither do I babes, but she is, and we will have to tread carefully. Neith clearly has no idea of Minju's true nature. If we move against Minju, Neith's first response will be to defend her.'

I drummed my fingers on the table. I hadn't thought of that. Of course, Neith would protect her. Would we have to immobilise Neith first? The idea was alarming.

How exactly did you stop Neith Salah?

Chapter Forty - November: Beta: Julius

By the following morning, we had a plan. And given the state of Clio's frown, she wasn't pleased with it. In three days' time, we were off to Russia and on to Alexandria, if things went accordingly.

I returned to Cambridge and put my affairs in order. I resigned from my job, explaining that I was now working for the Alexandria Company full time. College was pretty decent about the whole thing, which wasn't surprising, as I understood the group had funded a new science wing. I also let my neighbours know I was off travelling again, then took Dippy for an extra-long walk.

By the time I returned to London, everything was ready and Clio was smirking at me.

'I was reviewing the Kabul mission. That bit where you ran across the compound shooting up at the guards. I bet you thought you were James Bond or something.'

I decided Clio was teasing rather than being out and out rude, but it was always hard to tell.

'No dinner jacket. More Jason Bourne, I thought.'

'Jason Newborn, more like!' She laughed at her own joke.

I raised an eyebrow. 'Leave the jokes to the funny people, hey Clio? Now, what's the plan for you and me?'

She muttered something that sounded suspiciously like *dickhead*, then headed through to the kitchen and made a coffee. Just the one. Then continued to speak.

'From what Jack said, the meeting was taking place in the courtyard of the Kremlin senate. There was a lot of work on calibrating the landing zone. The days of landing half a mile and two centuries away are over. The engineers have been very busy. Anyway, we know where and when they are arriving, and we also know they are planning on bringing a lot of stuff back. Plus, they are going to be stepping over with fifty standard braces.'

'Fifty!'

'It's like I said. Minju has been importing personnel in large numbers. It's also the only way so far to carry stuff across.'

'So, how do we join the party?'

'We're going in as UN inspectors.'

This made sense. Ever since the failed invasion of Ukraine, Russia had been subjected to ongoing random inspections and penalties. It seemed we had learnt nothing from the Treaty of Versailles. For now, however, it meant that entry into the heart of the Kremlin would be relatively easy.

'There are a few issues.'

'No shit.'

'Language, Julius!'

I nearly apologised, then laughed. Just for a second, she had sounded like my mother.

'Go on, then. What are the issues, beyond wandering into the Kremlin whilst they are trying to do something very secretive?'

'Well, there's that, obviously. I suspect they would rather take us on a tour of their nuclear sites than let on they have set up relations with a whole other Earth. So we have to get past that, but we have to do it with a group of retired curators and a team of special service personnel.'

I stared at her. 'Are you kidding?'

'No. Apparently, Marcus has been speaking to someone called Brian Hastlethwaite. He's arranging access, but said that he would only help if we agreed to let some soldiers accompany us.'

'Does he know the full story?'

'No. Marcus has said we're about to expose an international art smuggling ring.'

At that point, Marcus wandered into the kitchen. Clio jumped up and offered him a cup of coffee.

'Thank you, Clio. Have you been bringing young Julius here up to speed, yes, yes?'

She nodded as she ground the coffee beans.

'Oh, if you're making a coffee, I'll have one. Cheers.' I smiled sweetly at her, then turned back to

Marcus. 'Clio was telling me about Hastlethwaite's demands. Is he buying into this smuggling ring story?'

'Not at all. It's one of the reasons why he's insisting that we have an escort. He doesn't trust us one bit, he just doesn't know why.'

'He sounds like a smart operator,' said Clio as she continued to grind Marcus' beans whilst making my coffee from a jar of instant.

'Very smart. We may be approaching the point where we have to inform him of who we are and what's going on. For now, though, I want to keep our privacy intact.'

'Okay, so say we get to the designated step zone. Then what?'

'Then we observe. If I feel we can intercept the people earmarked to wear a brace, we will take their place and step back. If we can't, we'll sabotage the step. But first we need to see what they are travelling back with. I am assuming they are selling Fabergé treasures. Ever since the Ukrainian war, Russia has been on its knees economically. It will be child's play for Alpha to re-float them financially. But no matter what treasures Minju wants for her new Arts Foundation, we cannot allow her to interfere in Beta politics.'

I felt that the curator's days of hiding in the shadows were coming to an end. If Minju was messing around with my Earth, it wouldn't be long before all hell broke loose. She might have experience with handling Grimaldi and quantum beings, but she was picking up a hornet's nest and trying to play basketball with it. The only thing in her favour was that Beta didn't possess Alpha technology, but when had that ever stopped any of our civilisations? If we encountered an enemy with superior force, we would retreat, drawing the enemy in until they were surrounded, and then we would attack. Or we'd simply steal their technology, or we would just quietly assimilate them. If Minju was planning on invading Beta, my bet was on the home team.

'You alright, Julius?' asked Clio.

Both Marcus and Clio were staring at me.

'Have we missed something?'

'No, I just—'

Something didn't feel right. Minju wasn't an idiot. I couldn't work out what she was doing, but I didn't think she was interested in Beta at all. I dismissed the thought.

'What's mine and Clio's role in all this?'

'You'll love this,' said Clio with a smirk. 'You get to be the hero.'

'What does that make you? My trusty side-kick?'

'Now, now, children. The plan, Julius, is that you and Clio wait to see what happens. When we get into the Kremlin, I need you and Clio to activate your concealment shields and separate from the group. If we successfully infiltrate the mission and step back, we need you on the other side, ready to help us. So when our braces are activated and bring us back to Alpha, you two will activate those nifty portable steppers and cross over. Clio has identified a location at the facility where you can arrive, then make your way to the step and help us secure the compound.'

'How many custodians are there, Clio?' I wasn't sure how we would manage on only a shoestring of curators.

'There's not many,' said Clio. 'Remember, Minju is trying to keep this place quiet, but there are a lot of Romans, Scythians, Samurais, Janissaries. You name it, Minju has gathered together trained killers from every era of Beta conflicts. From what I observed, these are warriors with no goal. They are out of their depth, confused and angry. Their discipline is shot to pieces. It will be easy to overpower them.'

I looked dubious.

'She's right, Julius,' said Marcus. 'Most soldiers don't enjoy fighting. They need something to fight for. These men should be easy to overcome.'

'And how do we stop our own soldiers, the ones that Hastlethwaite has assigned to us, from stepping over with you?'

'We'll slip them some wow-bangs if we need to. I think a bit of chaos is going to be our friend.'

And with that optimistic comment, we headed off for Russia.

Chapter Forty-One - November: Beta: Julius

The flight had been long and boring. Hastlethwaite had met us at RAF Northolt and introduced us to Major Greenacre. I expected Majors to be old and crusty with walrus moustaches. Greenacre was clean shaven, in his forties and whipcord lean. Behind him stood a small team of sorry looking soldiers who would act as our security guards. A less likely set of individuals, I had yet to meet. There was no discipline. I had expected ten identically built muscle-bound warriors all standing to attention. Instead, they resembled a bunch of undergrads after the exams. Two girls were playing patty-cake. One man had pink plaits and was wearing a straw hat. Another two were flexing their muscles, one older woman was reading a book, and so it went on. They certainly weren't going to pose any threat to a Russian soldier.

Observing Clio's scornful expression, Major Greenacre asked which one she thought was the weakest. She snorted derisorily, then grabbed a wow-bang from my belt and threw it in the air.

The second she snatched the device, they had reacted. The girls playing patty-cake sprang back. One of the muscle-bound men pulled a gun from his waistband. By the time Clio had flung the banger, the woman sitting in the shade of the aeroplane hangar was running towards Clio, the guy with the pink plait had whipped his hat off, caught the wow-bang from the air and was already moving away from the crowd.

'Enough!' shouted Marcus and Greenacre simultaneously.

Clio's wow-bang failed to detonate. The girl who had been running at her had ducked under Clio's punch and was a hair breath away from connecting with Clio's jaw when she stopped.

'Happy?' asked the girl, then sneered at Clio and stepped back, shouting at the woman who was still reading her book. 'Alright Jasmine? Anytime you want to step in and help would be good.'

The woman put her book down. 'Anytime I see a genuine threat, I will. Besides, I've just got to the good bit.'

She picked up her book again, and I was dying to go over and see what she was reading.

Their little display had convinced me I had dramatically underestimated them, and I decided their appearance was part of their cover. Who feels threatened by a man in a straw hat?

Clio returned the wow-bang to me with a small *humph* and headed off to a corner to brood. I suspected she hadn't liked how close that girl had come to landing a blow.

Once on the plane, our two groups had separated. There were our "guards", Clio and me, and four curators in their sixties and older. Pierre had tried to sit with me, but Clio had explained how he had once made a move on Neith and then told everyone she was frigid. It had been a pretty ugly exchange, and I understood why Clio had punched him.

However, I thought he deserved a greater punishment. I told him the woman with the book had been eyeing him up. As I anticipated, he went over to chat her up and tried to make a move on her. A few minutes later, he limped back. It was wrong to watch a man in his seventies gently cradling his balls, but I felt I had done a good deed and learnt to live with my lack of brotherly solidarity.

As she walked past me to go to the loo, she slapped me around the head with her book.

'Do your own dirty work next time.'

The book was *The Athenian Murders,* so naturally I forgave her. I nudged Clio, who appeared to be sleeping.

'Is this really going to work? A bunch of geriatric curators have to get past Russian security, then give the elite British soldiers the slip, then grab some braces, infiltrate themselves into a group of Russians and step across to Alexandria without raising any alarm?'

She tilted her head and opened one eyelid. 'Not a scoobie.'

'What?'

'Keep your voice down. You'll spook the camels.'

'Well, what do you think is going to happen?'

'No idea, there are way too many moving parts for this to go smoothly. But I appear to have ended up with two missions. I need to stop Minju, and now I also need to save these old timers from themselves.'

'Are you insane?'

She shrugged and closed her eye again. 'Stop talking. I need to rest. I suggest you do the same.'

Security through Sheremetyevo Airport was a very different affair to Kabul's. Mother Russia might have to accept our presence, but she wasn't doing it willingly. We were all travelling under diplomatic passports but, if anything, that was making things slower. The flight had taken six hours. Getting through security had taken almost the same amount of time and, if we thought it was cold in Afghanistan, Russia was a whole other level. I noticed that the heating in Immigration was severely lacking.

I'd tried to strike up a conversation with the woman reading, but she blanked me, calling me a pretty boy. It was good to see that my casual interactions with interesting women were as honed as ever. I sighed and settled down next to my seriously disturbing travelling companion, and wondered how the hell we could separate Neith from Minju.

Eventually, a very hostile official waved all of us through and we travelled in a convoy of armoured Strelas towards the Kremlin itself. Apparently, they had a guest wing. As we drove along, Marie-Louise loosened her many scarves and relaxed as she warmed up. The snow was falling heavily now. As we approached Red Square, the bulbous domes of St Basil's were only just visible. I wondered if this was normal for Moscow, or if a blizzard was coming.

Clio kicked my ankle, and I turned to find her face alarmingly close to mine. 'When we get out, switch your brace to cloaking. We need to separate from the group and get to the step.'

'No, we need to stick together.'

'You think the Russians will let the UN inspectors get anywhere near that location?'

Marcus leant across from the seat opposite and tapped Clio on the knee with his cane. 'Have faith. The Delta crew will create a diversion for us curators, and we have enough of our own little fizz bombs to create chaos. Remember, the Russians can't prevent the step opening. We just need to get to that location. Nothing can stop us. Once we are there, we'll see how things unfold.'

Chapter Forty-Two - November: Beta: Julius

'Delta Team. What's your status?'

The blizzard had played into our hands. As we were shepherded from the parking lot, Marcus added some smoke to the snow. Clio and I cloaked up and hitched a ride in the minivans. Major Greenacre hadn't wanted to let us out of his sight, so the curators had changed plans. Marie-Louise and Tam would stay with the Delta team, but when the minivan was unloaded, Clio and I would extend our shields to cover Marcus and Pierre. As far as the Major was concerned, Clio and I had remained back at the airport, providing tactical support away from the frontline. Naturally, he hadn't seen us as we boarded the minivan with everyone else.

Now the four of us moved carefully away from the team and headed towards the step zone. We knew the Russians would not permit the rest of the team anywhere near the zone, and we also knew that Greenacre wouldn't allow us to separate from the team, so this seemed the best option.

In the distance, I could hear Russian security voices shouting at the Delta team. Marcus and Pierre were missing, and Major Greenacre was shouting that the Russians had kidnapped them. The Russians were just as outraged and wanted to know where the hell the two

UN advisers were. A diplomatic incident was nicely unfolding as we slipped away towards the step zone.

According to Jack's coordinates, it came through into the larger of the three courtyards. We had uncloaked, as a cloaked body in snow or rain is almost as visible as an uncloaked one. The battery could run for days, but there was no point in letting people know we had that sort of technology.

We were now sheltering in the lee of a yellow painted wall, away from the main team. My stomach rumbled as I thought about lemon meringue pies, and Clio nudged me. It wasn't my fault that the building resembled a pie, the white snow piling up along the bright yellow wall. For the home of Russian intelligence, it was deceptively pretty. All four of us were hunkered down as the snow drifted around us.

'Everyone's in a tizzy,' I said, listening in to Marie-Louise's bug. 'Greenacre is shouting blue murder that you've been abducted. The Russians are screaming that we are all spies and are violating their integrity.'

As I spoke, Clio tapped Marcus on the arm and pointed. On the other side of the square we could see headlamps, the beams of light fragmenting through the snow. Instinctively, we all cowered down further as the truck drove forward. Four men in long black coats walked out from one of the buildings, shouting orders to the driver of the truck. Soldiers jumped down from the back of it as they hurried to unload the cargo, carefully stacking various crates onto the ground.

'Okay, we have eyes on the treasures,' said Marcus to Tam, who was waiting with the other team. 'Might be statues. Those are some heavy crates. Stand by.'

The more I studied the crates, the less comfortable I felt.

'Marcus. Do those look like the sorts of cartons used for transporting works of art?'

He picked up his binoculars, then passed them to Pierre.

'What do you think?'

'Who knows? The Russian economy is on its knees. We should be grateful they aren't transporting them in carrier bags.'

I was about to speak again when two men carried a crate between them from the back of the lorry and my skins automatically activated. I snapped my head towards Clio, who was equally encased head to toes. The skins had activated at full defensive level and our faces were covered by a near invisible barrier. Clean air was being fed to us. I checked my brace.

'What's happening?' hissed Marcus.

'Radiation alarm. Whatever is in that crate is radioactive.' My blood ran cold as everything finally fell into place. 'The Russians aren't trading treasures. They are trading weapons. That crate contains a nuclear bomb.'

Chapter Forty-Three - November:
Beta: Julius

The two curators stared at me in horror. No one had anticipated this, because no one could imagine anything so dreadful.

'Alright. This is no longer a reconnaissance mission,' said Marcus, and then spoke into his phone. 'Marie-Louise. The Russians are exporting nuclear weapons to Alpha. We're going to abort the transaction. I'm sending a report to Hastlethwaite. Can you do the same? And get out of here now.'

He paused as his face became tighter, a muscle in his cheek twitching.

'No. You will evacuate now,' he said. 'We need you in London. If I can, I will come back. If I can't, you were always the best of us. Yes, yes. I should have said that to you more.'

He hung up without waiting for her reply and then made a second call.

'Major Greenacre. Evacuate now. There are nuclear weapons at play. I have my own escape route. If she objects, knock her out. Now go. I can't delay what I have to do.'

Putting the phone back in his pocket, he turned to us, noticing that we had already overridden our full-face masks.

'The suit is exercising an abundance of caution,' said Clio. 'I don't want to waste the inbuilt oxygen supply.'

I nodded in agreement. Although I had to admit, I was not feeling as relaxed as she looked.

'Honestly, Julius, you'd get more radiation from a holiday to Cornwall,' she said.

I'd seen the readings and knew she was being flippant, but I tried to calm down. 'Well, what is in the crate?'

'Given the size, I would estimate a couple of suitcase bombs. Designed to be left in built-up areas and activated remotely.'

'Is Minju insane?'

'Insane? Who knows? But she is in charge of her faculties. This is not a mistake. And now we know how she plans to control Alpha. She's going to nuke them into submission.'

'We have to blow them up now,' said Clio. 'We can't have that reach Alpha.'

'And setting off a nuclear weapon in the Kremlin. How is that for our policy of non-interference in Beta politics?' asked Pierre.

'Better here than at home.'

'Stop arguing, the pair of you,' snapped Marcus. 'We are not blowing it up here. Pierre and I will travel back with the payload and deal with it there. Pierre. We're going to intercept the handover and step back with the bombs. We have to presume the curators are stepping across with additional braces for those soldiers.'

Pierre nodded and began to perform some micro stretches. I didn't like the man, but I had to admire the fact that here he was, in his seventies, preparing to infiltrate the Russian army and steal a nuclear bomb.

As we had been making plans, the Russians had been building up a small stockpile of crates. Twenty soldiers stood alongside them, no doubt to carry the boxes through. The step needed a human bio signature to activate, so these soldiers would have to be the mules.

'Clio. You and Julius need to travel back independently and be ready on the other side when we come through.'

The mission had moved from tricky to deadly. No doubt Minju knew she had nuclear weapons coming through the step and would be on high alert anyway, but the four of us would just have to find a way to immediately neutralise her. Out of the corner of my eye, I noticed a change in the pattern of snowfall.

'They've arrived,' I hissed as Clio and I muted our own braces and prayed that we hadn't been scanned as the curators stepped through. They wouldn't be looking for anyone so hopefully we hadn't been detected.

'Are you sure?' asked Pierre. 'I can't see them.'

'I can't either, now I've turned my brace off, but they were over by the lorry. Five of them carrying brace cases and lasers.'

After another minute, they became noticeable as their own deflector effect wore off. One of the men started waving his arms around and I recognised Ludo Bianco. The last time I had seen him, he was telling Luisa to pull herself together. He had walked around Charlie's study and scoffed at various books and pictures, whilst my memory began fading. I owed him a reckoning for his casual dismissal of Charlie's belongings, and for Luisa's life.

I'd like to think no crime went unpunished, but clearly, he was now working hand in hand with Minju. He must have turned after the battle. How had Minju convinced him? My money was on greed and vanity. God knows it wouldn't have been an intellectual debate. It made sense that Minju was using curators, but I wonder if Ramin knew?

Ludo and his team stood still as they waited for the distraction effect to wear off. They were clearly expected, and had nothing to hide and nothing to fear. We were about to re-educate them on that score.

'Showtime,' said Marcus.

Chapter Forty-Four - November:
Beta: Julius

Marcus and Pierre crept away from me and Clio. Hugging the wall, they inched around the square towards the guards. We watched as they crept up to two Russian sentries. I peered through the snow as two guards fell to the ground. If anyone had been paying attention, they may have noticed something amiss, but Pierre and Marcus removed the men's guns, coats and mufflers, putting them on themselves in seconds.

A minute later, they walked calmly towards the group of Russians and Alphas and each tapped a soldier on the shoulder. Marcus and Pierre were gesticulating and pointing back at the far wall. The two soldiers followed them, stubbing their fags on the floor. As they approached the two bodies shoved against the wall, the soldiers crouched down to examine them.

Pierre and Marcus struck again, then swapped their sentry uniforms with those of the soldiers. Once more, they returned to the group, just in time for wrist braces to be attached to their arms. They hugged and slapped themselves and I was grateful that my skins were keeping me warm against the extreme temperatures.

Clio and I shared an impressed glance. A perfect infiltration.

As I watched the group of soldiers, all wrapped up in winter gear, it was hard to determine which two were Pierre and Marcus and I was again impressed with how vigorous these old men were. Soldiers were picking up cartons, larger crates held between two. The step was imminent.

'Okay, Julius,' said Clio. 'Our turn. This portable stepper is a bastard. Jack has suggested we step back to one of the storage sheds out at the Glass Wastes. We're going to need some time to recover our wits.'

I didn't like the sound of that.

'When you stepped over, how quickly did you recover?'

'Five, maybe ten—'

'I think we can function during those ten seconds, Clio. Marcus needs us to bring our A game.'

'Minutes, Julius. Do you honestly think I would mention a side effect that impaired us for a few seconds? This is like having an anvil smashed against your head repeatedly, in zero gravity, whilst simultaneously vomiting and evacuating your bowels.'

'That last bit doesn't actually happen, does it?'

'It didn't last time. But what do I know? It was my first time and Jack said it was a prototype.' Her face soured. 'Oh, there is something else.'

Christ, what the hell could be worse than that? It sounded like she was describing the most fearsome quantum hangover ever.

'We have to hold hands.'

I stared at her, but she wasn't laughing.

'Jack says he has fixed splicing, but because we are both using our own steppers, we might get properly separated. He suggested holding hands.'

I wondered if I had a belt or a tie that we could use to tie ourselves together. The idea of holding hands with Clio was deeply uncomfortable.

'Stop pulling faces and switch on your stepper.'

I tapped it in the required sequence, the lights flashing accordingly. A holographic readout flickered in the snow above my arm, showing Alexandria with today's exact date and time to the nano second.

'Ready?'

'Yes. I suggest we activate each other's step,' I said. 'Let's shake with our left hands and with our right we tap the bangles on the count of three.'

'Why our left?'

'So that my shooting hand is free if we encounter trouble.'

Whilst I had picked up much of Neith's fighting skills I still instinctively favoured my right hand. Clio nodded approvingly, but it sounded like we would be too busy being spaced out. Still, it felt good to have a plan.

'Okay, the curators are telling people to stand back. Let's go.'

Across the snow I could no longer make out Marcus and Pierre, they blended in so well. Ludo was easy to spot, and I was looking forward to seeing him soon. I clasped Clio's hand and nodded.

Chapter Forty-Five - Unknown: Julius

We were in an ornamental park. Rows of cherry blossom trees were in full bloom. Groups of people sat around each tree, painting purple stripes onto the bark itself. In the distance, Mount Fuji framed the shot. This was not Alexandria, and it wasn't winter. Clio hadn't mentioned hallucinations, and the splitting headache felt real enough. She was off to one side, vomiting. I wanted to be sick, but was scared that if I moved, my insides would rupture. Great heaves of pain were rolling up from my legs and through my bowels. Defecating in public had never been on my bucket list. As I lay there sweating, the cherry blossoms fell lightly around me and I tried not to wince as they landed on my desperately tender skin.

'Clio,' I moaned. 'Are you okay?'

If she wasn't, there was sod all I could do about it, but it was the polite thing to do. She stood up and stumbled across the grass towards me, then slumped back to the ground.

'Okay, that wasn't as bad as last time. Although you look a state. Maybe the body starts to get used to it? Or maybe you're just weak.'

I wanted to nod, but knew that would hurt too much. 'Weak.'

'Here, have a bonbon.' Out of the corner of my eye, I saw her shrug. 'It might help?'

I blinked and felt a thousand shards of glass scratch across my eyeball. I tried to keep my lids open as I placed the sweet in my mouth. The flood of sugar and saliva felt like a shower of sugary summer rain, washing away the pain and filth. I gingerly pulled myself up to a seated position.

'I take it the step has gone wrong,' I groaned.

'You don't say?'

'But we have to get back,' I wheezed. 'Marcus needs us. We have to stop those bombs.'

Clio rolled on her back. 'I refer you to my previous comment. We'll try again when you can walk without vomiting.'

It took a few goes, but eventually I staggered all the way to the tree. I was so bloody grateful that Clio didn't make me walk back to her as she strolled towards me grinning and we clasped hands and hit step.

-

This time, I threw up directly into Clio's face as we fell backwards into a river. The water was racing towards thin air, my suit screaming emergency protocols as we hurtled towards the waterfall. Clio grabbed my wrist and slapped my brace.

-

The air was red. Before I could vomit, my skins went into full lockdown, sealing my face and body from the atmosphere. This time, my vomit rebounded off the visor and back onto my face. I whimpered and fell to my knees.

Clio's shaky laughter came through the intercom. 'How are you holding up? You'll stop vomiting soon, I promise.'

'Really?'

'You'll have nothing left.'

It was scant consolation. I'd dry heaved once before after a sixth form booze fest. It hadn't been pretty and, honestly, throwing up with nothing to actually expel hurt like crazy.

'Is this Earth?' I said.

'According to the brace, yes. But neither of ours. Or at least if it is one of ours, we are in the far past or future. There is barely any atmosphere. We're going to have to go again.'

I groaned and sat up. There was nothing to look at. Clio was sat beside me, and beyond the vomit-flecked visor all I could see was a heavy red cloud.

'My brace says this cloud is corrosive.'

'So is acid rain,' she said. 'We can rest for a few minutes if you need to recover.'

I shook my head. Clambering to my feet, I stretched out my arm.

-

As the knight careened towards Clio, I threw myself at her as we rolled out of his path. And hit the brace.

379

We were standing in a road. There was no traffic about just some vultures flying overhead.

'Julius. Was that knight riding a velociraptor?'

'That's what it looked like to me.'

She walked off the road and sat on a boulder. If I had to guess, I would say Arizona, but I would not put so much as a penny on that. This could be the M25 for all I knew.

'I need to stop for a minute. I have to check my skins.'

I didn't believe her for a second. Her voice was shaking, her skin pale.

'What do you think is going wrong?' I asked. 'Do you think Jack was wrong? Maybe we shouldn't be holding hands. Could that be throwing the step field?'

'Do I look like an engineer?'

There was a small orange grove over to one side, and I decided to explore. I expected a space sentry to fall out of the sky and shoot me, or a rabbit to materialise and explode, or the tree to disappear, but none of those things happened. I twisted off two fruits and headed back to Clio.

'Here. Probably poisonous, or disgusting, or full of worms or something, but it might just be a sweet juicy orange.'

Which it was.

We sat in silence as we quelled our stomachs and headaches and enjoyed the fruit, licking our fingers.

'This Earth seems okay?'

'So far.'

'No knights riding dinosaurs.'

'None that we can see.'

'Nice oranges?'

'Yes, okay.' She smiled. 'Nice oranges. I've been thinking about your theory.'

My head was still woolly, but I didn't remember postulating any theory.

'About holding hands.'

I looked up at the sky and noticed vultures had started to gather. Gliding in lazy arcs above us.

'Go on.'

'Well, you might have a point. According to the brace, it's not making a mistake as it sets off. Each step is supposed to take us to the Glass Wastes, but each time we end up elsewhere. And I'm thinking that combining the two braces by holding hands is screwing things up.'

The vultures were definitely in a circling pattern.

'I thought you said if we didn't hold hands, we might lose each other.'

'I know.' She sounded nervous. 'I'm beginning to wonder if we just have to take the chance.'

I thought about it. 'Did I ever tell you that I used to be a Young Ornithologist?'

She looked across at me and then shielded her eyes as she squinted at the sky. 'I don't think it's ever come up in our fireside chats. Why do you mention it?'

'Only, on reflection, I don't remember vultures being quite that large.'

'They are quite big, aren't they?' said Clio. 'But they could be quite close. It's hard to measure perspective with no other reference point.'

We both studied the birds as they wheeled high above our heads. As we watched, they loomed even bigger.

'Ah.'

'Ah, indeed.'

'They appear to be heading our way,' I said.

'So they do.'

'They really are quite large, aren't they?'

'Are those… teeth?'

'I'd say tusks.'

'Righty-ho. Alexandria, then?' Clio laughed as she slapped her brace. A wing cut through the air where she had been standing and I slapped my own brace.

Chapter Forty-Six - November:
Alpha: Neith

Two red custodians accompanied me as I flew back from the Glass Wastes. Jack had been trying to tell me something, and he looked terrified. Whatever Minju's plan was, it started tomorrow. I had run out of time, and still didn't know what to do.

The second stepper and the slave soldiers had undone me. I could no longer think straight and couldn't turn to anyone. It didn't matter, though. No one would believe me, and it would only result in their death and then mine. Once I played my hand, Minju would be forced to act.

I alone remembered her true nature. A coup and an assassination had only strengthened her position. She was cleverer than me, better connected, and had no morals. I couldn't unmask her. She'd outwit me in seconds. According to Jack, Minju was trading treasures for weapons, he didn't know what her end goal was, but I think Grimaldi had been the tip of the iceberg. Minju was pharaoh, and if that wasn't enough power, it became obvious that she wanted total control. And she was building an army to back her up.

There was only one solution. I had to kill Minju.

The only way to stop Minju was permanently, and the only way to do it would be to get past her bodyguards. That wouldn't be a problem, but she could probably fight me off long enough for them to rush in. The thought of physically trying to kill Minju made me queasy. I had never killed anyone in hand-to-hand combat. I knew how to do it, but we were always trained to immobilise. There would be no immobilising Minju. This was all or nothing.

I was going to kill Minju, which meant I would have to die as well.

As I drove home, I considered how I could do this. A bomb would work, but what if she had installed sensors? Plus, I couldn't be certain that there wouldn't be collateral damage. I couldn't risk anyone else getting hurt. I'd never get a gun past security. A knife would work, but could I get close enough to her without her realising the threat? And then soldiers would come running.

I considered immobilising the soldiers, and felt up to the task, but in the time it took to knock them out, Minju would simply run off.

What would Julius do? He would find a solution I hadn't even thought of. He'd probably offer up a prayer, but even knowing now that they did actually exist, I doubted they were listening. It's not as if they were actual gods. Plus, after Firenze had whipped their hides and banned them from ever returning, I doubted there was any help there. Even the idea of asking Firenze was non-sensical.

This was my Earth and my problem.

Eventually, I determined the only thing that would do was poison. I would lace a bottle of wine, then share it with her.

I didn't want to stop my life. I wanted the mouseion recovered to its former glory and for our society to flourish. There were other Earths to explore. Maybe we could help some of them. Julius would approve of that. I wanted us to grow, but in order for anyone to grow old, Minju had to be stopped.

I headed home and began writing farewell letters. It felt surreal talking about killing someone. I wondered if anyone would believe me. Would they even understand? I got up and paced around my room, the letters on the table haunting me. Who was I, to say ending Minju was the right thing to do? Maybe her vision for the future of Alpha was the right one. What did I know? Maybe getting onto an offensive footing was the smart option. What if another Earth invaded and enslaved us?

I kicked the cushions across the floor. Now I was thinking like those stupid chat shows, churning up fear and suspicion. It was more likely that we would be the Earth invading a lesser planet. Julius was already uncomfortable with how we treated his home. And he didn't know the half of it. We were exchanging treasures for slaves and weapons. God knew what was coming through the step tomorrow, but whatever it was, Minju was looking forward to it.

I strode into the bathroom and pulled down the emergency kit I always kept on hand. A good curator always carries a few extra tricks under her skins when heading out on a mission. I had enough sedatives here to stop a rhino. Adding an overdose to a bottle of wine would be child's play. It dispersed into liquid without taste or scent. I grabbed a syringe, walked back into the kitchen, and pulled out a bottle of red that I had bought for Julius.

Chapter Forty-Seven - November:
Alpha: Neith

The following morning, I woke and showered. I had slept without dreams, but now moved in a daze. I didn't want it to end like this, but I had run out of options. Tucking the bottle of wine into my bag, I placed my antidote in my bra. I couldn't wear my skins as they would activate the minute they sensed the poison in my system and Minju would be tipped off. The antidote wasn't for me, or for Minju, it was in case of emergencies, civilian engagement, a third party gate-crashing our drinks. I was trying to minimise all risks. Had any assassination ever been planned so carefully?

I headed in to work and waited for my summons.

All day at work we finalised the list of returned artefacts. What a mockery all this was. Minju was already returning items to Earth on the sly. No news of them appeared on Beta news feed, but suddenly Minju was importing weapons.

The day came to an end, and I relaxed. For whatever reason, Minju had granted me a reprieve.

My brace started buzzing. It was her. 'Neith, if you have a moment, could you pop up?'

I didn't know whether to laugh or cry.

Gaius Sulla was standing guard outside the door, and I took a momentary snatch of satisfaction that he was about to fail in his duty. One-nil to me, and that would be the eternal score card.

'Where's your sword, soldier boy?'

'I could snap your neck before you took another step.'

I smiled up at him, tilting my snappable neck.

'Really? You'd be pulling your teeth out of your arse before you'd even begun to attack me.' I smiled again. 'Would you like to try?'

To give him his due, he didn't. He weighed me up then dismissed the idea. I'd seen that look before. I recognised it from the mirror. Avoid engagement with an unknown enemy until you've witnessed them in battle. Clio would just pile in and learn what she needed as she went along. Ramin would assess and find a way to avoid engagement. I would watch and work out how to beat them. Gaius was clearly like me. And that he had already assessed that someone who was so much smaller and frailer than him could best him, added to his levels of intelligence.

'She's expecting me.'

I waved the bottle of wine in his face. Today was going to be at her pace. I could live with that. It turned out that today, I could live with a lot of things. They would all be my last and all the more valuable for that.

I walked in. Minju smiled at me and seeing my bottle of wine, raised her eyebrows.

'Are we celebrating?'

I shrugged. 'I've been out at the Glass Wastes and I think it's time we put our cards on the table.'

She waved me over to the loungers, collected two wine glasses and a corkscrew from a cabinet, and sat down opposite me.

I passed the bottle to Minju and leant back.

'Merovingian? Very special.'

I tucked my feet underneath me and relaxed into the cushions. 'Unless you'd prefer something else? I bet you have a well-stocked supply.'

She jabbed the corkscrew into the bottle and poured two glasses. As she handed mine over, I took a deep breath. It smelled wonderful, as well it should, the price it cost. I was also relieved that there was no other fragrance.

She was about to take a sip when she put the glass down.

'Look, come here.' She stood up, placing her glass on the table and headed over to her window. 'Tell me what you see.'

I reluctantly followed her, leaving my glass behind. Gazing down on Alexandria, I felt my heart swell with love for my home.

'I see a city that led this planet out of tribal wars and monetary gain,' I said. 'I see a society that put the needs of others on a footing with their own. In the harbour under the shelter of our lighthouse, I see the rising tide lifting all boats equally. From the children's skimmers to the family skiffs, to the large ocean-going haulers.'

'The river beyond reminds us that water sustains all humanity. The flora, the fauna. We have a beautiful world, and I will do anything to protect it.' Her fierce pride mirrored my own. 'From anyone.' She met my eyes. 'And anything.'

I nodded, and she returned to the sofa and sat down. I spent one last moment devouring the city and then joined her.

'Yes,' I said. 'From anything, and I understand the need for a second step. Those quantum dwellers or other such creatures could return at any moment.'

She lifted her glass. In the setting sun, the light shone through the crystal, illuminating the glorious red of the wine. I lifted my glass in acknowledgement of the toast and took a sip. As soon as I did, she joined me and drank her own.

'This is truly delicious. Do you know as a youngster I spent a time working in the vineyards? Drinking as much as I picked. I had a friend, Emce, and we would race each other throughout the day to see who could pick the most. Then, at night, we would race our way through the vats.' She laughed in recollection. 'The vintner allowed us our excesses because we would pick more in a day than the rest of the crew would in a week.'

'When was this?'

'One of the summers during basic training. Those were great days.' She took another sip. 'None of it tasted this good.'

I had to agree it was a special vintage. I took another sip. 'Ramin and I used to run crocodiles.'

'As cadets?'

'No.' I leant forwards, refilled her glass and topped up my own. 'As kids.'

Now she roared with laughter. 'Your mothers must have whooped you!'

'Ramin's did. Mine was gone by then.'

We drank in silence.

'I'm sorry,' said Minju. 'I had forgiven.' She frowned, then tried again. 'Forgotten.'

The poison was taking effect. I only needed to distract her for a few more minutes and she wouldn't be able to call for help.

I waved at her dismissively. As my hand flapped in the air, I felt a heaviness in my limbs and grinned at her.

'Don't apologise. Why would you know?'

'I knew them.'

I stared at her and tried to do the maths, but my brain felt sludgy. 'You knew…'

Now I was finding it hard to string my words together.

She shook her head and went to put her glass on the table. Her hand fumbled the placement, and it tipped over and broke. She stared at it, then at me, blinking.

'I swapped—' Her head lolled, and she tried again. 'I swapped glasses.'

'The poison was in the bottle.'

She glared at me, struggling to focus, then tried to stand, but her arm collapsed under her as she slumped back onto the sofa, her tail twitching.

'Noble fool.'

I smiled softly. As an epitaph, it would do. My sight darkened as my head slumped forward, froth bubbling on my lips.

Chapter Forty-Eight - November: Alpha: Julius

I was in a small room. The view out the windows was of a blue sky and strange multi-coloured sheets of glazed rock. No velociraptor, no man-eating birds, no poisonous gases, but I didn't know where we were.

'What is this place?'

'The Glass Wastes, the second stepper complex.'

We were home. Jack's gizmo had finally worked.

'What's with the outside?' I was trying hard to understand if what I was looking at was natural, or manmade. I had never seen anything like it.

'That's what happens to sand when you have a massive nuclear explosion.'

'And Minju wants to do it again?' I shook my head in bafflement.

'What better threat? We all know how bad it can get, and she is planning to target capital cities, no doubt. Force everyone to comply.'

It was bonkers, but I had long ago decided Minju was off her rocker.

'Okay, let's get to the stepper and help Marcus and Pierre.'

As Clio headed towards the door, she moaned and swayed against me. There were footsteps approaching and, wrapping my arm around her waist, I pulled her with me to hide behind a stack of boxes. As promised, we were in a storage unit. An open aperture led out onto a corridor, and whoever was walking past had just missed us by a hair's breadth.

Clio was panting as the footsteps approached, her skin had fully activated, sliding under my arms as I held her upright. There is nothing more unnerving in the world than being near a vulnerable Clio, and right then I was fully embracing her. The minute she recovered, I released her, causing her to stumble and fall.

I rushed to pick her up, but as she glared up at me, I decided she could probably manage.

'Thanks.' Clio had a way of saying thank you that ensured you never tried anything so stupid ever again.

'What happened?' I crouched down alongside her. Absolutely not ready to offer her any further assistance, should she need it, which she most positively would not.

'Check our timestamp.'

As she had said, we were exactly where we should be, and I smiled reassuringly at her.

'I didn't say where, stupid. I said when.'

Her colour was returning to her cheeks and her mental capacity appeared back to normal. I checked the brace.

'Oh, we're a day early.' And then I cottoned on. 'Oh hell! Was that you walking past just now?'

'Well done, Einstein.'

I didn't think the sarcasm was called for, but then she had nearly run into herself. I remembered how wobbly I had felt when I was at the Tower of London, and me and me were a passageway apart. Instead of offering her any sympathy, I waited for her to re-balance herself.

'Okay,' I said, trying to understand the timeline. 'How did you get here? How long were you with Jack? And what did you do afterwards?'

She winced, and I realised she was trying to access memories that had happened five days ago, and were also happening right now.

'Take it slowly.'

She nodded and took a deep breath. 'I've been spying on everyone for the past few months, ever since you were repatriated. I went into hiding and started to watch. Then last week, or rather today, Neith left the city following a visit from Sabrina the night before. Hang on.' Trying to recount your actions that happened in two different time frames was hard work on the brain. 'Anansi taught me a few tricks to handle simultaneous existence.'

She closed her eyes for a few minutes. A vein in her neck pulsed rapidly, and then she exhaled deeply.

'Okay, that helped. He wasn't all bad.'

She shrugged and I didn't comment. I didn't think you could judge gods in terms of good or bad, and I didn't care.

'So. You'd been keeping obs on everyone when Neith left the city.'

'Exactly. Once her destination became obvious, I hung back and masked my approach.'

'You knew something was going on out here?'

'I did. Or at least I knew the engineers were doing something. But they weren't the threat Minju was, so I was focused on her and the Arts Foundation.'

I was still surprised by how straightforward these Alphas were. Even ones that had spent a year travelling with a trickster god. If someone was drawing so much attention to something, in this case the Arts Foundation, I'd look elsewhere to see what they were hiding. I wanted to point out that the arts project was an obvious smokescreen, but that would achieve nothing.

'Anyway. I waited out in the dunes until Neith had left again with some custodians escorting her, and I snuck in.' She shook her head as she recalled what she had seen. 'I tell you Julius, I was almost impressed. Minju has built a second stepper, raised an army, and gathered together enough weapons to start and end a world war, and no one even noticed.'

'I'm not sure impressed is the right word. I'd be going with appalled. What did you do then?'

'I went to find Jack. He told me Neith knew nothing about this place and that she was going to try to help him. Minju found out that she was here and summoned Neith home. Jack didn't know what would happen to Neith, so I decided it was time for me to act.'

'So, when Jack told you what was happening, why didn't you go for backup?'

'I did.'

'Who? Sam? Ramin?' I sagged with relief. At least the cavalry was on the way. 'What about Giovanetti? Can we approach her? Who did you get?'

'I got you.'

I looked at her in silence and then, God help me, I had to smirk. 'In a moment of crisis, the best person you could think of was me?'

I didn't duck fast enough, but she did at least pull her punch. Even so, I was going to have a dead arm for a few hours.

'Yes. I thought of you. Now, if you are going to stop preening, can we please get on and sort out a plan of action? I need to wait until I have left, then go warn Jack that tomorrow a load of nuclear weapons will be arriving. We have to stop that happening.'

Chapter Forty-Nine - November:
Alpha: Julius

An hour later, Clio stood up.

'That's it, I've gone. Let's go grab Jack.'

I followed Clio as we ran along the empty corridors. Occasionally voices or footsteps could be heard in the distance but Clio navigated her way without incident. As we ran, I looked over my shoulder, protecting our rear. No one pursued us but I wasn't taking any chances. Clio may have known her way around, but I had just seen a payload of nuclear weapons on its way to this Earth. Nothing was going to stop me from stopping them.

We stopped outside a door. Clio opened it and walked in.

From inside I heard Jack's voice. 'Why are you back? Has it gone wrong?'

I walked in. Jack looked dreadful. My friend was running on empty and had been for a while. All my memories of him were of us laughing together. Mostly him laughing at my attempts to study higher maths and me laughing at him as he tried to handle alcohol. Now he looked like an undergraduate at the end of everything. His hair was dark with grease emphasising his sunken bloodshot eyes. His skin was pale and waxy except for the outbreak of angry red spots.

He turned to look at me and then a huge grin plastered across his face. Suddenly, I was looking at a puppy of a man. He ran forward and gave me a massive bearhug and lifted me off my feet, which was impressive given the size of him.

'It worked! You're here! Mate, I have missed you so much!'

'Not half as much as I've missed you. How are you? How's Sabrina? Please tell me you finally asked her out?'

'If you could save the bromance till later,' drawled Clio, 'we have work to do.'

Laughing, we finished slapping each other on the back and headed towards the chairs.

Jack's office was pretty sparse, although the walls were covered in mathematic workings-out. Clever Jack, always solving things, discovering stuff. It meant nothing to me beyond the fact that Jack was still plotting.

'Incidentally, these braces?' I gestured to my bangle. 'Holding hands is a very bad idea.'

'How so?' Jack asked.

'Vomiting,' said Clio. 'Much vomiting.'

'Plus we kept stepping to bizarre Earths,' I said. 'Velociraptors. Dead planets. Birds with fangs!'

'Fascinating,' mumbled Jack as he grabbed a pencil and started to scribble. 'It is possible that the molecular interaction between two or more particles causes a feedback loop in the quantum neural equilibrium, resulting in a self-reinforcing process that could potentially impact the overall stability and function of the quantum network…' His voice trailed off as he started to work out what might have gone wrong and I tried to remind myself that I wasn't actually stupid. When Jack started to theorise, I always felt like an utter idiot.

'Enough,' said Clio. 'We've got bigger problems right now.' And she told him what had happened on Beta.

Clio and I walked off the complex and into the desert under the cover of our cloaked skins. Despite it being November, the heat was uncomfortable and if our ride didn't turn up soon, we would be sleeping under the freezing stars. I'd done that in Afghanistan. I knew the Sahara would be worse.

When we told Jack he had to stop tomorrow's step, he explained why he couldn't. We had witnessed it, so now it had to happen. I hated time-travel paradoxes. We were taking a horrible risk but Jack assured us, breaking the timeline was a far bigger gamble.

Instead, he would neutralise the bombs as they arrived. If there was one thing the Glass Wastes had taught Alpha, it was how to deal with nuclear devices. After that, he would wait for us to get the rest of the plan in motion. Leaving Jack to greet and hide Marcus and Pierre, we headed off.

'Do you think he will come?' asked Clio, looking to the horizon.

'He said he would.'

'It's risky. He is a custodian, after all. Their sole purpose is to uphold the law, and you were repatriated.'

'You've made your point.'

As we trudged across the blue and green sands, the colours slowly turned back to beige as we walked further from the site.

'Do you think this will work?'

'God knows. But I can't think of anything else. It's going to take us a couple of days to get everything and everyone in place.'

'If anyone believes us.'

I frowned. Clio was being so negative.

'We have Jack's holograms. We can show people the step, the nuclear bombs, the slaves. If nothing else, surely that will trigger an enquiry.'

On the horizon, a black dot was wobbling in the mirage.

'Looks like our lift has arrived.'

'Or our death squad,' muttered Clio.

'That's the spirit.'

I uncloaked and waited as the hover came closer, speeding above the dunes. As it got closer to the ground, the sand plumed up around us. We were engulfed in a final cloud of dust as the driver skidded to a halt.

Kamal Shorbagy jumped out of the driver's seat and ran over to me, giving me the biggest hug ever. 'You are here! I wept. I wept for you. And you are here!' He turned to Clio. 'You marvellous, murderous miracle. I am your friend for life. I don't care what they say about you. Justice is restored if Julius is returned.'

Clio glared at him and he rapidly apologised.

She cut him off. 'Don't worry about it. It's not like they're lying. Right now, we need to get back to the city. I've got an apartment over in sixth. Can you take us there? Julius needs to remain hidden until we are ready to announce his return.'

'Yes, of course, jump in. But how have you come back? And why are you in the middle of the desert and why did I have to hide my journey?'

Shorbagy's questions were endless as we got into the hover and set off towards Alexandria.

'Give me two days and I'll explain everything. Can you do that?'

'Are you safe?'

Clio laughed. 'No, dear friend, we are not safe. So, like the man says, can you keep this a secret?'

Shorbagy straightened his jacket. 'In that case, you should both stay with me. I will protect you.'

Clio and I looked at each other with the same thought. Shorbagy was a skinny yellow custodian. He reprimanded citizens for litter dropping. No one could doubt his bravery. Like other yellows, he had risked his life to protect citizens during the Battle of the Gods, but this was a risk too far. I had a lump in my throat and had to cough before I spoke.

'You live with your wife and children. I could never bring harm to them.'

'Your presence would bring us honour.'

I was lost for words. The bravery of Alexandrian citizens slayed me.

'Custodian Shorbagy,' said Clio. 'Honour to your hearth and home. I will not allow you or your family to come to any harm. We will not stay at your home, but when this is done, I will commend you to Giovanetti for bravery above and beyond that required of any citizen.'

His face battled with his emotions. There was pride and relief, but also a glimmer of rebellion.

'Please, Shorbagy. You were my first friend here. Please don't ask me to live with the fear of risking your family.'

He nodded once and quickly wiped a knuckle under his eye. We rode the rest of the way in silence and, as we pulled up at Clio's, I returned his hug.

'I'm coming to yours for dinner this weekend though. Yes?'

He nodded and then smiled. 'Curator Masoud, would you care to join us?'

403

Clio looked back into the hover and blinked. 'If I'm free.'

I stared at her. She glared back, but then turned and smiled at Shorbagy.

'Yes. I would be honoured.'

The following morning, Clio headed off to talk to Asha Giovanetti. We needed her on our side and didn't have time to convince her. Nothing save brain surgery was going to work. Jack's holograms would take us so far, but to halt Minju in her tracks, the Director of Security needed the evidence of her own memories.

After that, Asha could release Ramin without alerting Minju, and recall Sam as well. She could also send troops over to the Glass Wastes and help Jack take the facility.

I paced Clio's tiny apartment all morning as I remained in hiding, waiting for her return. It was the afternoon when Clio's front door opened. I stood, laser in hand. If she had failed to convince Asha, I wasn't prepared to be arrested without a fight. I hadn't taken my bangle off and was prepared to step home if necessary.

Clio walked in, her face blank, with Asha Giovanetti beside her. It had been months since I had last seen her, and she was haggard. But then, she had just had brain surgery.

Asha stared at me, then closed the door behind her. 'I appear to owe you an apology.'

I exhaled loudly. 'You remember, then?'

'Yes. That little lesion was clearly caused by Anansi. Now we know what it is, we will remove it for all citizens. Though it might take years to get through everyone. In the meantime, we have to work quickly.'

We sat down in Clio's dining room and made plans.

'And what about Neith?' said Clio.

'Let's break into her place. Wait for her to come home this evening, then explain the whole situation. She's already been out to the Glass Wastes and knows what Jack has told her. If she doesn't believe us, we can suggest she has her lesion removed.'

Asha and Clio looked at me and nodded.

'Good call,' said Asha. 'Julius, I need you to remain cloaked. Your presence will get to Minju in a heartbeat.'

Chapter Fifty - November: Alpha: Julius

Half an hour later, we were standing outside Neith's front door.

'I'll kick it in if you create a diversion,' said Clio to Asha.

'I'm quite capable of kicking a door in without making a noise,' retorted Asha.

'How about we use the key?'

I looked up in surprise at the new voice. At the end of the corridor stood Rami, a huge beam on his face. 'Why are you two ladies always fighting? And who's cloaked?'

I couldn't help myself. I tapped my brace and undid the effect.

Rami did a double take and then barrelled me off my feet. I'd forgotten how fast he was as he sprinted towards me. We were laughing and punching each other when Asha cleared her throat.

'I believe I said incognito?' She tapped her foot. 'And did you mention a key, Ramin?'

As he handed her Neith's spare, we caught up as we made our way into her apartment.

Clio went to put the kettle on and Asha apologised again for placing Ramin under house arrest.

'And you are certain,' said Ramin, 'that Minju was behind everything?' He paced back and forth. 'I mean, are you sure?'

'Trust us,' shouted Clio from the kitchen. 'Julius and I have been living with this knowledge for the past few months. That was why Minju had him repatriated, and I went to ground.'

Rami called over to me as I wandered around Neith's apartment. 'I knew you were innocent!'

'Anyone with a brain knew he was innocent,' called Clio, and I swore I saw Asha wince. She had a lot of self-reflection to do.

I looked away. I couldn't blame her. Her memory had been altered and then she had been played. She had been tasked with protecting an increasingly fearful society and had happily gone along with the new troops without questioning the ethics. It seemed Minju had told her about the new Beta soldiers and the second step. Now that she understood the reality of Minju, Asha feared for the planet.

I walked over to Neith's desk. I could picture her here, sitting looking over the quantum facility. The better views were in the living room towards the sea, but Neith was a curator through and through. There was a collection of letters on the table. Bizarrely one was addressed to me, although how she ever expected me to see it, I had no idea. I couldn't wait to see her face as she walked through the door.

I picked the letter up, slid the folded paper out of the envelope and began to read.

'Julius? Are you okay?'

I looked up. The other three had turned to study me. I must have moaned out loud.

'She's known all along.' I handed the letter to Clio. 'There's one for you as well. She says when she woke from the coma, she knew Minju was bad. Anansi's effect never touched her.'

Ramin sat down, taking his letter. 'She was clinically dead for a few moments. Maybe that's why she was immune? So why hasn't she said anything?'

'It's all here.' I waved the letter and read on. 'She didn't know who to turn to.' I paused as I processed her sentences. 'Oh, God. No.'

Asha stood up and joined us. 'What? What's going on?'

'Neith is going to kill Minju. This is her suicide note.'

I dropped the letter and ran. I could hear their voices, but ignored them as I clattered down the stairs and out onto the pavement.

Clio and Ramin kept pace with me. She tugged my sleeve as Ramin flagged down a hover. Seconds later, we had evicted the driver and were clocking up speeding violations racing towards the civic building.

As the automatic brakes slowed the hover, Ramin shouted into his brace.

'Asha, we're in Taxi 326. Release the safety modifications.'

Seconds later, we sped up, scattering other traffic, then screeched to a halt outside the building. Crowds of tourists fled away as a cohort of reds ran towards us.

'Move!' I drew my laser. I didn't want to shoot them, but nothing was going to stop me.

'Wait,' their commander shouted.

I took aim, fired and missed, rolling behind a nearby column for cover. I prepared myself for a counter-strike, but instead, I saw that the custodians had formed a shield wall and looked ready to shoot me if I tried anything else stupid. I was happy to oblige. No one was going to stop me getting to Neith in time.

'Giovanetti says to assist you in all actions,' the commander roared and threw his laser on the floor to emphasise his point. 'She's on her way with further reinforcements.'

I had been expecting a fight, but as I stood up, they fell in behind me.

We ran through the corridors, our boots echoing on the marble floors. Directors and officials leant out of their offices and then quickly pulled their heads back in. Recent memories still haunted the population.

'The Romans will fight,' said Clio. 'They are loyal only to the pharaoh.'

'Understood.'

As we approached the outer office, the door was closed, two goddamn Romans blocking it. I had been forewarned about the Romans but the reality was still astonishing. The sight was so surprising that I almost stopped. Romans in Alexandria, and everyone else had just got used to it. Hell, every curator fought them in the simulator and now they were just part of the team. It was hard to swallow.

The two soldiers drew their swords, ready for a fight. I could see the determination in their eyes, and knew this was going to be intense.

'Attack!' shouted the red custodian at my side, and we all ducked as he stepped forward and fired a sonic wave at the Romans.

They were caught off guard, and one of them went down, clutching his chest.

I charged forward, laser in hand, ready to bypass the other soldier, when I heard more heavy feet running towards us. Their guttural battle cries rang along the corridors.

My indecision nearly cost me my life as a Roman sword cut the air above my head.

Clio had tackled me to the ground and swept around to deflect his second strike. 'Custodians! To me!'

As she called them to action, I stumbled to my feet, firing my laser at the oncoming soldiers. Within seconds they created a wall of men and were advancing on the red custodians. The Roman shield wall had been enhanced by Alpha technology. One long, electro-magnetic pulse wrapped each individual shield, creating an undulating wall of defence. Behind the barrier the soldiers held lasers rather than swords. I knew the fight would be a bloody one and soon the two sides were fully engaged.

I wanted to stay. The fight was here, but my battle lay further beyond the antechamber.

I ran towards the door, jumping over the bodies and shouted instructions to those following. In the distance, I could hear even more Romans running to join the battle. But now I had to go.

The office within was quiet. There was a large desk with some papers on it, but no signs of Minju and Neith. To one side was a smaller room, and I ran through. Sat opposite each other on two sofas were the still forms of Neith and Minju. Eyes closed, bodies slumped, white foam around their mouths. Between them stood a bottle of red wine. One glass had fallen over. A pool of red wine staining the rug.

Leaping over the sofa, I shook Neith. My fingers bit into her shoulders as I attempted to revive her. She'd lost weight and her hair had grown out. These were stupid observations, and I sobbed as I screamed her name.

'Check her clothing,' shouted Clio, who had run in behind me. I looked at Clio in confusion, just long enough for her to push me aside as she ripped open Neith's top.

'She always carries an antidote when she uses poison in case of accidents.'

Clio grabbed a vial from Neith's bra and, clicking a small button, plunged the needle into Neith's chest.

'Save Minju,' shouted Ramin, as the fight between the custodian and Romans continued in the anteroom.

'Are you mad?'

'If Minju dies, Neith will be tried for murder.'

I tried to work out how to administer the syringe, my fingers fumbling as I looked at Neith's deathly form. Ramin snatched it from me and a second later plunged it into Minju's arm.

The three of us stared at each other, panting. I checked Neith's pulse. It was erratic, but present. I nodded my head tiredly. Rami did the same for Minju. As we slumped to the floor, Asha walked in.

'Report,' she said.

Clio jumped to her feet. 'Both alive, but you'd better call Bitsoi. They are going to need attention.'

'We don't know how much poison Neith placed in the bottle, or how long they've been unconscious,' said Ramin.

The sounds of battle from beyond the doors had ceased.

'Asha. Are we secure?'

'Against the Romans?' she scoffed. 'Yes, of course. Now let's see what we can do to secure ourselves against *her*.'

Chapter Fifty-One - November:

Alpha: Neith

I slowly became aware of voices.

'She's waking up.'

I was groggy, my limbs on fire, but I felt certain that I recognised Ramin's voice. I opened my eyes and groaned.

Minju was also beginning to stir. I had failed.

She would smooth talk her way out of this, and have me silenced for good. I watched her, too tired to react as she struggled to sit up.

'Asha. Arrest Neith, she tried to kill me.' Minju's voice was croaky and hesitant, but her intention was clear.

'Not a chance,' said a male voice from behind me. I knew that voice and saw Minju's eyes flick open in alarm. I tried to turn around, but my arms felt like lead, my neck full of concrete. Someone moved behind me and walked around the side of my sofa. I stared up at the beautiful silly Julius Strathclyde and burst into tears.

His alarm was so funny that I cried more, watching him panic, desperately trying to find a handkerchief.

'Come here, you daft fool,' I sobbed and leant against him as he sat down beside me and held me close.

'Is she okay?' It was Ramin's voice, sounding concerned.

I slumped on the sofa, a warm body beside me, and I smiled weakly at Julius and Ramin.

'Yes, I think she passed out again,' said Julius uncertainly. 'Where is Bitsoi?'

Clio was sitting bolt upright on the other sofa next to Minju.

'Minju's the same. She's drifting in and out.'

'No, I'm not, you fool,' muttered Minju. Her voice getting clearer each time she spoke. The antidote was working just fine, but it could take a little while before either of us would be walking. That is, if Minju ever let me walk again.

'Hang on,' I said, trying to marshal my thoughts. 'When did you get back?'

'Yesterday. Clio and I have been busy.'

I had a moment before Minju could stop me.

'Julius. Minju is the enemy. She has deceived everyone. She led the uprising, not Grimaldi.'

'I know, knucklehead. That's why she got rid of me. Why didn't you tell anyone?'

'Because she was killing people and getting rid of them.'

'What about me?' said Ramin. 'Why didn't you tell me?'

'And what if she suspected you knew something? She nearly killed you when you discovered something. I wanted to keep you safe.'

'Wally, I was trying to keep you safe.'

Minju cleared her throat and scoffed. 'This is all nonsense, but I can see I shall have to convince you.' She tapped her brace. Asha seemed unconcerned that Minju still had access to her communications, so I relaxed.

'Tybalt?' She tapped the brace again and repeated herself. 'Tybalt?'

I smiled as a hologram of Jack appeared in the room. 'Good evening, Minju. How very glad I am to see you looking so dreadful. Is that spittle on your chin?'

Minju hissed at Jack. 'Have you forgotten our arrangement? Put Tybalt Jones on at once or I promise you—'

'What? You'll kill Sabrina. My parents. My friends. Not going to happen.' He smirked at the screen. 'Incidentally, Tybalt is under arrest. And those nuclear weapons you imported this afternoon? All disarmed. We've been calling in the troops and letting people know what you did. Sam is on his way back. Footage of your actions has been sent to world leaders. News of the Anansi lesion and how to repair it will soon be disseminated to all medical centres.'

'How did you know?' asked Minju in shock.

416

'We tipped him off.'

An old man had walked into the room with First Engineer, Hypatia Smith. 'It's over, Juju. What were you thinking?'

The man was well-dressed, possibly Kenyan, although his accent was odd. No one recognised him.

Minju was staring at him closely. 'Marcus?'

He nodded.

Minju wiped her chin and tried to stand up, but her legs were still too weak. 'You're alive.'

He nodded sadly as he looked at her. 'Oh, Minju. How could you have become this?'

Tears filled her eyes. 'Emce, you have to understand. I did this for Alpha. You don't know how weak we've become. The engineers have been hiding secrets for centuries. We've been attacked by creatures from other Earths. We need to defend ourselves. I'm trying to save us.'

'By destroying us?'

'You don't get it. You can't bring about change without pain. Not if you need to be quick.'

I watched the pair of them in confusion and turned to Julius.

'Who is Emce?'

'Emce, stands for M.C. I guess. Marcus Caractacus.'

'Caractacus?' asked Ramin in awe.

'The one and only. Your young man there,' he said, pointing towards Jack's hologram, 'has found a way to

417

travel without the steps. He sent Clio to rescue Julius and found me and a bunch of other curators. Since then, we've been undoing Minju's scheme.' He turned to me. 'And you are the famous Neith Salah, I take it?'

I nodded in awe. Marcus Caractacus was a living, breathing myth.

'Thank you for having the courage to single-handedly take down a tyrant, but remember, we curators work better in teams. Yes, yes?'

Julius squeezed my hand and Ramin ruffed my hair, presumably because he knew I couldn't muster up enough energy for a fight.

'Do that again and I swear—'

'You swear what?' he said ruefully. 'You'll arrest me?'

I groaned and laughed weakly. 'So, what are we going to do about her?'

Hypatia Smith spoke. 'We will deal with Minju in good time. A lot has been happening and needs to be investigated. Including your role in this, Special Adviser Salah.'

'Hang on,' cried Clio. 'Neith nearly sacrificed herself for this country. Don't you dare—'

Hypatia held her hand up, and Clio trailed off.

'Neith, if you had come to me and explained what you knew, things would never have got to this state. I was informed that Jack was out running new test experiments, and I allowed this with my blessing. Had

I known the extent of his discoveries and applications, I would have intervened.'

'You wouldn't have believed me.'

'What has belief got to do with it? If you had given me the facts, I am well capable of extrapolating the probability of your statement.'

I snorted. I could manage that much. 'Oh yes,' I said. 'The highly trustworthy, open society of engineers. Not exactly covered yourself in glory these past few years, have you?'

She had the grace to look put out.

'As far as I knew, you could have been neck deep in quicksand with Minju. If I extrapolated the probability of you being on my side, I'd have come out with a very low number.'

Now Hypatia snorted, but she didn't reply. Instead, she turned to the screen and addressed Jack. 'What's the situation at your end?'

'Step is shut down. Platoons of reds have arrived and are monitoring the camps. All weapons have been made safe and artefacts are being packed up to return to the mouseion. When the nuclear weapons came through, there was a gun fight and some of the Scythians got a bit excited and shot the men stepping through. Three were shot on sight, including Ludo Bianco. Once we know what to do with the Betas, we can shut this place down.'

He smiled and gave me a goofy double thumbs up, which I returned.

'Very good, Jack. I suggest you come home now. See if you can convince your Sabrina to stop bothering me. And bring me the schematics of this personal stepper you've created. That sounds fascinating.'

Jack's holo switched off and I relaxed. Everyone was accounted for and almost no one had had to die.

'Julius, Clio. Your bangles, I believe you call them?' Hypatia held her hand out.

Julius slid his off his wrist and handed it to the First Engineer. She held it up in the light and examined it. 'Extraordinary. That boy is a marvel.'

She stepped towards Clio, who had just slid her bangle off when Minju's hand shot out and snatched it from Clio's grasp.

In the distance, I could hear ringing bells running closer towards us as Sabrina exploded into the room.

'You bitch!' she screamed at Minju. 'You threatened my life? To force Jack to work!'

'Sabrina, step back,' roared Hypatia. 'She has a stepper in her hand. Minju, put the bangle down or I will shoot you.'

Minju slowly stood up, her tail waving to and fro. Long agitated arcs as she tried to activate the device.

'I mean it,' said Hypatia. 'Put it down and let's talk.'

Clio had edged away from Minju, no doubt not wanting to inadvertently get caught up in the step effect. The room was now full, and I struggled to my feet. I had started this. I felt the need to end it as peacefully as possible.

'Minju—'

At that moment, she began to shimmer. No doubt she had finally worked out how to activate it.

'What's she doing?' shouted Sabrina. 'She can't escape!'

Asha fired her laser, but the beam hit the shimmer and ricocheted off, causing all of us to duck. Hypatia yelled in alarm as a blast of energy tore through her hat.

Sabrina ducked, jumped up and ran at Minju. At the last second, she slammed to a halt and grabbed Minju's bangle.

Several things happened at once.

Minju disappeared.

Sabrina fell to the floor screaming as blood pumped out of her severed wrist.

And in the void where Minju had been standing, the bangle fell to the floor, two severed hands still attached.

Asha dropped to Sabrina's side, muttering as she applied a tourniquet to her arm. 'What were you thinking?'

'She couldn't escape. She had to answer for her crimes.'

Julius was shouting at Hypatia to return his bangle. 'We have to go after her. God knows what she will do on Beta.'

Hypatia refused.

I watched numbly as Sabrina, sweet, clever Sabrina in her silly bell boots continued to bleed out.

Clio grabbed Julius and whispered something and he stopped shouting, and then Bitsoi ran into the room. He had come for me, but Sabrina came first, so I passed out instead.

Chapter Fifty-Two - November: Alpha: Julius

Three nights later, eleven of us were sitting in Kamal Shorbagy's dining room. Jack and Sabrina sat side by side as he carved her food for her. Her hand had been reattached, but was still healing. Rami and his partner Xandro were at the far end, beside Clio and Neith. Sam was also at the table complaining about having missed all the fun. Marcus and Hypatia were chatting animatedly about time-travel and multiple universes.

Shorbagy's children had come in earlier, giggling excitedly at the presence of so many recognisable faces until I stuck my tongue out at them and they pretended to scream and ran off to bed.

'Behave yourself, cadet,' teased Shorbagy, and I remembered our first encounter.

'Hard to believe that was only three years ago.'

Shorbagy's wife was a lady called Kimi, who shyly offered me some pickled root. It looked dreadful, but Shorbagy beamed with pride.

'Only the best for our honoured guests.'

I saw delight spread across the faces of all at the table and I smiled bravely as she piled up my plate.

Everyone hooted with laughter as my eyes watered after the first mouthful. I suspected they had been fried in chillies, then pickled in ammonia. Clio leant over and speared a few from my plate and munched down on them, singing her praises to Kimi. Kimi brought me a bowl of yoghurt and I kissed her hand.

'So, what happens next?' said Sam to Hypatia. As the most senior person in the room, she had been stuck in meetings for the past three days. On the first day, she had publicly exonerated and then praised Neith. After that, Asha Giovanetti had offered her resignation, although as yet it hadn't been accepted.

'The first step is a proper election for the new pharaoh and then an entire range of checks and balances to be installed. Transparency in all departments.'

Clio coughed.

'As I said,' continued Hypatia, 'all departments, including the engineers. We are also making serious proposals for an open exchange with Beta. Julius and Marcus, I imagine you will be involved with that. We are going to need ambassadors.'

Marcus nodded his head. 'I can think of a few curators back on Beta who will be excellent candidates. It will be my pleasure to introduce you all to Marie-Louise, a quite formidable lady.'

Hypatia nodded in acknowledgement. 'It will be quite the undertaking. But, for now, the pharaoh comes first. I have already declared my preference to the council, but of course it will be an open election that anyone can stand for.'

She picked up her fork and speared her fish, examining it closely before taking a mouthful. We all stared at her.

'Come on, Hypatia,' I laughed. 'You can't say that and then just carry on eating. Who are you proposing?'

She laughed. 'Do I have to spell it out? Do the maths. Apply some logic. Use your flabby minds and come to the inevitable conclusion.'

Everyone looked blank.

'You nominated yourself?' I said, and she laughed harder.

'I think I would make an excellent pharaoh, but there is a possibility that no one else would agree.' She dabbed her napkin on her mouth and turned to Neith.

'How does a butterfly hide on a corpse?'

Neith frowned and then smiled back at Hypatia. 'I get it! It's a rebirth thing, isn't it? You have to be prepared to die to be worthy. It's metaphysical, isn't it?'

'Yes. You see, that baffles me. I understand rules and logic, but I'll never understand sacrifice. That's why I nominated you, Neith Salah. You are and always will be the best of us.'

Around the room, I saw the same awe and acknowledgement on everyone's faces. It had taken Hypatia's words to make us see the truth of what was right in front of us.

I scraped back my chair and raised my glass. 'To Neith Salah. Pharaoh.'

As everyone else stood and toasted Neith, I watched as my friend desperately waved at everyone to sit down, laughing through her tears.

An hour later, after a delicious pudding, we had moved on from Neith's campaign strategy to the strange Earths that Jack's bangle had taken us to.

'Do you think that's where Minju ended up?'

'I have no idea,' said Clio. 'As I removed my bangle, I cleared all the previous coordinates and just punched in some random calculations. Wherever she ended up, it wasn't Alpha or Beta.'

'Well, wherever it was, I hope they are ready for a one-handed, long-tailed, great deceiver.'

It was a sobering thought, but personally I thought her days were numbered. If she survived the arterial bleed from her severed hand, she still needed to hide her tail. She had no way home and no resources.

'Wherever she is, I hope Juju's life is short and painless,' said Marcus sadly.

'You should never have let her escape,' said Sabrina darkly.

'I know,' said Clio. 'But I knew this Earth would never do what was necessary and kill her. She was too dangerous to let her live. This seemed like the only solution.'

She put her spoon down and looked at Sabrina. 'But I regret your injury and I remain in awe of your sacrifice.'

Sabrina squirmed. Praise from Clio was very uncomfortable.

'I lost my temper. That was all. It was stupid, really.'

As I looked around the room, I had a silly grin on my face. Hypatia may have had one or ten drinks too many and was gesticulating wildly as Marcus laughed shaking his head shouting 'Yes, yes!' with each point. Shorbagy had his arm around Kimi, a proud smile on his face as he gently squeezed his wife's waist. At the other end of the table Jack, Neith and Ramin were mucking around seeing who could fit the most chillies in their mouths. Neith spluttered as she grabbed for the pitcher of water. And then there was Sabrina, looking awkward.

I picked up my glass and got to my feet.

'Here's to stupid curators, may we always preserve.'

The others rose to their feet, glasses in hand, and smiled back at me.

'We preserve!'

Author's Note

Greetings to your hearth and home!

Here we are at the end of this first run of Quantum Curator adventures. I have adored writing these books, but I wasn't ready for how Minju was going to derail the story. It was great fun battling her, but now I have her back under control and she's gone. For now. Honestly, I'm not sure that we will ever see her again. But now I can get back to treasure hunting, time jumping adventures. I have a new antagonist in mind and you are going to love him, he's really dreadful.

For the second series I have so many ideas to explore. The young princes, multiple Earths, the history of the stranded curators, Alpha and Beta working together. So many directions. And in all of them we will have Julius and Clio bickering and fighting their way through their missions.

You may have noticed that there isn't a pre-order link for book six. That's because I'm working on another project at the moment. I can't say much about it right now but the subtitle is *Maps, Murder and Magic*. And I am very excited about it.

To hear more about it or to be the first to be told when book six of the Quantum Curators comes out, please sign up to my newsletter.

I also have a bonus scene, if you are interested? I had to delete this chapter but I enjoyed it so much that I kept it. Just tap the link and I'll e-mail it to you.

https://dl.bookfunnel.com/3t401ybtoc

A quick note on the Romans. There is some evidence that the Ninth Legions may have left Britain and gone to the Netherlands, but it's uncertain. I think my explanation is more fun. Regarding the Roman salute, there is no contemporary evidence for it, maybe they simply nodded? But I didn't feel a nod was dramatic enough for the scene in which Neith challenges the centurion, so a salute it shall be. Again, dramatic licence is a grand thing.

This book was over a year in the making and I need to thank everyone that stood in the wings, whilst I ranted and bewailed ever finishing it. My thanks to my editors Mark Stay and Julian Barr, and my Alpha readers, Anna and Al, and an excellent team of advance readers. All of them helped pull me though the doldrums, and without them I don't think this book would have shone anywhere near as brightly as it does.

I have also loved chatting with you, either via e-mails or on social media. Your comments and compliments have spurred me on and I really like the community that we are building.

Finally, my thanks to my friends and family, but in particular to my husband and sons who have had to endure the greatest of my personality swings, but have also shown me nothing but one hundred per cent confidence in my ability to get it done. Also, it is so cool when you impress your children.

Chat more in the next newsletter.

TTFN

ESJ

Printed in Great Britain
by Amazon

42931097R00249